I0601161

THE
SUMMER
TWINS
book two

second chance
SUMMER

DEBRA ST JAMES

SECOND CHANCE SUMMER

The Summer Twins | Book Two

DEBRA ST JAMES

Second Chance Summer | The Summer Twins – Book Two

© 2021 by Debra St James

No part of this publication may be reproduced, distributed, or transmitted in any form or by any means, including photocopying, recording, or other electronic or mechanical methods, without the prior written permission of the publisher, except in the case of brief quotations embodied in crucial reviews and certain other noncommercial uses permitted by copyright law.

This novel is a work of fiction. While reference may be made to actual historical events or existing locations, the names, characters, places, and incidents are products of the author's imagination. Any resemblance to people either living or deceased, business establishments, events, or locales are purely coincidental and not intended by the author.

Any trademarks, service marks, product names, or named features are assumed to be the property of their respective owners and are only used for reference. There is no implied endorsement if any of these terms are used.

Website: *www.debrastjamesbooks.com*

Email: *debrastjamesbooks@gmail.com*

Published by: Debra St James Author

Edited by: Double AA Author Services

Formatted by: Debra St James Author

ISBN: 978-0-6454536-6-9 [Paperback]

ISBN: 978-0-6454536-7-6 [Discreet Edition Paperback]

ISBN: 978-0-6450483-2-2 [Ebook]

inspiration

This story was inspired by the lyrics ...
—> *No Such Thing by John Mayer* <—

reader discretion required

This book contains incidences of domestic violence, which
may be upsetting to some readers.
Check here for a more comprehensive explanation on Debra's
website.
https://debrastjamesbooks.com/second-chance-summer-content-warning/
The above explanation <u>does contain spoilers</u>.

characters in this story

SOME CHARACTERS IN THIS STORY ARE DEAF OR HARD OF Hearing. They are depicted using American Sign Language (ASL). ASL is a common form of sign language used in the United States and many parts of Canada. It incorporates these five parameters: hand shape, palm orientation, location, movement, and facial expression/non-manual markers.

It has its own grammatical rules and syntax. Therefore, some of the dialogue, shown within quotes, throughout this work is a translation of ASL to English for this novel. Please be aware that when it states someone is signing and speaking simultaneously, they are communicating through Simultaneous Communication (SimCom), which is different from ASL. This is a common form of communication between hearing individuals and those who are Deaf or Hard of Hearing.

The use of capitalization for the terms Deaf and Hard of Hearing demonstrates that the person identifies as a member of the Deaf Community.

I would like to take this opportunity to thank Kimberly and Fiona for their insights into the Deaf Community and their invaluable suggestions, which helped to make these characters as authentic as possible.

playlist

No Such Thing ... *John Mayer*
Crush ... *Jennifer Paige*
Love Song for No One ... *John Mayer*
Vultures ... *John Mayer*
I Just Wanna Live ... *Good Charlotte*
Style ... *Taylor Swift*
Love Me Do ... *The Beatles*
Sweet Home Alabama ... *Lynyrd Skynyrd*
Three Little Birds ... *Bob Marley and the Wailers*
Isn't She Lovely ... *Stevie Wonder*

You can check it out here:
https://tinyurl.com/secondchancesummer-spotify

ONE

-toby-

[senior year]

SITTING AT THE TABLE IN THE FAR CORNER OF THE CAFETERIA, to avoid notice, I watch Cassia walk in with her group of friends. They're all laughing and having a great time, something I generally find difficult to do in mixed company. I'm not sure why I'm the way I am. I generally only feel comfortable around my family and some close friends (which are limited). Music takes a lot of space in my head—I tend to get lost in there quite a bit—which doesn't make for a good friend, in most people's opinion.

As usual, Cassia looks beautiful with her chestnut hair falling below her shoulders in soft waves. As she looks up, our eyes lock across the crowded room. Sounds cheesy, right? But it's the norm for us. I'm connected to her on some fundamental level I don't understand. I also find her incredibly hot. She just has to walk into the room and my dick misbehaves, embarrassing me to the point where I have to escape being in her presence as soon as possible. The way I always leave whenever she's around, I'm sure she thinks I hate her.

Cassia excuses herself from her friends, then walks toward me with a shy smile. Luckily, I'm sitting down, so she won't see my hard-on. Stopping in front of me, she tucks her silky hair behind her ear. "Hey, Toby."

"Uh, hi, Cassia. How are things?" I manage to sound somewhat put together, which is a bonus.

"Great. The girls and I were just talking about prom. You going?"

I wouldn't be caught dead going to prom. I don't want to see her dancing with that douche she dates on and off, Jake Simmons. Kate's going with Michael Fitzpatrick, who hangs out in the same group as Jake. I don't think Michael and Jake are best buds, but they *are* friends. I told Kate that I think she'd be better off going to prom with her girlfriends than with Michael. He seems like a dick to me.

"Nah, not my scene." I look down at the table because I don't want to see the pity in her graphite-colored eyes.

"Oh, that's disappointing. I was hoping we could share a dance."

My head snaps up to hers. "I thought you'd be going with Jake."

She shakes her head in the negative, swishing the long, silky waves around her shoulders. Her lips spread in a half-smile. "Nope. We broke up." She rolls her eyes. "Again."

She doesn't seem too upset about another breakup. I don't know what that guy's problem is. He's constantly breaking up with her, then chases her down after realizing his mistake, begging for forgiveness. If she were my girl, I'd never let her go.

Shane wanders toward us, coming in behind Cassia. He wiggles his eyebrows when he sees we're talking. He knows I have a crush on her, so he likes to take every opportunity to tease me about it. "Hey, guys. What's up?"

Cassia turns toward Shane with a genuine smile, one that

lights up her entire face. "Oh, hi, Shane. We were just talking about prom. Toby's being a boohoo and not going. What about you? Are you going?" She looks hopeful.

He tucks his hands into his pockets, looking between the two of us. "Maybe. Not sure yet."

"It should be a fun night. You two should definitely come." She looks over her shoulder to acknowledge her friends, who are calling her back to their table. "Anyway, I need to go. See ya in last period, Toby."

"Yeah, see ya around."

I watch her long legs carry her away from us, wishing I wasn't such a loser. Shane looks at me with raised eyebrows as he sits down. "You should definitely go to the prom. I hear Jake broke up with her again. This could be your chance, bro."

A large body moves in front of me. When I tilt my head up to see who's blocking my stellar view, I find Jake.

"Whatcha lookin' at, Emo Boy?" His beefy arms are crossed over his bulky chest. Just because he's the captain of our school football team, he thinks he rules the school. Actually, he *does* rule the school, and I hate him. I hate him because he has Cassia and doesn't treat her with the respect she deserves.

I don't even bother making eye contact with the jerk. "Nothin'."

"Good, keep it that way, Emo Boy. She's no one to you. Got it?" He snarls down his nose at me. Since I'm sitting while he's standing, he's pretty much towering over me like a giant brick wall.

"No problem." I'll say anything to get the guy out of my face. He seems satisfied with my answer, raps his knuckles on the table, and walks away to join his so-called friends. I'm pretty sure half the guys he hangs out with are only friends with him because it's safer for them. If you're not his friend, it leaves you open to being bullied by him.

"You should tell him to fuck off," Shane suggests, knowing I'll do nothing of the sort. "So, are you gonna go to prom?"

I doodle in my notebook that I always carry with me. "Nah. They'll probably get back together by then. It's not worth the hassle."

The last period is music appreciation, my favorite class. Music centers me, quiets all the noise in my head, and allows me to be who I really am. My teacher, Mr. Hastings, pretty much lets me do my own thing, guiding me when I need it and leaving me alone when I don't. I also like the class because Cassia Phillips is in it—the only class we share. She is in no way musically inclined, only taking the class because her mom wanted her to take it. She wants her to be 'well rounded'. She plays the flute, which causes all sorts of issues with my dick, as she purses her pouty lips to blow across the embouchure hole. She struggles to maintain the appropriate pressure, causing a lot of frustration on her part, while all I can think about is kissing her soft lips.

Since I'm not a chatty person, everyone pretty much leaves me alone, but Cassia always sits next to me during our music history session. "Hey again." She smiles at me, making my insides flip upside down.

Struggling to make eye contact with her, I flick my eyes over her shoulder. "Yeah, hey." I sound like a douche. I get so damn nervous when she's around. For once, I wish I could be the cool kid.

"You ready to learn all about Dylan's crash and burn when he decided to use an electric guitar instead of his trusty acoustic at the Newport Folk Festival in 1965?"

I'm impressed she's interested in Dylan. He's definitely one of my idols, and I aspire to be as famous as he is one day. I raise my eyes to hers. She's fidgeting … biting her lip …

looking unsure. Raising an eyebrow, I nod slightly as one side of my mouth lifts to give her the approval I think she's looking for. She stops fidgeting, then smiles back. "It should be an interesting discussion."

"Yeah, it'll be interesting to find out what everyone's views are. I, for one, think Dylan's music was great, whether he played acoustic or electric guitar. It was all about the lyrics, the storytelling." I think it's the most number of words I've said to her, ever. The surprised expression on her face supports this idea.

Mr. Hastings walks in, interrupting our bonding moment over Dylan.

TWO

-cassia-

I'M CERTAIN TOBY HATES ME. TODAY WAS THE MOST HE'S EVER said to me, and it was only because we were talking about something close to his heart. Maybe that's the key? He usually only says a few words to me because I approach him to strike up a conversation. Otherwise, he would never speak to me. I love hearing the timbre of his voice when he talks—and when he sings, oh my gosh, *so good*—so I purposely go out of my way to chat with him. My friends always tease me because they know I have a huge crush on him. He makes my heart beat faster and my belly flip. Watching him work his guitar, I imagine the way his hands would feel on my body. Today, when he looked at me with his denim-colored eyes, I'm sure the breath in my lungs seized.

Perhaps if I stopped going back to Jake, I'd have a chance with Toby. Probably not—he always seems to be in a hurry to get away from me, and I'm not sure why. I've repeatedly gone back over the years in my memory, trying to pinpoint if I ever did anything to him to make him dislike me, but I can't think of anything. Two thick arms wrap around my torso from behind, scaring the crap outta me. Glancing over my shoulder, I put a face to the arms. Ugh, Jake. "Let me go, asshole."

"Now, that's no way to talk to your boyfriend." He squeezes me tighter with one arm, while the other comes up to grab my boob, hard. "Ouch. Let me go."

"I'm never lettin' you go, Sia." Stupid idiot. This is what happens. He breaks up with me and then he acts like nothing happened.

"You already did remember?" Wiggling free, I turn to face him. "You broke up with me because I didn't want to have sex with you on Friday night. Or did you forget?" He had a game on Saturday, so I'm sure he hooked up with someone else. Jake can't go without sex for more than two days at a time. He figures that if he breaks up with me before he hooks up with someone else, it doesn't count as cheating.

"Awww, you're upset. I didn't mean it. You know I never mean it." He pulls me into his huge body, snuggling down into my neck the way I love. He may be an idiot, but he can be so sweet to me. I like having a boyfriend; it makes me feel special and important to someone outside of my family. He pulls back, taking my school bag to carry, then grasps my hand to lead me out to his car. Throwing my bag on the back seat, he pins me against the side of his car, kissing me with apology and sweetness. Pulling back, he looks into my eyes. "I'm sorry, Babe. I was stupid. Please forgive me."

As I'm about to forgive him, *again*, Toby passes by with Shane and Kate. Toby looks my way and our eyes connect on a deeper level, as they always seem to. I'm sure I'm the only one who feels it, though, because he never seems affected. He doesn't stop, just keeps on walking, shaking his head … *in disappointment*, maybe? I'm pretty sure him being disappointed that I'm with Jake is wishful thinking on my part. Then he turns away down the sidewalk, exiting the school grounds without giving me another look. Looking back at Jake, I see the sincerity in his eyes, and I know he'll spend the rest of this week making it up to me.

I put on my sternest voice. "I forgive you. But this is the last time, Jake. I mean it."

He leans forward again, taking my mouth in a hard kiss filled with relief. He doesn't mean what he says and does half the time. He doesn't think things through, and he can be a spoiled brat when he doesn't get his way. Friday night was like witnessing a toddler's tantrum. He wasn't getting his way, so he wanted to hurt me by breaking up with me. I'm certain he's learned his lesson this time.

THREE

-toby-

[present]

"Hey, Xanthe," I sign, "I'm early."

Shane makes himself comfortable on a seat in the front lobby area.

Her face lights up as she leans in for a hug, then pulls back to greet me. "Hey, Toby." Signing as though she's playing guitar for my sign name. I'm proud to have recently been given a sign name by the people I interact with within the Deaf Community—it took almost four years to earn it after I became somewhat capable in ASL—which I still struggle with at times. Xanthe is Hard of Hearing, so she always signs with me to help me practice my newly acquired skills. I have a lot of time for Xanthe and her husband, Louis, who have worked tirelessly to set up and establish this brand-new facility for Deaf and Hard of Hearing kids. "I'm happy you could make it today."

I use my hands, facial expressions, and body language, combined with clear speech, to allow for lip-reading, as my signing is still a little clunky to communicate in ASL with

Xanthe. "I can't wait to get started. Show me where I need to set up."

She indicates for me to follow her, taking me on a tour of the impressive facility and explaining the purpose of each area. She then shows me to a large room with wooden floors and large windows. There's a heap of colorful balloons spread around the room, making it look like a party is about to take place.

"The kids will be surprised to have a real-life musician play for them today." She shows me where everything is so I can set up and then leaves me to my own devices. I take a moment to tune my guitar, strumming a new melody I've been experimenting with.

I'm so lost in my head that I fail to notice the little girl who's now resting her hands on my guitar. Her eyes are closed, her lashes resting on the apples of her cheeks as she's absorbing the vibrations of the strings through the body of the guitar via her hands. She's wearing a serene smile as she enjoys the melody I'm playing on repeat until I get it perfect. I don't want to stop because she's obviously enjoying the experience. After a few more minutes, she opens her eyes, revealing gorgeous pewter-colored irises, and smiles up at me. She's a cute little girl.

She signs to me, "I liked that."

"Thanks. I'm still working on it," I sign back to her.

"I love the guitar."

"Yeah?" I smile. I love it when I find a fellow guitar enthusiast. "I hug the guitar, too."

She giggles. "I think you mean you *love* the guitar, too."

"That's what I said."

"No, you didn't, silly. You said, 'I *hug* the guitar, too'." She shows me the difference between the two signs. They're so similar. I still get some signs muddled. "I've always wanted to learn how to play."

"Really? Why?"

"Why not?" she immediately responds.

"Because it would be hard," I sign. Her face drops a little. I'm still a newbie within the Community, and occasionally I make a faux pas, and I fear I've just made one. My ignorance surrounding the capabilities of Deaf and Hard of Hearing people still colors my thinking sometimes, but I'm working to shut those old thoughts down.

"That's okay. I like learning things that can be hard." She smiles at me. "Would you teach me?"

Uh, this was meant to be a one-off session to entertain the kids as part of their school vacation program. She's making a puppy dog face while holding her hands together in the begging position. I must be a complete sucker because this is going to require a regular commitment from me. "Okay. Okay." I laugh at myself and the situation I now find myself in.

She jumps up and down, spinning around with the biggest grin on her little face, and now I'm glad I've agreed to teach her. Not that I know where to even begin to teach a kid how to play the guitar. I've never done it before. I'll have to ask Mom for help since she's the music teacher of the family.

"Thank you. Thank you. Thank you," she excitedly signs.

I can't stop the spread of my lips in response to her sheer happiness at my agreement to teach her how to play the guitar. But then her face suddenly drops, as if she's remembered something terrible. "What's wrong?"

She shrugs. "I don't have a guitar to learn with."

"Oh, no problem." I wave away her concern. "I possible bring one of my old ones that you possible use while you're learning until you possible get one of your own." Her face lights up yet again, and she giggles. It doesn't take much to make this kid happy. I have several old guitars sitting at Mom and Dad's from when I was younger. I'm sure one of them will be the perfect size for her.

"Oh, you're silly. You kept saying *possible* instead of *can*." She shows me the difference between the two signs. "See the difference?"

That's twice I've stuffed up my signs. "Uh, yeah, thanks. I'll try to remember." I practice the two signs, trying to commit them to memory.

"That's okay. I sometimes make mistakes, too."

"You'll need to get permission from your parents." Her smile widens as she nods energetically. We're interrupted as a handful of kids of various ages make their way into the room. My new friend stays close to me but welcomes her friends with a wave. They've all spent quite a bit of time together over the past few weeks, and probably most of them attend the same school. Xanthe's close behind. She notices my new friend standing next to me, away from her friends.

She signs to me, "I see you've met Poppy." Looking at the little girl with affection.

So, her name is Poppy; it suits her. She's vibrant, like the color of the flower I assume she's named after. I nod, then let Xanthe know she conned me into giving her guitar lessons. She bursts into laughter before letting me know that Poppy's very good at getting people to do her bidding. *Oh, great*, I've been had by a kid. Kate's going to get a real kick out of this.

Xanthe introduces me to the kids by fingerspelling my name, then using my sign name from there on out. She explains how we met, and the kids' faces light up as they all wave to me. I'm not convinced Poppy got all the information because she was fascinated with stroking the timber of my guitar. I plug my guitar into the amplifier, put in my earplugs, and cover them with headphones for double protection. The amplifiers are loud to increase the vibrations through the wooden floor, so I make sure to protect my hearing. The kids lay on the floor, close their eyes, and lose themselves in the vibrations as I strum my way through a couple of my slower songs. Normally, I have my band playing with me during a concert or recording an album. Today, it's just me and my trusty guitar. After a couple of songs, Xanthe gets the kids to stand up. They grab a balloon each, and she does what she does best.

Sign my music to the kids.

Which is how we met four and a half years ago. I saw her signing at a concert, and I was hooked. I knew I had to get her to work with me, signing my concerts, and making them accessible to the Deaf Community. She's already familiar with my music, so it's smooth and fluent for her and the kids. The kids' faces light up with lips stretched wide as they experience my more upbeat songs for the first time.

I'm on top of the world.

Poppy's front and center, moving to the music with evident enjoyment written all over her body. Being part of this experience with these kids, who seem to have a natural rhythm, could easily become addictive. They're so appreciative and open with their joy. Maybe it won't be so bad to spend time with Poppy and teach her how to play the guitar.

After the class is over, Poppy comes over to me. "That was so good."

I bow, flattening my right hand, then placing the tips of my fingers to my lips before moving it out and down toward Poppy with a smile. "Thank you." We stand, smiling at each other until she realizes it's time to go. "I'll come back next Friday at the same time. See you then, Poppy."

"Okay," she nods. "See you then." She uses my sign name the way Xanthe showed the kids.

I touch her shoulder gently to gain her attention because she's already turned to leave. I wait until she's looking at me. "Make sure you get permission. Okay?"

She nods emphatically, waving over her shoulder as she runs out of the room.

I pack up my guitar to head out to find Xanthe and Louis before I leave, so I can let them know I'll be back at the same time next week for my first lesson with Poppy. I didn't think to check with them if it would be okay before agreeing to teach Poppy. Thankfully, they give me the all-clear. Me teaching Poppy how to play the guitar is exactly the sort of thing they want to happen in this space. Their mission is to bring the joy of music and dance to kids in a deaf-friendly way. They got into it because they have a passion for music and dance and wanted to share that with others. As their own hearing deteriorated, their love for and appreciation of the arts never waned.

"Why the balloons?" I sign to Xanthe. I was puzzled why the kids were holding onto the colorful spheres during the session.

Her eyebrows rise along with a knowing smile. "They're great at amplifying the vibrations of the sound waves in the air. It adds to the entire experience for them."

"That's so freaking clever. I would never have thought of that." I shake my head in amazement at the different approaches that can be used to share the music experience. I never used to even consider that a Deaf person would be interested in music since they can't hear. After spending time with Xanthe and Louis, I've learned it isn't true. They've dispelled a lot of myths.

As I'm leaving the building with Shane, I spy Poppy climbing into a car with an older lady. She looks like she could be Poppy's nan. They're signing animatedly when the lady glances up, making eye contact with me. I nod in acknowledgment, and she smiles in return as Shane and I keep walking toward my car.

"What was that all about?" Shane observes.

"That's Poppy. The little girl who conned me into giving her guitar lessons, starting next Friday." I huff out a laugh, brushing loose strands of hair behind my ear.

Shane does a double-take between Poppy and me in disbelief. "*She* conned you. You're a grown-ass man, for god's sake. You need to learn to say no occasionally, bro." He shakes his head. "You have enough going on at the moment writing your next album. You shouldn't be adding more shit to your schedule." He shakes his head at me.

I know he has my best interest at heart, but I want to do this for Poppy, and well, for me, too. I think it'll be fun. I've just gotta work out where to start. "It's cool, Shane. I'm pretty sure this won't be a problem. It might even give me some inspiration. Win-win."

He shakes his head at me with a half-smile. We've known each other long enough that he knows I won't change my mind. He won't get in my way or try to stop me. "Where to next, Boss Man?"

I look at the time. Mom should be home. I might visit her so I can find out how to teach guitar to a kid. She'll be able to give me some idea about how to get started, at least. "Let's head to my folks. I need to ask Mom how to teach guitar."

That's enough to cause Shane to burst into laughter. Deep, happy laughter sounds fantastic coming from my long-time best friend and bodyguard. He's seen so much shit during his time in Syria as part of the Special Forces Operational Unit. To hear him laugh eases a deep worry inside me. He's not been the same since he came home, and I worry he'll never be the Shane I knew before he signed up.

FOUR

-toby-

ARRIVING AT MY CHILDHOOD HOME, MY SHOULDERS RELAX slightly as I step up to the front door. I'm a pretty laid-back guy, but I'm wound up because I don't want to let Poppy down. I'm hoping Mom can give me some guidance on where to start, as well as what techniques I should use, since she's been a music teacher for over thirty years. It's not like I can use a standard teaching approach.

Maybe I bit off more than I can chew?

I knock on the door out of politeness, then walk straight in with Shane on my heels, calling out to Mom as I go. She steps out of the kitchen, wiping her hands on a dishtowel. Her face lights up when she sees the two of us coming toward her. "Hey, Mom." I wrap my arms around her in a tight hug, then step back to let Shane hug her, too.

"Hey, Mrs. S."

"Hello, boys, this is a lovely surprise. I didn't think I'd see you until your birthday on Sunday. Come through. I've made a brownie slice."

Shane and I smile at each other because we both love Mom's brownies, and if my nose doesn't deceive me, I have a feeling these are still gonna be warm. It takes me back to my school days, coming home from school with Kate and Shane to the smell of fresh baked goods. Following her into the kitchen, we find the brownie slice on the cooling rack in the middle of the counter.

Oh, yeah, they're still warm.

Mom potters around, making us each a cup of coffee, and then cuts the brownie into equal portions. She knows Shane and I love this treat, so she cuts and plates a generous serving for each of us. We sit around the table so we can catch up.

"Have you heard anything from Kate and Oliver?"

"Oh, yes. They checked in on Wednesday to let us know they arrived safely on the island. Kate was stressing out about her engagement ring because she found out how much it was worth on the honeymoon." Mom laughs.

"Well, it wasn't going to be cheap if Oliver had anything to do with it. What did she expect?"

Shane shakes his head. "Kate's gonna have to get used to how much money that guy spends on things. He can afford it."

Mom and I nod in agreement.

"So, what have you boys been up to today?"

"We just finished at *Music for my Heart*. Remember, I said I was volunteering there for an afternoon?"

"Oh, that's right. How was it?"

"It was great. Interesting and loads of fun."

"Your son got conned by a little girl," Shane adds with a smirk. He thinks it's hilarious that Poppy conned guitar lessons out of me. Mom's eyes flit between the two of us, waiting for an explanation. I explain how I met Poppy, our conversation, and that I've agreed to give her guitar lessons starting next Friday. I even tell Mom that I've offered the use of one of my old guitars. I must remember to get it out of the attic for her. Before she can play it, I need to fit new strings.

Mom's entire face softens as a smile curves her lips. Eyes,

exactly like mine, look at me with pride and affection. "I'm so happy you're using your talent to teach others. What sort of hearing loss does this little girl have?"

"She's profoundly deaf, according to Xanthe. She was feeling the vibrations through the body of my guitar. The kids also used balloons. I've never seen anything like it before."

"Oh, my. That's amazing. I would have never thought to use balloons. I might try that with some of my younger students. It'll be fun." She pauses. "You'll need to employ some different techniques than what you normally would for a hearing child."

"I know. That's why we came over. I wanted to ask for your advice. First, I've never taught anyone how to play the guitar. Even though I'm competent, I'm not sure I know where to start with lessons, let alone for a Deaf person." I'm realizing that I *am* in over my head.

"She's going to rely on touch and vibrations more than a hearing person. *Feeling* the vibrations of the lower notes will send the signals to the brain, the same as ours receives the signals through *hearing* the sounds."

"Yeah. That's what we did today. The kids laid on the floor. We turned the speakers up loud, and they experienced the music through the vibrations. Then Xanthe joined in, signing the lyrics and music to the kids to give them a more robust experience as they held the balloons. They loved it."

"There's a music teacher I've heard about in London who teaches guitar to Deaf and Hard of Hearing children. Maybe look him up. I'll try to find his name for you."

"Thanks, Mom. That'd be great."

"No problem. Just remember to have fun with it. Remember, you want to build a love for the instrument, not just learn how it works or how to play it." She pats my hand to reinforce her point.

"I will, Mom. Promise. I'll do some research to see what I

can find. I need to get one of my old guitars out of the attic, so she has one to use." I stand to take my dishes to the sink. "Be back in a minute."

I turn on the light in the attic and make my way to the area where I've stored my guitars since childhood. I have several sizes that Mom and Dad bought me as I grew. I find my half-size guitar, which I had when I was about six or seven. I'm not sure how old Poppy is. She looks quite small, so this should be a good size for her. I suppose I could buy a new one, but I like the idea of her using one of my old guitars. I grab the guitar, dusting it off as I leave the attic in the dark once again.

I step into the kitchen to find Mom washing the dishes and Shane wiping them. "I found my first guitar." Holding it up, I show her the small instrument. It brings back a lot of memories for me. Wonderful memories of Mom and me sitting together practicing *Love Me Do* by the Beatles. Two simple chords for most of the song, introducing a third in the bridge. "I think our first song will be the same one you taught me. Do you remember what it was?"

"Of course I do. *Love Me Do* by The Beatles. Such a fun little song and a brilliant choice for a first song to learn. I'm sure she'll love it."

FIVE

-cassia-

I DRAG MYSELF IN THE FRONT DOOR AFTER NINE, WHICH IS usual for a Friday night—especially lately. A lot of my work is for weddings, which predominantly happen on the weekend. Therefore, the latter part of my week is always busy, requiring me to work late most Friday nights.

Ever since I donated the floral arrangements for a big fundraiser for *The Parkerville Project*, I've been run off my feet. Most of the attendees—make that all the attendees—were very wealthy, and they seemed to like the quirky arrangements I put together for the table centerpieces. When Mr. Stone contacted me to ask if I would be interested in helping, I jumped at the opportunity. I was flattered that he had been impressed with my work whenever he purchased flowers from me, that I offered to provide all the floral arrangements for free. Even though I did it to help the kids, I've benefited tenfold from the event with the uptake in sales; it's put my little business on the map. Where I used to have at least two weekends a month off, I'm working events every weekend now, and it's all thanks to those centerpieces. I'm going to need to employ another staff member to help, so I don't spend every weekend away from my daughter.

The front of the house is dark, so I make my way toward the back of Mom's home. I moved back after I found out I was pregnant and would be going it alone. I needed Mom's help and support. I find Mom on the couch with my little girl curled up next to her, wearing her favorite purple pajamas, sound asleep.

"Hey, Mom. Sorry, I'm so late. The order for the wedding tomorrow was huge, and I needed to make sure the arrangements made it to the venue intact. I'll have to head over tomorrow morning to place everything and deliver the bouquets to the bride and boutonnieres to the groom. It should only take about four hours. Thank goodness." I sigh. "I need a break and I miss hanging out with my girl."

"It's no problem, Cassia. It's why you moved back home, remember? So I could help you. I love looking after my granddaughter." Mom looks lovingly at my little girl as she strokes a lock of hair that's fallen over her cherubic face behind her ear.

"She tried hard to stay awake to see you when you got home. She has some exciting news to share with you, but it's gonna have to wait 'til tomorrow." Mom stands up, ready to carry my baby upstairs to bed. Not that she's a baby anymore. She just turned seven.

"I can carry her, Mom. You sit down."

"Okay. I'll go up to get her bed ready so that you can lay her down."

I drop my purse on the table as Mom quickly walks ahead of us to prepare her bed. Carrying her behind Mom, I place her carefully on her pale purple sheets, kissing her forehead before Mom bends down to do the same. Mom leaves the room, allowing me time with my girl.

I use the light spilling in from the hall to take a few minutes to watch her sleep, then lean down to tuck her in and kiss her goodnight one last time. I wasn't quite as stealthy as I should have been, causing her to stir. When she sees it's me, her entire face lights up in happiness, which makes every single part of my heart feel close to exploding. She's the best thing I've ever done in my life. My greatest joy. I turn on the lamp next to her bed to make it easier for us to communicate.

She sleepily signs, "Hello, Mommy."

I sign, "Hey, Baby Girl." I brush the hair away from her face.

"Guess what happened today?"

"You won a vacation to the moon?"

She laughs. "No, Mommy. Don't be silly."

Sitting on the side of her bed, I settle in for a chat. "Well, tell me then. What happened today to make you so happy?"

"I'm going to learn how to play guitar from a real-life guitarist."

I'm not sure what qualifies someone as a 'real-life guitarist'. "Oh, yeah, anyone I know?"

She signs his name as the universal sign for 'guitar'. Well, that's an apt name for a guitarist, I suppose.

"How did you manage to get someone to agree to give you guitar lessons?" She's skilled at convincing anybody to do anything she wants. I'm not sure how she does it, but her success rate is extraordinary.

She shrugs her shoulders, giving me her most innocent face. "I just asked, Mommy, and he said 'okay'. He's even going to bring a guitar for me to use." Her little hands are flying fast and furious, conveying her excitement.

She's been asking to learn the guitar for the past two years. I'm not sure why she has such a fascination with the instrument, but it's something she really wants to do.

"You'll need to make sure you practice at home in between lessons."

She nods vigorously.

"When will you have these lessons?"

"On Friday afternoon. I already asked Gramma, and she doesn't mind taking me after school." She holds her hands in the begging position. "Please say it's okay, Mommy."

I bet that's how she got the guitarist to agree to give her lessons. "Of course it's okay, Baby. If Gramma is happy to take you and you promise to practice between lessons, I think it will be great for you."

She springs forward, wrapping her little arms around my neck, kissing me all over my face in absolute joy. We chat about her afternoon at *Music for my Heart* and how she spent the rest of her day. I let her know that I have work in the morning, but then I'll be free for the rest of the weekend. She snuggles back into her comfy bed, and I tuck her in again, kissing her goodnight. "I love you more than all the stars in the sky and grains of sand on the earth." She smiles at me, and I turn off her lamp to head downstairs to catch up with Mom.

"You were up there a while. I assume Poppy told you her news. She was so excited, bouncing in the back seat all the way home." Mom laughs.

"Yeah, she did. She's so freaking excited. I'm thrilled for her. Thanks for agreeing to take her to her lessons."

"No problem. I think it'll be fantastic for her. A challenge."

I nod in agreement. "She loves to be challenged. This will be just the thing." I lean forward to hug Mom. "I'm gonna have a shower, then head to bed. I'm exhausted."

"Sure thing, Honey. Sweet dreams."

"You, too. See you in the morning."

"I want Lisianthus flowers in their double form in purple, pink, and white in my bouquet and for our table centerpieces, at the church, and anywhere else we need flowers. I want them everywhere. I want to be swimming in them. They're just so beautiful." The bride-to-be is fierce in her love for the floral bloom. They are beautiful flowers, and I can envision the displays clearly.

"For your bouquets, I can do a tight round design using a minimum of fifty blooms wrapped in satin ribbon to match the dresses. For the table centerpieces, I would suggest a more whimsical display, softer with more movement. I can incorporate the same blooms, tying them in with some Lavender and Baby's Breath." I pull out my extensive collection of photo albums, which I keep on hand for clients. Flipping through, I find the collection I'm looking for, placing the open album on the table between us. Her eyes light up as she nods in agreement. "Something like this?"

"That's perfect. Exactly what I had in mind," she gushes.

We spend the next forty-five minutes finalizing the number of tables, bouquets, boutonnieres, and pedestal displays at the entrance of the church and reception. The wedding is three months away, so I make sure to put all of my notes into the system. I activate my calendar alerts to order the flowers and for the event itself. I set the order up in the system, which takes a significant amount of time because I have to calculate the number of flowers I'll require. When I place the order, I add an extra five percent to the quantity to allow for damaged blooms.

The bell over the door tinkles, letting me know someone's entered my store. I love my little shop, which belonged to my gramma, who is also a florist. I spent many afternoons and school vacation days here helping her with designs and arrangements. She still comes in every Friday morning to help me out with my weekend event orders. Stepping out of my office, I'm almost bowled over by my rambunctious daughter, followed closely by my mom. She hugs me tight around my waist, and I lean down to kiss the top of her head.

"Hi, Mom. It's so great to see you guys. You just missed Gramma Iris." I sign as I speak, so Poppy knows what I'm saying. I generally sign for Poppy, so she's not left out of conversation wherever it's appropriate. Some conversations aren't for little people, so I don't sign those if she's in the room. She gets mad at me sometimes, but I've explained to her that some conversations aren't meant for children.

"Poppy wanted to show you her guitar and tell you all about her lesson this afternoon."

I look down at Poppy and sign, "Was it as good as you hoped it would be?"

"It was better, Mommy." She shows me her guitar. "The best. Look at my guitar."

"It's not yours. Just on loan."

"No, he said I could keep it. It used to be his when he first learned to play. He was even younger than me." She's moving her hands so fast that I'm having trouble keeping up with her. "He even put different-colored strings on it for me to help me learn the different chords. Isn't it cool?"

"So cool." I smile at her. "You are one lucky girl."

"Let me show you what I learned today."

She sits on the chair opposite my desk, straps on the guitar, positions it tightly against her stomach, and places her fingers on the strings. She's focusing hard on getting them in just the right place. Then she strums the first chord. My heart's in my throat as moisture fills my eyes. I'm so happy she's doing something she's been wanting to do for ages. I'm so proud of her for making her dream a reality. I never want her to miss out on any of the things she wants to do.

"That sounds awesome, Poppy. I'm so proud of you." I glance over at Mom. She has the same look of pride as I do. "Did you have fun?"

"Oh, yeah. So much fun, Mommy. He's really funny, and

he said that I might be able to go on tour with him when I'm older."

Geez, he needs to slow down a bit. Talk about getting her hopes up. "Uh, we'll see, Baby Girl. You need to get through school before you start thinking about touring the world with a band." Plus, I don't want to think about her growing up and moving away from home—not just yet, anyway.

SIX

-cassia-

My phone lights up with an incoming call from my sister. I quickly answer it because she rarely phones me, especially on a Sunday.

"Hey, Vi."

I hear sniffling on the other end before she answers. "Hey, Cass. I'm sorry to bug you on a Sunday, but I didn't know who else I could talk to."

"It's okay, Vi. You know you can call me anytime. What's happened?"

"It's Allen." She sniffles.

"Is he okay?"

"Well, if you call him getting shit-faced every weekend and hooking up with anyone with a vagina, okay. Then yeah, he's okay," she spits at me.

"Oh my gosh! I had no idea, Vi. How long's this been going on?" Far out. I had no idea they were having trouble in their marriage. I mean, Allen's always been a bit of a dick. He's often flirted with me behind Vi's back, but I shut him down, never giving it a second thought.

"Since I got pregnant with Jasmine, if I'm honest. But it's

escalated over the last twelve months or so. I don't know what I should do." Her voice is shaky as she shares her secret.

"Have you spoken to him about his behavior? Told him it's unacceptable?"

"Yeah," she sighs. "When I call him out about it, we always end up in a huge argument. I'm tired of going over the same shit with him. Either he wants to be in this marriage, or he doesn't. If Jasmine and I aren't what he wants anymore, then I would prefer him to leave rather than act like a nineteen-year-old frat boy."

"I hear ya, Sis. It's not good enough. Do you think he's waiting for you to end the relationship rather than manning up to do it himself?"

"Possibly. But I need *him* to leave. I don't want to have to move and uproot Jas if I can help it."

"You can always move in with us. There's plenty of room here. I don't know what I would've done without Mom's support. She's been a godsend."

"Yeah, I know. Thanks for reminding me, Cass." She pauses. "I guess now that I've admitted my marriage is in trouble, it makes it easier to ask for help. I haven't wanted to say anything to anyone before this, but last night was the last straw."

"What happened last night?"

"Nothing worse than usual, but he stumbled into the house after three this morning, his shirt all undone, stinking of another woman, and I don't just mean her perfume. It was disgusting." That would be awful. I remember Jake coming to me after we'd broken up, wanting to get back together, smelling of someone else. It was foul.

"Oh, Vi. I sort of know how you feel. Jake used to do that all the time, but we weren't married. I'm sure it's a thousand times worse for you."

"Don't devalue your experience because you and Jake

weren't married. It's still just as bad. Men think they can do whatever they want and it'll be okay."

"Why don't the two of you come over for the afternoon? Leave the asshole to stew. Mom and Poppy made shortbread."

"Yeah, I think I might do that. I'll see ya soon."

"Great. I'll let Mom and Poppy know you're coming over. They'll be so happy."

"Okay." She pauses. "And, Cass. Thanks."

The call disconnects, and I'm heartbroken for my big sister. After what Dad did to Mom, and what Jake did to me, I always looked at Violet's marriage, hoping that not all men were immature assholes. But I guess they are.

I walk downstairs to let Mom know Vi and Jas are coming over to visit. Poppy's ecstatic because she adores her little cousin and dotes over her whenever they spend time together.

"You'd better put away anything unsafe for Jas. Okay?" I sign.

"Okay, Mommy." She darts upstairs to tidy her bedroom, making sure it's safe for her three-year-old cousin. Not that her cousin will play in her bedroom because it's upstairs, which isn't safe, but it's a great way to get Poppy to tidy her bedroom. Yep, I'm totally winning at this mom gig.

Mom smiles, winking at me because she's the one who taught me the strategy. I update Mom on what's been going on with Vi.

She hangs her head, then looks back up at me. She looks livid. "What is it with men? What's so hard about being a decent human being toward the people you supposedly love?" She slaps her thighs, shaking her head in disbelief. She just verbalized precisely what I was thinking.

"I don't know, Mom. What's so hard about owning up to your responsibilities and acting like an adult?"

"Exactly, Cass." She starts cleaning up the kitchen like a

madwoman. Wiping over the counters as if they've wronged her.

I check the playroom to make sure Poppy's put away her Lego blocks, which would be dangerous for Jas. I'm finishing up when there's a knock at the front door and Jas runs in, looking for Mom.

"Gamma. Gamma. Gamma." Her little squeals precede her through the house.

I step out of the playroom to greet my sister with the hug she needs. Without words, I wrap my arms around her, pulling her in tight to me. Her body sinks into mine as she absorbs my support. "Things'll work out, Vi. I promise."

She nods, pulling away from me to wipe the tears from her face. Vi's coloring differs from mine. She takes after our father more than I do. I look more like Mom. Mom steps out of the kitchen carrying Jas on her hip, immediately pulling Violet into her for a fierce embrace. I wrap my arms around both of them, making a huddle of support for my heartbroken sister. She must have been through hell these past years, and not once has she let on to us that there was a problem. It must be a relief for her to have it all out in the open now and be able to lean on us for support. We separate to make our way into the kitchen, where Mom sets about making us each a cup of coffee to have with our shortbread. I flick the light switch, which flashes the lights throughout the house, to let Poppy know to come downstairs.

It doesn't take long before we hear Poppy's feet on the stairs and Vi braces herself for Poppy's onslaught. Sure enough, Poppy throws herself at her aunt's body. That's my baby girl all over. Luckily, she's gentler when she greets her younger cousin. She gets down on her knees to greet Jas. They hug so tightly that they fall over in fits of giggles; watching the girls instantly improves the mood in the room. We all sit to enjoy the yummy shortbread and hot coffee for the grown-ups, while the kids have a cup of milk. Poppy updates Violet on her guitar lessons, offering to play for her later; I have to translate a little because it takes Vi a little while to get back into the swing of ASL whenever she visits. After they've caught up, Poppy takes Jasmine into the playroom.

Mom reaches across the table, taking one of our hands in each of hers, squeezing in silent support. "I'm sorry, girls."

Vi and I glance at each other in confusion. "What are you sorry about, Mom?"

"I … I think I've done a disservice to you both." I attempt to interrupt her, but she stops me with her hand held up in the universal sign for stop. "Your father leaving left its mark on all of us. I never bothered to put myself out there again to meet a decent man, and I think I may have done more damage than I thought. You girls have never had a positive male role model in your lives. Your father left when I was pregnant with Cassia. Then my father died when you girls were so little, and then, well, then I put all my focus on raising you girls while working to put a roof over our heads. I never bothered to build another relationship, to model a positive relationship for you girls." Her head drops between her shoulders in defeat. She looks back up at us. "I'm so sorry."

Vi and I climb to our feet, embracing Mom on either side. "No, Mom. It's not your fault. Our relationships, or lack thereof, have nothing to do with you. You've always taught us to be strong and independent. To get on with what needs to be done and move forward. That's a great lesson. The best." I tell her.

"Yeah, Mom. The only people at fault here are the guys who seem to have difficulty acting like decent human beings."

"That's the thing. You girls never had that male role model."

"Once again, not your fault, Mom. Honestly. Don't carry

that on your shoulders." I hug her extra tight to make sure she gets the message.

Violet looks at me, then at Mom. "You never told us why Dad left. I think we're old enough to know now."

Mom looks between the two of us, and I can see the war inside her—whether to keep us in the dark or to share her experience with us. I quickly check on the girls in the playroom to find them playing together happily. As I sit down, Mom begins to share her story.

"Your father and I were happily married, and we'd always talked about having a family, but he only wanted one child." She looks at me sympathetically. "I wanted more, but I accepted that he only wanted the one. We were ... well, I *thought* we were happy. Things were going along smoothly enough, I suppose, with a baby in the house. Then I got sick with the stomach flu. Didn't really think anything of it," she shrugs, "but not long after that, I started feeling ill and my boobs were sore. When I sat down and thought about things, I realized I'd missed my period. So I took a pregnancy test without telling your father and found out I was pregnant." She gets up to make us all another cup of coffee. I sense this is difficult for her to share with us, even after all these years. "I was terrified to tell your father I was pregnant again. Obviously, the stomach flu caused the pill I was taking to be ineffective, so I felt completely responsible for the situation. I kept putting it off and putting it off until I couldn't hide the swell of my stomach any longer. He noticed my boobs had become bigger and my stomach wasn't as flat as it usually was. He confronted me about it." She sighs, carrying the coffee back to the table. "I don't know what I was thinking; not telling him straight away. What did I possibly think could be the result? Anyway, he was furious with me. Accused me of trapping him with another child." She braces herself, looking directly at me. "A child *he* never wanted." She squeezes my hand. "I'm sorry, Cass. This is painful, and I want you to know it wasn't your fault that he left. It was his own. There was never a time I didn't want you."

I can only nod. Some part of me always felt it must have been my fault he left, and Mom just confirmed it for me.

"So, he packed his things and left. I've never heard from him since that day. Technically, we're still married because we've never divorced."

Now that *is* a shock. "You need to track him down and divorce his ass, Mom," Violet rightly suggests. "If Al walks away from me, I'm gonna divorce his ass as soon as I can."

I see red. "Why are you waiting for Allen to walk away from you? You can walk away from him, you know? Take the power away from him."

"You are more than welcome to move in here. The three of us could make a formidable team, working together to raise the girls. Supporting each other." Mom reminds Violet.

"I know I could and should walk away from him. But I want him to do it. It'll make it easier for me when it comes time to divorce his ass. I don't want him to have access to Jas. I'm hoping a judge will be less likely to award Al time with his daughter if he's the one to walk away."

"Maybe, maybe not." I wrap my arm around her shoulder. "Whatever happens, know that we're here for you. Okay?"

"Yeah, I know."

Violet decides to stay for dinner, so we head into the playroom to play with the girls. Then we take them to the park to get some fresh air for a while.

Saying goodbye to them both after dinner hurts my heart. Knowing what they're going home to makes it hard to let them go.

SEVEN

-toby-

"Hey, bro. You ready to head over for your lesson with Poppy?"

Shane's voice startles me. I was caught up in this new song I'm writing and I didn't hear him come up to my studio. If it weren't for him, I'd miss heaps of appointments when I'm in the zone.

"Uh, yeah. Sure thing." Before I lose the notes I was working on, I place my Fender on its stand and write them down. I grab what I need for today's lesson, then follow Shane downstairs to the garage. I'm really excited to show Poppy the new app I downloaded onto my laptop. It uses the computer microphone to convert the sounds from the guitar into interesting visual interpretations. I found out about it from the guitar teacher in the UK that Mom was telling me about. He uses it with his Deaf and Hard of Hearing students. I think she'll like it and I'm pretty sure it'll make our lessons fun.

"Have you decided whether you're going to the reunion tomorrow night?"

"Yeah, when I FaceTimed Kate on our birthday, she convinced me to go. She gave a compelling argument about taking the opportunity to apologize to Cassia for always blowing her off in high school. She thinks it'll be good for me."

"I think she's right. It's something that's weighed on your mind. It would be good for you to close that door."

"Yeah, I guess." I brush my hands through my hair, looking out of the car window as we drive. "I just don't want to spend time with anyone else. None of those assholes gave me the time of day back then."

"You don't have to talk to anyone else. I'll make sure to keep everyone else away from you. After all, that's my job. Right?"

"Right."

Arriving at *Music for my Heart*, we exit the car and make our way inside. Xanthe is the first person we see. Her whole body expresses her happiness when she sees us. Her joy is unmistakable.

"Hey, guys. So, you're definitely making this a weekly thing with Poppy?" she speaks as she signs.

"Hi, Xanthe. Yeah, I committed to her and I intend to keep it. I found this awesome software which I think will make our lessons so much better for her. I even purchased an extra copy for her parents to load onto their computer at home." Shit, I hope they have a computer at home. Most people have computers, right? I guess I'll find out today. If she doesn't have one, I'll get her one.

"I've heard about that program. We're still setting everything up, but we should definitely get it for the center. You're taking this seriously."

"Absolutely. You know I don't do anything by half," I sign as I speak.

Xanthe laughs, nodding in agreement. "Oh, I know. You're a workhorse."

She walks me to the room where Poppy and I had our first two lessons. She's picking it up surprisingly fast for someone so young—much the way I did. As I set up my computer, Poppy runs into the room with the guitar I gave her, throwing herself at me in greeting. The guitar she's holding whacks me on the back of my legs. She's an incredibly vivacious little girl. I can't help but fall for her, which sounds weird. We step apart, and her little hands move wildly, telling me all about her at-home practice this past week. I'm equally excited to share my discovery with her, so I show her the program on my laptop.

I play our song to show her how it *should* look on the computer using the program I downloaded. While her eyes are on the laptop screen, her hands are on the body of my guitar. She looks mesmerized by the patterns being created on the screen in time with my playing.

Poppy signs to me. "Wow. That's amazing."

"I know. I think it's going to help you learn how to play the guitar."

"Me, too."

"Do you want to show me how you're doing? Then we'll look at how it comes out on the screen."

"Okay."

She puts on her guitar with the different-colored strings, pressing the body close against her stomach to maximize the vibrations, and begins to play as she watches the laptop screen. The smile forming on her cute little face is magical to watch. As she plays, she makes minor errors here and there, and I make a note of them on the music tabs so I can show her when she finishes. I can't correct her as she goes because she's focused on her fingers and the screen; I also don't want to distract her. I've caught on quickly that I need to give all of my instructions before she begins playing. I also ensure I have direct eye contact with her during any breaks. That's why I wait until she looks up after the last note to sign, "That sounds great, Poppy. I can tell you've been practicing."

"Oh, yeah. I practice all the time."

"I can tell. Do you like the program?" I point to the laptop.

"Yeah, it's really good. I can *see* my playing." She smiles proudly. "I'm making those sounds." She points to herself, then to the screen.

"Yes, you are. I bought a second copy of the app." I give Poppy the thumb drive. "You can load it onto your computer at home."

She nods as she takes the thumb drive from me. "Thank you."

"No problem. Do you have a computer at home you can use?"

"Yeah, we do. Gramma needs it for drawing the gardens she builds, but she lets me use it sometimes."

She never seems to mention her dad. It's always Mommy or Gramma. "What about your mom or dad? Do either of them have a computer they're not using, so you don't take time away from your gramma's work?"

"Oh, I don't have a daddy. Me and Mommy live with Gramma. I guess I can use Mommy's when she's home. She doesn't use it much because she works so much that when she's home, she likes to spend time with me." I had a feeling that was the situation, but it's none of my business. Heaps of parents don't live together anymore.

"I'm sure you have a daddy. You wouldn't be here without one." I nudge her shoulder.

"Oh, yeah, I guess so. I've just never met him." She shrugs as if it's not a big deal. I'm at a loss as to what kind of asshole abandons his daughter—especially a daughter as cool as Poppy.

"Let me know if it's not working out. I can get you a laptop."

Poppy jumps up, giving me an awkward hug, trapping her guitar between us. "Thank you. Thank you. Thank you. You're always so kind to me."

"I'm happy to help. I'm playing teaching you how to ..." I shake my head and wave my hand as though I'm erasing my words. "I mean, I'm *enjoying* teaching you how to play the guitar. It brings back memories from when my mom taught me how to play." I explain that Mom's a music teacher. It's because of her that I started playing guitar.

We get back to our practice for the rest of the hour. I'm in awe of her determination to master the chords, to master this instrument. She has a quiet determination about her, and I know she's going to succeed in her quest to master the guitar. Her mom must be so proud of her desire to succeed. I know I am, and I've only known her for a few weeks.

I get the feeling that Poppy makes everyone she meets fall in love with her.

EIGHT

-cassia-

OUR PROM THEME WAS VEGAS NIGHTS, SO THE ORGANIZING committee used the same theme for our ten-year reunion. I don't know how to feel about tonight. I'm excited to see old classmates, but I'm dreading running into Jake. I have nothing to say to him. I don't want to have a confrontation in front of other people. My stomach turns at the thought of facing him tonight after what happened the last time I saw him.

Searching through my closet for something to wear that suits the theme and makes me look somewhat sexy and sophisticated. I push hanger after hanger aside until I come across my dressy black jumpsuit that I'd forgotten I had. If I pair it with my patent leather stiletto sandals, I think I can look somewhat sexy. It comes down low in the front as well as the back, which means I'm gonna need my boob tape and adhesive bra to keep the girls relatively contained. As I'm searching through my dresser for the tape, my thoughts switch to Toby. I wonder if he'll show up tonight? Ever since I received the invitation to this reunion, he's the one person who has been foremost in my thoughts; he's the one person I truly want to see. He didn't bother attending prom. I don't want to get my hopes up, especially now that he's famous.

I would love to see him again so I can congratulate him on his success. *Oh, who am I kidding?* I want to see his hotness up close and personal. I've followed his career via social media, and I'm really proud of his success—and from what I've seen, he's one hot dude. Women throw their panties at him when he's on stage; he's *that* hot.

Poppy's at a friend's house until tomorrow, allowing me to take my time to pamper myself so I treat myself to a bath with my favorite cinnamon bun bubble bath. Soaking quietly in the tub, my thoughts wander back to Toby in high school. He was always so withdrawn. He never socialized with too many people. He barely tolerated me chatting with him, finding any excuse to escape my presence. I know the jocks used to give him a hard time, but he wasn't the only person in high school to be subjected to their immature, self-inflated egos.

I'm lost in my thoughts, not noticing how cool the water's become until I shiver. I release the plug and step into the shower to finish my routine. I wash my hair, shave everywhere that needs shaving, then use my cinnamon scrub to make sure my skin glows. It's time to work out what to do with my hair that can't seem to decide if it's wavy or straight. Before I had Poppy, I had nice, even waves in my hair. After pregnancy, my hair doesn't know what it wants to do. It drives me crazy, and most days, I end up tying it up in a messy ponytail to keep it out of the way. I straighten it, then put in some loose waves. My hair is longer now than it was in high school, reaching halfway down my back.

I wonder how different everyone looks?

I don't get the opportunity to dress up or go out very often, so I'm taking my time to put some effort in for tonight. Plus, I'm hoping to catch a certain someone's eye, *if* he shows up. Putting on my makeup, I go for dramatic eyes with subtle lips and then choose my jewelry. Mmm, what to choose? Looking at my selections, I gravitate toward the butterfly pendant Poppy gave me last Mother's Day. I remember how excited she was to give it to me. When I asked her why she chose it, she said it was because butterflies are deaf, just like her. She thought it was awesome, while my heart cracked a little for my baby girl. Wearing the pendant she gifted me will help me feel confident and strong because she's the strongest person I know—the way she goes after what she wants with such determination is inspiring. Taking one last look in the mirror, I'm reasonably happy with what I see. I look pretty good for a mom—not that everyone there will know I'm a mom.

As I make my way downstairs, I realize it's nice to be dressed up as a woman, not just a 'mom'—I feel sexy instead of practical for a change. Mom steps in, taking my hands to hold them out from my sides. "You look gorgeous, Cassia."

"Thanks, Mom. I'm a little nervous, to be honest. I'm hoping Jake won't make a scene."

"Surely he won't do that sort of thing in front of everyone." Mom grumbles. "If he starts anything, just hold your head up high and walk away from him. He doesn't deserve a second of your time or your breath."

"Thanks, Mom. I'll do my best to avoid him. I'd better get going—my Uber's waiting. Don't wait up. I'll see you in the morning."

"Have fun, Love."

"I will. Night."

Stepping into the function room, I'm surprised at the amount of effort that went into the decorations. It looks amazing; the organizing committee did a fantastic job. I take a minute to get my bearings before stepping all the way inside the room.

Peering around the ample space, it takes me a little while to recognize the faces from my senior year. Locating my high school girlfriends grouped over near the drinks—*of course, where else would they be?*—I make my way toward them, but I don't get far before a beefy body steps in my way. I haven't even been here for five freaking minutes, and he's already all up in my grill.

"Hello, Sia. You're looking mighty fine tonight."

I look at him closely. He looks okay. Still bulky, but not so much in a muscular way like he was in high school through to college. "Hi, Jake. I don't want any trouble tonight. I just want to spend time with old friends and have a good time." My heart's racing in my chest as though I've run all the way here. Why did he have to be the first person to speak to me? I haven't even had the chance to have a drink to settle my nerves.

"I'm not looking for any trouble, Babe. You're lookin' hot, but I wanna have a good time with old friends, too. Maybe we can catch up for old times' sake?" He finishes with a sleazy wink as he trails his finger up and down my arm. I shift slightly, so he's no longer touching me. *Uh, whatever.* I feel like I need to go home to bathe again now.

"Not interested, Jake. Not even in the slightest. Now, if you'll excuse me, I see some old friends I want to say hi to."

He blocks my escape. "Who's looking after the kid tonight?"

Who does he think he is? Like he cares. "That's none of your concern, Jake. Remember, you didn't want to complicate your life with a kid. Certainly not a deaf one," I spit out the last sentence.

Stepping around him, I plaster a smile on my face, then make my way toward my group of friends from high school. We lost touch when I found out I was pregnant. Our lives were moving in totally different directions; while they were out partying, I was throwing up and growing round with a baby. I don't begrudge them for losing contact. I was concentrating on growing up, getting ready to be responsible for another human being, while they were focusing on how many shots they could down and remain standing. The girls spot me, squealing in delight. I walk faster to make it to them, and we share an excited group hug. It's great to be surrounded by my old friends. It almost feels as though no time has passed. As our excitement calms, I take in each of my friends, noting changes in their appearance. Of course, we all look older, that's to be expected, but the girls all look fantastic. My eyes stop on Sam's belly; it seems to me as though she has a slight baby bump. My head snaps up, and she signals for me to keep my discovery to myself. I nod discreetly to confirm that I'll keep my lips sealed.

"How are my girls?" I look around the group. "You all look so incredibly gorgeous."

"Not as gorgeous as you do, girl. You're one hot momma." Jessica touches her finger to her hip like its sizzling. All I can do is shake my head, smiling at her antics. She hasn't changed one bit.

We spend the next hour drinking while catching up on the last ten years. Everyone seems oblivious to the fact that Sam's not drinking any alcoholic drinks. I'm surprised to find that none of the girls have settled down. They're all still single, foot-loose, and fancy-free—even Sam. I internally consider this prospect. Would I want to be like them? No, I don't think I would. I love my daughter, the life I've built, and my little shop. I don't think I would change a thing at this point in time. Suddenly, the entire room quiets. I look around, attempting to work out why. When I look toward the entrance, I find my answer.

Toby Summer has arrived.

This'll be interesting to watch. No one gave him the time of day in high school, but now that he's famous, I'll bet everyone wants a piece of him. He's with his twin sister, Kate, and his best friend, Shane. There's also another man I recognize as a regular client of mine—the one and only Mr. Stone. I recently worked on his wedding, not that I interacted in person with him or his wife, who I figure must be Kate by the way he's holding her close to his side. The foursome make quite an impact standing at the entrance. Kate's the first to break away, making her way toward her group of friends from school; her husband hot on her heels.

As I look back toward the entrance, my eyes connect with Toby's. With our gazes locked, it's like no time has passed at all. Those same tingles I used to experience every time he was near take hold.

He's totally smoking hot. Hotter than any image I've seen of him online. In person, there's a presence about him that wasn't there ten years ago.

He says something to Shane, then makes a beeline straight for me. Stalking forward like a panther. *Oh, wow!*

He's different; there's a confidence about him he never used to have. The lanky kid who would sit out of the way to avoid people now draws the eye of everyone in the room as his sure strides bring him to me. People attempt to get his attention, but he ignores them without breaking stride, as though I'm the only person he sees. He stops directly in front of me, making me tilt my head back to take him in. Those tingles I mentioned before, they've become a full-on assault on my senses now he's this close to me. He smells so freaking good, matching how good he looks in his casual suit. His hair's longer now, tied up in a bun, and that beard. *So freaking sexy.* What I wouldn't give to feel the rasp of it between my thighs.

"Hey, Cassia." His voice is so much deeper, richer than it was when we were seventeen.

"Uh, hey, Toby." My shaky voice exposes my nervousness. "I'm surprised you came tonight." Maybe I shouldn't have said that. It sounded pretty rude, so I quickly add, "I'm glad you could make it."

"It was touch and go there for a while, but Kate and Shane convinced me to come along."

"Well, I'm happy to see you. You look ... uh ... good." *Geez, girl, get it together.* You're being ridiculous. You used to talk with him all the time, whether he wanted to or not.

"I'm happy to see you, too, Cassia. You look as stunning as ever." The girls behind me let out a collective sigh. I can *feel* their eyes ping-ponging between the two of us. "I was hoping we could chat for a couple of minutes." *Oh, wow.* This is new. He never once sought me out in high school. "Would you mind joining me at the bar for a drink?"

I'm a little shocked, but manage to respond with a nod of my head. I turn to the girls, waving awkwardly, letting them know where I'm going. Not that I needed to tell them. They had a front-row seat to our conversation. They're all either fanning their faces, widening their eyes comically, or signaling for me to hurry and follow after Toby. Stepping away from the group, I hurry to catch up with him as he heads directly to the bar. He situates himself at the far end, away from everyone else —I see some things haven't changed. I sit beside him after he pulls out the stool for me, which is welcome since I've been standing in these heels for over an hour now. They may look sexy, but they are so freaking uncomfortable.

He studies me intently for a few seconds, as though he's cataloging the changes he sees in me. "What would you like to drink?"

"I'll have a lemon drop martini, thanks." I love my Vodka-based drinks.

He orders himself a beer along with my drink. We don't speak while we wait for our drinks to be served, but it doesn't feel awkward. It gives me the time I need to recalibrate. Once the bartender places the glasses in front of us, Toby slides my drink closer to me, then picks up his beer, indicating he wants to make a toast.

"To second chances." His toast is a bit cryptic. He taps his beer against my glass before taking a swallow of his drink. I watch, mesmerized by the dance of his Adam's apple, before realizing I should take a drink of my own. Sipping my drink, I sigh in appreciation of the sweet but tart taste of the cool liquid. When I open my eyes and look across at Toby, I find him staring at me.

Wiping gingerly at my mouth, I ask, "Do I have something on my face?"

NINE

-toby-

GOD, SHE'S STILL SO FUCKING BEAUTIFUL—NO, THAT'S NOT true, she's even more beautiful now—I can't take my eyes off her. When I stepped through the doorway to the function room, my eyes automatically started seeking her out. When I finally decided to come to this reunion, I decided my first action would be to apologize to Cassia for the way I treated her in high school. How I always made excuses to escape being in her presence. Now that I'm here, standing next to her, I'm too overwhelmed to say what I need to say. My wayward dick, as usual, is misbehaving in her presence.

I snap out of it to respond to her. "Uh, no. Nothing on your face, Cass."

"Oh, okay then. That's good." She takes another delicate sip of her cocktail. I watch her throat work to swallow the concoction and all I can imagine is her throat working over my cock. *Shit, that's not helping my situation.* "I believe congratulations are in order." I'm not sure why she's congratulating me. My confusion must show because she clarifies, "For all of your success. I knew you were a talented singer and guitarist in high school, but I never imagined the success you would go on to have. It must feel amazing to have followed your passion and have it all work out so well for you."

Ah, okay, that's what she's talking about. I shrug my shoulder, tucking a wayward lock of hair behind my ear. "I guess so. I just did what I love; what I'm good at. The rest sort of followed on from that." I sip my beer because what I'm about to say next is going to sound ungrateful, even though I *am* incredibly grateful for all of my successes and achievements. "I don't enjoy being in the limelight, though. I would rather be left alone." I glance over my shoulder, noticing several people who wouldn't give me the time of day in high school waiting for a chance to talk to me. Shane's doing his job and keeping them away from me—as he promised he would.

"Yeah, you always preferred your own company back then. I figured with your fame, you'd be used to all the people by now."

"Nah. I don't think I'll ever get used to that side of things." We're quiet for a few minutes; she drinking her martini, me drinking my beer. I'm generally not great with conversation or making small talk, so I don't know how to broach the subject of high school, but I'm determined to apologize to her. I guess now's as good a time as any. "Uh, Cass, I've thought about you a lot over the years." Her eyes widen in surprise as she chokes on her drink. *Oh, shit,* that didn't sound good. I pat her on the back to help her out. "Uh, I mean. Fuck, I don't know what I mean. What I wanted to say was I've often thought about how I treated you in high school." I take in her puzzled face. Clearly, she's forgotten all the times I would make a hasty exit. "You know, always making excuses to leave. Not participating in the conversations you made an effort to strike up with me." She nods as if she now remembers. "I owe you an apology for all of that."

"Don't worry about it, Toby." She waves off my apology. "Sometimes I was too much for people. I've toned down a lot over the years. I'm possibly more tolerable now." She laughs. I can't believe she thinks she was too much for anyone.

"It wasn't that. It was …" Fuck, this is going to be embarrassing. "Me. All me. I was the one with the problem because I had a crush on you." There, I said it. I don't think her eyes could get any bigger as her lips part in surprise. With my stomach rolling from nerves, I huff out a laugh. "Every time you came near me, my teenage dick would stand to attention. I had to get away from you because I was terrified I'd embarrass myself." Well, there—I've laid it out as plain as day. She can laugh at me and tell me what an idiot I was.

She lays her hand on my arm. The heat from her touch burns through my skin. "Oh, Toby." She's smiling. I guess that's a positive sign. Maybe she doesn't feel creeped out by my confession. I never meant to tell her *why* I acted the way I did. I only wanted to apologize for my behavior. "You weren't alone. I studied up on Dylan like I was going to be graded on it so that I could hold a two-minute conversation with you." My head snaps up to study her face, seeking any dishonesty—all I see is sincerity. "I had the biggest crush on you, too." She gestures to her friends. "They all used to tease me relentlessly about it. They gave me a hard time for dating Jake when I should have been with you. If you had asked me to go to prom with you in the cafeteria that day, I would have said 'yes' in a heartbeat."

I can't believe what I'm hearing.

She felt the same way I did.

Everything I thought I knew about high school has been tilted off its axis. What I thought was a fantasy could have been a reality. One I could have acted on had I been courageous. But who's courageous at seventeen or eighteen, really? I mean, I was fearless with my music, not so much with people.

How would things have been different if I'd manned up

and asked her to the prom, as Shane suggested? I'm trying to collect my equilibrium when she returns her hand to my arm.

"Toby, are you okay?"

I turn to face her directly. "I wish I'd been brave. I can't believe I missed my chance with you." My disappointment floods through me like a giant wave.

She smiles slowly, biting her full bottom lip as she does. The same one I used to imagine kissing. "Who says you missed your chance?" She clinks her glass against my beer. "To second chances, you said."

My lips spread wide as I return the gesture. "To second chances." We each drink, smiling at each other as if we've shared a secret.

Kate and Oliver break our moment. Kate and Cassia do the usual girly hug in greeting. They weren't close in school, but they were friendly. Kate's come into her own since dating Oliver. He's been great for her confidence.

She turns to me excitedly. "Guess what just happened. No, you'll never guess. I'll just tell you." She looks up at her husband, and he winks at her. "Michael Fitzpatrick just apologized to me for setting me up to go to prom alone. Can you believe it?"

Oliver looks like he wants to smash something when Kate mentions Michael's name. I guess she filled him in on what went down.

Cassia smiles. "It seems it's the night for apologies." She winks at me, but Kate and Oliver are completely caught up in each other, so they miss it.

Kate turns her attention to Cassia. "What have you been up to the last ten years, Cass?"

Shit, I'm such a douche. I didn't even ask her what she's been doing. What is her life like? Is she with anyone? Maybe not, because she sort of insinuated that we might have a second chance. Well, I hope that's what she was saying. She tucks a silky chestnut lock of hair behind her ear. "Well, I went to college, like most other people. Then I took over my gramma's florist shop."

"Oh, wow. That's so cool. Would I know of it? What's it called?"

"I'm pretty sure you do." She smiles, looking between Kate and Oliver. "I did the floral arrangements for your gala *and* your wedding."

"No way!" Kate and Oliver appear stunned. "You own *Blooms and Balloons*? That's your shop?" Cass nods. "Your flower arrangements are freaking awesome." Kate's almost squealing.

Oliver holds out his hand for Cass. "I thought you looked familiar." Kate looks between Cass and Oliver, trying to work out what's going on. "When I ordered the flowers I had delivered for you, I stopped in at *Blooms and Balloons*," he tells his wife. "That's how I became familiar with her work. When I was organizing the gala, she seemed like the perfect person to put our table centerpieces together." He looks back at Cass. "You did outstanding work. I had no qualms in recommending you to our wedding coordinator when it came time to organize the flowers."

"I loved, loved, loved what you did for our wedding. Oh, and the balloon drop for the gala. That was ah-mazing."

"Why, thank you." She does a little curtsy. "I was proud of that balloon drop. I was trying to think of something that would be memorable when you guys reached your goal."

Jake comes in behind her, wrapping his beefy arm around her waist and snuggling into her neck. My entire body goes into alert mode, my pulse increasing as my muscles tense. I had the impression that Cassia was unattached when she suggested we might get a second chance, but here's Mr. Beefcake wrapping himself around her like the snake he is. *What the fuck?*

I relax slightly when Cass tries to extricate herself from his hold, but he won't release his grip; if anything, he holds on tighter, sending a smarmy look my way. She continues to push against him, whispering something in his ear. I move forward, ready to step in if necessary; Oliver must read the cues too, because he seems to stand taller, looking more formidable than usual. Finally, Jake releases Cassia. The relief emanating from her body is palpable. It's obvious she doesn't like the man anymore, which is somewhat of a relief. He tries to move back into her space, but she pushes him away.

"Leave me alone, Jake. I told you, I'm not interested."

Oliver steps forward. "The lady asked you to leave her alone. I suggest you do so." His tone would typically be enough to get anyone to do his bidding, but Jake's not just anyone.

"Who the fuck are you?" he slurs. It's obvious he's had too much to drink. "Think you can tell me what the fuck to do." Kate puts her hand on Oliver's arm to calm him.

Shane quietly joins the group, sensing there's going to be trouble. He's no longer the skinny kid from high school; he's a trained killer now. Jake senses he's outnumbered *and* outmuscled. Looking around at our group, he raises his hands in surrender, sways, and steps away from Cass.

To us, he says, "Later." To Cass, he points and says, "I ain't done with you." Stepping backward from us, he turns, leaving the function room. We all turn to Cass to ask if she's okay, but she's folded in on herself, her arms wrapped around her waist.

She looks scared.

I step closer, checking with her if it's okay to hold her. She nods a little, so I wrap her in my arms, pulling her close. She fits against me like a missing puzzle piece and smells fucking sensational; spicy and sweet. I whisper in her ear, "You okay?"

She nods slowly in response.

"You want another lemon drop martini?"

"Yes, please."

Oliver steps up to the bar to order drinks for everyone in our group. The mood has dropped from the happy, upbeat vibe of before as we sip our drinks. We make light conversation about what we've each been up to over the past ten years. I do my best to ignore old classmates who think it's okay to interrupt us to get a piece of me. They didn't want a bar of me back in high school—they can fuck right off now. I only came hoping to catch up with the woman still in my arms.

Cass's friends join our group, expanding the circle and lightening the mood considerably. After several hours of reminiscing about various high school events, stupid shit different kids got up to, and bitching about some of the teachers; people start calling it a night and the crowd dwindles. Her high school girlfriends all want to head out to a club, but Cass declines. I need to think of something so that I can spend more time with her—I'm not ready to let her go yet. I want to know what that was about with Jake.

"You wanna get a drink somewhere?"

She smiles broadly, seemingly happy that I want to spend more time with her. "Yeah, that'd be great."

-toby-

I'M CURRENTLY THANKFUL SHANE DROVE SEPARATELY TO THE reunion tonight because it means I'll have Cassia all to myself in my car. Walking to the parking lot, I guide Cass with my hand firmly pressed against the curve of her exposed lower back, right above her sexy ass. The feel of her warm, silky skin against my palm is testing my resolve to be a gentleman. It's taking all of my strength to stop my hand from sliding down to cup her firm behind.

"Is this your car?"

"Yeah, this is it." I'm proud of this baby. When I found it for sale, I knew I had to have her. I'm a fan of Sam and Dean, and well … I just had to have her. She's not exactly the same as their beast, since mine's a convertible.

She glides her hand along the front panel. I can't believe I'm jealous of my car. "Is this like the car from *Supernatural?*"

I think I'm in love.

"Same make and year. However, theirs is a hardtop."

I open the door for her, and she gracefully lowers herself into the passenger seat. She looks mighty fine sitting in my car.

Stepping around the front of the car, I join her inside. After starting the car, I turn to Cass. "Where would you like to go?"

"Uh, do you have issues with being out in public? Like, do people bother you a lot?"

"Yeah, it bothers me. It's something I've had to get used to."

"How about we just go back to your place then?"

My eyebrows almost hit my hairline with surprise at her suggestion. If I have her alone at my place, there's no telling what we might get up to. I'm not sure I have the self-control to keep my hands off her, especially if this is my only chance to have her. "Yeah, I'm not sure that's such a good idea."

"Why not? Then we don't have to worry about you being spotted by your fans, and we can talk in a quiet space." She tucks her hair behind her ear. "Or maybe you don't want me in your private space?"

"I would love to have you in my private space, Cass. Maybe a little too much." I clear my throat. "I'm not sure I could keep my intentions pure or my hands to myself."

She smiles across at me. "That's okay with me."

Okay then. I put my foot down, making my way home in record time. She seems restless in her seat, adjusting her position every few minutes. Not another word is spoken, but I sense the tension building between us. That spark that was there in high school ... yeah, it's intensified into a low-burning ember.

Pulling into the garage, Cass speaks for the first time. "I like your place. It's very rock star." She clasps her hands tightly together; her lips press closed suddenly.

I laugh. "You think? I bought it for the view from every room across to the bridge, which looks spectacular at sunset."

We step out of the elevator that brought us up from the garage, entering the foyer on the lower level of my three-story home. It's all timber, steel, and glass.

Cass has her mouth on mine before we make it five steps

inside, surprising the hell outta me. I've been waiting for this kiss for longer than a decade. I want to take my time; savor it, slow it down, and enjoy it. Pressing my lips against hers, I cradle the back of her head while tugging her hips forward, ensuring there's zero space between us—the press of her full tits against my hard planes—the silkiness of her hair in my hand, and the softness of her plump lips against mine are more than I ever imagined. Her arms wrap around me, her hands coming up to press my shoulder blades, pushing me into her ever closer. Our mouths open, and our tongues meet for the first time. I know, in this moment, there will never be another woman for me.

She's it.

Cass moans into the kiss, stealing my breath, while all the blood in my body redirects to my cock. It's throbbing in the confines of my pants, trying to find its target. I walk her backward, trapping her against the glass of my living room window. The only light is provided by the moon. I press my hard cock into her soft body so she can feel what she's done to me.

"Are you as wet as I'm hard, Cass?"

"Why don't you find out for yourself?" she responds without missing a beat.

Oh, yeah, don't mind if I do, but I have no fucking idea how to get her out of these clothes. I step away, manhandling her until her back faces me to check for a zipper or something. The thin straps tie in the middle of her spine. I kiss my way along the graceful curve until I reach the ties, biting and tugging them undone with my teeth. Releasing the ties, I loosen the front, hoping it's enough to expose her breasts. Preparing myself to see what I've only imagined since I was sixteen, I turn her back toward me. Slowly, my eyes wander down from her captivating face, her slender neck, to her delicate collarbones, and finally to those mounds I've imagined holding. Her top is somehow still stuck to her chest. I don't understand why it hasn't fallen to her waist as I expected. I gently pry the material away from her supple skin, but it doesn't release as I would expect. She looks down, peeling the fabric away from her skin gently.

"I had to use boob tape. I didn't want to expose myself inadvertently at the reunion. Give me a sec." She gives a breathless laugh as she peels the fabric away, giving me a perfect view ...

Wait!

How come I can't see any nipples? I look up at her face, and I'm sure my confusion is apparent. Her boobs are pert, but there are no nipples as far as I can see in the little light available.

She blushes. "Sorry. I couldn't wear a regular bra with the design of the top. Give me a minute, and I'll have these off." She turns her back to me—I'm not having it. I want to watch her reveal herself to me.

"Uh, uh, uh. Let me watch."

She's looking down, not making eye contact with me. "I'm a little embarrassed. I hadn't planned to get naked in front of anyone tonight, and ... well ... this isn't very sexy."

"Maybe it's not the sexiest, but it's you. You went to a lot of trouble to get dressed—to look good. No, more than good—you look fucking sexy tonight, and I want to see how you made that happen. Let me see you."

She bites her bottom lip, so I press in to take over, biting the plumpness gently before sucking out the sting. Pressing my lips harder against hers, I swipe with my tongue, requesting permission to enter. She opens and our tongues reacquaint, sliding against each other, learning each other's taste. I pull back to allow her to remove whatever it is she's wearing in place of a regular bra. As she works on one side, I gently peel the second side. She's careful not to pull too hard or fast, holding her skin taut to reduce the sting as the adhesive pulls away, so I mimic her technique.

Finally, *fucking finally*, her tits are fully exposed for my perusal. I soak them in, admiring their fullness, and the slight teardrop droop to them. Taking one in hand, I test the weight before closing my hand over the globe and squeezing gently, realizing the bra has left behind a significant amount of sticky residue.

"How do you get this stuff off your boobs?" I marvel at what women go through to look good in their clothes. Men just have to put on pants and a shirt, and we're done. I wouldn't have the patience to be a woman.

"Oh, uh. I don't use these very often because I rarely go out. When I do, I usually rub it with some olive oil. It seems to do the trick. Maybe we shouldn't bother. I can just head home." She tries to cover her embarrassment with a deprecating laugh. "Can we forget this happened?"

"That'd be a no." I walk into the kitchen, dragging her behind me. "I have olive oil in the kitchen. Let's get this shit off your magnificent breasts so I can get down to business."

She giggles at my determination to get her into the kitchen. I know I'm acting like a madman, but I'm not willing to wait any longer to get my hands and mouth on her. It's been more than ten years, and from what I can see, it's definitely been worth the wait. Wrapping my hands around her trim waist, I lift her easily to sit her ass on my counter, so I can source the materials I need to get this show on the road. I find what I need, then carry everything over to Cass. I tip some olive oil onto my palm before rubbing my hands together to get it warm. Gently, reverently, I massage her soft breasts, paying particular attention to the areas with the most adhesive. I rub, caressing her until her nipples form peaks and goosebumps cover her skin. Teasing her nipples with gentle touches, squeezing the globes with firm pressure, makes her breaths come faster, the pulse at the base of her neck fluttering rapidly. Her hands come up to the back of my head, sliding into my hair as she pulls at the elastic I used to keep it in place. Trying to maintain my focus while her fingers comb through my hair, I work her breasts over until I feel the sticky residue dissolve. I desperately need to get my mouth on her. Reluctantly pulling away, I find a soft, clean cloth in the drawer. As I wipe the excess oil off her body, I manage to tear my eyes away from her breasts to peer at her face. Her eyes are molten, searing into me.

"Toby, please kiss me."

I don't have to be asked twice. I throw the cloth into the sink, moving forward at the same time as Cass to meet in the middle.

This kiss is slower—seeking, tempting, teasing.

Using only our lips, we slide back and forth gently, building up to something more, something intense and life-changing. I can't resist slipping my tongue out to glide along her plump bottom lip. Cass sighs softly, her warm breath moving across my mouth, and I use the opportunity to slide inside, deepening our connection. Her hand tightens in my hair, as though she doesn't want this kiss to end.

Me neither, Gorgeous. Me neither.

I need to get my mouth on her tits. I used to fantasize about her breasts in high school, and now that I have the opportunity before me on a silver platter, I'm not willing to miss out on getting my fill. I trail my kisses down to Cass's jawline, then further down her neck until I reach her collarbone. Nibbling, licking, and kissing my way further down, I finally reach my target. Leaning forward, I suck a nipple into my mouth. I taste it with my tongue before pulling back slightly to nip and bite around the areola; she tastes like olive oil with a hint of cinnamon. I swap over, paying the same attention to the other globe. She moans in pleasure, grasping the back of my head to hold me in place. "You like my mouth on you, Cass?"

"Yeah, yeah, I do. Don't stop. Please don't stop."

Not planning on it anytime soon.

I glide my hands slowly down each side of her body, grazing her rib cage with the aim of removing her pantsuit, but it's stuck on her hips. It must have a zipper somewhere. Cass reads my intention, releasing the zipper on my behalf, allowing the fabric to slip down to pool on the counter. Encouraging her to raise her hips, I slide the material down her body until it's free of her sexy shoes. Starting at her ankles, I glide my hands slowly up the inside of her silky legs, pushing them wider apart as I go. In this position, I can smell her arousal even before I nudge my nose into the apex of her thighs. Dragging upwards, seeking her clit, I rub gently with the tip of my nose, garnering a sigh from my girl as she pulses her hips forward, seeking more friction. I search out the top of her underwear so I can remove the lacy fabric from her body. She lifts her ass again, and as I slide the lace down her legs and over her strappy shoes —they're staying on—they're sexy as fuck.

Standing to my full height, I pull her ass forward so she's balancing on the edge of my kitchen counter and slam my mouth down onto hers. I need this woman to come so that I can get inside her pussy. I press in as close as possible to grind my hard length against her exposed pussy, which I noticed is groomed to perfection. Her heat sears me through my trousers and boxers. I can't wait to feel her internal muscles squeezing the cum out of my cock.

Trying to slow myself down, I tenderly press her back so she's lying on the counter. Slowly, I glide my hands down the length of her body before squatting down to position her feet over my shoulders, opening her as wide as possible to my mouth and fingers. I can't resist watching her opening tremble as I delicately run my fingertips along her outer lips from the base to the top, pinching her clit gently. Her body shoots up from the bench with a jolt as she releases a long moan. I'm finally living out my fantasy, but I'm worried any moment now, teenage me is going to wake up, and this is all going to be a dream.

I press her body back down. "Don't move. Take what I'm gonna give you."

Her clit pulses. Oh, yeah, she likes my command. I can't believe how fucking lucky I am to be touching her like this. I'm determined to make this an experience she'll remember forever. I double down on my efforts, kissing her pussy like I would kiss her mouth. Biting and nipping her lips as I insert first one finger, then another into her tight channel. My dick leaps in eagerness to be where my fingers are, feeling her muscles pulsing and tightening around it in readiness for release. I work at a slow, steady pace to tease her along. I don't want to rush this. I intend to take my time, cherishing every moment, and tucking it away in my memory banks for inspiration. Cass begins the slow climb, and I feel her walls tightening, strangling my fingers.

"You're so fucking wet. Listen to my fingers sliding in and out of your hot pussy."

The slick noises seem loud in the quiet darkness. Cass moans as her pussy walls tighten and begin to flutter. I carefully bite her clit, pressing down with my tongue while pressing more firmly against her g-spot. She shatters, her walls pulsing relentlessly against the invasion of my fingers as I slow my movements, gentling as she convulses. Her legs tighten around my head, her heels digging into my back, holding me in position. This experience with her is better than anything I've had up to this point, which shouldn't be a surprise.

After all, it *is* Cassia.

ELEVEN

-cassia-

WOAH. I KNOW IT'S BEEN A LONG TIME FOR ME, BUT I DON'T ever remember having an orgasm that powerful before. He's as masterful with his fingers as I imagined he would be. The sounds my pussy made while they were inside me were almost obscene. If I hadn't been completely caught up in the moment, I would have been embarrassed. My muscles are relaxed, but I'm still turned on.

I don't allow myself to date, and I definitely don't do one-night stands, because Poppy is my priority. I highly doubt someone as famous as Toby does repeat performances, so this will be the only night I'll have with him, and I'm certain it's going to be one I remember for the rest of my life. I'm going to take full advantage of my one night out.

"Did you like my mouth on your clit and my fingers in your tight pussy?" God, he has a dirty mouth. I never knew that could be such a turn-on.

"Yeah, but I want your dick."

"You'll get it when I'm good and ready to give it to you."

He's put me in my place, and embarrassment floods me. I close my legs to regain my modesty, but Toby blocks my attempt with his body—which, I might add, is still fully clothed, putting me at a further disadvantage. Turning my head to the side, I try to block him out, but he's not having that either.

"Uh, uh, uh. What's up, Cass?" He gently directs my eyes back to his, holding my chin between his fingers. "Talk to me, Bun." I search his face. I'm not sure what he means. Was he calling *me* Bun? Why? He must read my confusion. "You smell like a cinnamon bun. All sweet, with a hint of spice." He nuzzles his nose up the side of my neck to that sensitive spot behind my lobe, where he licks me, then places the softest kiss.

"Nothing," I whisper. I'm embarrassed that I got so carried away that I basically demanded he fuck me. Maybe he doesn't want to go that far with me. I mean, I did pounce on him the minute we entered his home. I'm not sure what came over me. He doesn't know me, and I don't really know him. I'm mortified as I mentally run through my behavior since we arrived.

"I felt you fold in on yourself. So don't tell me 'nothing' when I know there's something."

"Really, it's nothing. I should probably get dressed and get out of your hair. I've already taken up too much of your time." I'm struggling to avoid his eyes in my embarrassment.

"If you want to leave, that's your choice. I won't hold you here against your will, but I don't understand the sudden change. Did I do something wrong? Have I upset you?" His eyes implore me for an answer, but I'm not sure what I can say as his voice drops to a whisper. "Talk to me, Cass."

"Uh, I'm a bit embarrassed. I ..." I try to look away—once again, he's not having it. "I, uh, got caught up in the moment and ... uh, well ... I'm not that girl."

"What girl?" He's completely confused.

"The girl that pounces on a guy I barely know. The one that gets so caught up in what's happening that I say things I wouldn't normally say; act in a way I wouldn't normally act. To be honest, I'm mortified with myself."

"I'm confused. So, are you saying you weren't into what was going down?"

Geez, this is unbelievably awkward. "Of course I was into it. But I got all demanding, and then you basically told me to slow down. You don't want to go that far." *Ugh. I just want to be invisible.*

His head tilts to the side. I can see him thinking. "When did I say I didn't want to 'go that far'? Because let me make something absolutely clear. I've wanted to get in your pants since I was sixteen years old."

Oh, uh. Wow. I'm shocked speechless. It takes me a minute to process his words, then formulate my response. "I guess I assumed when you said you'd give me your dick when you were 'good and ready' that you didn't want to go that far tonight." I try to sit up, but he folds his body over mine, pressing his clothed chest to my bare breasts. His breath tickles my face as he closely studies my eyes. He presses in closer, taking my mouth savagely. His kiss alone brings me back to life, sending all of my pulse points pounding out a rhythm I can't ignore. I try to rub my pussy against his hard shaft, but the way he has me pinned makes it impossible.

"What I said is 'You'll get it when I'm good and ready to give it to you'. Which means you need to trust me to take you where you need to go. Don't try to take over. I'm in charge here, and I make the decisions. Outside of the bedroom, I'm more than happy to be on equal terms, but here, I won't tolerate you attempting to take over. Understood?"

I swallow hard, and his eyes snap to my throat as he releases a groan. I can only nod in response to him laying down the law.

"I need your words, Cass." He nuzzles the side of my face

before whispering, "I need to know you understand what I'm saying, Gorgeous."

I nod again. "Yeah, I understand what you're saying."

"Good girl." He tucks his arms underneath me. "Now wrap your legs around my hips. I'm taking you to bed."

My clit throbs, and my pussy pulses in response as I wrap myself around his body. He lifts me easily, carrying me upstairs to his spacious bedroom. We land on his massive bed as one unit, his body weight forcing all the air from my lungs. Toby studies me closely, then pushes himself up to stand at the edge of the bed.

"Move up the bed, rest your head on the pillow. Spread your legs. I want to see your wet pussy." I quickly situate myself as directed, pushing down my internal discomfort at being on display to follow his instructions. His eyes travel languidly down my body like a caress as he removes his jacket. Leisurely, piece by piece, he methodically removes every stitch of clothing, revealing a muscular swimmer's body. His muscles flex and contract as he moves about, making my mouth water for a taste.

"Run your fingers along your slit. Show them to me. I want to see how wet you are."

He stands completely naked, waiting for me to comply. I slide my eyes over his body, stopping at his cock, standing gloriously hard and proud. While keeping my eyes on his cock, I slowly run my hands down my body, passing over my breasts, across my soft abdomen (thank god only the moonlight lights us), to my pussy which is so ready for him, it's pulsing. I gently caress the outer lips from the bottom to the top before moving inward, collecting my natural lubricant on my fingers. His cock bobs forth as if it's trying to get to me. I hold my fingers up for him, and he lunges forward in one fell swoop, taking them in his mouth and licking them clean.

Holy shit. That's so hot!

He guides my fingers back to my pussy, sliding them the same way he used his fingers, collecting more of my juices. He makes a show of licking my fingers clean. "Mmm, my new favorite flavor." Pressing down, he takes my mouth in a hot kiss. I can taste myself on his tongue, and even though I wouldn't have thought it could be sexy, it is. Everything he does turns me on more than I thought possible. I get lost in the kiss, my heartbeat increasing against his, my mind focusing solely on the moment we're sharing. I need to remember every detail so that I can draw on this experience on lonely nights.

"Turn over. I want to see your sexy ass while I fuck you." He pulls away, leaning over to the bedside drawer, retrieving a condom. I take the opportunity to turn over, scrambling to my hands and knees. I realize I haven't touched his cock. I haven't done anything except kiss him and hold on to him. I feel slightly cheated. Looking over my shoulder, I watch him roll the latex down his long, thick shaft. He's beautifully well-proportioned, and I can't wait to have him fill me up; just the thought has me almost dripping. I drop my head between my shoulders in anticipation of the first push of his cock into me; instead, he smooths my hair back from my face, clasping it firmly in his hand. His other hand comes around from behind, cupping my chin, directing my head where he wants it to go. He kisses me again, roughly this time, dominating my mouth, holding me hostage in our lust. Using his grip on my hair, he tugs my head back further, exposing my neck to his mouth. His soft beard grazes the sensitive skin, feeling fantastic and adding to the sensations overwhelming me.

His warm breath touches my ear just before his whispered words. "Are you ready for my cock, Cass?"

He thrusts fully into my core, forcing me forward, not allowing me to respond. I'm only stabilized by his hand holding onto my hair. I gasp for air, trying to regain my balance, but it's difficult. He leans back down over my body. "Your pussy's like heaven. So fucking tight around my cock." He kisses my neck again. "You feel how good my cock fits in your tight hole?" I can only whimper in response. Keeping his dick situated deep, he rotates his hips, hitting my g-spot, sending shudders throughout my body. My toes curl in preparation for his onslaught.

"You ready, Bun?" His chest leaves my back. I immediately feel the loss of his heat. "Answer me."

I suck in a breath. "Yeah, I'm ready." I try to brace myself, but the way he's holding me makes it difficult. He secures my hair tightly, then grasps my hip with his other hand before withdrawing his cock until only the tip is inside me. Biting my bottom lip, I prepare for what I anticipate will be a rough fuck. He slams back in, fast and hard. Pause. Swivel. Slow withdrawal. Pause. Slam. He sets up a fierce rhythm, and I match him. Pushing back into his firm body as he thrusts into me. He feels divine—I can't hold back my moans or my whimpers. His pace increases as he releases my hair and grasps both hips firmly. Taking over completely, he pulls me onto his cock—over and over and over again. His fingers feel like a branding iron on me, searing my skin, and even if he doesn't leave a visible mark, an indelible one will remain there forever in my mind. My breaths come in short pants. My skin's slick.

"I can feel your hot pussy tightening around my cock. Worshipping it. Trying to squeeze the cum out."

His words are so hot. I moan, "Oooooh, god!"

"You want my cum?"

"Mmmm. Yeah."

My body tightens from the tips of my toes to the tips of my fingers. My heart's pounding so hard, I'm not sure if it's trying to escape my chest. Like a supernova, I explode. Shattering into a thousand pieces, the brightest light scorches me to my very core.

Oh my god!

I try to collapse forward, but his grip on my hips prevents it. My ass is still high in the air while my head and shoulders rest on his soft bedding. He hasn't slowed down through my orgasm, still chasing his own. In this position, his dick is rubbing my g-spot without needing to twist his hips. His thrusts increase in speed and power as his hand comes around to massage my clit.

"Oh, god." I moan out. Low and deep, all the way from my belly. I think I'm gonna come again. I never believed having multiple orgasms was real.

"Come for me, now, Gorgeous."

After a few more thrusts, he pinches my clit, setting me off again. I'm going to pass out from orgasm overload.

His dick pulses as he lets out a long, low, sexy groan. Holding me in place, he presses tightly against my ass as he fills the condom with his release. His rough fingers tighten their grip on my hips to the point of pain—interestingly, I like it. I need to know he has hold of me, as I float out of my body during my moments of bliss.

Maintaining our physical connection, he lies to the side, pulling me with him, spooning me from behind, our sweaty bodies connected at every available point. Toby wraps his arms around me, each hand grasping one of my boobs. We lay in silence as we each catch our breath. That was possibly the most amazing sex I've ever had. Mind you, I've only had sex with one other person, while Toby's probably had heaps of sex with loads of different women.

As sated and as comfortable as I am lying here in Toby's arms, I need to pee. There's no way I want to end up with an infection.

"Uh, Toby. I need to go to the bathroom." I try to wriggle my way out of his arms, but he squeezes me tighter.

"Just give me a few more minutes," Toby whispers in my ear.

A few more minutes before he kicks me out? Or will he want me to stay the night? Which I can't do, anyway. I need to get home before Mom wakes up and notices I haven't come home. *God, I feel like a high schooler staying out beyond curfew.*

I guess I should luxuriate in his solid arms for as much time as he'll allow. It's not likely I'll get this chance again. I snuggle back into his embrace, the cooling sweat of our bodies causing our skin to stick together. He kisses the back of my head, making my whole body sigh at the sweetness of the gesture, which is such a juxtaposition to how he showed affection during sex. It's like he's reverted to the sweet Toby I remember.

I must doze for a moment because I wake to Toby quietly extricating himself from the bed and me. I'm assuming to deal with the condom. I take the opportunity to get up so I can deal with my own business in the bathroom.

"Sorry, I didn't mean to wake you. I needed to deal with the condom. You can stay there. I'll be right back."

"Oh, that's okay. I need to go to the bathroom myself."

We both deal with our business. I'm unsure whether he wants me to leave or stay. I wouldn't mind snuggling a little more with him. Stepping out of the bathroom, I find Toby lying in bed, with the opposite side of the bedcovers pulled down, inviting me to join him. I would definitely love to join him; however, I should head home.

"Come on. Get in."

"I should probably head home. It's late." His eyebrows slash down over his gorgeous blue eyes, and his jaw tenses beneath that short beard of his.

"What's the rush? Got someone waiting for you?" *Shit.* I don't want to tell him I live with my mom and daughter. I don't want to tell him I have a daughter. She's already been rejected by the one man who should never have done so. What would Toby, a musician, think of Poppy? This isn't anything serious. I'm not about to share *everything* about me and my life with him.

"Uh, no. I just figured you'd want me out of your hair."

"Nope. Not ready to let you go yet, Bun. Come on." I step closer to the bed, and he reaches out, grabbing my hand to pull me down on top of him. A surprised laugh escapes, leading to a round of giggles from both of us. It feels good to laugh, to relax.

Toby raises his head off the pillow, brushing his lips gently across mine. "I want you again."

I pull back to study his face. He's deadly serious. There's no way I could take his dick again after the rough sex we just shared. It's been a while for me, so I'm raw and sore. If we go again, I'm worried I'll do some serious damage.

This is embarrassing, but I need to let him know it won't be happening anytime soon. "Uh, I don't think so. My hoo-ha couldn't take another round like that tonight."

Doesn't mean I can't get him off, though. I didn't get a chance to touch or explore his body before, and I don't want to explain that I'm tender because it's been so long since I've had sex. I kiss my way down his body, starting at his beard-covered chin. I tickle my fingers through the soft bristles before moving down, kissing down his throat, torso, and abdomen—which is cut like granite. I follow the sexy trail of hair that leads to his hard dick, which is bobbing on his stomach. His hands slide to the back of my head, clutching my hair. His hips lift, seeking my mouth. Tentatively, I touch my tongue to the tip of his cock, running it over the head like a lollipop. He groans at the contact, then pushes my head down further. Shifting to make myself comfortable, I take his penis as far as I can without choking and swallow around the shaft. His hips shoot up in response as he releases another groan.

"Your mouth feels so good around my cock. I used to picture this exact scenario when you were playing the flute in high school. Your pouty lips blowing across the embouchure hole used to get me so hard."

I can't believe what I'm hearing. He gave me the impression he didn't like me—*at all.*

I swallow against his cock in response, garnering another low, sexy groan. Working my hand and mouth in tandem, I slide up and down his shaft in precise glides, squeezing the base each time I slide down. The lubrication from my mouth makes the movement easy. He guides my head in the way he wants, thrusting his hips up and hitting the back of my throat. I have to work hard to breathe through my nose because he's restricting my airway.

As sore as I am, my pussy feels empty as my clit throbs in time with my strokes.

"Swallow on my cock again," he moans.

So I do. His cock pulses, so I gently grasp the heavy sac below, massaging it with my other hand. That seems to push him over the edge because he tries to pull my head back to release himself from my mouth, but I stay firm.

I want his cum in my mouth.

I want the opportunity to taste him, just as he tasted me.

One last squeeze and swallow and he releases his orgasm on a long groan, his hand squeezing my hair so tight it's making my eyes water. I must look a sight at the moment, with my eyes watering as saliva runs down my chin. Slowing my hands and mouth, I coax him through his release, swallowing his salty cum before licking his shaft clean.

His hands loosen around my hair, then he reverently smooths it away from my face. "You didn't need to do that, but I'm glad you did."

I position my hands on his firm abdomen, resting my chin on them to look up at him. "I wanted to. I felt duped that I didn't get to touch you before."

"I'll remember that for next time." My eyes widen involuntarily at his statement. I'm surprised he's talking about a 'next time'. I figured this would be a one-and-done scenario for someone as famous as he is. "Now that I've had you, I'm gonna need to do that again, and if you won't let me have you again tonight, then it'll have to be another night. Soon." He gently brushes a lock of hair behind my ear, then places his hands underneath his head, looking down the length of his body at me. "I don't wanna wait another ten years to see you again."

"Oh." Is all I can say. This development is completely unexpected; one I'm uncertain about.

"Are you interested in catching up again?"

Does he mean like a booty call? Part of me would definitely be up for more of what we did, but the other part of me needs to shut this down.

"It might be difficult with my schedule at the shop. I get very little downtime, and I'm pretty busy when I'm not working." *Looking after my daughter.*

"Pretty sure we can work around your schedule. Mine's pretty hectic, too. I'm in and out of the studio, writing and laying down my new album, which will be followed by a tour when it launches."

For a moment, I forgot he's a famous musician, so he probably *is* only looking for a booty call. I was getting ahead of myself. He pulls me until I'm lying flat on top of him, one leg sliding between both of his. He groans at the contact. I try to pull away because I'm worried I've hurt him.

"Uh, uh, uh. You're not going anywhere." He directs my head to lie on his chest. His heartbeat is strong and steady. It's profound to listen so closely to the part of him that's keeping him alive and vital. Time passes without words; it feels comfortable to spend this quiet time with him—as though this is common practice for us.

We must have fallen asleep because I wake to the very early rays of the new day. I quietly and carefully remove myself from Toby, collect my shoes, and head downstairs to get the rest of my clothes. Dressing quickly, I step out of his spectacular home to call myself an Uber.

TWELVE

-toby-

I CAN'T REMEMBER THE LAST TIME I SLEPT SO SOUNDLY. I always have some melody or lyrics making themselves known at the oddest times. If I don't get them down, I've often lost them by morning, never to be retrieved again. I roll over, seeking Cass's warm body, only to turn up empty-handed. I sit up, looking around my bedroom.

Shit, I hope I didn't dream last night.

Getting up, I notice her shoes are missing, so I jog downstairs only to be filled with disappointment to find her gone. Slapping the granite counter with my palm, I run my hands through my hair, searching for something to tell me it was real.

That it wasn't a dream.

A fantasy.

The cloth I used to wipe the oil away from her tits is still in the sink, and the olive oil bottle still sits on the counter, making me feel marginally better, but pissed that she snuck out while I was sleeping. We didn't even exchange fucking phone numbers.

God, I'm stupid.

She never did answer me properly about catching up again.

Maybe it was a one-and-done thing for her, something she can check off—*fucked a famous musician.*

I stomp back upstairs to have a shower and get dressed, remembering how she felt against me. How my cock felt inside her pussy. How we *fit* together like the perfect rhythm and melody.

Feeling motivated, I spend most of the day in my studio writing a melody that's stuck with me for the last couple of days. It's come through strong this morning, so I need to get it out. The words to complement it come quickly after waking up alone this morning.

Why can't you see me for me
Instead of the man you think me to be
I'm standing here in front of you
A simple man asking you to see
The man I am; the man you need

Shane steps into the studio, making me realize I must have lost track of time because he was set to pick me up for our regular Sunday dinner at my parents'. He doesn't come to dinner as my bodyguard but as my long-time friend. He's spent many Sundays at my parents' home, so he's casual and relaxed since he's not on the clock.

He smirks at me. "So, last night, huh?"

I glare at him, telegraphing that I don't want to talk about Cass.

"Jake's still a dick. Nothing much has changed there. He just looked softer around the middle." He smirks, patting his taut midsection.

I nod in agreement. "Yep. I agree with you there, brother. Nothing much has changed with him."

"I wonder what's going on between him and Cass? Do you think they're still together? Did you get a chance to talk to her after we all left?"

I got to do a whole lot more than talk to her last night, but I want to keep that to myself. It feels wrong to talk about what we did with anyone outside the two of us.

"I don't think they're still together; the way she pushed him away last night." Fuck, I hope they're not still doing that on-again, off-again shit like they did in high school. Maybe that's why she didn't give me an answer about seeing each other again. If she thinks she can leave me hanging, she has another thing coming. "He seemed pretty pissed last night."

"Yeah, maybe." He brushes his hand over his short hair. "You gonna catch up with her again?"

I stand up, placing my Gibson on the stand in the corner. "I dunno, man. I'd like to, but I'm busy, and she's probably busy with her business. Our lives are pretty different." I'm definitely hoping for a repeat of last night, but I want more than just great sex with her.

It's Friday, and I'm waiting for Poppy for our fourth lesson. She's picking it up quickly. She says she practices every spare minute and performs for her mom and gramma. I hope I can focus on her because I've done a shit job at it all week. My mind has constantly drifted back to Cass and the night we spent together before she snuck out on me. I'm kicking myself because I didn't even see her face as she came, and now I may never get the opportunity.

Poppy runs in with her usual excitement, throwing herself at me and hugging me in greeting. She's such a loving little girl.

I'm not sure why her dad's not around, but he's missing out big time. We catch up for a few minutes as she updates me on her vacation adventures.

"Gramma took me to the movies and the park. But I've still been practicing every single day. I love playing the guitar," she rapidly signs. "That app is awesome. Mommy and Gramma love watching the patterns it makes when I play."

"That's great. It's fun watching the music come to life on the screen. Show me how far you've come this week." With the amount of work she puts in, she'll have our first song mastered in no time. "How are your fingers holding up?"

She shows me her little fingers; they're pretty red. The blisters, which are common for new players, seem to be starting to heal over. "They're okay. They've been a bit sore, but Gramma soaks my hands in warm salty water. It seems to help." Smart lady.

She situates herself on the chair before putting on her guitar. It's the perfect size for her, and it makes me happy to see my first guitar being used once again, rather than gathering dust in Mom and Dad's attic. The colored strings have helped Poppy pick up the different chords easily. While she's getting organized, I set up my laptop, loading the *Whitecap* program ready for Poppy to play. The program, together with the colored strings, helps her to *see* the music as she plays. She has a natural talent for the guitar, which contributes to the speed with which she's picked it up.

She starts the intro perfectly, G, C, G, C, and strums through to the bridge, introducing D, C, G, D, C, G. She plays through the song, hitting most of the chord changes correctly, making a few small errors here and there. As she finishes, her face lights up as her cheeks lift; her gray eyes sparkle with joy. She's so damn proud of herself, and I'm equally proud of her. For only her fourth lesson, she's done a remarkable job. We high-five, and then we laugh with joy over her success. My heart feels full to overflowing knowing I was the one to teach her, bringing this joy into her world.

"You are an awesome guitarist, Poppy. I'm proud of you."

"Me too. Mommy and Gramma have been listening to me every day. They're proud of me, too."

"I bet they are. Are they sick of listening to that song yet?" I laugh, remembering the countless number of times I played this song until I had it perfected. Kate and Dad grew sick of it, but Mom understood how important it was to me to get it just right. "Hey, how about you take a break and I'll play this new song I'm working on."

Poppy nods, removing her guitar so she can sit close to me. She places her hands on my guitar, watching the laptop as I play. It starts as a simple melody, which builds in difficulty and intensity as the song progresses. Once I've finished playing, Poppy looks up at me as a broad smile takes over her lips.

"I really liked that. Have you finished it with the words yet?"

"Not ..." Uh, what's the word I need here? Oh, that's right. "Completely. I'm still tweaking it. I wrote some lyrics this morning. They haven't been easy to come by."

Poppy frowns. "Why?"

"I've been distracted this week. I'm sure they'll come soon."

"I bet they will." It's a little weird getting support from a seven-year-old. The thing is, I know it's genuine from her.

"I thought you could start learning a new song. It uses the same chords, C, G, D, and introduces F on the solo. What do you think? Are you ready?"

She jumps up and down with her usual excitement. "Oh, yes! I'll still keep practicing the first one, but it would be great to learn a new one, too."

I find Poppy quite an interesting child. She has that child-like wonder and exuberance, yet at times, she shows a level of maturity beyond her years.

"Come on then. I'll play it for you." She places her hands back on my guitar, and I play *Sweet Home Alabama* by Lynyrd Skynyrd. We spend the rest of the lesson going through the intro for the song. Poppy's eagerness is contagious. I feel motivated to head back to my studio so I can work on my new song after the lesson's finished.

Poppy's gramma arrives to pick her up at the end of the lesson, and for the first time, she comes inside. She's standing in the doorway with a ghost of a smile, watching Poppy and me play together, as Poppy watches the colorful patterns move and change on my laptop screen. Poppy hasn't noticed her yet, but I heard the door open, so I looked up to see who was there. I motion with my head for her to come further into the room. Poppy notices my movement and turns to see what's going on.

She stops playing and removes her guitar quickly, then she runs to meet her gramma with the same enthusiasm she greeted me at the beginning of the lesson. I watch their exchange, full of happiness and love. I guess they would be closer than many grandparents to their grandchildren because they live together. I step forward to introduce myself, but Poppy beats me to it, signing my name sign—guitar—to her gramma. I don't bother correcting her, stepping closer to shake her hand.

"Hi, I'm Rose, Poppy's gramma. It's nice to meet you. Poppy talks non-stop about you and practices the guitar religiously," she signs as she speaks to me.

"Hi, Mrs.—" I realize I don't know her last name.

"Oh, please call me Rose." She waves me off.

"Well, Rose, it's nice to meet you, too. I can tell how hard Poppy's working on perfecting her technique and the song by how quickly she's mastered it. You must be sick of listening to *Love Me Do* by now," I sign as I speak.

She laughs as she nods. "Only a little." She says it with a grin, so I know she's not too bothered.

"Well, we started learning a new song today. She can switch between the two, giving you guys some variety."

"Oh, that's great." She stops signing. "Look, I stopped in today because Poppy's mother wanted me to thank you for teaching Poppy and to ask if we needed to be paying you for your time."

Poppy stomps her foot, looking frustrated. "Gramma, sign, please!"

"It's my pleasure. I've never actually *taught* anyone how to play guitar before. My mom had to tell me where to start." I laugh lightly. "She's the music teacher in the family." I shove my hand through my hair. "You don't need to pay me anything. I'm really enjoying spending time with Poppy."

Poppy interrupts. "Your mom's a music teacher? That's so cool."

I nod to Poppy. "Yeah, she taught me."

"Oh, okay. So you're not a music teacher then?" She seems confused.

"Uh, no." She doesn't seem to know who I am, which is fine by me. "I play and sing. I've been playing since I was younger than Poppy. I'm competent, but I'm not a teacher, as such."

"Sorry, I … we assumed you were a music teacher. Are you certain you want to keep teaching Poppy? We could probably get her a proper teacher."

"No, Gramma. I want to keep learning with Guitar." Her little eyebrows are drawn down low over her silver eyes.

Oh, shit. I don't want to stop working with Poppy. I've grown fond of the little girl. I love her spark, her energy, and her determination to learn and master something that would be quite difficult for her. There I go again with my assumptions about the capabilities of someone who is Deaf or Hard of Hearing—I mentally kick my ass.

"If you feel she would do better with a proper music teacher, you're more than welcome to seek one out for her, but I would love to keep working with Poppy. If that's okay?" I pause, hoping she sees as well as hears my sincerity. "Teaching her has helped me just as much as it's helping her. However, I understand if you would prefer she is taught by a professional."

"Oh, no. Poppy loves working with you. I didn't mean to imply you weren't professional. I didn't want to impose on your time if this isn't what you do. Are you sure we can't pay you for your time, at least? What about compensation for the program you sent home?"

"I'm certain. I don't need or want any payment. Not even for the program. It's fine, I promise."

"Okay then. Thank you so much. She's thoroughly enjoying these lessons. Poppy's wanted to learn to play the guitar for some time, and it's great to see her being challenged," she signs to Poppy, "Are you ready to go?"

Poppy nods and then collects her guitar. She hugs me goodbye and confirms that we'll meet again next week for her lesson.

THIRTEEN

-toby-

I CAN'T KEEP GOING LIKE I AM. IT'S BEEN JUST OVER TWO weeks, and thoughts of Cassia have invaded every minute of my day since the reunion. The only time I've had a break has been when I've worked with Poppy. I may not have her phone number, but I *know her flower shop's name*, so I plan to pay her a surprise visit today after my morning swim.

From the outside, *Blooms and Balloons* is a cute little shop. Cassia has flowers in various-sized pots outside the windows, made of smaller panes that curve in toward the door. I stop, watching her through the window. She's busy putting flowers together in some type of complicated arrangement. She has a serene smile, one that shows she genuinely enjoys what she does.

I feel like a bit of a creeper, so I step inside and, instantly, am overwhelmed by the scent of flowers. Hundreds of flowers in various colors, sizes, and shapes. The bell over the door tinkles, alerting Cassia to my arrival. When she looks up, she freezes—I've caught her by surprise.

I tuck my hands in my pockets to keep myself in check. "Hey, Cassia."

Her back straightens as she stiffens. "Uh, hey, Toby." She finishes tying off the ribbon on the arrangement she's working on, then places it gently on the counter. She makes no move to come to me, so I step forward.

"You left before I woke up the other morning." I push my hair back from my face. "Why?" I sound pissed. Which I am, but I don't want her to think … actually, I don't know what I want her to think or not think. I'm just pissed, and to be honest, hurt that she left the way she did.

Her eyes are darting everywhere but at me. That just won't do. I step around the counter, which looks to be made from wooden pallets, to get into her space. She can't avoid me when I'm this close to her. The pulse point at the base of her neck is fluttering like crazy, and she's biting that delectable bottom lip. That was her tell in high school. I see it hasn't changed. She feels uncomfortable and nervous about my question. *Good.*

She looks gorgeous, her hair tied back in a simple ponytail, minimal makeup, and her pale pink *Blooms and Balloons* apron. I reach forward to tenderly tuck a loose lock of hair behind her ear, my fingers following the line of her jaw to her chin, directing her to look up at me.

I whisper, "Tell me why you left, Cass."

She doesn't retreat from me or pull away from my light touch, which is a good sign, but I can see her thinking. As though she's formulating a response for me. "I needed to get home. That's all."

"That's all, huh?" My eyes inspect her face for deceit. In my line of business, people lie to me all the time. While I can tell she's not lying, she's also not being completely honest with me. "You couldn't wake me up to say goodbye?"

"Well, there was no need for both of us to be awake so early. You were sleeping peacefully. I told myself that if you didn't wake on your own when I got up, I'd leave you to enjoy your sleep."

"So, you were being ... thoughtful?" I tense my jaw. "Considerate?"

She latches onto those words, nodding eagerly. "That's right. I was being considerate."

"Sure you were. I was hoping to cook you breakfast and spend at least part of the day with you. I was ..." I look away, searching for the correct word. "disappointed. Disappointed to wake up and find you gone; no note, no goodbye."

Cassia's lip-biting has taken on a life of its own. I want to take that bottom lip between my teeth and bite it, suck it, lick it. *Fuck!* That doesn't help the constant issue I have with my dick whenever I'm around this woman.

"Sor-ry?" She seems uncertain in her apology.

"You need to make it up to me. Have lunch with me this week. A friend of mine owns a Greek restaurant close to here; good food, and the atmosphere is private. A quiet place where we can talk."

She's fidgeting, her eyes darting around her shop while I'm waiting for her to refuse. The expressions that cross her beautiful face suggest she's working through various responses and weighing up her options.

FOURTEEN

-cassia-

I CAN'T BELIEVE I AGREED TO HAVE LUNCH WITH TOBY. THIS week is crazy busy, and I don't have time, but more importantly, I'm surprised he wanted to see me again. I felt terrible to refuse his request, so I agreed to meet him for lunch today at his friend's restaurant. He offered to pick me up, but I told him I'd rather make my way to the restaurant than have him pick me up.

I've never been here before, and as soon as I step inside, it's like I've been transported back in time to a traditional Greek taverna. Not that I've ever been to a traditional Greek taverna —I'm basing my impression on what I'd imagine it to be like. It's darker inside than it is outside, and it takes my eyes a moment to adjust. If the delicious aromas are anything to go by, the food is going to be amazing. It's more upmarket than I was expecting, and I feel underdressed in my skinny jeans and work shirt—but I *am* on my lunch break. It's not as busy as I would have expected, but I guess it *is* a weekday.

The host greets me with a smile. "Welcome to *Cristo's Taverna*. How may I help you?"

"I'm meeting a friend. I assume he has a reservation. Toby

Summer?" I finish as though I'm asking a question. I'm not sure if he would have made the reservation under his name or not. I'm not sure how secretive he has to be when he goes out.

"Your lunch companion has already arrived. Allow me to show you to your table." She guides me through the taverna to a table hidden away in the back corner. I guess Toby has to take some measures to maintain his privacy when he's out in public. We reach the table to find Toby on his phone. He looks up, noticing my arrival as the host steps away to get back to the greeting podium. He quickly finishes the call, then stands up to pull out my chair, encouraging me to sit down.

"Hey, Cassia. I'm so happy you could make it." He sits down, his knee touching mine beneath the table, sending electricity shooting through my body. He picks up the water bottle, motioning toward my glass, waiting for my approval before filling it.

I quickly sip my drink before responding. "Hi. Of course, I made it. I said I would join you for lunch." I glance around the taverna. "I've never been here before. It feels as though I'm in Greece. Not that I've ever been to Greece. I mean, it feels like I could be in Greece. I mean, it feels authentic." *Geez, Cass, shut the hell up already!* Toby presses his lips together; I think he's trying to contain his laughter.

"It's pretty authentic. My friend Cristo is of Greek descent. His family has owned and operated this taverna for three generations. Before that, they owned and ran a taverna back in Greece. So it's in their DNA. The food is amazing. You're in for a real treat."

"What do you recommend?" Hopefully, he knows what's best, which will save us some time with the ordering process. I only have an hour.

"I thought we could start with their Thursday special: a tasting plate which includes Epiros Feta, Dolmathes, Octapodaki tou Yiorgou, Garides Skordates, and Soutzoukakia. Then

I thought we could have Moussaka for our main meal, and we'll see how we go for dessert." He puts down his menu to check with me. "How does that sound?"

"That sounds delicious, but it seems like an awful lot of food for the two of us."

"I'm hungry. I'll eat whatever you don't." He pats his trim stomach for good measure. I remember exactly how amazing those abs of his felt beneath my hands.

The waiter stops at our table with a bottle of wine Toby must have ordered before I arrived. I really shouldn't have a drink because I have to go back to work, but I think I'll need a glass to get through this lunch. My nerves are running rampant. I got the distinct impression the other day that he was upset with me for leaving before he woke up. I'm worried about how he's going to deal with the *'issue'* today. The waiter pours us each a glass of wine before placing the bottle on the table, then takes our order.

Toby picks up his glass, then indicates for me to pick up mine. "To second chances, Cassia."

I tip my head in acknowledgment. "To second chances." We clink our glasses together, then drink.

"How's your week been so far?" he asks.

"Busy. I have two weddings this weekend, so it's rather hectic. I can only spare an hour for lunch today." He nods. "It's great to be so busy. I have Sally, a trainee, who puts together basic arrangements. She does the more straightforward stuff, but I prefer to handle the more complicated orders myself. I'm a bit fussy, wanting every single order that leaves my store to be truly unique. I really need to employ someone else, though, even if it's just doing office management and ordering, freeing me up to make the arrangements." I tuck a lock of hair behind my ear. "How about you? What have you been up to?"

"I'm currently writing songs for a new album, which I'll record before the end of the year."

"How do you come up with new ideas for your music?" I'm genuinely curious about where his inspiration comes from.

"From experiences, people, how I'm feeling, things happening around me. Anywhere, really. I have a great song that I'm thrilled with, but I can't seem to get the lyrics straight for it."

I take another drink of wine. "Is that how you work? The music comes first, and then the lyrics come second?"

"Sometimes. Other times, it's the other way around. It depends. Sometimes a bridge will come to me, and I work around that to write the rest of the song. I don't think I've written two songs the same way. It's weird like that."

The server delivers our tasting plate, interrupting our conversation briefly. The food looks divine and smells fantastic —I can't wait to taste it.

"This looks amazing." I place the napkin on my lap as Toby begins scooping a portion of each item onto my plate, then repeats the process with his own. We both take a bite of food, and I can't help the appreciative noise that escapes me. Embarrassed, I look up from my plate to see if Toby noticed. He's looking at me with his food paused midway to his mouth. "Uh, sorry. Couldn't help myself. This octopus tastes delicious. So fresh and tasty with the zesty lemon and subtle oregano."

"Never apologize for enjoying your food. The food here is always fresh and tastes delicious."

Discussion ceases momentarily while we enjoy the various foods and flavors. Everything is so scrumptious.

Toby wipes his mouth with his napkin. "Did you enjoy the reunion?"

"Yeah, it was great to catch up with old friends. Most people looked pretty much the same, just older. Though I don't think I would have recognized Shane if I fell over him in the street. He looks so different from what he did in high school."

Toby nods in agreement. "Time serving overseas in the Special Forces will change a guy."

"Oh, I didn't know. Where did he serve?"

"He spent some time in Syria. Saw some horrendous shit over there. Since he's been home, he hasn't been the same. He doesn't talk about it. He, uh, actually works for me as my bodyguard." He looks sheepish sharing that information with me, as though he's embarrassed he's so famous he needs a bodyguard.

"It must be hard to go through war over there, then have to come home and function as if you haven't seen and done terrible things. I didn't know he worked as your bodyguard."

"Yeah, I don't need one, but I wanted to keep an eye on him, so I created the position. He doesn't know that, though, so please keep that information to yourself." What a kind, generous thing to do for a friend. It makes Toby that much more attractive in my eyes—a man who takes responsibility with his actions rather than his words.

"Sure. No problem." Does that mean he thinks I'll be seeing Shane again? The server comes to clear our dishes, topping up each of our glasses with wine at the same time.

"So, do you keep in touch with anyone from high school?"

"No. The other night was the first time I'd seen the girls since we were nineteen. I got busy, and we lost touch." That's an understatement. I wonder what he'd think if he knew the reason why I became so busy.

"What about Jake? You still see him?"

"Uh nope. The last time I saw him was just over five years ago now." I don't want to talk about Jake or why our relationship ended for good. It'll expose Poppy, and I don't want to do that. She's had enough rejection. I refuse to open her up to more. "I don't want to talk about him. He's of no importance to me."

He nods thoughtfully as the server returns with our main meal, which smells out of this world. The béchamel sauce looks as though it's been baked to perfection. The next few moments are silent as we dig into our Moussaka; enjoying the combination of flavors on my tongue. I'm about halfway through when Toby puts me on the spot. "At the reunion, Jake still seemed … interested in a relationship with you. What was that about then?"

"Toby, I don't want to be rude, but I don't want to talk about Jake. We're done. Over. Have been for a long time. I'm happier for it. That's all there is to it, as far as I'm concerned." He doesn't look like he wants to drop the discussion about Jake; however, he must conclude there's nothing left to discuss.

We continue eating in silence. The atmosphere between us is awkward; however, I'm not sure how to break the sour mood. "So, do you have any humorous stories from your tours?"

He places his knife and fork down, taking a moment to think. "Actually, I do. My nan thought she'd surprise me by turning up to one of my concerts. I had no idea she was there, and I don't know if you're aware, but women often throw their panties on stage when I'm playing." He blushes, which is adorable. "Well, she noticed the women were taking their underwear off to throw them onto the stage. She was mortified and worried that I would be touching 'dirty' panties." He huffs out a laugh. "I don't know how she did it, but she managed to get on stage and used my bass player's mic to tell off all the 'filthy young ladies' in the audience. She said, and I quote, 'If you want to give my grandson your panties, bring a clean pair. Don't be throwing your dirty, smelly underwear at my Toby.' Security managed to guide her gently backstage, where she waited for me to finish my set before proceeding to lecture me about touching other people's dirty underwear."

I can't believe what I'm hearing and burst into uncontrollable snort-laughter; Toby joins me. Once we settle down, I ask, "Are you serious?"

He deadpans, "Completely."

"Oh my gosh, your nan sounds hysterical. How embarrassed were you?" I'm still giggling.

"Utterly embarrassed. It was a few years ago now, yet I *still* get asked about it in interviews sometimes." He shakes his head. "I wonder if it will ever go away?"

When I asked him if he had any humorous stories, I never imagined a story involving his nan. It makes him even more appealing in my eyes. He could have easily shared something that would portray him as the star he is; instead, he chose a funny anecdote involving his family. It suggests how close they are. I touch his hand. "I think it's sweet she was worried about you."

He uses the opportunity to turn over his palm so he can hold my hand. "We're a pretty close family. We catch up every Sunday when we're all in town; we enjoy spending time together. Most of the time, it's me who can't make it because I'm on tour, and I miss them when that happens."

"I think it's pretty rare these days to find families who *like* to spend time together. I'm close to my mom and sister, too."

"I didn't know you had a sister."

"Yeah, Violet's two years older than I am. She didn't like to be seen with her little sister at high school, so it wasn't common knowledge we were related then. She's married and has a three-year-old daughter with her husband."

"Cool. Do you like being an aunt? I can't wait for Kate and Oliver to start a family. I'm gonna be the coolest uncle." He puffs out his chest as though it will be his most outstanding lifetime achievement.

"I'm sure you'll be the coolest." I giggle. "I do love being an aunt. It's truly special to be part of their lives."

His mood suddenly changes from light and happy to serious as he squeezes my hand. "Are you ready to tell me the real reason you snuck out of my place early on Sunday morning?"

I knew this was coming, so I've been thinking about what to tell him. I figure I can go with part of the truth. People always say to stick with the truth as much as possible. "Look, it's a bit embarrassing, but I moved back in with my mom about eight years ago. I didn't want to arrive home after she had woken up and make her aware that I had spent the night somewhere; it feels disrespectful to her, and she would have asked me loads of questions." I bite my bottom lip. "As it was, I felt like I was back in high school breaking curfew." I give a light laugh, hoping to lighten my statement.

The surprised expression on his face shows he wasn't expecting that as my answer. "I didn't know that. Fair enough. I understand not wanting to be disrespectful to your mom. I would have probably done the same thing." He squeezes my hand, bumping my leg with his own to regain my focus. "I still would have preferred you to have woken me before you left."

"I'm sorry about that. I didn't know the protocol in that situation. I never do one-night stands. I figured you'd want me out of the way."

"Never. I don't want you out of the way. *Ever.*" The sincerity in his voice suggests he means this. But what does that really mean? Does he want us to hook up again? I'm not sure I could do it. My heart's already begun to get involved, and that's definitely not something I want to happen.

"When can we catch up again? I know you have two weddings this weekend, but are you free next weekend?"

Oh, shit! What can I say? I don't want to ask Mom to look after Poppy so I can go on a date if that's even what he's asking for. She already helps me out so much with her. "Um, what did you have in mind? I'll have to check my schedule."

"I enjoy going to *Brady's Pub* now and then on a Saturday night to watch live bands. I was planning to go next Saturday night with this guy I met a while ago through Oliver to watch an up-and-coming band. It would be great if you could come along, too." Oh, so it's not a *date*. I'm unsure if I'm disappointed or not. It sounds as though he's inviting me out as a friend.

"That sounds like fun. I'll have to let you know after I check my schedule for that weekend."

"Fair enough." His lips lift in a half-smile. "That means you'll need my number."

"Yeah, I guess I do." He gestures for me to get my phone out, so I reach down to pick up my purse. The strap catches under the leg of my chair, and everything spills out onto the floor—how freaking embarrassing. I mean everything. Tissues; wet wipes; band-aids; tampons; the arm from Poppy's Barbie doll. It's a genuine mom purse, you know—all the things I need to carry at all times. I try to scoop everything up quickly before Toby notices, except he's already bent down to help me.

"Wow, you sure carry a lot of stuff in your purse. It must weigh a ton." He laughs as he picks up the doll's arm, raising an eyebrow at me.

"Uh." I laugh awkwardly, thinking quickly. "That belongs to my niece, Jasmine." He hands it to me, and I add it to the collection in my purse. I glance at the time and am shocked to see that lunch has taken well over an hour. "I really need to get back to work. I have a lot to do."

He stands, then pulls out my chair for me. "I'll walk you back. I still need to give you my number." He pays for our meal, and I thank him for buying me lunch today. Shane steps in behind us, taking me by surprise. I didn't realize he was in the restaurant.

"Hey, Shane."

He tilts his head. "Hey, Cassia. How're things?"

"Great, thanks."

Toby holds my hand as we walk back toward my shop, and

I marvel at how nice it feels to hold a man's hand in this way. Every time we've touched, whether it be our hands or our legs, I've felt that spark with him. Hell, I don't even need to be touching him to feel the spark between us. As we arrive, he pulls me around in front of him, wrapping his arms around my waist. Pulling me in tight to his body, he kisses my lips gently, as though he's unsure of my reception, but I press in tighter, returning the kiss. Toby pulls back to whisper in my ear. "It's hard to do, but I'm keeping it PG in front of your shop to be respectful of your business. Now give me your phone so that I can give you my number."

I pull out of his embrace and tackle the mess that is my purse to find my phone, unlocking it before handing it to him for his number. He inputs his information, then sends a message to his phone to get my number. He kisses me once again before we part ways with my promise to let him know about next Saturday night.

FIFTEEN

-cassia-

I NEVER GO OUT THIS OFTEN, BUT I'M STANDING IN FRONT OF my mirror checking out my reflection once again. When I told Mom I'd been invited out by a high school friend I reconnected with at the reunion, she all but pushed me out the door. She was unbelievably happy to see me going out to spend time with friends. I didn't tell her the person was of the male persuasion; that would have led to too many questions and too much excitement. I've lost count of the number of times Mom's lectured me about 'putting myself out there' and 'you'll never meet anyone if all you do is work and hang out at home with me'.

I've chosen to keep my outfit simple. Pairing my black ripped skinny jeans with my white boyfriend shirt and the stiletto sandals I wore to the reunion. No boob tape or adhesive bras in sight—*just in case*. I've straightened my hair and put on minimal makeup. I've always been a bit of a no-fuss kinda girl, which suits my busy lifestyle since becoming a mom and business owner. I also don't want to look like I'm trying too hard to impress anyone, or Mom will get suspicious.

Saying my goodbyes to Poppy and Mom, I tell them not to

wait up for me. Poppy's not used to seeing me dressed to go out socially, so she makes a big deal about how pretty I look, hugging me extra tight. I remind her to behave for Gramma, not that I need to. She's always such a good kid. I'm incredibly fortunate to have her in my life. I know Mom will spoil her tonight, giving her extra dessert.

Arriving at the pub on time, it's unsurprisingly busy for a Saturday night. I can't hear a live band playing, but there is definitely music pumping over the din of conversation. Unfortunately, the place is bigger than I expected, and as I make my way slowly through the crowded space, I'm not sure I'll be able to locate Toby and his friend here. The next thing I know, I'm wrapped in two arms and lifted off of my feet, causing me to squeal in surprise as I attempt to escape the stranger's grip.

"Fancy seeing you here, Sia."

Ugh, I know that voice. I heard it three weeks ago for the first time after a five-year absence. "Put me down, Jake." My tone brooks no argument. I'm livid that he thinks he still has the right to put his hands on me after all this time and everything that's gone down between us. "Now, Jake. I mean it." He squeezes me tighter, pushing all the air out of my lungs, so I increase my attempt to break free. I remember the shoes I'm wearing, so I thrust my foot back into his leg, causing him to release me, finally.

"You fucking bitch!" He raises his hand, ready to strike me when a couple of good Samaritans standing close by step in to help me. They step in between the two of us, using their bodies as a shield.

"You need to leave the lady alone, man. She doesn't seem interested." Samaritan number one says.

"Don't you fucking tell me what to do. She's my woman. I'll do whatever the fuck I want!" He sneers at the guy.

Samaritan number two looks over his shoulder to check the accuracy of the statement. "I'm not his woman. He's crazy."

When I look around, I notice we've attracted quite a bit of attention from the surrounding people, one of which is Toby. He's moving toward me with malice in his eyes. Shane's close behind with a third guy bringing up the rear.

"What the hell is going on?" He looks at me. "Are you okay?"

Good Samaritan number two speaks up, "This guy's been giving her a hard time. He says she's his girl. She's saying she's not." He shrugs as if he doesn't know who to believe. Toby looks across, noticing Jake for the first time. If he was concerned that Jake and I were still together before, he's really going to think we're still on and off now.

I feel like I need to clarify the situation. "I'm NOT with him. We haven't been together for years." Of all the places we could bump into each other, it had to be in a place where Toby would be, too. It's unbelievable in a city this size that we happened to be in the same place at the same time—I guess it happens. Toby pulls me to his side, offering his support.

"What the fuck? Are you with Emo Boy now?" Jake sneers at me. The good Samaritans have stepped away, and I don't blame them. Jake looks about ready to explode. I can only hope he doesn't mention Poppy. He looks at Toby. "You always did have a hard-on for her in high school." He spits on the floor at my feet. "Enjoy her while you can, Emo Boy. She *always* comes back to me." Jake turns on his heel and storms away, pushing his way forcefully through the crowd. I finally release the breath I was holding in anticipation of the possible bombshell he could've dropped—fortunately, he didn't.

Toby pulls me into him, holding me tight as he strokes my hair. "You okay?" he whispers in my ear. I'm shaking now. I guess the release of adrenalin has kicked in, and I can only nod. "Come on. Let's go sit in our booth." He guides me across the tiled floor to the other side of the bar. Toby helps me sit, and I slide across the seat, allowing him to join me. Shane and the other guy slide into the other side. Toby pulls me back into his body, helping me to feel secure after what's transpired. He pulls his head away to study my face. "You sure you're okay? You're trembling."

I finally find my voice. "Yeah, I'm okay. It was just unexpected. I haven't seen him for years, then suddenly I see him twice in one month. Each time, he seems like he's been drinking too much and has acted like he still has the right to touch me. Which he doesn't." I look pointedly at Toby to make it clear that I'm not comfortable with Jake touching me. Toby tips his chin in deference. I hope it's the end of the conversation. He looks at Shane and the other guy. "This is my friend, Jase Parker. He works with Oliver, Kate's husband. And you already know Shane."

I smile at the guys. "Hey, Shane, good to see you again. Nice to meet you, Jase."

"You, too." He smiles. I feel like I'm sitting with the hot guy club among these three men. Looking around at my surroundings, I notice several women eyeing the men at my table. Yet I'm the lucky one sitting here with them. A couple of women step closer to our table as though they're going to approach the guys.

Shane stands. "What would you like to drink? We have a tab running." He situates himself between the women and our table, effectively blocking their approach.

"I'll have a Vodka tonic. Thanks." He acknowledges my request, then heads off toward the bar. The drink will help calm me down. Toby places his hand on my thigh under the table, and the heat that travels up my thigh to my core is instantaneous.

"So, you've known Toby since high school, huh? Any embarrassing stories you're willing to share about our boy here?" Jase smiles as he winks at me.

"Uh, not really. We didn't hang out in the same circles, and whenever I tried to strike up a conversation with him, he'd find some excuse to leave."

"Hey, I've explained and apologized for that." Toby laughs, his breath rushing across my cheek. I look at him, appreciating the beauty of his face relaxed with joy.

"I feel there's a story here. C'mon, don't leave me in the dark, man." He looks at Toby.

Shane returns partway through the conversation. "It's because Toby had a crush on Cassia in high school. He couldn't be in the same room with her without getting a ..." His words fade away as he gestures to his crotch. The guys laugh at Toby's expense and, the good sport that he is, he joins in with them. The conversation lightens the mood and has everyone laughing. He doesn't seem to mind being the butt of the joke.

Conversation flows freely after that, then at ten, we make our way downstairs to the basement where the pub showcases live bands on a Saturday night. I didn't know this part was down here. The wooden floors look well worn, with years of patrons enjoying music in the space. Wooden paneling on the walls makes the space feel intimate. Green Tiffany pendants dangle from the high ceiling, providing dim light for the ample space.

We listen to the first set. The guys seem to enjoy the music, although it's not my style. I prefer Toby's style more than anything. That pop, rock, sometimes acoustic sound he seems to pull together. These guys are playing really heavy rock, and to me, it just sounds like a whole lotta noise. Jase has gone off to catch up with some other friends, while Toby wants to talk with the band during the break, so I stay with Shane.

Shane steps closer to me. "Hey, Cassia, I wanted to check something with you."

"Yeah. What is it?"

"Are things really over between you and Jake?" I'm uncertain what my relationship with Jake has to do with Shane. "I don't want Toby to get his hopes up, that's all. If you're still on and off with Jake, you need to make that clear to Toby. Don't let him think there's hope where there's none."

I think it's sweet that he's looking out for Toby, just as Toby's looking out for him by giving him a job. "Shane. I'm not involved with Jake in any way, shape, or form. You needn't worry about that. I promise. But what makes you think there's anything between Toby and me?" I'm interested to know if Toby told Shane about our night together.

"You know his high school crush?" I nod. "It never went away. You were the primary reason he attended the reunion. He was hoping to reconnect with you, maybe see where things could go between the two of you if you were single."

Wow. Toby hasn't said it in so many words, but he sort of implied he wanted me in his life. I wonder how Toby would feel if he knew what Shane's just told me? I'm starting to think I need to cut this, whatever this is, with Toby off. As much as I like him and thoroughly enjoyed spending time in his bed, a relationship between us would never work in a million years. There's no way he'd be interested in me if he knew I had a daughter. With Jake, no less. His world revolves around sound, while the most precious person in my life lives in a world of silence—even though she's learning the guitar. He travels all over, performing to thousands upon thousands of screaming fans, meaning he's away for probably most of the year. He probably sleeps with women worldwide; that's why he's so talented in bed. I doubt he's looking to settle down and be a committed partner. I'm not prepared to expose Poppy to his lifestyle or his possible rejection of her.

What in the hell am I doing here?

Toby's nowhere in sight, but I feel the urgent need to leave. "I've gotta get going. Can you please tell Toby I needed to leave?"

Shane seems surprised by my sudden need to leave. "Uh, sure. Of course. Do you need a ride? We can take you home."

"No. No, that's okay. I'll get an Uber. Bye, Shane." I step away from him. "Enjoy the rest of your night." Turning to leave, I make my way as quickly as possible through the crowded room, up the stairs, through the packed pub, and out the front door. By the time I reach fresh air, I'm almost gasping with an impending panic attack. I calm myself down with solid deep breaths, then use my app to request an Uber. Walking down the street to an open café, I wait inside for it to arrive.

My phone rings in my back pocket, so I pull it out to read the display. Toby. *Shit!* I contemplate sending it to voicemail, but that feels wrong since I just abandoned him in the pub.

Before I can get a word out of my mouth, he frantically speaks. "Where are you, Cassia?"

"Didn't Shane tell you? I had to leave. I wasn't sure how long you'd be, and I couldn't wait around." Sort of true.

"Is there some kind of emergency or something?" Or something, I guess.

"It was just time to leave. My Uber's arrived. Gotta go. Bye." I disconnect the call as I confirm my ride is actually my ride. As I'm settling into the back seat, my phone rings again. It's Toby.

Should I send him to voicemail?

I need to cut ties with him.

It would be best this way.

I've been contemplating what to do for too long, and my voicemail picks up the call, deciding for me. I breathe a sigh of relief that I don't have to talk to him now as the alert on my phone tells me he's left a message. I'll listen to it later. My phone rings again. Shit, he's not giving up. I probably should answer the damn thing.

"Hey—"

Toby cuts me off. "Don't hang up on me again. Do you

understand?" he snaps before pausing. I open my mouth to answer, but he keeps on talking. "You have a habit of leaving me without the opportunity to say goodbye or to set up another time to catch up. Do you have some kind of issue with me?"

The only issue I have with him is the perceived future I imagine playing out. I can't express that to him, though.

"Am I a checklist item on your bucket list or something? Fucked a famous musician. Tick," he grumbles.

"What in the hell did you just say to me?" I can't believe he said that to me. How dare he speak to me like that. I'm the total opposite of some groupie who just wants to sleep with him. "Don't you dare presume something so crass about me. You don't know me. Who I am. The things that are important to me." I huff out a breath. I don't think I've been this mad for a long time.

"I'm sorry, Cassia. I don't know what else to think. You keep blowing me off." He releases a huge sigh. "I like you, okay. I fucking loved being inside you. I would like to explore a relationship with you, but I'm getting the distinct impression I'm on my own on that front."

He's sincere in his words; I can tell. "Look, Toby. You're not on your own. I like you, too. And I loved what we did at your place. It was by far the best sexual experience of my life." The Uber driver looks up at me through the rear-view mirror, reminding me I have someone who can listen to my conversation. I drop my voice to a whisper. "I'm not sure a relationship with you is possible with your career. That lifestyle is not something I'm interested in. I have other commitments and priorities that must come first for me at the moment. I'm sorry, but I think it's for the best if we leave things be." I'm greeted with silence on the other end of the phone. I look at the display to check he's still there. "Toby. You there?"

"Yeah. Just taking a minute to digest what you said and come to terms with the disappointment. But you're probably right. I don't want to force you into something that doesn't *appeal* to you—I respect you too much for that. Unfortunately, my lifestyle isn't conducive to a steady relationship, no matter how much I want one. See ya, Cass." He sounds resigned. As though he's acknowledging the prospect he'll have to face his entire future alone. I'm sure that's my imagination, though. I bet he has women lining up for him after his performances. I doubt he spends too many nights alone.

He disconnects the call before I can say goodbye, giving me a taste of my own medicine. Well, he gave up quickly. I guess he's not genuinely interested in a relationship with me, and he was looking more for a hook-up—which isn't me.

He's like all the other men—out for a good time.

Slumping back into the seat, I feel hollow inside. I never imagined tonight would go the way it did. First with Jake, and now with Toby. If only I felt like I'd made the right decision.

SIXTEEN

-toby-

WELL, I GUESS THAT'S THAT THEN. OVER BEFORE IT EVER really started. I'm confused as to how our night turned out so ... *shitty!* I was confident she felt the same sparks, the same connection I did whenever we touched. Hell, we didn't even need to touch for me to *feel* it—but I guess I was on my own. It reinforces the notion I'm not going to find someone to accept me as long-term partner material with my career. Ever since Kate settled with Oliver, I've been thinking about my life and how I want it to look; and I know, without a doubt, that I don't want to be alone.

I'm still staring at my blank phone when Shane pats me on the back. "What's up, bro?"

"Uh, nothing. I think I'll call it a night. You guys enjoy the band. I'll catch up with ya tomorrow. Let me know when the next decent band's playing, Jase."

I don't give either of them a chance to ask any further questions, waving over my shoulder as I make my way through the crowd to head home—*alone.*

Poppy comes running to me as soon as she enters the room, launching herself at me. I've learned to brace myself for the onslaught of her exuberant greetings. She's always so happy to see me and show me how much she's improved since our last lesson. She pulls back, studying my face.

At least someone's happy to spend time with me. I sound like a crybaby, but Cass's rejection still fucking stings.

Her head tilts to the side. "Are you okay? You look sad."

"Yeah, Poppy. I've been sad, but seeing you makes me feel happier." If she's astute enough to pick up on my mood, I'm not going to lie to her. People experience all types of emotions in life. There's no need to pretend you always feel fantastic when you don't. I don't need to give her any details—just acknowledge that her assessment was accurate. "Come on, show me how you're going with your new song."

"Okay." She steps back into me, throwing her little arms around my hips, squeezing me tight. She steps back and signs. "When I'm feeling sad, Mommy gives me the biggest hugs, and that always makes me feel better. So I'll give you this hug now, and then I'll give you another one before I leave. Hopefully, they'll make you feel better."

My throat feels tight, making it hard to swallow. This kid slays me. She's so open and honest with her affection and friendship. She is a true credit to her mom and gramma. "Thank you. Your mom is right about hugs. Just seeing your smiling face made me feel better, but that hug. It was the best hug I've ever had. Thank you." I muss her hair before indicating for her to get her guitar to show me how she's going with her practice.

We settle into our lesson. I'm more than impressed with Poppy's progress on the new song. I only introduced it to her three weeks ago, and she started back at school this week, so I assume she's had less time to practice.

"You pretty much have it nailed. Anyone would think

you've been playing guitar a lot longer than you have." I sign to her when she finishes. The smile that lights up her face is magnificent. She's proud of herself and with good reason. I don't understand why her father's not in her life, because she's a daughter I'd be proud to have. "Okay, now show me *Love Me Do*. Have you been practicing that one, too?"

She nods. "Yes, I have. I don't have as much time now I'm back at school, but I still make sure I practice every day."

"How has your first week back at paper been? Do you like your teacher?"

She giggles at me. "You're funny, Guitar. It's school, not paper." She shows me the difference between the two signs. They're very similar. Instead of brushing the base of my palms together, I need to clap them without making a sound.

"Thanks, Poppy. So, do you like your teacher?"

"Oh, yeah, she's nice, and all my friends are still in my class."

"That's good. It makes a difference when you have a teacher you like. My sister's a kindergarten teacher."

"I want to be a kindergarten teacher when I grow up. Can I meet her?"

"I'll ask her. Maybe she could come to one of our lessons."

"Cool." She spins around in her excitement.

Once she calms down, she settles in, and she's pretty much spot on with every note. I wave my arms in the air for her as she finishes, then she curtsies to me. We're having a good laugh when Xanthe steps further into the room. I was so focused on Poppy that I didn't notice her enter.

"Poppy, you sound fantastic. How many lessons have you had now?" Xanthe signs, speaking at the same time.

Poppy looks at me tentatively, showing the number eight.

Shaking my head with a smile, I correct her. "Seven. You've only had seven lessons."

Xanthe makes a big show of looking surprised. "You play

like you've been playing for a lot longer than that. You were born to play guitar, girl."

You can almost see Poppy glowing with pride right before our very eyes. She should feel damn proud of herself—her consistent hard work and determination have brought her to this point quickly.

"I stopped in to ask a favor," she signs to both of us. "You know the Labor Day concert we have coming up?" Poppy and I both nod. "One of our performers has had to pull out because they've had a change in circumstances. I was wondering if you guys would be interested in doing a duet?" She holds her hands up in the begging position.

I look at Poppy and sign, "It's up to you, Poppy. I'm happy to do whatever you decide." I really am. If she feels up to the challenge of performing in front of others, I'll support her, standing by her side all the way.

She barely takes a moment to think it over, agreeing readily to the duet for the concert. She is one brave young lady since we only have two lessons to get prepared for it.

"Great. If you could let me know what song you guys want to perform so I can add it to the running sheet, that'd be fantastic. Oh, I'm a happy girl. I can't wait to see you guys play together on stage." She hugs each of us before bustling out of the room.

I look at Poppy. "Which song would you like to do? *Love Me Do* or *Sweet Home Alabama*?"

"Can we do *Love Me Do*?"

"Of course. Let's get started on working out an arrangement."

We work solidly for the rest of the lesson, working out the parts we'll play together. The parts I'll sing, and some parts Poppy can sign while I play. I feel energized and possibly more excited than when I play to a packed stadium. When we part ways at the end of the lesson, I stop in to let Xanthe know which song we'll be performing.

SEVENTEEN

-cassia-

I DRAG MY EXHAUSTED ASS IN THE FRONT DOOR WITH thoughts of a warm shower to ease my tired legs, then flopping face-first onto my bed. As much as I love my daughter and can't imagine my life without her in it, I'm hoping she's already in bed so I can just sneak in to kiss her goodnight. I've worked my schedule so I only have to work tomorrow morning this weekend. Walking through the house, I find Mom and Poppy in the kitchen making hot chocolate; it *is* only seven-thirty, after all. Poppy has her back to me, so she doesn't know I'm watching her.

She's growing up so fast. I miss the baby years: holding her while she slept; that yummy baby smell; her coos, giggling, and babbling. She was always such a happy baby; she's still a happy child. I thank my lucky stars every single day that I have her in my life. She turns around, noticing me, and immediately stops what she's doing to run to me. Throwing herself at me, I pick her up to hold her close. She grasps my cheeks, drawing her face back to look at me closely, then kisses the tip of my nose—she's such a sweetheart.

"Hello, Mommy."

I put her down so I can sign. "Hello, Baby Girl. What are you guys doing?"

"We're making hot chocolate with marshmallows." She shows me the bag of marshmallows as I notice the remnants of icing sugar on her cheek.

"Oooo, marshmallows. The best."

We work together to get the hot chocolate prepared, then carry it into the living room.

"You're home earlier tonight," Mom observes.

"Yep. I only need to work tomorrow morning, then I have the rest of the weekend off," I speak and sign at the same time so Poppy knows we have lots of time together this weekend. She jumps up and down with excitement. I spend a lot of time feeling guilty for the limited time I spend with my daughter. I've put an ad in the local community paper looking for an office manager in the hopes it will free up some of my time, allowing me to leave work earlier during the week.

"That's so good, Mommy. I have some news, too."

Mom winks at me with the biggest grin, making her look younger.

"I'm going to do a duet with my guitar teacher in a concert at *Music for my Heart* over the Labor Day weekend. You'll come to watch, won't you, Mommy?"

"I wouldn't miss it for the world, Pop. That's amazing. Does your teacher think you're ready?"

"He let me decide. We're going to do *Love Me Do*. We were working out the best way to play it today. Wait 'til you see what we're going to do. I'm so excited." I can tell she's excited. She has so much energy that I don't think she'll sleep tonight. She's almost jumping out of her skin. "I'm going to practice extra hard. We only have two lessons until the concert."

"You'll be great, Poppy. You're already doing so well with

that song. You're going to smash it for the concert." I hug her close.

We all catch up on our days over hot chocolate. I feel revitalized after spending this time with the people I love most in the world.

"Come on, Pop. Time for bed."

She says her goodnights with hugs and kisses before trudging upstairs to get ready for bed. She works through her nightly routine independently while I get her bed ready for her to hop right on in. Tucking her down, ready to read a story together, she stops me.

"Mommy."

"Yeah, Baby Girl. What's up?"

"Why don't I have a daddy like everyone else?"

I knew one day I would need to answer this question. So I've been preparing my answer for her depending on how old she was when she asked. She's astute enough to pick up when I'm not completely honest with her, but I don't want to go into too much detail. "You *do* have a daddy, Pop. Or else you wouldn't be here. It takes a mommy and a daddy to make a baby."

"Where is he? How come I've never met him?"

"He was my boyfriend for a long time during high school and through college. When I told him I was pregnant, he wasn't ready to be a daddy, and that's okay. Not everybody is ready to be a mommy and a daddy at the same time. I moved back here with Gramma so we could all be a big family." I smooth her hair down her back. "Why are you asking about your daddy, Baby Girl?"

She shrugs. "I was just wondering."

"That's okay. You can talk to me or ask me about anything. Okay?"

"Okay, Mommy. Can we read the story now?"

"Sure."

We snuggle down together while I read the next chapter of *Charlie and the Chocolate Factory*. One of my favorites from my childhood. It's a little slower than usual to read and interpret it in ASL, but I'm so happy to share one of my favorites with her and have her enjoy it as much as I did.

I pop the book on her side table before hopping out of bed to tuck her in for the night, but she stops me.

"Mommy, do you think I could ask my guitar teacher to be my daddy?"

I startle at her question. I have to temper my response because I'm so surprised. "Why would you want to ask him?"

"He's really nice. He's kind to me, and he's been very patient. He's been sad, and he said I make him happy." She smiles at me. "I like it when I can make people happy. I really like him, Mommy. He's the best."

"That's great, Poppy. I'm glad you like him, and he's good to you. But you can't ask somebody to be your daddy." Her little face drops, so I rush to add. "There's no reason he can't be your friend, though." I brush a lock of silky hair behind her ear.

"You wait until you meet him after the concert, Mommy. You'll want him to be my daddy, too." Only if her guitar teacher was someone like Toby, I think to myself.

"Maybe, Baby Girl. We'll see, okay?"

"Okay, Mommy. I love you."

"I love you more than all the stars in the sky and grains of sand on the earth."

I kiss her goodnight, turn off the light, and step out of her room. Then close myself in my room, down the hall. Leaning against the door, I look up at the ceiling to prevent the tears from falling; I had no idea she had been thinking about not having a father. I didn't know it bothered her to the degree that she wanted to find herself a dad. Once I get myself somewhat together, I make my way downstairs to speak with Mom.

Mom knows me too well. She reads the defeat in my posture and the look of failure on my face. She knows something's up. "What's up, Cass?"

"Poppy just asked about her dad or lack thereof." I brush my hand through my loose hair, reminding myself I really should get it cut.

Mom places her hand on her heart. "Oh, I guess we knew the questions had to come one day."

"Yeah, I know. It's just that … she wants to ask her guitar teacher to be her daddy."

A smile breaks out across Mom's face as her eyebrows almost hit her hairline. "Well, she has good taste. He *is* rather handsome, *and* he's been very good to her."

I chuckle mildly. "Oh my god, Mom. She can't go around asking just any man to be her daddy. I didn't realize she was missing having a father. That we're not enough for her."

Mom wraps her arm around my shoulders to comfort me. "Of course, we're enough for her. She's just at that age when she's noticing what her friends have and wondering why she doesn't have the same things. It doesn't mean we're not enough or that she's missing out on anything. She's just making sense of the world around her." She nudges my shoulder. "You were about her age when you asked me the very same question. Mind you, you didn't have someone lined up to be your daddy."

I'm shocked I would do such a thing. "No way. I would never have done that."

"Well, you did. It's only natural, Honey. Wait 'til you meet him at their concert. You may just want him to be her daddy, too." She snickers. *Oh, she's so damn funny.*

"I doubt it very much, Mom." I kiss her forehead. "I'm going to bed. I need to start early tomorrow."

"Night, Love."

"Night, Mom." I turn to head back upstairs. Halfway up the stairs, I turn around. "Thanks, Mom."

She nods, then heads back into the kitchen to shut off the lights.

EIGHTEEN

-cassia-

POPPY AND I STEP OUT OF THE FRONT DOOR TO VISIT THE PARK, followed by ice cream from her favorite ice cream shop, *Brain Freeze*. She loves the quirky characters the ice cream artists make out of ice cream and candy. As we're closing the front screen door, my sister's car pulls into the driveway. We haven't heard from her much since last month's visit, so I wasn't expecting her today. Poppy runs toward her car once it's parked. I follow along behind with a sinking feeling in my gut. As I get closer and see her face—her red, swollen eyes and messy hair—I know my gut was right. I step around to open her door, crouching down until I'm at eye level. Her tears burst forth, and I lean forward to engulf her in my arms. It's awkward, but I do my best to offer comfort. Her body shudders as her tears wet my shoulder.

Poppy's climbed into the back of the car entertaining Jasmine, while Vi and I cry together. I feel the pain of losing her marriage, as my hope fades for my own happily ever after with the demise of my sister's. Finally, I pull away, gently wiping my sister's tears with my thumbs.

"C'mon. Let's go inside." Undoing her seatbelt, I help her

out of the car, then lean into the back to retrieve Jasmine. She's smiling and chatting happily as she squishes my cheeks between her chubby hands.

"Herro, Aunt Cass!"

"Hello, Jolly Jas!" I nuzzle her nose with my own, squishing her impossibly closer. This poor baby doesn't understand the turmoil her mom is going through at the moment. As we turn toward the house, Mom comes down the front porch steps, walking quickly toward Vi with her arms open wide. Violet runs into her arms, sobbing as Mom embraces her eldest daughter tightly.

"Come on, Love. Come inside." She guides Vi inside, as I follow behind with Jas and Poppy. I can't explain to Poppy that we won't be going to the park or for ice cream today because I have my hands full, but as soon as we get inside, I'll explain it to her; though she probably already has an idea that things aren't all that great with her aunt.

I explain the situation to Poppy without going into too much detail. She's such a gorgeous girl that she automatically responds it's okay, we can go to the park and get ice cream another day. She then gently guides her cousin into the play-room after I've done a quick check that there's nothing dangerous for a toddler in the room. Unfortunately, I may have to move anything hazardous upstairs to Poppy's room because I think Violet and Jasmine will be here for a while.

We get the kids settled in the playroom, then settle ourselves at the kitchen table, which always seems to be the location of choice for our discussions. Finally, Mom gets us all a drink—alcoholic, of course—it's the obvious choice for an occasion like this.

"He kicked us out!" Vi blurts. More tears are pouring down her face.

"He did what?" Mom and I respond at the same time.

"He said we're dominating his life. He feels like he can't breathe because we're always there."

I'm at a loss. Isn't that what a marriage and family are? Am I missing something here? "What does he mean, 'you're always there'? Isn't that where you're meant to be?"

"How am I supposed to know? He says Jasmine's too needy, that I'm so focused on her I don't pay him any attention other than to tell him what needs to be done around the house. He said, and I quote, 'you don't treat me like a man'."

How dare he act like an immature asshole, kicking my sister and his child out of their home. I feel like the top of my head's going to explode like the emoji.

Mom scoffs, "That would be because he's not acting like a friggin' man." She takes another drink. "If he wants to be treated like a man, he needs to behave like one. Kicking his wife and child out of the family home is certainly not acting like a man in my book."

"Why didn't he just leave? Why did he kick you guys out? What an asshole!" I feel positively violent on her behalf.

"He said his wage paid the mortgage, so it's his home, not mine. It doesn't matter that my wage paid the other bills and put food on the table." All I can do is blink in disbelief. I can't imagine how my sister feels.

"Are you serious?" Mom's voice is growing louder the angrier she gets. "I feel like I never even knew him." She's hurt. And to be honest, she should be. She welcomed Allen into our family as if he were her own son. This isn't just a breakup for Violet. It's a breakup for the whole family.

"Deadly. He thinks because he contributed more financially, I have fewer rights." She looks between both of us, her bottom lip quivering. "He said he doesn't love us anymore. There's nothing about the two of us that interests him. He's outgrown us." Her sobs break free.

We both lean in to hold Vi tight, offering her support in the only way we can right now, as all of our hearts break for her and for Jasmine. I'm not sure how long we stay like that, but the girls find us embracing in the kitchen and join in the hug fest. Eventually, we pull ourselves together and get busy organizing sleeping arrangements, pulling together essential items to get Vi and Jas through a couple of days. She left with nothing. The asshole didn't even give her a chance to pack a bag. Luckily, my sister and I are similar sizes, and I still have Poppy's old clothes that don't fit her anymore, ready to give to my sister. She's going to have to go back at some point to pick up their things, but she needs a few days' grace period to pull herself together.

-cassia-
_____

TODAY'S BEEN PRETTY QUIET FOR ORDERS, SO I USE THE opportunity to catch up on paperwork in my office. Checking my emails for responses to my office manager ad, I find I have one reply, so I click on the attachment to read through the application. Disappointment fills me as I read, finding they have zero experience in office management. I'm all for giving people an opportunity to expand their skills, but I need someone who can walk straight into the position and get started without training them *how* to be an office manager. I shoot back a response, thanking the applicant for her interest and letting her know she was unsuccessful in her application.

My phone rings. The screen displays Sam's name.

"Hey, Sam."

"Hey, Cass. How are things?"

"Oh, Sam, where do I even begin? I'm so busy, I don't know where to start. Today's been my quietest day, so I'm catching up on paperwork." I respond with a chuckle.

"Oh, no. I was hoping we could catch up for lunch sometime."

"I could catch up today since I'm doing office work. I've

already put together my orders for the day, plus a few extras, so I have enough arrangements on display for any last-minute call-ins."

"Sounds good. How about I pick up something, then come to you? That'll save you some time."

"You're an angel."

"I know," she says with a laugh. "I'll see you soon."

We disconnect the call, leaving me feeling lighter, knowing I'm going to have some girl chat time. I haven't had the opportunity to catch up with girlfriends since falling pregnant with Poppy. There was a playgroup when she was little, but the other moms seemed to pity me—which I didn't need or want. I found it difficult to bond with them, so I kept my distance. Once she started school for Deaf and Hard of Hearing children, I took over the shop from Gramma, which didn't afford me the opportunity or time to catch up with other school moms. I get stuck into my work, so I don't feel I have to watch the clock while Sam's here.

The bell over the front door tinkles, alerting me to someone entering my shop and forcing me out of my small office. I put on my best welcoming expression for the potential customer only to find Sam holding a large paper bag filled with what I hope is our lunch. We squeal in happiness, moving forward simultaneously to hug. We pull apart to spend a moment taking each other in. It's been just over four weeks since the reunion and Sam's bump has become more prominent.

"Are you going to tell me about this and why I couldn't say anything at the reunion?" I gesture toward her baby bump with my chin.

"I've been dying to talk to you about it. You're probably the only one who'll understand." I nod because I get it. I was in her shoes when I found out I was pregnant. None of my friends could relate to my situation and weren't interested.

"Come through. We can eat in my office. The space is small, but we can make it work."

We get ourselves settled. Then Sam pulls out the delicious-smelling food from the paper bag she was carrying. The first few moments are silent as we dig into the chicken and avocado paninis Sam chose for our lunch today.

"Come on, girl, spill. How many weeks along are you?"

"I've just hit sixteen weeks, so I'm feeling quite good. Unfortunately, I had terrible morning sickness which seemed to last all freaking day."

"I hear ya! I was the same during my pregnancy. Felt great during the second trimester, then started getting tired easily during my third trimester." It feels like such a long time ago, yet it seems like it was only yesterday. It felt amazing to be growing a human inside my body. "Do you want to talk about the father?"

Sam sucks in a deep breath before shrugging. "Not much to tell." She wiggles in her seat, looking away from me. "We'd been on and off for a while. Then, when I got pregnant, he wanted me to get rid of it. I couldn't do it, Cass." I can only nod because her story sounds so similar to mine. "He wasn't interested in continuing the relationship if I didn't have an abortion—he's not interested in being a father. I guess I'm on my own." She shrugs.

"He sounds like a real douche. He's certainly not someone you would want in your baby's life." He sounds exactly like Jake. "You've made the right choice for you, Sam. If he's not prepared to join you in this experience, then it's his loss."

She nods. However, I sense she's not convinced. "I know. It would just be nice to have a partner who's as invested in this baby as much as I am." She looks up at me with glassy eyes.

"I understand. I was in the exact situation you are in now. That's why I moved home. I needed help physically, emotionally, and financially. I couldn't have done it without Mom."

"My sister wants me to move in with her so that she can help. I'm seriously considering the offer. But I also need to get out of corporate. I can't put in the long hours expected with a baby on the way. Then, after the bean is born, I want to spend some time at home with him or her."

"What type of work do you do in corporate?" I take another bite of my delicious lunch.

"A bit of this, a bit of that. Anything from office organization to financial stuff." She shrugs.

Oh my gosh, could Sam be the answer to my prayers? I wonder if she'd be interested? I have nothing to lose by asking.

"I'm looking for someone at the moment who can take over running the office side of things. It's taking too much time. I need to focus on designing and constructing the arrangements and meeting with clients." I'm excited about the prospect of offloading the office stuff I hate so much. My passion is working with flora and balloons. "I'm not sure I can pay what you're earning in corporate, but it would be fewer hours, with only four days a week."

Sam's face lights up. "Are you offering me a job?"

"Uh, yeah. I'm offering you a freaking job." I can't keep the excitement from my voice. "Do you think you'd be interested?" I have every finger and toe crossed, hoping she says yes.

"Hell yeah. I'm interested. I'd have to give notice where I work, but I could start immediately after that." She pauses, looking around my office. "What about the time I'd need off when the baby's born? I wanted to have some time off before putting him or her into daycare." She caresses her small bump.

"I could pay for some time off, but probably not as much as you would get with your current job because you'll have been with me for less than six months. After the baby's born, we can look at reduced hours for a while, and you could even bring the baby into the office if you like." I'm thinking on my feet here. "We can work it out as we go along. You could even do some of the office stuff from home, to be honest. Anything to make life easier for you." Which will also make life easier for me, too.

Sam jumps up out of her chair, pulling me up before engulfing me in a hug, her hard stomach pressing against my softer one. We jump around like a couple of loons, me excited to have solved my time issues, her for simplifying her life. Finally, we settle down to work out some of the initial details, completing the employment forms, benefits, and banking info. We finish lunch, then Sam heads back to her office while I get stuck into my paperwork. Ugh!

"Thanks for making that adjustment. You saved my ass." It's a relief to have the issue sorted out.

"No problem, I'll update the order and then send through a confirmation email."

"Excellent. Talk to you next week."

"Bye."

I end the call with one of my suppliers just as the bell over the door alerts me to a new customer. It's been hectic today for some reason. I step out of my office with a smile on my face, ready to greet whoever is visiting my little shop. When I look toward the door, my heart drops to my feet. *What in the hell?*

"Hey, Sia." Jake's eyes wander down my body, making me thankful for my work apron.

"What are you doing here, Jake?" I can't keep the disdain out of my voice.

"Aren't I allowed to buy flowers?"

"Of course you are. But this seems a little too contrived for my liking. I haven't seen you for five years, and suddenly, since the reunion, you seem to be making regular appearances. What's going on?"

"Nothin', Babe." He steps closer to me. "I told you, I ain't done with you."

"Well, I'm done with you. Please leave my shop and don't come back." I cross my arms in front of me, adding an extra barrier.

"And I told you, I'm here to buy flowers." His voice has a hard edge to it.

I narrow my eyes, sensing a lie. "Who are the flowers for?"

"Mom. She's been sick, so I thought I'd get her some flowers."

My shoulders release as I drop my hands to my sides. "Oh." I feel terrible now. "What's wrong with her?"

"She has bronchitis. Had it for over a week now." I'm relieved it isn't too serious. I always liked Jake's mom. Though I was hurt she never reached out to me when I got pregnant with her grandchild.

"Well, I hope she recovers soon. Do you have an idea of what type of flowers you'd like to give her?" I remember she loved peonies.

"I dunno. What do you think I should get for her?"

"Well, if I remember correctly, her favorite flower is the peony. So I could put together a simple arrangement for her."

"Sounds good."

"It'll take me about thirty minutes. You wanna come back?"

"Nope, I think I'll wait." Ugh, I was hoping he'd leave and come back. I don't want to make small talk with him.

"Okay. I'll just collect everything I need."

I can't leave the front of my shop unattended for long periods. It's okay to step into my office to answer a quick call, but to work out the back on an arrangement will take too long. Normally, in this situation, I make the client's arrangement and chat with them about the recipient and the reason behind the gift. I enjoy hearing the different stories behind someone's choice to purchase the gift of flowers or balloons.

I step out back and take a deep breath. I don't want to have to spend any time with Jake, but I have to maintain a degree of professionalism, no matter who he is. I wish Sally were here. I hate being in the shop with him by myself.

I collect a rope-style pot, gorgeous pale pink peonies, a hydrangea bloom, a couple of flowering cabbage, and some biodegradable oasis foam. I carry the items out to the front of my store, placing them carefully on the counter. Jake's made himself at home on the stool on the opposite side. I don't bother making conversation. I always pre-soak my oasis so it's ready for use, but I have to shape it before placing it in the pot. Once that's done, I anchor one side of the pot with the flowering cabbage, then the opposite side with the white hydrangea bloom, leaving room down the center for the peonies. Cutting and trimming to get the right height, I carefully place them to fill the space between the flowering cabbage and the hydrangea. I wander out back to collect a couple of peony buds to add interest to the arrangement. I finish off the display by adding them in, then adjusting the other stems slightly, looking at it from different angles to make sure it's balanced and interesting from all perspectives.

"How's this?" I present the pot to Jake.

He looks between the arrangement and me several times before speaking. I'm worried he doesn't like it. "It looks beautiful, Sia. You're great at this." Well, I hope so. It *is* my business, my livelihood.

"Thanks. I would hope so since I rely on this for my income."

We sort out the payment; I add on an extra twenty percent as a douche tax. *Ha!*

"Can I take you out on a date tonight, Sia?" I hate that he calls me Sia. It's not my name, and it isn't cute.

"No. I'm busy."

"Busy with what?" He straightens up. "You seeing that loser, Emo Boy?"

"It's none of your business, Jake. I'm not interested in spending any time with you now or in the future. Say 'hi' to your mom, and I hope she feels better soon."

"No, I want to know. What are you so busy doing tonight?"

"I said." I pause, looking him directly in the eye. "I'm busy. It's none of your damn business."

He steps around the counter so quickly. I have no time to react. He grasps my throat, lifting me slightly, so I'm balancing on my toes. My heartbeat picks up speed. I'm honestly scared. I don't know *this* Jake. The old Jake used to have a temper, but he would never put his hands on me like this. I bring my hands up to claw at him, trying to get him to release me, but I'm not making any headway.

"Tell me, what the fuck you're busy doing tonight?" He shakes me. "And don't give me none of that attitude." He loosens his grip slightly, allowing me to speak.

"I ... I'm looking after our daughter, Jake. I can't go out at the drop of a hat. I have to make plans." He releases me, and I take in gasping breaths. Reaching up, I rub my throat, which is tender from his hard grip. He leans into my space again, and I'm too paralyzed to move. I don't know what to expect when he nuzzles down into my neck, kissing the red marks I'm certain he's left behind.

"Sorry, Babe. I didn't think about that. How about tomorrow night?"

Is this guy for real?

I'm not sure what he expects from me. I've told him repeatedly that I'm not interested in a relationship with him. His recent behavior is scary, which makes me even more determined to stay away from him.

"I ... I can't. I can't get a babysitter at short notice like that.

Plus, I don't like leaving her with a babysitter on a weeknight. She has routines and school and stuff." Hopefully, reminding him I'm a mom puts him off.

"Saturday night then?"

"I can't Saturday night. Poppy has a concert that I can't miss."

"What the fuck does a deaf kid do in a fucking concert?" I don't want to give him any information about Poppy. He doesn't deserve to know anything about her.

"It doesn't matter, Jake. It's important to me to be there for her. I won't miss it." Especially to spend time with him.

He steps back from me, huffing out a breath, mumbling something to himself. Then, grabbing the arrangement I made for his mom, he walks toward the door. "As I said, Sia. I'm not done with you. I'll be back next week. You *will* go on a date with me. I guarantee it." He opens the door, leaving my shop before I can respond.

Tears stream down my cheeks as I begin to shake. I have to sit down so I can control my breathing before I fall. I get the sense that he's not going to leave me alone until he gets his way.

Somehow, I have to remind him I'm a package deal.

It's not just me.

I have a daughter.

His daughter.

The one *he* never wanted.

It takes me some time to collect my thoughts and feel stable enough to stand up without feeling like my jelly legs will fail me. I'm beginning to wish I'd never gone to that damn reunion and put myself in Jake's sights again.

TWENTY

-toby-

"NO WAY, PETA. I'M NOT GONNA EXPLOIT THE LABOR DAY Concert to promote my upcoming album." I slash my arm through the air, gesturing my displeasure at the idea. Peta's been dying to use my guitar lessons with Poppy to our advantage. In her eyes, this is the perfect opportunity. Poppy's family has put their trust in me—a complete stranger—allowing me to work with her at *Music for my Heart*, assuming she's in safe hands. Using her in this way feels underhanded and filthy. I won't allow it. "That's the end of it. Find another way to start promoting my new album. That's what I pay you for."

"Come on, Toby. You said yourself she's a cute kid with a ton of potential. It's not gonna hurt anybody if we record your duet at the concert and leak it to social media."

I adore Peta. She works hard for me and always has my best interest at heart, but I can't agree to this, especially since she doesn't want to get permission from Poppy or her family. She doesn't even want Poppy to know anything about it, to ensure she comes across naturally on camera. I'm not up for exploiting a kid, especially one who has burrowed her way into my life as deeply as Poppy has. She brings out the protective side of me, and I'll do anything to prevent exposing her to the public and their oftentimes vicious scrutiny.

"Poppy and her family don't even know who I am. They thought I was a music teacher. There's no way they would agree to your proposal, and I refuse to do it without their permission. Forget it. Think of something else." I brush the loose hair back from my face. "What's wrong with the usual press tour? It's always been effective in the past. I don't see why we can't do the same. I don't even mind doing some behind-the-scenes footage in my studio showing me working through the songs."

Peta holds her hands up in surrender. "Okay, okay. Alright, I won't use this golden opportunity to promote your new album. I want to show your compassionate side; remind everyone that you're a great guy." Shane snickers from behind me, so I throw him the bird over my shoulder in thanks. "Would you agree to visit the children's ward at the hospital again?"

"Sure thing. I don't have a problem with that scenario because it's set up for that purpose. I'm not blindsiding anyone." Peta should know me well enough by now. I'm pretty easygoing when it comes to my promo, so long as it's all above board. "Set it up, then let me know when and where. I'll be there." I stand up, ready to leave. "Remember, I have a standing commitment every Friday afternoon. So that won't work."

"Okay. See you next week for our regular meeting."

I wave over my shoulder as I clear the doorway. "Let's head over to *Brady's* for a couple of drinks."

It's one of the few places I can hang out on a weekday where people generally leave me alone. Maybe it's because I've been a regular there for a little while now—ever since Jase introduced me to Finn, the owner. I enjoy watching the new bands on Saturday nights, and their Wicked Wings Wednesday special is a favorite of ours.

"Sounds good to me," Shane responds. We head across town toward the pub. I can already taste the wings.

Stepping inside, I can't help but think about the last time we were here with Jase and Cassia. That night certainly didn't end the way I was hoping it would. I had plans to take Cass back to my place. I was hoping we could ... I don't know what I was hoping for. Yes, I do. There's no point lying to myself. I wanted to repeat our night together after the reunion. I was caught entirely off-guard that she called an end to something that had only just begun.

We locate a booth toward the back and relax. A waitress, who's so busy eyeing up Shane I'm surprised she hears a word we say, takes our order. After she steps away, Shane locks his gaze on me. "What's going on with you, bro?"

I give him a 'what are you talking about' look, which is completely disrespectful because Shane probably knows me better than almost anybody. He returns the look with interest that says, 'what the fuck, man'.

"C'mon, what's up? You haven't been yourself since the pub the other Saturday."

We're interrupted as the waitress delivers our drinks, lingering longer than necessary, hoping to gain Shane's attention. Good luck, lady. He ain't interested. She eventually gets the hint and leaves, allowing us the privacy to return to our conversation.

"I dunno. You know I had a crush on Cassia in high school." He nods. "When we reconnected at the reunion, she admitted she had a crush on me, too. I thought maybe something could grow between us, but then she suddenly went cold and shut me out. I guess I wasn't enough in high school, and

I'm still not enough now." I shrug, attempting to play down how hurt I feel because I don't want to come across as a pussy. "I think she's still on and off with Jake, even though she won't admit it. He seems to be all up in her space every which way she turns."

"When I spoke to her, she said she wasn't involved with him in any way. She seemed pretty adamant." He looks away, pulling at the collar of his shirt, then looks back at me, but not directly at me. "Uh, I may have put my foot in it and said something I shouldn't have."

He immediately has my attention. "What did you say?"

He pulls a grimace. "Uh, I may have told her your crush from high school never went away, and if she's still on and off with Jake, she should be upfront with you and not mess you around."

What the actual fuck! That explains the sudden turnaround. I glare at him.

"Sorry, bro. I thought I was helping you. I didn't think I would scare her off. You want me to clear things up with her?"

I know his heart was in the right place; my brother had my back. "Nah, man. If she scares off that easily, she wasn't interested. It's probably for the best. My career isn't conducive to a steady relationship, anyway. I'm not sure what I was thinking."

Our wings arrive, halting our conversation as we pretty much inhale the food. The wings taste so fucking good, and it allows me to reassess things internally. Cass *is* the type of girl I would change my lifestyle for: slow down and stop touring so I could spend more time with her. It isn't like I need any more money. I could record an album every couple of years, then be selective about where I perform and how long I tour. Other artists do that and manage to stay relevant. They've even found that by making themselves less available, they have greater success. But I'm getting ahead of myself. I would actually need to meet someone who wants to be with me—the person—not the me that's famous for my music. I hoped that could be Cassia.

We go over our schedule, then Shane drives me home before heading to his place. I lay in bed, reminiscing about fucking Cass here; how her body felt against mine. It was as though we were meant to fit together like lyrics and melody.

-toby-

PETA MEETS US OUTSIDE THE FRONT ENTRANCE OF *MERCY VALE General Hospital* with a grin that takes up almost half of her face. She's practically bouncing on her toes with delight. She lives for these PR opportunities. Because I've been locked away in my cave and not in the public eye so much these past few months, this is the first public appearance I've had in a while. Saturday will be the concert, but I refuse to let her use Poppy and *Music for my Heart* for my gain. She leans in, wrapping her slim arms around me. She's so tiny that the top of her head only comes up to the middle of my chest. "Hey, Toby. Today's gonna be great."

We've worked together for a long time, and she's like another sister to me. We often rib each other. She can be pretty sassy at times, but she's a genuine person who wants me to be as successful as possible. Our relationship has quietly built over the years; the level of trust and respect we have for each other is based on a solid foundation. Not that we don't have our moments. "I'm looking forward to it."

She steps back, gushing, "The hospital was incredibly

happy to have you back again. You know how much they love you."

"You know I always enjoy coming here to play for the kids and their families. It reminds me how lucky I am." I've never had serious health issues, nor has anyone in my family. My heart breaks for the kids and families I visit here now and then.

"You and me both. You ready to make our way upstairs to the ward?" She seems to be ignoring Shane, making me wonder if they've had words. Occasionally, they clash over Peta's expectations and Shane's need to control a situation; I often end up in the middle, being the peacemaker.

"Absolutely. Let's get this show on the road."

Shane nods, following quietly behind Peta and me as she gives me a rundown of the program for this morning, speaking quickly.

Glancing over my shoulder to check on Shane, I catch him shaking his head. "What's up?"

He looks at me. "Nothin'." He opens and closes his hand like a talking mouth behind Peta's back, as he rolls his eyes with a half-smile.

I remind Peta that Poppy and I have our last practice session this afternoon, ensuring she remembers I need to finish up here by two-thirty to make it across town for our lesson. As we step out of the elevator, we're met by the hospital's PR people who run through their expectations for our visit, reminding us of their rules, who we can record, and who we can't film or photograph. We're then led through to the ward, where we're greeted by the Registrar, who will stay with us throughout our visit, ensuring we follow protocols.

Shane tries to be as unobtrusive as possible, and to be honest, he didn't need to be here today; it's not like I'm in a high-security risk situation here.

We step onto the ward, and the smell of disinfectant and bleach immediately assaults my nose. At least the children's ward walls are a cheery yellow color as opposed to the usual beige you see in the rest of the hospital. They've also gone the extra mile, painting murals of superheroes and princesses along the solid lengths of wall. It certainly brightens the space, making it feel more welcoming. We walk past a playroom designed for younger kids and step into a room designed for older kids, complete with TVs and gaming stations. The atmosphere is one of anticipation, with half a dozen kids waiting with their parents for our arrival. A hush moves through the room as the kids realize we've arrived; smiles fill their sweet little faces as their eyes light up. I can't imagine what these kids and their families are going through, spending more of their life in the hospital than out of it. The stress on these parents as they watch their sick kids, unable to fix whatever the problem must be … is unfathomable. Some of these kids are very sick. Like so ill, they may not make it.

"Hello, everyone! How are we all today?"

I only hear positive replies: "We're great!"; "Never been better."; "I'm fantastic."

It blows me away that they can be so unwell, yet still be so positive. Every time I visit and spend time here, it's always been the same. They're beyond grateful for every day they have; for every minute they feel well enough to leave their bed and experience some normality in their day. It makes me feel on top of the world that I can add something positive to their day. That I can give them something else to focus on, even if it's only for a couple of hours. Scanning the room, my eyes land on a familiar face. I nod in acknowledgment as my heart cracks for him and his family. They were hoping he was in remission the last time I saw them two years ago, but here they are again. I make my way toward them, greeting them like the old friends they are to me.

"It's great to see you again, Toby." Fiona leans in to hug me, and her husband, Daniel, shakes my hand. To be honest,

I'd rather not be seeing them here again. It means Mathew is unwell again, but I return her hug and his handshake before crouching down to chat with Mathew.

"Hey, Mat. How's my man?" We fist bump, and Shane steps closer to say 'hi', sharing a fist bump, too. We've gotten to know this family quite well over the last three years; we even had them come to my final concert on my last tour, complete with backstage passes. He got a real kick out of it.

"Good, man. How's your new album coming?"

"Not too bad. I should be further along than I am, but I've been distracted. I have some excellent stuff, though. You want me to play something new today?"

His entire face lights up. "Yeah, would ya? That'd be so freaking cool."

"No problem. How've you been feeling?"

He shrugs, glancing over to his parents; they're busy talking with Shane and Peta, so they're not paying any attention to us. "I put on a good face for Mom and Dad, but I'm tired, Toby. Tired of fighting this disease. Tired of seeing Mom and Dad so worried about me, spending all of their time coming back and forth to the hospital when they should be spending time with Flo and Georgie."

I reach out, grasping his shoulder, and give it a gentle squeeze. "I can only imagine how tough it is for you and them. But you know they would never not want to be here with you." I make sure I have his eyes locked with mine. "They love you, man. They want to spend as much time with you as they possibly can. When you're feeling tired, lean on them; take your strength from their love for you." I muss the little hair he has left. "I'd better say hi to the other kids and families. Okay?"

"Thanks, Toby. I needed that pep talk. I'm sorry I was a downer."

"You're never a downer, Mat. Let me know what you think about my new stuff, okay?"

"You know it. I'm your biggest fan. I'll always tell you how I see it." We fist bump.

"I know, Mat." I wink at him. "Talk later?" He smiles, lifting his chin to me.

I make my way around the room, probably spending about an hour chatting with the kids and their families. Shane and Peta also spend time engaging with them, and when the kids learn Shane was a real-life soldier in a real-life war, the questions come flying thick and fast.

Attention then focuses on me, and why we're here today, so I grab my guitar and situate myself on a stool in the center of the room. I start out playing my more familiar songs, strumming and singing the popular tunes, gradually moving toward less familiar songs, and finish with some of my new stuff that nobody's heard yet. I'm always nervous about sharing my recent work. I never know how it's going to be received, whether my fans are excited by it or disappointed.

I'm relieved to receive a positive response to my new material from the small gathering, giving me hope a wider audience will receive it well. I mean, I still have quite a bit of work to do to complete the album, and some of the songs I performed today may sound different by the time I've finished, but the bones are there, and I'm happy with them so far. I'll be locking myself away with my band to begin recording them shortly, so I need to have them pretty close to being complete before then; I don't want to waste anybody's valuable time.

-toby-

TODAY'S OUR LAST PRACTICE BEFORE THE CONCERT TOMORROW night. First, I want to practice the song we're performing to ensure we have smooth transitions between our parts so it flows cohesively. I'm setting up my laptop when Poppy comes running in with her gramma hot on her heels. Poppy throws herself at me in her usual greeting, and I wave at her gramma as she smiles at us with affection.

"Hi, Rose." I hope I remembered her name correctly.

"Hi, uh, 'guitar'?" She says in a questioning tone, signing at the same time, using my sign name. I laugh in return.

"My name's Toby." I fingerspell my name.

"Well, Poppy only ever uses the sign for 'guitar' when she talks about you. I figured you had a regular name. We just didn't know what it was." She smiles warmly.

"That's okay. Are you coming to the concert tomorrow night?" I sign as I speak.

"Absolutely. I wouldn't miss it for the world. Poppy's mom will also be there. She's hoping to meet you after the concert, so she can personally thank you for the time you've spent teaching Poppy the guitar." She smiles at Poppy. "Do you know if I can purchase additional tickets? My other daughter and granddaughter will also be coming along."

"Uh, yeah. If you see Xanthe in the front office, I'm pretty sure she can sort that out for you." Well, I hope she can. I'm not sure about ticket sales. Poppy and I didn't have to pay because we're performing, though I've given a large donation to support the center.

"Okay, thanks." She signs to Poppy. "I'll be back in an hour to pick you up. Okay?"

"Yeah, Gramma. See you later." Poppy kisses her gramma, hugging her goodbye before she comes back to me. Rose leaves the room, closing the door with a click.

"Hey, Poppy. Are you concerned about the concert?"

"Why would I be concerned?" She fingerspells concerned, her eyebrows drawn low over her silver eyes.

Damn, I think I've mixed up my signs again. "Sorry. I meant … are you *excited* about the concert?" I fingerspell excited.

The smile that graces her face is magnificent. Her eyes are alight with joy and excitement as she nods eagerly. Then she shows me she's a little nervous by rubbing her thumb and index finger together.

"It's okay to be nervous. Nerves help to keep you alert. They also help you play your best." She nods in understanding. "How's your week been?"

"It's been really great. I love having my aunt and cousin living with us now. It's so much fun playing with her every day, and she likes watching me play my guitar."

"How old is your cousin?"

"She's three, and she's so cute." She certainly loves her little cousin. "She's gonna come to watch the concert tomorrow night with my aunt."

"Well, we'd better get on with our last practice before the big event."

"Yay. Let's get started."

We play through the song once, the way we planned to play it tomorrow night. Poppy stops, looking thoughtful.

"What if we changed this part and did it like this?" She shows me what she means. I really like the thought she's put into it. Her change makes sense, making the transition smoother. She has a genuine talent for the guitar and a unique approach to arranging music.

I nod. "I really like that. Let's do that. C'mon, let's practice it."

We practice it a couple more times until we're both comfortable with the arrangement and the adjustments we made today. We have a little time to spare, so we do another run-through of *Sweet Home Alabama*, which is coming along nicely. Poppy is a quick study. Her dedication to the guitar shows in how fast she masters the chords and melodies of each song she's introduced to. I think her family will be proud to see her performing for others so quickly after first picking up the guitar. Even though they've been privy to her daily practice, it's going to be very different for them to watch her perform on stage as part of a duet. Even though I perform for a living, in front of thousands of people, this is the most excited I've been to perform in a long time, and it's because I'm going to be performing with such an amazing young girl.

"Well, I think we're ready."

"Definitely." She nods. "Are you still wearing blue jeans with a white T-shirt?"

"Yep. You?"

"Definitely. Although Mommy will probably want me to wear something girly." She rolls her eyes in disgust. "I'll tell her it's our costume. She won't be able to change it then."

I can't help the laugh that bubbles out of me. This girl cracks me up. She certainly knows how to get her way. "I'm sure you can be very convincing." Especially since I've experienced her skills firsthand.

TWENTY-THREE

-cassia-

DAMN IT! I LOOK AT MY PHONE. ON ONE OF THE MOST important days of Poppy's life, I'm running late. I don't want to miss her very first performance. Finishing up quickly, I rush to my car, hoping to make it home with enough time to get ready quickly. Thankfully, traffic is on my side for once, allowing me to make the drive in record time. I barge through the door, run upstairs, and jump straight into the shower. Ten minutes later, I'm out, dried off, and dressed in black linen pants and a sleeveless blouse. I wrap my ponytail up into a bun, put on a coat of mascara, and run downstairs with my sandals in my hand to find the rest of my family.

Bursting into the kitchen, I find everyone ready to go. Poppy leaps forward, grasping me around my waist in greeting. She's wearing her jeans with a white T-shirt. I would have thought she'd wear a pretty dress for the performance. I look at Mom, hoping to telegraph, 'what were you thinking?' to which she shrugs. Then, gently pushing Poppy away from me so that I can sign to her, I ask, "Why are you wearing this? I thought you might wear a pretty dress."

She smiles up at me. "It's our costume. Guitar is wearing the same." Oh, how adorable is that.

I nod, smiling in return. "Okay. Are you ready?" I'm nervous for her, but I bet she's not nervous at all.

"Yeah, let's go." She pulls on my hand, leading me out of the house with Mom, Violet, and Jasmine hot on our heels. Poppy's practically bouncing out of her skin as she grabs her guitar as we step out of the front door. We lock up the house, piling into my car with Mom in the front while Poppy, Vi, and Jas get situated in the backseat. I had a car seat installed for Jas once my sister moved in with us. I figured it would make life easier than transferring one car seat between our cars.

Arriving at the venue, Poppy quickly jumps out of the car, ready to take off inside. I manage to grasp her shoulder, gaining her attention. "I wanted to tell you how proud I am of you, Poppy. I'm excited to be watching you on stage doing something you've wanted to do for such a long time. I love you so much, Baby Girl."

I hold her close, hugging her tight as I breathe in her little girl strawberry scent. I feel unexpectedly emotional about this milestone in her young life. When the specialists first told me she was profoundly deaf, never in my wildest dreams did I imagine a future for Poppy which included her playing guitar at a concert in front of a couple of hundred people. This is a dream come true for her. At only seven years of age, she's made it happen. I'm in awe of her. I marvel at what the future holds for my little girl with determination so strong and goals so solid she lets nothing stand in her way.

She pulls away from me, excitement all over her angelic face. "I gotta go, Mommy." She kisses me, then grabs her guitar to make her way to where she's supposed to be. I stand watching my baby go until she disappears through the doors. I'm not sure how long after that I stay lost in my thoughts of how grown up my baby has become. It's not until Mom and Violet embrace me on either side that I manage to tear my eyes away from the building.

"My baby's not a baby anymore," I whisper, more to myself than anyone else.

Mom squeezes my shoulder. "No, she isn't. She's growing up and taking life by the horns. Heaven help us when she becomes a teenager."

Her statement is enough to send the three of us into a fit of giggles, making the tears that had welled in my eyes fall onto my cheeks. Once we've settled ourselves down, we walk inside to find the auditorium. A young man greets us at the double doors, offering earplugs for the audience members to protect our ears because the music will be loud. We each accept a pair, then find our seats inside. Unfortunately, our seats are toward the back, as Mom swapped out our original seats to have four seats together. It's okay. I'll sneak down to sit on a lower step so I can record Poppy's performance on my phone. There will be fifteen acts tonight—Poppy is number eleven, so I have a while to wait until I see my little girl.

I take the opportunity to ask Violet how she went today. She had plans to return home to grab some more of their clothes and some toys for Jasmine.

"Ugh. Don't ask. I don't want to ruin our night out." Violet sighs heavily.

"What happened?" Vi and Mom share a look. Violet looks like she wants to punch something, or maybe someone.

"He wasn't going to be home, so I thought it'd be safe to collect some of our things." I nod because I already knew this part. "Well, the good news is he wasn't home. The bad news is there was another woman's clothes hanging in our closet and filling my drawers. All of my stuff had been dumped on the guest bed."

I'm pretty sure my jaw hits my knee. "What in the hell is that man thinking?" I reach over to grasp my sister's hand in a show of support as the lights in the room dim. Xanthe and her husband, Louis, take to the stage. A spotlight shines down on their proud, smiling faces as some people applaud, while others wave their hands in the air.

Louis speaks as Xanthe signs for the audience. "Welcome to our Labor Day concert, ladies and gentlemen." More applause and hand waving greet him. "When Xanthe and I first had the idea to create a space for Deaf and Hard of Hearing kids to learn how to dance and play music, we never imagined how successful it would become. It's been a dream of ours for a long time to bring the joy of music to everyone. Making music accessible no matter whether you are a hearing person, a hard of hearing person, or a profoundly deaf person is a goal that we can proudly say we have finally achieved." More well-deserved applause and waving fills the auditorium for the pair who have brought so much joy into the lives of all these kids and their families. "Ladies and gentlemen, we have quite the lineup for you tonight. A special guest is accompanying one of our students in her debut performance. So, keep an eye and an ear out for that special treat." A hum makes its way, like the build of a slow wave, through the audience. "Without further ado, please welcome our first performer, Adelaide Scott, dancing to Lady Gaga's *Poker Face*." Wild applause breaks out through the auditorium in welcome for the teenager, dressed in a teal outfit complete with black ankle boots, reminding me of the famous video.

As the evening progresses and performers come and go on the stage, my arms become sore from waving, my feet tingle from all the stomping, and my face aches from smiling so much. The happiness that shines out of each performer is contagious. I challenge anyone here tonight to walk out of here not feeling blessed to have witnessed such talent and utter delight. The tenth performance of the night is finishing up, so I gesture to Mom and Vi that I'm going to head down to sit on the steps to record Poppy's performance. As I'm getting situated, I glance across, spotting Kate and Oliver in the row adjacent to the step I'm sitting on. They're deep in conversation, so I'm unable to catch their eye. The lights change, indicating that the next performer will be coming on stage, so I get my phone ready to record, pressing the button to ensure I don't miss a single thing.

Poppy steps onto the stage holding her guitar. Her cheeks lifted high as a smile fills her beautiful face. She must feel the vibrations of everyone's feet stomping on the floor throughout the auditorium. My heart fills my throat. It's difficult to swallow down the emotion I'm feeling seeing my Poppy on the stage, standing proudly in front of a packed house for the very first time. Not one single ounce of nervousness. She takes her seat, then looks off to the side of the stage she just stepped out from. I guess her guitar teacher is about to join her. I zoom my camera out so I can capture Poppy *and* her guitar teacher as he enters. As a man steps out, it takes a moment for my mind to register who it is. My heart, which had taken up residence in my throat, has made its way down to my toes as the bottom falls out of my stomach while I fight for breath.

Toby Summer.

The Toby Summer.

My high school crush and famous musician, whom I hooked up with mere weeks ago, is *my* daughter's guitar teacher.

This has to be some weird cosmic joke.

How can this be?

Seeing him walk toward my daughter with a proud smile on his face to match hers is surreal—they obviously share a solid friendship. I think back over all the conversations I've had over the last two months with Poppy about her guitar teacher.

My stomach rolls as I remember ... oh my god! She wanted to ask *him* to be her daddy! She said that once I met him, I would want him to be her daddy, too. A nervous giggle escapes me as I think how right she was. I'd love for him to be her daddy—how crazy is that? He takes the seat next to Poppy. They both situate their guitars, with matching colored strings, against their bodies. Poppy looks so small next to him, and she hasn't stopped smiling at him, just as he hasn't stopped smiling at her. Then, with a wink, they begin to play together ... and it's magic.

Beautiful, soul-filling magic!

As I watch my daughter pause her playing to sign the chorus while Toby continues to sing and play, my face heats with the memory of his hands on my body. His fingers coaxing me toward completion, his whiskers close to my ear as his deep voice whispered words of encouragement. It takes a Herculean effort on my part to remain focused on Poppy's performance while keeping my phone steady for the recording. I sit, absorbing their rendition of *Love Me Do*, tears filling my eyes as I watch my daughter discover a love for performing that I hope will stay with her forever.

As the song comes to a close, the audience stands, stomping their feet with abandon for the two entertainers on the stage. I know a lot of it is for Toby. He's obviously the special guest Louis mentioned at the beginning of the evening. Still, I also know in my heart that Poppy shone in her debut and deserves the show of appreciation. She worked damn hard to get that song perfected for tonight's show—she did such a fantastic job. As the crowd applauds the two, they stand, hold hands, and bow—all the while smiling at each other. Their bond is plain for anyone to see, and I now understand why Poppy was keen to ask him to be her daddy. It's clear that Toby cares for and respects her—a connection beyond that of teacher and student.

They both seem to really admire one another.

They leave the stage while people return to their seated positions, so I turn to head back up to my family. As I do, I catch Kate's eye. She smiles as she waves at me. She looks back and forth from me to the stage and back again; I see the moment that understanding dawns on her. Her expression changes as she tips her head in acknowledgment.

I have to face Toby after the show.

He's going to find out I'm a single mom, and that Poppy is my daughter.

The daughter I never told him about.

I don't know how I'll make it through the last few performances without being sick. I'm light-headed at the thought of the conversation we're going to have. I only hope he doesn't make too much of a big deal out of it in front of Poppy.

Joining Mom, Vi, and Jas back in my original seat, they excitedly congratulate me on Poppy's performance—as if I had anything to do with it. I'm not even certain where she gets her talent from; it certainly isn't from me. Vi makes some off-hand comment about how hot Poppy's guitar teacher is while Mom looks on with a knowing smile. She knows Poppy wanted to ask Toby to be her daddy. She's met and spoken with him a couple of times; even hinted that Poppy had good taste in her choice of a daddy, but I don't think Mom truly knows who he is.

It's then I note the change in Vi's expression. She places her hand on my arm, leaning in close to me as we watch the video I recorded on my phone. "Um, isn't that Toby Summer? *The* Toby Summer. Didn't you go to school with him?" Her eyes widen as she remembers our teenage discussions late at night when we were supposed to be sleeping. "You had the biggest crush on him in high school, but you kept dating that douche, Jake," she whispers. A wide smile spreads across her face, and then she looks at me knowingly. "Wow. Just wow." Is all she says as she slumps back into her seat, still smiling at me. Wiggling her eyebrows up and down, she slaps her thighs. "Well, I think our night has just become a whole lot more interesting, Mom."

Mom looks completely confused. "Why? How do you know Poppy's guitar teacher?"

"Um, we went to high school together. We were in the same music class."

"Oh, well, isn't that nice. What a coincidence that he's the one teaching Poppy how to play the guitar."

"You said he wasn't a music teacher, that he said he was 'competent' and enjoyed working with Poppy." Mom nods while Violet laughs. "He's not just 'competent', Mom. He's a successful and very famous singer-songwriter."

All Mom can manage is a simple 'oh' as she nods her head. I don't think she fully comprehends the magnitude of Toby's fame or how amazing it is that he took time away from his work to teach our Poppy the guitar.

That guitar she has—*is his!*

He's the one who's gone over and above to provide Poppy with every opportunity to succeed in pursuing her dream of playing guitar. I have a whole new level of respect for him while simultaneously feeling terrible that I assumed he would reject Poppy because she's deaf.

Obviously, that wouldn't be the case at all.

I wonder how he's going to react when he finds out that Poppy's *my* daughter. I struggle to contain my nervousness for what's going to happen after the show's over—I have no hope of concentrating on the final performances of the night. As the concert finishes and all the performers return to the stage to take a final bow, my back aches from the tension gripping me from the inside out. Within the next few minutes, I'll come face to face with Toby, and my truth will be exposed.

We make our way out of the auditorium, walking toward the meeting place we prearranged with Poppy. My nerves are shot and my legs feel like jelly. I'm having trouble keeping my breaths even. Looking around, I spot Poppy at the same time she spots us. She runs toward us, leaping into my arms.

TWENTY-FOUR

-toby-

THAT PERFORMANCE WAS PROBABLY UP THERE WITH MY MOST memorable to date. Playing alongside Poppy was … *amazing*. Amazing isn't enough to describe the feelings that performance with her evoked in me. I was unbelievably proud of her. It was an honor to be the one playing beside her for her debut.

Waiting in the meeting area with Shane and Poppy, Kate, Oliver, Mom, and Dad quickly come out of the auditorium. After I told Kate about Poppy wanting to become a kinder-garten teacher, Kate's been itching to meet her. They walk toward us en masse, broad smiles on their faces. Hugs and pats on the back are gifted all-around in greeting before I get down to business introducing Poppy to my family. These are the most important people in my life, and I'm introducing them to someone for whom I have a lot of respect.

Kate's the first to step in to hug Poppy and tell her how much she loved her performance. The rest of my family steps in to greet Poppy and tell her how amazing she is. I interpret by signing on their behalf as people steadily file out of the auditorium.

Poppy looks up, taking off at the speed of light—she must

have spied her family. I try to keep her in my sights, but there are too many people between us. The six of us stroll forward in the direction Poppy went. People stop me, congratulating me on my performance, but I'm short with them because I want to get to Poppy. I spot Rose smiling down at someone, so I follow her line of sight. She's fondly watching a woman crouched down, hugging Poppy tightly. She stands as Poppy wraps her legs around her, holding on tightly. Poppy waves at me over the woman's shoulder, who I assume is her mom.

Poppy directs her mom to turn around, and as she does, her face comes into view.

Everything around me stops.

All sound vanishes.

The breath in my lungs expels in a gush.

I shake my head, closing my eyes, hoping when I open them again, the person I see isn't the person I just saw. I open them slowly, hoping that my eyes deceived me. Looking directly at her, our eyes lock for a moment as she tucks her luscious bottom lip behind her teeth. She's struggling to make eye contact with me, her eyes darting between my family and me. Her delicate eyebrows slash down low over her steely eyes as she slightly shakes her head.

If she thinks I'm going to pretend that everything's fine between us, she has another thing coming. I'm furious with her, but more than that, I'm hurt. She never told me she had a daughter. As I run through our previous interactions, I *know* I didn't miss any clues. Even when I discovered the doll's arm in her purse, she brushed it off as belonging to her niece.

She obviously didn't trust me with her truth.

My family steps as one toward Poppy's family as my senses come back online. Kate's clearly excited that Cassia is Poppy's mom, as she hugs them both tightly, as though they're best friends. Which, to my knowledge, they're not.

I tilt my head. "Cassia."

She nods slightly. "Toby."

Rose steps into me, surprising me with an embrace. "Hello, Toby. Thank you so much. That was just wonderful. Wonderful to see Poppy so happy while in her element up there with you. It was amazing," she gushes as she signs.

"It was my privilege, Rose. It's been fantastic working with Poppy; to watch her grow. Her determination and grit are inspiring." I sign as I speak. I want Poppy to know that I admire her determination.

Rose steps back. "I believe you already know Poppy's mom, Cassia." I nod. She then directs my attention to another woman holding a toddler. "This is my eldest daughter, Violet, and her daughter, Jasmine."

I reach my hand out to shake Violet's hand. "Nice to meet you, Violet." Smiling at Jasmine, I speak directly to her, "Nice to meet you, too, Jasmine." She giggles, tucking her chin into her chest so she can burrow further into her mother's embrace.

I return Rose's gesture as I introduce my family. While they all engage in the initial getting-to-know-you conversation, my eyes never leave Cassia. She doesn't even look at me, and my temper boils. Past teenage hurts rising to the surface, reminding me I wasn't good enough back then, poking at the scabs, suggesting I'm still not good enough now.

Looking between Cassia and Poppy, I'm stumped as to how I missed the resemblance. Poppy's the spitting image of her mother, right down to the gray eyes. Mind you, Poppy's gray eyes are on the lighter side, more like silver, while Cass's eyes are darker, more like storm clouds. She looks my way, catching me watching her with her daughter. Cass smiles timidly as she places Poppy back on her feet before moving closer to me.

She lowers her voice to keep the conversation private. "Um … I don't know what to say. I had planned to thank Poppy's guitar teacher for everything he's done for her, but never in my wildest dreams did I imagine that person to be you." Her eyes dart away, checking to see if anyone's paying any attention to us. "Toby …"

I shake my head, stepping back, putting space between us.

There's nothing she can say to me to make this situation better at the moment. I'm too caught up in the fact that she kept such an important secret from me. Perhaps I had no right to know about Poppy for the short amount of time we spent together, but even before that, she kept her secret when catching up at the reunion.

Isn't that something you share when people ask what you've been up to for the last ten years?

She steps forward again, placing her hand on my arm. The sensation burns through my skin, shooting sparks up my arm before heading down to my dick. I'm frustrated that my body still reacts to hers in such an acute way. Obviously, my dick hasn't got the memo that we're pissed at this woman.

"Toby, let me explain. Please."

I'm at war with myself. Do I want to know what could possibly be her excuse for not sharing such important information with me? Or should I walk away, never to look back, protecting my heart? But, in all honesty, it's like shutting the gate after the horse has bolted. It's already too late; I'm already too invested—in her and her daughter.

I'm fucked.

Completely and utterly fucked because I know, without a doubt, that I'll allow her to explain. Just not here. Not in front of my family and hers. Not in front of Poppy, whom I adore; how could I not?

"Not now. Okay?" My voice is low and firm as I indicate with my eyes and head that there are too many people around us. This needs to happen in private. It's something that needs to be sorted out between the two of us.

"Okay." She swallows as she nods. All I can imagine is her swallowing around my cock and how it felt as her throat tightened and released around my shaft. "But Toby ..." She waits until she has my attention. "Thank you for everything you've done for Poppy. The guitar, the strings, the program, your time and patience with her. She adores you and looks forward to your Friday afternoon sessions."

I nod stiffly. "You're welcome. I adore her, too. Her dedication to the instrument has been inspiring."

Cass smiles then, and it's everything to me. Poppy has her smile. Her positive energy. Though Cass's has dimmed somewhat since high school, it's still there, lying in her depths. "I'll call you. If that's okay?"

"Sure." I feel the need to put her at ease, so I offer her a small smile, which does what I hoped. Her shoulders drop, and she appears to relax slightly.

Cass turns back toward our families. "Well, it's getting late. We'd better get our superstar home to bed," she signs, as she talks for Poppy's benefit. I love that she doesn't exclude Poppy from the conversation.

"Aaaaah, Mommy. Can we at least go for ice cream to celebrate my performance? Can we? Please." She has those same begging hands and puppy-dog eyes she used on me to get me to teach her the guitar. She's one gifted kid at manipulating people to get what she wants. I'll be shocked if Cass can resist.

She looks up and around at all of us, rolling her eyes with a beautiful smile on her face. "Oh, okay. Come on then. Let's go."

Poppy jumps up and down in delight, punching the air to celebrate her success. "You'll come, won't you, Toby?"

Ugh, what? How did I become part of the celebratory party? Poppy leans closer to me, putting me under the same pressure as she did her mom. I'm powerless to resist, even though I don't feel up to spending any more time in Cass's company tonight. Maybe if I invite everyone along, it'll make it easier.

"Okay, Poppy, I'll come, too." I look around at everyone.

"Ice cream for everyone!" Cheers go up all around, and we make our way to the exit and our respective vehicles.

Cass asks, "Everyone familiar with *Brain Freeze*? It's Poppy's favorite ice cream shop." We all nod. You'd have to live under a rock not to be familiar with the place. It's only the best ice cream shop in the city. We all get into our vehicles, making our way to Poppy's favorite ice cream shop. This is the Saturday night of a rock star!

I get in the car with Shane, drop my head back against my seat, blowing out a long breath. I can sense Shane's eyes boring into the side of my head.

"Well, that was fucking awkward." He rubs his hand over his cropped hair. "Did you know Cass was Poppy's mom?"

Without lifting my head from the seat back, I turn to glance at Shane. "Nope."

He bursts into laughter. I'm not sure what's so damn funny.

"Only you, man. This shit could only happen to you. What are the fucking chances that the only time you decide to teach a kid you don't even know from a bar of soap how to play the guitar, she's the daughter of your high school crush?"

It's unbelievable, is what it is. What *are* the fucking chances?

Shane pulls himself together, starts the car, and we make our way to meet everyone for ice cream. "You realize I haven't had a chance to vet this place or book it out, so you're not bothered by fans?"

"Yeah, I know. Sometimes it's okay to be spontaneous. We'll manage."

We all arrive within moments of each other, moving into the shop together. The girls lead the way, with me, Shane, and Oliver following close behind. My eyes automatically lower to check out Cass's ass in those black pants that hug those sweet globes I had my hands all over mere weeks ago. Everyone orders their favorite selection and I pick up the tab—even for my billionaire brother-in-law, Oliver. Ha!

I make sure to keep at least one or two people between Cass and me at all times. I don't want to get into anything with her in front of our families. I don't want to spoil Poppy's big night or our celebration of her debut performance.

My phone lights up with a text from Peta.

PETA

I thought you said I couldn't use tonight as PR for your new album.

ME

What do you mean?

PETA

I mean, check out whose images are trending across social media as we text

I switch out of my text messages to load my favored web browser. Typing in my name before clicking across to images, my stomach falls to the floor as I let out a curse—image after image of Poppy and me at the concert tonight. Videos of our performance are trending. I feel sick to my stomach, my hands shaking with pent-up rage. I switch back to my messages.

ME

What the fuck, Peta?

PETA

I had nothing to do with it

Don't look at me

But I'm not gonna say sorry it happened

This is great for you

ME

Get them taken down

I don't care how much it costs

I'm fucking fuming. Shane notices the change in my mood and quietly steps closer to me to check out the problem. I show him my search results, and he sucks in a breath.

"I thought you told Peta to leave the concert out of any PR?"

"I did. She says she had nothing to do with it."

"And you believe her. She'd do anything to advance your career. You know this." His expression is one of disbelief that I'm taking Peta's word about this.

"I believe her. I trust her, man. She respects my decisions."

He raises his hands in surrender. "Okay, man. If you say so."

"I say so. There were a couple of hundred people in the audience. Any one of them could have taken that video and those photos and shared them on social media. What other people do is out of our control. You know this."

He rubs his hand over his cropped hair. "Yeah, I know." I know it irks Shane when he doesn't have complete control over situations.

I should warn Cass and her family that Poppy's performance has gone viral. They need to prepare for the onslaught of attention that's about to come their way. Whoever uploaded the images and video named Poppy directly, meaning there'll be no escaping the spotlight for her. Moving closer to Cassia, I lightly touch her elbow to gain her attention. "Can I talk to you quickly about something that's just come up?"

She looks around. Her eyebrows slashed low as she tries to make sense of the fact I want to talk with her now, but agrees. I gently guide her away from the group.

"Look, I've just been made aware of a situation involving Poppy." Her body goes rigid as she pulls her elbow away from my touch. The best thing to do is to show her the images and video that's gone viral. I take out my phone to show Cass the search results. "I'm really sorry, Cass. I never intended to put

Poppy in the spotlight like this. I've already asked my manager to get the images taken down. Unfortunately, they've already been shared hundreds of times, which will make it very difficult to remove all evidence of them."

Her hand covers her mouth, eyes wide, as she looks at my screen in what I can only imagine is horror. But when she drops her hand, her lips are spread wide. "Oh my gosh, Toby. Poppy will think this is totally awesome."

Um, what!?

-toby-

I EXPECTED HER TO BE FURIOUS, DEMANDING I GET EVERY LAST image removed. "But the photographs and video name Poppy. Even though it doesn't say her last name, it says the concert's venue. It won't take much for someone to put two and two together to find her. This could be bad, Cass. I don't think you understand the gravity of this situation. Someone could take a liking to her and attempt to kidnap her. She could be in danger because of me." I brush my hands through my hair in agitation. I'm having trouble standing still. I need to pace, to smash something.

She places her hand on my arm again to draw my attention back to her. That sizzle gets me every time. "Toby, calm down. I think you're overreacting. Nobody's gonna try to kidnap Poppy. She'll get a real kick out of seeing her video going viral. Surely that's gotta be good PR for *Music for my Heart* and for you?"

I can't believe how flippant Cass is being. "Well, yeah, but PR, no matter how good, should never happen at the expense of a child without their permission. Poppy's a really cute kid.

What if someone takes an unhealthy liking to her, Cass? I couldn't live with myself if something happened to that little girl. I fucking adore her." My heart's pounding wildly in my chest cavity. My adrenaline is coursing through my system, its fight or flight response kicking in. Anxiety fills every pore. I want to punch myself in the face for bringing danger directly to Poppy and Cass's door.

Before I can react, Cass has her arms around my torso, pressing her body against mine. "Toby, it'll be okay. I'm not sure why you're so worked up about this, but I don't think anything bad will happen. Take a breath."

Wrapping my arms around her, I tighten our embrace, kissing the top of her head. "Social media can be dangerous, Cass. You don't know what sickos are out there or what they'll do." I smooth my hand up her back, grasping her nape. "It's okay, though. I'll have Shane watch over her. At least until I feel comfortable that nothing's gonna happen to her."

She pulls back, studying my face closely. She must see my determination, my unshakeable resolve to keep Poppy safe because she nods once in acquiescence. Her agreement makes me feel marginally better, releasing some of the tension from my muscles. Only then do I notice the position I find myself in with Cass while both of our families look on. I quickly drop my hands and step away from Cass. It feels almost painful to disengage from her physically, but she doesn't want me in that way. I can't keep putting myself in a situation where I'm constantly rejected—it's too painful.

I need to speak with Shane about the changes to his schedule. I'm making my way over to him when I feel my phone buzz.

PETA

I have my guy working on removing as many of the images as possible

Don't expect miracles

ME

Thanks Peta

PETA

No problem

Still think it's great PR for you though

Of course, she thinks that. As my manager, it's her job to put me front and center of as many people as possible as often as possible. I know I make her life difficult by enforcing certain limitations on her. We've had many heated discussions because of those limitations. I remember the huge argument I had with her when I helped Kate work on the *Parkerville* house renovation. I thought she was going to quit on me; that was probably our biggest disagreement to date. She thought my fans had every right to see me sweaty, dirty, and shirtless. I disagreed.

I stand next to Shane. "I'm gonna need to change things around a bit with your schedule." He nods thoughtfully. "I want you to keep Poppy safe. These images could draw out any number of crazies. I don't want anything to happen to her because of me."

"If anything happens to Poppy, it won't be because of you. It'll be because of whoever took the fucking images and uploaded them to social media without thought or consideration for the little girl." He seems as pissed about the whole incident as I am, and that's saying something. "Of course, I'll keep an eye on her. No problem, but what about you?"

"I'll be fine. At the moment, I'm stuck in my studio most of the time. I only go to Poppy's Friday lesson, our regular meeting with Peta, and my parents' place on the weekend. No biggie." I shrug.

He nods thoughtfully. "Maybe we should get someone else on you while I'm on Poppy. I'd feel better."

"I don't need anyone, Shane. Honestly. If I have to go anywhere, we can work something out. Okay?"

He reluctantly agrees.

Cass gains everyone's attention. "As wonderful as this evening has been, it's time we get this superstar-in-the-making home to bed."

I'm the first to step forward to say goodbye to my amazing duet partner. "It was a privilege to perform alongside you tonight. It was an honor to be your partner for your first public performance. Thank you." I lean down to embrace her. When she wraps her little arms around my neck, pulling me in closer before placing a kiss on my cheek, my heart fucking melts like an icy pole. This kid is so easy with her affection, her joy, and her sheer happiness. I can't help but be affected by her.

She signs to me. "Thank you, Toby. For everything."

I can only nod in response because I'm too choked up. "See you next Friday, okay?"

Poppy nods to me before making the rounds, thanking everyone for coming and saying goodnight. I say my goodbyes to her mom and aunt, who's carrying a very sleepy Jasmine in her arms. After they've all left, I turn to my family, who are watching me like I've stolen the last cookie out of the cookie jar.

"What?"

Mom's the first to speak. "Oh, nothing! You and Cassia looked rather cozy there for a minute, and Poppy is the most adorable little girl I've ever met." Her voice gets higher in pitch as she finishes the sentence.

Kate comes up, linking her arm through mine. "You still have that crush, brother. Only now you can act on it. So why don't you ask her out on a date?"

I look at Shane. Only he knows what went down between Cass and me recently—not that he knows everything. I don't feel like spilling my guts to my sister in front of everyone, though, so I just shrug it off without saying anything one way or the other. Of course, Cass still owes me an explanation, which I'll be sure to collect.

TWENTY-SIX

-cassia-

THE MINUTE I SAW TOBY'S FACE WHILE I HELD MY DAUGHTER after her performance, I knew ... *I knew* I'd made a huge mistake shutting him out. Now I need to make it right. I need to pull up my big girl panties and face the music. The way he worried about Poppy's safety filled my heart more than anything else he could have ever done or said. His care for her was obvious from the minute he joined her on the stage, which carried through to him agreeing to ice cream, as well as the concern he had for her safety. He's still the great guy he was in high school. He deserves an in-depth explanation of my behavior. I'm not looking forward to telling him who Poppy's father is, but he's possibly already guessed.

I was waiting to see if he would still follow through with Poppy's guitar lesson yesterday—I wanted to know if he was going to cut ties with her because of me, but he didn't.

I should have known he wouldn't do that to her.

He still showed up, working with my little girl as though nothing was amiss, showing me who he really is deep down. He also followed through with having Shane watch over Poppy. I think it's too much, but Shane's been taking Poppy to and from school, as well as to her lesson with Toby yesterday afternoon.

Knocking on his front door, my heart's beating a gazillion miles a minute—my legs are shaky. I didn't check if he'd be home, wanting to catch him unaware. I figured I'd have a better chance of explaining things if he didn't have time to work himself up about what I did, as well as how I've behaved toward him.

It's taking an age for anyone to answer the door. I'm beginning to think he's not home. I step back down the steps, looking up from the street, noticing the large glass doors to his bedroom are open to the balcony. I think I can hear him playing his guitar. Perhaps he can't hear me knocking on the door over his playing.

ME

Hi, I'm at your house

Can you please let me in

We need to talk

It seems to take ages for a response, but it's probably been less than a minute.

TOBY

On my way down

That sounded curt. I hope he's not still mad at me. Before I have the chance to contemplate his mood, the front door opens to reveal a shirtless, barefoot Toby wearing only ripped jeans sitting low on his hips, exposing that beautiful V I never got to lick. He seems annoyed I'm standing on his doorstep if his scowl is anything to go on. My idea to catch him by surprise may not work as well as I was hoping.

"What are you doing here?"

Not the greeting I would like, but I guess I have to expect it after the way I treated him.

"Uh, hi, Toby. I was hoping we could talk."

He pauses for a moment, then shakes his head. "Sure." He steps to the side, allowing me to pass. The scent of him instantly heats my blood from memories of our night together. "Is everything okay?" Even though he's pissed at me, he still takes the time to check in. I feel like such an asshole.

"Yeah, everything's okay. I owe you an explanation as well as an apology for … well, everything." I feel sheepish. Now I'm wondering if he was even bothered enough to want to know my reasons.

He gestures to the couch and as I sit; I look toward the window he had me pressed up against the night I was here. I look around the room, taking it in for the first time in the daylight. It's homely and comfortable. Not a place I would have imagined a famous entertainer, such as Toby, would live. "I'm just gonna go put on a shirt. Be back in a tick."

While he's gone, I get up to wander around the space. Looking out of the large windows, I admire the view across to the bridge. This must look spectacular at sunrise and sunset, with the colors and shadows playing across the structure. Stepping into the kitchen, memories of him carefully wiping oil over my breasts to remove the adhesive assault me. The memories make my nipples pucker and my breasts heavy. Everywhere I look in this room, there's a memory associated.

I don't know how Toby's lived here.

"You're everywhere in this room." His voice startles me. "Here as well as in my bedroom. One night and the memories won't fucking leave me alone." He runs his hands through his unruly hair, his jaw tense under his neat beard.

So he *does* feel it, the magnitude of that night. I'm glad to know I'm not alone. Maybe I should apologize first. "Toby …" He looks at me with such interest, as though he can't wait to hear what's going to come tumbling out of my mouth. "I'm, uh … I'm sorry."

He shoves his hands into the front pockets of his jeans. "What exactly are you sorry for, Cassia?" There's a bite to his tone, which I completely deserve.

"I'm sorry I didn't tell you about Poppy. I'm sorry I didn't give you a chance. I'm sorry I ended us before we started." I run my hands through my hair, as all of my apologies gush out in a rush. Trying to get my words straight, I pause, looking around the room. "I was protecting Poppy."

"Protecting her from what exactly?" he snaps back at me without pause.

This is the tough part to share because I've painted him with the same brush as Jake when I knew deep down he was nothing like him, but I did it just the same. I step back to the couch, taking the seat he offered me when I first arrived. He must sense the difficulty of what I'm about to share because his voice softens. "You wanna drink?"

"Yeah, thanks. Water would be great." He prepares two tall glasses of cold water, carries them over, and hands one to me. I eagerly sip the cool liquid, trying to soothe my dry throat.

Toby sits on the edge of the couch opposite me, elbows resting on his knees, hands draped between his legs. He studies me for a moment. "What were you protecting Poppy from, Cass? Because the longer you take to tell me, the longer I have to create all sorts of terrible scenarios in my mind."

"I was protecting her from rejection." I sigh. "Her father never wanted her. When he found out I was pregnant, he demanded I have an abortion." He sits up straight, sucking in a harsh breath. "When I refused, he left me. That's when I moved back home." I give him a meaningful look, hoping he remembers I *did* share some of my history with him.

He shakes his head. "I'm sorry, Cass. Obviously, the guy's a dick."

I nod in agreement. "I decided to raise Poppy on my own with my mom's help. I figured that was the end of it." I shake my head to myself as I remember Jake coming back around, claiming he wanted to be a family man, to bring our family together.

God, I was stupid. I brush my hand through my hair, then take another sip of my water, my hands shaking.

Toby moves to the cushion next to me, his knee pressing gently against mine, giving me the encouragement I need to keep going.

"I didn't hear from him for nearly two years. Then he started coming back around." I can't bring myself to make eye contact with Toby, looking at the glass in my hands instead. I wipe the condensation from the surface for something to do.

"He wanted to be a family—said he was sorry. He seemed genuine, so I gave him a chance. We started dating again, but I was reluctant to introduce him to Poppy until I was sure he was serious about hanging around." I sneak a look at Toby to find him listening intently. I wonder if he's worked out who I'm talking about. "Anyway, after a few weeks, he insisted on meeting Poppy. In hindsight, I probably should have warned him she was deaf, but I never did, for one reason or another. When he met her, he thought she was ignoring him. That's when I explained she wasn't ignoring him. She couldn't hear him." Toby leans in closer, the side of his body touching the entire side of mine. He wraps his arm around my shoulder, pulling me in tight, kissing my temple.

"He lost the plot completely. He was furious I hadn't told him, furious that the child he fathered wasn't perfect in every way. He tried to punch her in the head, but I stepped in between, taking the strike. I pushed and screamed at him until he left. He thought the punch would 'sort her out'."

Toby pulls back suddenly. "What the fuck! Who in the hell thinks it's okay to strike a child? What in the actual fuck?" His voice is getting louder, angrier. "How could anyone think Poppy was less than perfect? In every single way?" He's completely pissed on Poppy's behalf, so I place my hand on his hard thigh in an attempt to calm him down.

"He said some truly horrible things. He accused me of trying to trap him with a freak for a child. I gave him back as much as he gave me. I was furious that he couldn't see the treasure that Poppy is, while feeling devastated on her behalf that her father rejected her in such a horrible way. Her parents are supposed to love her unconditionally." Toby presses in, kissing my forehead, before tilting my face toward his. With his hands cupping my face, his thumbs wipe away the tears tracking down my cheeks. "He said he didn't want her, and since I was her mother, he didn't want me either. Which I was fine with, but I was heartbroken for Poppy. I was hopeful for her to have a father figure in her life; I wanted more for her than I ever had."

"It's his fucking loss. Poppy *is* amazing. I would be proud to have a daughter like her. Any man would. He sounds like a fucking bastard."

"Anyway, once I came to terms with everything, I sought a lawyer and requested, no demanded, he sign away his rights as her father. He happily signed the paperwork, which made me feel better knowing he had absolutely zero rights when it comes to her. I didn't want him to be able to come back into her life in the future or to have any say." I sigh. "I'm so thankful Poppy's too young to remember his visit or the subsequent argument." I gather my courage to look at Toby. "I guess you're wondering who Poppy's father is."

He huffs out a breath. "I have a feeling I already know who the bastard is, but maybe you should tell me." He brushes his hand through his hair as he looks out of the window. The tic in his jaw tells me he's bracing himself.

I whisper, "Jake. Jake's her father. We were still on and off—"

I don't get the opportunity to finish my sentence when Toby suddenly bolts up from the couch, storming over to the windows. He rests his arm on the frame, his shoulders tense, his face like thunder. "He was always a fucking asshole. Even in high school. I could never understand why you kept going back to him."

I stand up, angry at him. "Don't you dare throw my mistakes back in my face. You don't know me, my background, what I was feeling, what I was searching for."

He storms back to me, stopping mere inches from me, and getting right in my face. His anger rolls off him in waves, smashing into me. "Only because you didn't deem me worthy enough to date back then." His voice is harsh as he brushes the hair out of his face. "I wanted to be with you, Cass; I would have treated you so much better."

"You! You never gave me the time of day. You treated me like I was somehow less than. I thought you hated me!" I snap.

He huffs out a breath, gentling his voice. "I've apologized for that and explained my behavior." He looks away, glaring at the window before softening his features to look back at me. "I would have treated you with the care and respect you deserved. I may have been a teenager, but I would have been better to you than he was." He gently, carefully cups my face in his hands, using his thumbs to wipe my tears. "Let me show you now."

I freeze in place. My body locked from head to toe. I can't possibly put Poppy at risk like that. She already loves Toby so much that she wants him to be her daddy.

If we don't work out ... we couldn't possibly work out ... with his career, his lifestyle.

He leans forward, gently pressing his lips against mine in a tender touch. His breath caressing my mouth, his eyes locked on mine, twilight blue to stormy gray. "C'mon, Cass. Give me a chance. I'll be the man you and Poppy need."

My head shakes back and forth in the negative without my permission, my last form of defense against him. "I can't, Toby. I can't risk Poppy like that. It's not just about me and you—I'm a package deal. I have to put Poppy's needs above my own." I sob. "I'm sorry, Toby." Breaking away from him, I grab my purse and run out of his home. Making it to my car, I quickly start it and drive.

I drive aimlessly, ending up at the riverside.

I need to get myself under control before I go home, or Poppy'll know something's wrong, so I go for a walk to settle my thoughts.

The woman inside me was desperate to say yes to Toby— to beg him to be with me, and if it was just me, I would have jumped in with two feet and my eyes wide open. But ... the mother in me, the protective momma-bear, can't put Poppy at risk of falling in love with a father figure, only to have him walk away when parenthood and family life are no longer what he wants—it's too scary. Her grandfather did it, her own father did it, and even her uncle's done it. Everywhere I turn, I see examples of men who don't live up to their promises, don't man up or stick it out when things aren't exciting or they're not the sole focus anymore—even the father of Sam's baby. Toby may think he wants this life, but it's not compatible with his career. Touring and performing across the country isn't conducive to a healthy family life—I know that, and deep down, he knows it, too. His high school crush blinds him.

-cassia-

THE BELL OVER THE DOOR ALERTS ME TO SOMEONE ENTERING the store but I have my hands full out the back with gorgeous sunflowers for a tall vase arrangement, so I call out to Sam to get the door. That woman's been heaven-sent—I don't know why I waited so long to employ someone to help with the business management side of things. I keep working on my arrangement, confident that Sam can handle basic customer inquiries after her two weeks of training until I hear a familiar male voice speaking loudly to her.

Of course, Sam knows Jake from high school, but she's probably never seen him like this. I quickly step out from the back to diffuse his temper before it gets out of hand like last time. Before I can make my presence known, I hear Jake cursing at Sam.

"What the fuck are you doing here?"

Sam's arms are crossed. Neither of them has seen me yet. "I work here, Jake. What are you doing here?"

"You fucking work here? Are you fucking with me? You've always been a trouble-making bitch!" He leans over the counter with menace in his eyes, dropping his voice. "You'd better not fucking tell Sia that I'm the father of that kid in your belly." He points at her stomach like he wants it gone.

"I haven't told her anything. I have no intention of ever telling anybody about the biggest mistake I've ever made. Don't worry. Your miserable secret is safe with me, asshole," she snaps back.

I suck in a breath as the shock of this revelation hits me.

That fucking asshole!

How many women has he knocked up and repeatedly refused to take any responsibility for? I steady myself, preparing to face this jerk head-on. I'm almost certain he won't put his hands on me in front of Sam, so I'm going to lay everything out on the table. Stepping out of the doorway, I catch them both by surprise. Sam's obviously uncomfortable with the thought of me knowing that Jake is her baby daddy as she fidgets with her shirt buttons, looking everywhere but at me. Jake continues to shoot daggers from his eyes at Sam. He finally turns toward me with a smile as if he wasn't just cursing out my friend, and employee, and the mother of his child.

"Jake."

"Hey, Sia. You're looking hot as usual." I can't believe he's speaking like that to me, in front of his baby momma, no less.

Crossing my arms in front of my body, forming a barrier, I step in front of Sam. "What are you doing here, Jake?"

"I came to follow up. I told you I'm not done with you—I meant it, Sia." Out of my periphery, I see Sam leave the front room to head back into the small office. I can't believe he's doing this in front of her.

"And I told *you*, Jake, I'm not interested. I can't believe you think it's okay to come into my shop and curse out my staff. A woman who is carrying *your* baby, then thinks it's okay to pursue me in front of your baby momma. You're a disgusting pig."

He steps threateningly around the counter, getting into my

space, the same way he did last time. I suck in a breath because I thought I would be safer having someone else in the shop while he was here. Obviously, he doesn't give a shit. Stroking the side of my face, he whispers, "You jealous, Babe?"

Ugh! As if.

Pulling my face away from his hand as though it's burned me, I step back quickly, breaking physical contact with him. "Why would I be jealous? I don't care what you do anymore, Jake. I haven't cared for a long time because there is nothing between us—not for the last five years since you attempted to punch Poppy in the head and treated her as though she was less than because she's deaf!" My anger is ratcheting up. I'm finding it difficult to keep control of my emotions or the tone of my voice level. "Nothing's changed on my end, so I'm not sure what you think is going to happen here?" I wave my hand between us.

He softens his tone. "I miss you, Babe. I want you back." He grabs hold of my hips, rubbing his pelvis against my belly. "We were good together. Remember?"

Ugh. Actually, I've had much better in recent times. I try to pull away, but his grip tightens on my hips. "I'm a package deal. Remember?" I hold his eyes with my own. "The package you never wanted. Remember?"

He releases me, stepping back as though I've scolded him. "Let's just spend some time together, you and me."

"No, Jake. It'll never be just you and me because Poppy and I are a package deal. Stop wasting your time." I turn to walk away from him, hoping he gets the message to leave, but he stops me with a tight grip around my wrist, dragging me into his body.

"I fucking told you, I ain't finished with you yet. Get that through your pretty little head." He drops my wrist forcefully and pivots around, walking out of my shop. My whole body sags in relief, shaking from the exchange as Sam pokes her head out of our little office.

"Is he gone?"

I give her the side-eye because she damn well abandoned me out here with him. Where's the loyalty? "Yeah, he's gone." I spin around on her, pointing to her bump. "You wanna explain what's going on?"

She looks sheepish but is saved by the bell over the door and a new customer. I spend the next twenty minutes with my customer, who wanted to buy an arrangement for her grandparents, who are celebrating their sixty-fifth wedding anniversary. I know there are plenty of couples who have long, happy marriages in my line of work. I just don't have any positive examples in the people close to me. It always seems like it happens for everyone else, but never for me.

As soon as she leaves, I step toward the office and lean on the doorframe, arms folded, waiting for Sam to notice I'm there. After a few seconds, I know she's seen me but is pretending she hasn't. I huff out a breath, drop my hands to my sides, and take one step into the room. "Sam?"

She ducks her head. "I feel ashamed of myself. I never wanted you to know Jake was the father of this baby. He certainly didn't want to be the father." When she first told me the father of her baby wasn't interested, I remember thinking her story was so similar to mine—I never contemplated that it was *exactly* like mine.

"Oh, Sam." I lean in, awkwardly wrapping my arms around her. "You have nothing to feel ashamed about. He's the asshole who gets women pregnant, then doesn't face his responsibilities. That's on him, not you."

"But, you see, this time, it's on me." Tears track down her face. She looks utterly miserable. "I got pregnant on purpose."

I feel as though she's slapped me, and the words tumble out before I can stop them. "What were you thinking, Sam?" I realize after they're out of my mouth that I sound like a judgmental bitch. "I don't mean it like that. It's your choice to start a family, but why Jake?"

"I've loved him since high school." Shit, I feel like she just knocked me on my ass. My eyebrows shoot to my hairline, and I'm surprised they didn't fly off my face completely. "I'm so sorry."

"I had no idea, Sam." She nods, looking away from me, obviously finding it difficult to face me with her truth. "Why didn't you ever say anything when we were in school?"

"You loved him, and I know he loved you. I was an easy lay whenever the two of you had a break." She shrugs her shoulders, looking down.

"There was a reason we kept having 'breaks,' Sam. We didn't work. We were all wrong for each other, but I was desperate to keep him because it made me feel special; like I was important to someone outside of my family." Laying my teenage thoughts out like that to Sam makes me feel exposed. "You already know I didn't have a dad in my life, and looking back now, I was desperate for male attention. *Any* male attention was better than nothing in my mind back then." I look away because I feel ashamed of myself now. "I was young, insecure, and stupid back then."

Sam stands to hug me tight as we sob into each other, coming to terms with our self-imposed shame. I'm ashamed of my back and forth with Jake in my late teens, while she's ashamed for loving someone she thought I loved. Back then, in my teenage heart, I thought it was love, but looking back with an adult mind, I know it wasn't. I gesture for her to sit, then I sit opposite her, the desk between us.

"So, what happened?"

"I hadn't seen Jake since high school. Then I bumped into him in a bar about six months ago. We hooked up, and he started coming around regularly. He made it pretty clear it was only for sex, but I wanted more. I still loved him." She fiddles with a piece of paper on her desk. "I thought ... no, I hoped if I were pregnant with his baby, he would stick around. It was my pathetic attempt at trying to keep him. I'm so stupid." She sobs. "He's never wanted me. It's always been you. Even now, I'm pregnant with his baby, and he still wants you." She doesn't say it with jealousy, more in resignation that things haven't changed in all these years.

"He doesn't want me. Not really. I'm not sure what game he's playing, but I'm not interested. He didn't want me when I got pregnant. When he found out Poppy was deaf, he certainly didn't want her because, in *his* eyes, she's defective." My anger rises back to the surface just thinking about how he exploded that day five years ago. I look back at my friend. "What are you going to do?"

"Stick with my plan, I guess. I'm having this baby. I already love the bean to pieces. If Jake doesn't want to be involved, that's his right, I guess. Especially since *I* did it on purpose."

"I'll help you wherever I can, okay? You realize Poppy's your baby's big sister?" As the tears in her eyes build again, she nods, accepting our ties through family as well as my help. "You're not alone." We hug again, sealing my promise.

-cassia-

THE BELL OVER THE DOOR TINKLES, SO I LOOK UP TO FIND
Gramma Iris in my doorway. Happiness fills me as my eyes
land on her. "Gramma." I step out from behind the counter to
embrace her.

"Cassia, lovely girl. How are you doing today?" She
squeezes me extra tight before we release each other.

"I'm great. I thought you weren't coming in today."

"Well … I wanted to surprise you. I thought you could take
the afternoon off. Sally, Sam, and I will look after the shop for
you. I know you only have one event over the weekend, and
I'm sure you're already organized for it." She looks me up and
down. "I've booked you a hair appointment and a pedicure—"
I try to cut in, but she keeps speaking over the top of me. "No
arguments. You never do anything for yourself. My treat."

I lean back in, squeezing her extra tight in appreciation for
her thoughtful gesture. She's right, I never take time to do
anything for myself. If I'm lucky, I'll be able to make it to
Poppy's guitar lesson this afternoon. She'll be so surprised.
"Thank you, Gramma. I'm not gonna say no. I can't

remember the last time I had my hair done or my feet treated. What time is my appointment?"

She looks at her watch. "You need to get a move on. You have twenty minutes." I kiss her cheek, then step into my office to grab my purse and coat, saying goodbye to the girls.

"Thanks, Gramma. See you on the weekend for lunch on Sunday." I kiss her cheek again, waving over my shoulder as I step out of the shop before she answers. I'm so freaking excited for a couple of hours of pampering. I know the shop's in expert hands, meaning I can relax and enjoy the afternoon.

I step out of the salon, feeling like a million bucks. Gramma had organized a shampoo, highlights, cut, and blowout. While the highlights were working their magic, I had my pedicure. It felt completely decadent to be pampered for a couple of hours —I feel like a new me!

I manage to get to *Music for my Heart* halfway through Poppy's lesson with Toby. Shane's sitting just inside the doorway as I enter. "Hey, Shane, how are things?" I don't see him all that much because I'm gone by the time he arrives to take Poppy to school and I generally don't get home until closer to dinnertime.

"Hey. Good, thanks, Cass. How 'bout you?"

"Good thanks. Um, so I was wondering how much longer you're going to be watching over Poppy?" I can't believe he's still driving her everywhere, as well as watching over her whenever she's out of the house. It seems like overkill to me.

"Until Toby decides things are safe for her, I guess." He shrugs as if it's no big deal.

"And when might that be?"

"Dunno. You need to ask him. But I don't think he'll be in

a hurry. He had an unpleasant experience with a stalker a few years back. He doesn't want anything to happen to Poppy."

I didn't know; now his response to the video going viral makes sense. "Oh, okay. I guess I'll talk to him about it then." I gesture toward the room Mom told me they use for the lesson. He nods and goes back to looking at whatever's on his phone. He's never been much of a talker.

I make it down to the music room and peek in through the glass window in the door. My breath gushes out of my lungs at what greets me. Toby's sitting behind Poppy, his hands over hers, showing her the correct position for her fingers on the neck of the guitar. Her head's resting against his chest as he adjusts her fingers accordingly. The smile on my daughter's face is breathtaking. The level of comfort they have together is clear for anyone to see.

I'm not sure how many minutes pass before Toby looks up, noticing me in the window. He nudges Poppy, pointing toward the door. Once she sees I'm here, she scoots away from Toby, takes off her guitar, and runs toward the door. I open it, stepping inside to catch her little body as she slams into me, both of us laughing. I set her on her feet as Toby slowly makes his way over to where we are.

"Hey, Cass, this is a surprise." He seems reserved, greeting me as he would any acquaintance. I guess I can't blame him for being guarded.

I sign as I speak, so Poppy knows how I came to be here. "My gramma surprised me with an afternoon of pampering. I finished in time to surprise my girl." I slide my hand down Poppy's hair. "I wanted to watch you practice." I look at Toby. "I hope you don't mind?"

His eyes are locked on me. "Of course not. You're welcome here anytime." He looks down at Poppy. "Wanna show your mom what we've been working on?" She nods eagerly, then heads back to where they were when I arrived. They settle in and, with the biggest smile on her face, Poppy begins to strum a song I recognize instantly. It's upbeat and modern compared to the two songs she's already mastered. It was played to death on the radio when Poppy was a year old. I remember dancing around the house to this song, shaking my ass all over the place, and making Poppy giggle like crazy. I'll have to tell her when she finishes.

After she finishes, she asks me, "Do you know that song, Mommy?"

"Of course I know *Shake It Off.* When you were a baby, I used to dance with you around the house to this song. You used to giggle like crazy. You loved it so much." She's so excited that I know the song, while Toby smiles.

"I'd pay to see that." He signs as he speaks. "You shaking that sexy ass of yours." He tucks his hands into his pockets for the last part, smirking at me. I'm thankful he didn't sign that in front of my daughter.

I glance across at her to see if she has any idea what he just said, but I think the angle Toby's standing probably blocked the movement of his lips from her view. Sometimes, she can pick up the odd word here or there by watching a person's mouth while they speak, but it's a lot for her to take in.

He smiles, rubbing his thumb across his bottom lip—he's so freaking sexy, and he doesn't even need to try. I tuck my newly styled hair behind my ear, darting my eyes anywhere but at Toby. Maybe it was a mistake to turn up here. I should be doing my best to avoid him at all costs.

Poppy signs to Toby, "Let's play all the songs I've learned for Mommy, like a concert." Toby nods in agreement, so Poppy situates a chair for me. She regularly checks between the computer monitor and Toby as they play. Her love for him is evident every time she looks at him. It's heartwarming while being scary at the same time. I'm worried she's getting too attached to him since I'm sure he'll have to abandon these lessons at some point. When his album's finished, he'll have to tour, meaning he'll be away for months. I make a mental note to speak to Poppy about it so I can prepare her for when the lessons stop. I tear my eyes away from my daughter to watch Toby. My heart stutters to see my daughter's affection returned —he truly cares for her.

As they finish, Toby encourages Poppy to bow. I wave my hands in the air and stomp my feet as heavily as I can on the wooden floor. I walk over, picking up my baby to give her the biggest hug. My heart feels so full with her in my life; I'm incredibly proud to call her my daughter. It's the end of the lesson, so they pack everything up. I notice Poppy put her guitar in a case. "Where did you get the case?"

"Guitar gave it to me today." Now I know that Guitar is Toby's sign name, it makes more sense.

My eyes shoot up to him. "Thank you, Toby. You didn't have to do that. You've already done so much for her." I sign directly to Poppy. "Did you say thank you?"

Toby answers instead of Poppy. "Of course she did. It was my pleasure to give her a case for the guitar. After all, she *is* a professional." He signs that last part, especially to her, as he winks.

"Mommy, can we go for ice cream, please?"

Well, if I can't take my girl for ice cream on the one day I get off from work early, there's gotta be something wrong with me. "Of course, Baby Girl. Get your stuff, then say bye to Toby."

"No, Mommy. Toby can come, too. Please." Oh, boy, she's put on the puppy-dog begging eyes, which will make me look like an asshole if I say no.

"Toby's probably busy—" I don't get to finish before he butts in.

"I'm not busy at all. My afternoon's wide open, so I'd love to come for ice cream with two beautiful ladies." Poppy jumps up and down in excitement, while I brace myself to spend the next hour or so with the man who sets my body on fire and my heart into a crazy rhythm.

"Okay then. Let's head out. We'll meet you at the ice cream shop. You remember Poppy's favorite place, right?"

"Of course. But I'll come with you guys. Shane can follow in my car." *Oh, shit!* I don't know if I can be stuck in such close proximity to him, but Poppy's celebrating like crazy.

"Okay, let's go." We all make our way out of the building, collecting Shane on the way. Toby gives Shane an update on our afternoon plans. I can tell he's surprised by the turn of events, by the way his head snaps up and his eyes capture mine.

I hear ya—*I've been railroaded, too.*

Before I get the chance, Toby helps Poppy into her booster seat, ensuring she's strapped in safely with such care and attention. He then opens my door because I'm frozen in place, watching his interaction with the most precious person in my world. Eventually, we get on our way, so I use the opportunity to speak to Toby about Shane.

"I wanted to ask you how much longer you think Poppy needs to have Shane driving her around?"

"Until I feel there's no threat." Oh-kay then, his tone brooks no argument. He doesn't elaborate either, but she *is* my daughter, and I need to know what's going on.

"Shane mentioned you had a stalker a few years ago. Are you worried that person might come after Poppy?" His body tenses, including that jaw of his I love, as his eyebrows slash down, causing creases in his forehead. I don't think he's happy I know about his stalker.

He looks out of the window before looking forward again. "He shouldn't have told you about that. It's not relevant. I'm just more aware than the average person of how social media can impact your private life." He briefly glances across at me.

"I feel better knowing Poppy's safe. It helps me to sleep better at night." His voice is soft, vulnerable.

Without taking my eyes off the road, I nod in acceptance, whispering, "Okay." Tightening my hands on the steering wheel, I tell him, "If you ever want to talk about it, I'm a good listener." He nods, his jaw tense. "Thank you for keeping Poppy safe."

His body relaxes into the seat as he looks out of the window. "I would do anything for that little girl." After watching them together, I believe him.

TWENTY-NINE

-toby-

WELL, HOW PERFECT IS MY AFTERNOON TURNING OUT TO BE. Ice cream with the two girls I want in my life.

I was pissed at Cassia for running out on me before I could have my say. I've gone back and forth between feeling pissed, hurt, and hopeful that she cared enough to talk to me in the first place. She's scared, and I get that. I get she feels the need to protect her daughter, but she needs to realize she doesn't need to protect Poppy from me—I'm not the enemy here. I could have bought Poppy all the ice cream in the world when she wanted me to come with them, unknowingly giving me the opportunity I needed to spend more time with her gorgeous mom.

Poppy and Cassia make their ice cream selections: peanut butter crunch in the form of a penguin for Poppy, while Cassia goes with the chocolate chip. I place their order along with mine (macadamia crunch) and Shane's (raspberry swirl). A couple of teenage girls think they're being covert as they snap photos of me on their phones while I order. Shane approaches them with our usual request—I'm happy to have a selfie with them if they delay posting the photos to social media for a couple of hours. Most people readily agree, allowing me the opportunity to enjoy whatever I'm doing without hoards of people descending on us. This time, though, I'll also ask the girls to delete any photographs they have of Poppy and Cassia. Once they agree, I pose for a couple of selfies with each girl with the promise they'll delay posting them, allowing us to enjoy our ice cream in peace.

We opt to sit outside to enjoy the pleasant fall weather we're blessed with today. With Poppy completely focused on her ice cream, I take the opportunity to study Cass with her daughter. They're very similar in appearance, but also in their mannerisms. They both light up when they're in each other's company. Their love and bond with each other is so strong; it's beautiful to watch.

"—huh?" I glance at Shane. He said something that I missed because I was too busy watching my girls.

He lifts his chin, gesturing across the road. "Jake was watching the girls from over there. You want me to follow him?"

I search around but can't see any sign of him. "He's gone now, but make sure you keep an eye out for him. I don't want him causing trouble." I'm not sure if Cass wants it to be general knowledge that Jake is Poppy's father, but it's fucking creepy that he was watching them from the opposite side of the street.

Poppy breaks me out of my head when she thrusts her ice cream in my face, gesturing for me to have a taste. I check in with Cass that it's okay with her since I'll be licking her daughter's ice cream, but she just shrugs as though it's not up to her to decide. I take a lick, making a big show of liking the flavor. She screws up her face when I allow her to taste mine.

"I don't like vanilla ice cream. It's too boring," Poppy signs one-handed. Cassia bursts out laughing as my eyebrows hit my hairline. I pass my ice cream to Shane so I can defend my ice cream choice to a freaking seven-year-old.

"It's not *just* vanilla. It's macadamia crunch. It's delicious." I make a big show of taking another taste, followed by a lick of my lips.

Glancing up at Cass, she's squirming in her seat, looking everywhere but at Poppy and me—it's good to know I have *some* effect on her. Poppy laughs, screwing up her face yet again, shaking her head in the negative. I guess she's entitled to her opinion on ice cream flavors, even if she *is* wrong. Handing my ice cream back to Shane, I tell her exactly that, eliciting more giggles from her as well as her gorgeous mom.

Once we've finished our ice cream, Poppy insists we should visit the park. She's obviously enjoying having her mom home early from work and is planning to take advantage of every minute. She looks across at me with her sweet face. "Can you come, too?"

I don't even bother to check in with Cass. I'm enjoying my time with them way too much to have her deny me. "Of course. Let's go."

The four of us walk to the park, Poppy holding Shane's hand, while Cass and I walk behind them. "You don't have to come to the park. You're allowed to say no to her."

"I know I can say no to her, but I don't want to." I nudge her shoulder with my arm. "Unless we're encroaching on your mommy-daughter time?"

"Oh, no, it's nothing like that. I do my best to make sure I get regular time with my girl, not as much as I'd like with running the shop, but whenever I'm not there, I'm with her." She tucks her hands into the pockets of her coat. "I just figured you probably have other stuff to do that's more important than hanging out with us."

I *do* have plenty to do. These songs won't write themselves. "There's nowhere on this earth I'd rather be than sharing ice cream, followed by a visit to the park with you and Poppy on this fine afternoon." I mean it, too—this is exactly where I want to be. I smile at her, then laugh at the way Poppy jerks Shane's arm back and forth as she skips her way to the park. Cass notices, too, letting out a giggle of her own. It's a rather comical sight—Shane's a big guy, yet he's willingly being yanked around by a small child.

As we arrive at the park, I step forward, picking Poppy up by the waist to run ahead with her until we reach the swings, causing her to giggle all the way. After situating her on the swing, I check with her if she likes to go high or stay low. She tells me she wants to go high, so I swing her high and higher still while she squeals with girlish delight, kicking her little legs back and forth the whole time.

Cass stands in front of her, signing like a crazy woman to hold on tight—maybe I got a bit carried away because she looks worried. I stop pushing for a bit, allowing the swing to slow, gradually reducing its height so Cass can relax. Finishing on the swing, Poppy takes off for the climbing frame.

She climbs up like a monkey, and my heart plummets to my feet as I realize I can't call out to her to keep her safe. I glance across to Cass to find she's watching Poppy like a hawk, clutching onto the lapels of her coat. I look back up, finding Poppy higher now, so I quickly climb up behind her, ready to break her fall if she loses her grip, but she makes it to the top with no mishaps. Then she proceeds to scare the absolute shit out of me by letting one hand go so she can celebrate getting to the top, throwing her little fist up in triumph. I quickly step up behind her, trapping her between the climbing frame and my body to keep her safe. We both climb down until we have two feet securely on the ground. I release the breath that had been trapped in my lungs in relief, knowing she's safe on the ground, where she belongs.

Cassia steps forward, hugging her close, before signing.

"You always need to hold on tight with two hands when you climb up high."

Her little bottom lip trembles as her chin drops to her chest. "Sorry, Mommy."

She raises Poppy's chin with her finger. "That's okay, Baby Girl. Just remember next time. Promise Mommy."

Poppy nods. "Promise, Mommy." Cassia holds her close, brushing her hair back from her face affectionately, studying her. After a few moments, Cass ruffles her hair playfully, and we walk together toward the obstacle course. All four of us, including Shane, goof off through the obstacles, allowing Poppy to take the lead. She runs across the open grassed area to the next obstacle, which is quite a distance away. Other kids are playing baseball, while others are running laps around the edge of the grassy field. Chasing after Poppy, I see a kid hit a ball full-on with his baseball bat out of my periphery, then hear the distinct crack of maple against hide. As I look back toward Poppy, everything seems to happen in slow motion as the trajectory of the ball heads straight for the back of her head.

I can't call out to her to get out of the way, so I pick up speed, sprinting forward and dive, putting myself between the ball and Poppy. Twisting around, the ball collides against my shoulder, taking Poppy and me down to the ground—*motherfucker!*

It hurts like a bitch.

Shane and Cass come running up to us, dropping to their knees beside Poppy and me. Shit, I dropped Poppy when I got hit. Quickly sitting up, I check to find Poppy's okay. After Cassia's checked her over for herself, she turns her attention to me.

"Oh my god, are you okay? That ball hit you so freaking hard." The color drains from her face as the realization dawns on her that the ball should have hit Poppy. She looks back and forth between her daughter and me as tears fill her eyes. Her shaky hand comes up to cover her mouth, her wide eyes watching me as her other hand comes up to my arm where I'm holding it. Her shaky fingertips tenderly brush over my hand. Before I can brace myself, she throws herself at me, wrapping her arms around me, squeezing me impossibly tight. A grunt escapes unbidden, and she realizes she's unwittingly hurt my injured arm and quickly leans away.

Shane bends down to help me stand. I climb to my feet, feeling the effects of the impact on my arm. I bet I'm gonna have a fucking huge bruise. I try to lift my arm, but the pain is too much, so I drop it back down, holding it across my chest.

Poppy wraps her arms around my hips, burying her face in my stomach. I lightly smooth my hand down the back of her silky hair, holding her close. My heart's still beating like crazy at what just happened. In the blink of an eye, we could have lost this precious little angel.

The kid who hit the ball comes running over to us as Shane picks up the ball. "I'm sorry, Mister. I didn't mean to hit you." His wide eyes flit between all four of us, and his heavy breaths reveal his worry that we're gonna ream him out.

"That's okay, bud. It was an accident." Shane hands the kid his ball.

His body shifts, his expression changing from worry to recognition. He points at me. "Hey, you're Toby Summer. My sister has your poster on her wall."

I nod. "Yeah. I am. Would you mind keeping this between us?"

"Sure. Sure." He looks down at the ball in his hand. "Uh, would you be able to sign this for my sister?" He thrusts the ball forward.

"No problem. Are you sure?"

"Uh, yeah?" He doesn't seem sure. The ball is probably his, and if I sign it to his sister, he'll have to forfeit it. Shane keeps small photos of me on stage in his pocket for this very reason. He pulls one out, then hands me a pen.

"What's your sister's name, bud?"

"Ruth."

I sign the photo to Ruth, then hand it to the kid.

"Thanks, Mr. Summer." He walks backward, heading toward his friends. "Sorry again."

I wave him off. No point in getting mad over an accident. He's probably only about ten years old and he was thoughtful enough to ask for an autograph for his sister. Gotta give him kudos for that.

Cass still looks as white as a ghost, so I shuffle forward with Poppy still attached to me and wrap my good arm around her, pulling her into a group hug. I'm not sure how long it lasts, but I could get used to holding the girls this close. The upbeat mood has been broken, so I suggest we make our way back to the parking lot to head home. My arm's throbbing, and I desperately need to get some ice on it. Back at the parking lot, I manage to get Poppy strapped into her seat securely. "Be good for your mom. I'll see you next Friday."

"Thanks for looking after me, Toby." She wraps her little arms around my neck, kissing my cheek.

I tap the tip of her nose with my finger. "Anytime." I wink as I stand to my full height, wincing at the pain in my shoulder. Cass is standing close by and notices.

Drawing her eyebrows down low, she bites her bottom lip. "Our place is closer to here if you wanna come home with us. I can take care of your arm. Make sure you're okay."

If I were a better man, I'd say no and go home to take care of myself, but I'm not a good man because I'm going to use this opportunity to my advantage. I'm gonna take her up on her offer. I look across at Shane, catching the hint of a smirk because he already knows what my decision will be. He nods slightly, letting me know he'll take the car home, then come back to collect me when I'm ready. "You don't have to." I'm not sure how I manage to say the words with a straight face, but I'm proud of myself.

"It's the least I can do. Please. I'll feel better if I know you're okay."

"Okay. It beats going home to my empty place to take care of myself. But only if you're sure it's not too much trouble."

"Really, it's no trouble at all. I promise."

"Shane, would you be able to come and pick me up later?"

He plays along for Cass's benefit, looking at his watch, then back to Cass and me. "Sure. No problem. I'll see you guys later." He pops his head inside the car, waving to Poppy, then heads over to our car to leave.

-toby-

CASS HELPS ME SITUATE MYSELF IN HER PASSENGER SEAT, leaning across me to buckle me in, putting her magnificent cleavage right in my line of sight. Her hair smells different from last time, more of a chemical smell, not the cinnamon scent I've come to expect. As she pulls back, our eyes connect and lock, charcoal to cobalt, our lips mere inches apart, breaths melding together. It takes everything inside of me to keep my good arm by my side, rather than grasping the back of her head to pull her to me so I can take her mouth the way I've been dreaming since we spent the night together. She breaks the moment when she pulls away to close the door. Walking briskly around the front of the car, she grants me the pleasure of watching her.

Clearing my throat, I thank her as we make our way to her home. I've never been there before; we didn't mix in the same circles, which was mostly my fault because I kept to myself, rebuffing her attempts at establishing a friendship. I was a stupid fool when I was a teenager.

We make our way inside the neat home, and Cass immediately switches into caretaker mode, signing to Poppy to get the medical kit. Looking around, it seems we're the only ones here. "Where's your mom?"

"Oh, well, when I found out I had the afternoon off, I let Mom know so that she could make plans. She and Violet decided to take Jasmine out to an indoor playground center, followed by pizza for dinner and maybe a movie." She gestures for me to follow her. "Come on; let's look at your arm."

I follow her into the kitchen, which includes a dining nook. "Can you lift your sleeve?"

The ball hit me at the top of my arm, so I don't think I'll be able to lift my sleeve that high, but I try.

"Just take your shirt off, Toby. I'll get some ice."

I struggle to get my shirt off in the usual way, so I have to take one arm out, then take it over my head to drag the material down my injured arm. I'm studying the bruise that's already forming when I hear Cass suck in a sharp breath. Looking up, she's right there with a bag of frozen peas, her eyes wide, but they're not on my bruised arm. Instead, she's looking at my bare upper torso. I unintentionally flex in response to her heated gaze on me, causing her eyes to snap up to mine, locking our gazes in an intimate moment. Poppy breaks it as she comes running into the kitchen with the medical kit, which I'm sure is unnecessary.

Cass immediately goes into action, assessing the bruise. "Shit, I can see the stitches from the ball imprinted on your arm." She gently presses the imprint, causing me to wince. I'm trying to be all manly, but it hurts something fierce.

Poppy drags a chair close to me on the other side and rests her head on my good arm, which I move out to wrap around her small shoulders. She's been very subdued since the incident in the park, which is unlike the Poppy I know and have grown to love. I squeeze her in close, kissing the top of her head. Cass pulls a chair closer on my injured side, carefully pressing the peas against the bruised area.

"I could have lost my baby today," she whispers. "You saved Poppy's life. I'll never be able to repay you." Her plush bottom lip trembles, and I want to take it between my teeth to bite, then kiss it better.

"I told you, I would do anything for her, and I meant it. In the short time I've known her, I've grown to care for her ... a lot—even before I knew she was your daughter." I love Poppy, but that might be too much, too soon, for Cass. I don't want to sound like a weirdo. Our eyes meet and lock again, and she nods slightly, smiling timidly. "She's been quiet since the incident." Cass nods. "Is she gonna be okay?"

"Yeah, I'll talk to her about it later. Make sure she's alright." She lifts the icy bag from my arm. "We should put some arnica on this; it'll help with the bruising." She picks through the items in the medical kit until she finds what she's looking for. Opening it, Cass gently applies a liberal amount to the bruised area, which seems to be spreading rapidly. At this rate, my entire upper arm is going to be black and blue. I'm not complaining, though, because I would rather have this outcome over the other possible one, which I never want to think about. "We'll give the ice a break for a bit, then put it on again." I nod. "Do you want some Tylenol?"

"Yes, please, if you don't mind. It's throbbing quite a bit." She rises to get a glass of water, then places two small pills in my hand along with the cool glass of water. I eagerly take the medicine, hoping to lessen the pain radiating from the site.

"Poppy, let's make some pancakes for dinner." That perks the little girl up. She jumps out of her seat to help her mom in the kitchen. I get up to help the girls, but Cass insists I stay where I am. I'm not complaining—I have the perfect view from where I'm sitting. The ladies get to work, and before I know it, they place a stack of pancakes on the table along with a variety of toppings and several flavors of ice cream. Poppy sets the table, and we all sit to eat. It's comforting to see her smiling again, the sparkle returning to her eyes.

Taking a pancake from the stack, I load it with strawberries, then drizzle chocolate sauce over the top before finishing it off with ice cream. Taking my first bite, my taste buds delight in the flavors and the light, fluffy texture of the pancake. "Mmm, these are delicious." I sign to Poppy, as I make a show of licking my lips. Cass's eyes are locked on my mouth, so I draw out the show, especially for her. We make short work of the stack in the middle of the table, after which Cass repeats the process with the frozen peas on my arm. Then we clean up the mess from our breakfast for dinner.

I don't want to overstay my welcome. I know Cass was reluctant to have me join them this afternoon, so I excuse myself to head home.

"Can't you stay to watch a movie with us?" I look up to Cass to check her reaction to Poppy's invitation. She smiles slightly, tilting her head to the side as though she's awaiting my answer.

"I can if you want me to." I look between the two as they both nod their heads. This is definitely my lucky day. Cass willingly spending time with me is something I thought I'd never have after the way we left things between us. "What movie are we gonna watch?"

Poppy jumps up and down. "*School of Rock*, of course."

"Of course." I laugh.

"Can we make popcorn, Mommy?"

"Sure. Go put your pajamas on. I'll get the popcorn." Poppy races upstairs without complaint, as Cass tells me to get comfortable in the living room after giving me the frozen peas for my arm. I situate myself on the side of the couch that will keep my bruised arm safe from any bumps or knocks, holding the peas gingerly against my bicep.

I'm lost in my head when Poppy runs into the living room,

throwing herself onto the middle of the couch, before snuggling into my side. I soak up her warmth, her vitality. Breathing in her little girl scent as I thank my lucky stars, our afternoon didn't end up the way it could have. Cass steps into the room with an enormous bowl of popcorn, placing it on Poppy's lap as she sits on the other side of her daughter, kissing the top of her head and then turning on the TV to pull up the movie. As the film begins, captions display across the screen for Poppy's benefit.

We're about fifteen minutes into the movie when Poppy snuggles further into my side, so I drop the frozen peas to the floor to wrap my arm around her small body, tucking her in close. When I look up from her, Cass is watching us, her lips slightly tipped up at the corners; the love she has for her daughter written all over her beautiful face. My fingers itch to touch her, and I easily could, but I refrain. She's made her feelings toward me clear; she's not interested in a relationship with me and as much as I would love for this to be my life, to share times like these on the regular, I know it's not in the cards for me.

Rose and Violet pop their heads in to say hello briefly when they get home before taking Jasmine upstairs to bed. I wait for them to come back down to join us, but they never do.

About three-quarters of the way through the movie, I notice the little girl who's stolen my heart has slipped down to my lap; her breaths slow and steady. I pretend to be too caught up in the movie to notice because with her asleep, there's no longer a reason for me to stay. As the movie ends, I dread the conclusion of our evening. The credits roll, so I know my time is up when Cass presses pause; however, she surprises me when she turns in her seat. "Um, thank you again for today. I don't know what I would have done if you …"

Her words trail off as she looks down at Poppy. My need to soothe her surpasses my need to protect myself from further rejection; lifting my hand from her daughter, I squeeze her shoulder, then gently caress her cheek with my hand. Her silky smooth skin presses deeper into my palm until I'm cupping the side of her face, her eyes fluttering closed as I caress the softness of her cheek. The moment between us feels deep. Deeper than any we've shared before, even the night we spent together, which was all about connecting on a physical level. Slipping my hand behind her neck, I pull her toward me and press my lips against her forehead in a barely there touch. She tilts her face upward, making it oh so easy to take her mouth, but that would be all kinds of wrong with her daughter asleep in my lap. "You don't have to keep thanking me. I would do it again in a heartbeat to keep her safe." I look down at Poppy. "You want me to carry her upstairs to her bed?"

"No, that's okay. I can manage."

"You don't have to manage while I'm here. Let me do it. Please." I implore her.

Nodding her head slowly, she relents. "Okay, thank you." I carefully adjust my position to allow me the space to scoop her up. Hiding my wince, I lift her without her waking, following Cass upstairs to Poppy's bedroom. I take in the explosion of purple as Cass pulls back the comforter and blankets, readying the bed for a sleeping Poppy. I place her as gently as possible onto her pale purple sheets, then step back slightly to allow Cass to do her motherly thing, tucking her daughter in. Once she's tucked in to Cass's satisfaction, we step out of the room to head downstairs.

I message Shane to pick me up. It would be easier to call a cab or an Uber, but the grief Shane would give me for doing that wouldn't be worth my while. Saying goodbye is the awkward part of the evening: do I kiss her like I desperately want to? Or do I keep it purely platonic, the way she wants to? Standing by the front door, waiting for my ride, I tuck my hands in my pockets to stop myself from reaching for her.

"Thanks for everything, Toby."

I wave off her thank you. "Please stop. Thanks for looking after me." I gesture to my arm, which is still throbbing like a bitch. "And for inviting me to spend the evening with you." I shuffle on my feet as I brush loose hair out of my face. "I, uh, had a really great time."

She looks surprised, huffing out a laugh. "Oh, yeah, this must have been a real highlight in your rock 'n' roll life." She tucks her hair behind her ear, her eyes skipping around everywhere but at me.

I pause, waiting for her to look at my face so I can respond. "Actually, yeah, it was. It's the best Friday night I've had in a really long time. I wouldn't mind all of my Friday nights being just like this one." Headlights shine through the window near the front door, highlighting that my time with Cass has come to an end. Her eyes widen in surprise at my confession, so I use the opportunity to lean in and cup the side of her face, pulling her forward to press my lips gently against hers. She doesn't pull away, so I press in firmer, using my tongue to lick at the seam of her lips. She opens for me, welcoming me inside her mouth. Moaning, I take the kiss I've wanted for weeks—my hand in her hair, my lips on hers, my tongue dueling with hers.

THIRTY-ONE

-cassia-

STANDING IN THE DOORWAY, WATCHING THE RED TAILLIGHTS disappear while pressing my fingers against my puffy lips, I wonder if anyone else's kiss will ever sear my lips the way Toby's kisses do.

"What are you doing, Love?" Mom startles me out of my daze, so I quickly close the door, keeping the cold air out where it belongs.

"Uh … I was … uh … just saying bye to Toby."

"Oh. I must say, it surprised me to find him here." There's no judgment in her voice, but there *is* a hint of curiosity.

Turning around, I face her, and the fear I felt from the afternoon washes over me. There's something about being in Mom's presence that permits me to let go. Tears well in my eyes from nowhere, tipping over the lower lids to stream down my cheeks.

"Oh, Mom. Where do I even start?" She recognizes how upset I am and guides me into the kitchen, sitting me at the kitchen table. Mom makes us both herbal tea before joining me.

"What's upsetting you so much?"

I tell Mom about the afternoon, from the time I left my shop until now. I'm sure to include every detail, not leaving out a single thing. All the color drains from her face as she learns how close we came to losing Poppy today. If it hadn't been for Toby's quick thinking and action ... I dread to think. Poppy was at a definite disadvantage. If Toby had been further away from her, or the timing had been different, then ...

"I need to be with my baby. I'll see you in the morning. Okay?" She only nods at me. Still shell-shocked by the events of the afternoon. I ensure I lock the front door, then make my way upstairs.

I get changed into my pajamas, going through my nighttime routine, before climbing into Poppy's bed with her. She immediately rolls over, snuggling into me, as though she senses I need her close. I breathe in her little girl scent of strawberries, feeling the life inside of her wrapped in my arms and the tension finally releases from my body. Lying with Poppy safe in my embrace, I permit myself to think about tonight. Having dinner, then watching a movie with Toby felt almost ... like being a family. It felt right having him here. Poppy's clearly in love with him, which Toby obviously reciprocates easily.

Maybe I could let him in.

Then, I remind myself of his career and his fame, and I can't see a way it could possibly work. I *know* he has women throwing themselves at him every which way he turns—I've seen it happen when I've watched him on television or followed him on social media.

Why on earth would he be interested in a single mother who could never really be part of all that?

But that kiss—it was incredibly intense—I could feel his blatant need for me. He asked me to give him a chance the day I apologized.

Should I?

Could I?

I look down at my sleeping daughter. She's already in love with him and I can see he feels the same way.

What if it doesn't work out?

She'd be devastated if she loses him from her life. If things don't work out between us, would he still be there for Poppy?

THIRTY-TWO

-toby-

IT'S TIME TO PUSH FORWARD WITH CASS. SHE'S NOT GOING TO come to me, and I know I want her and Poppy in my life from here on out. I know she's scared. From the little she's told me, I don't think she's had a man stick around in her life for one reason or another. I get the impression she's assuming things about me based on my career—that I'll be yet another man in her life who doesn't stick. She couldn't be more wrong, though. I just need the opportunity to show her.

Walking along the cracked sidewalk with the sun shining down, the closer I get to her shop, the more my heart rate increases. When I arrive out front, I breathe deeply several times to prepare myself to be rejected yet again, but I've decided I'm not giving up easily.

"Do you mind waiting out here?"

"Don't you want a witness to your crash and burn?" Shane laughs. It's great to hear him laugh, to see him lighten up, but I would prefer it wasn't at my expense. I already feel as though I'm stepping up to the gallows.

"Haha. Smart ass." I give him the bird over my shoulder.

Stepping inside Cass's small shop, the scent of hundreds of

blooms infiltrates my nose. I stand in place, giving myself a moment for my eyes to adjust to the light inside.

What greets me makes my fists clench and my jaw tighten. Jake has Cass pinned against the wall with his body. I clear my throat loudly, attempting to garner their attention since the bell over the door failed to do so. Then, moving closer to them, I round the counter as Jake looks over his shoulder. When he spots me, he smirks slyly, then turns back to Cass, nuzzling her neck.

"What the fuck is going on?" I snap, sharp as the crack of a whip. I hear Cass suck in a sharp breath.

"What's it look like to you, Emo Boy?" Jake responds without turning around. His body jolts as though he's being jostled. I get the impression Cass is trying to push him away, but I can't be sure. Everything she's ever said about him leads me to believe she's not interested in a relationship with him, but then why is he here?

"Jake, move," Cass firmly states, though he ignores her, pushing his body further into hers. She clearly doesn't want him touching her. I step forward. Grabbing the back of his collar, I put all of my strength into pulling him away from her. He barely budges, but it's enough to give Cass room, allowing her to raise her arms to push at his chest as I pull at his shirt. He takes half a step away from her, glaring between the two of us.

"You two still fucking?" he spits out.

Before I can respond to defend Cass's honor, she snarls, "It's none of your goddamn business, Jake. I've repeatedly told you to leave me alone."

I step forward, getting in his face, my jaw tense, my fists ready to brawl. "You heard the lady, asshole. She's not fucking interested in you. Leave her the fuck alone."

"And I fucking told her I ain't finished with her yet," he grinds out to Cass before turning to me. "This is between her and me. Stay out of it, Emo. It's none of ya fucking business."

I step up to him. He has a couple of inches on me and probably close to eighty pounds, but I don't give a shit. "It's my fucking business because she's with me." Cass's eyes widen at my statement. I hope she catches on to what I'm putting down and plays along. "Get your filthy fucking hands off my girl." My tone brooks no argument. The bell over the door alerts me to another person entering. Glancing over my shoulder, I see it's Shane. He must have been watching through the window. He remains close by the door, holding it open for Jake and making it clear it's time for him to leave. These days, he's an intimidating motherfucker. He could easily kill Jake with his bare hands.

Jake turns toward Cass, pointing his finger sharply in her direction. "I ain't finished with you, bitch. Have your fun with Emo Boy, but you'll be coming back to me."

He turns to step past me, striking my shoulder with the side of his body, but I stand my ground. If it had been last week, I would have keeled over like a pussy after a nudge like that against my bruised arm.

"Have my sloppy seconds while you can. She'll tire of you, then come back to me. She always does." He heads for the door, closing in on Shane. He says something in a low tone that I can't hear. Shane follows him out, closing the door behind him, and returns to his position out front.

I remain standing where I am, looking out of the front of the shop for a few moments, gathering my calm. Dropping my head, I turn toward Cass when a woman steps out of the office, seemingly oblivious to my presence.

"Has he gone?"

My head snaps up at her question. I'm fucking pissed she left Cass out here to deal with that cocksucker on her own.

Cass shakes her head and huffs out, "Yeah, he's gone." She

walks slowly toward me, as though she's unsure of my reaction to her. My eyes don't leave her as I hold out my hand. She doesn't hesitate to slide her smooth palm against mine, and I close my hand around hers, squeezing it in reassurance. She returns my gesture with a small smile, stepping closer to me. Then, using my hold on her, I pull her in, wrapping her in my arms.

"You okay?" I whisper.

Her eyes connect with mine, and I know what she's about to say is the truth. I see nothing but sincerity in her clear gray gaze. "Yeah, I'm okay. Thanks for stepping in." I nod, trying to rein in my anger and worry about what might have happened had I not been here. I came on the off-chance I could take her out to lunch, or at the very least set up a date for another time.

What would Jake have done if I hadn't stepped in?

Her employee obviously wasn't going to help her out. Glancing back at the woman who stepped out of Cass's office, I recognize Sam, one of her high school friends. My eyes drop and I notice a significant bump, which she instinctively covers with her hand when she sees me notice.

I lift my chin. "Hey, Sam. You okay?"

She seems surprised at my question but nods in answer. Cass goes to step away from me, so I drop my hands, feeling the loss immediately. Whenever I'm with her, I always want to touch her in some way. I look between the two women, wondering why Sam was in Cass's office.

"Sam works for me now," Cass answers my silent question. "She makes such a difference to my workday. I get home at a decent time now."

"I bet Poppy loves spending more time with you."

Cass's shoulders relax as she smiles. "She sure does."

"Does that mean you can spare an hour for lunch?"

Cass looks over her shoulder at Sam in question. "You

don't need to check in with me, Boss Lady. Off ya go." She smiles at Cass, wiggling her fingers in a shooing motion.

"Okay, let me get my purse." She slips past Sam into the office, emerging quickly with her purse slung over her shoulder. Placing my hand on the small of her back, I guide her toward the door. We both wave to Sam over our shoulders as we leave. Stepping out into the pleasant fall day, she acknowledges Shane standing outside her shop. "Hey, Shane."

"Hey, Cass." He looks between us. "You need me to deal with Jake for you?"

Cass's step stalls for a moment, her eyebrows slashing down over her eyes. She looks at me as if to ask, 'Is he serious?' then turns back to Shane. "Uh, I don't think that would be a good idea. I wouldn't want you to get into any trouble. He'll get tired of coming around." She looks down at the ground. "Eventually."

Now that gets my attention. "How often does he come around hassling you?"

"I dunno. It's random." She glances between Shane and me before rushing to add. "I haven't led him on. In fact, I always tell him I'm not interested in anything with him. I don't understand why he's started coming around. My situation's the same as it was when he rejected Poppy five years ago."

"Have you called the police about his visits?" I'm agitated thinking about him touching her. He has no right to put his hands on her.

"What can they do? It's random. I can't predict when he'll show up or what he'll do."

I huff out a breath as I flick my eyes to Shane. He knows exactly what I want to do. Without me having to ask him, he lets me know with a nod of his head that he's onto it. I feel somewhat better knowing Cassia will be safer once Shane gets a guy over here to watch her. I grasp her hand as we make our way to the local diner a few blocks away from the shop. We order a couple of subs while Shane sits away from us to give us privacy. After a few moments of silence, as we take our first bites of food, Cass is the first to speak.

"So, I'm with you, huh?" Her metallic eyes are sparkling, and she has a cheeky grin on her beautiful face.

I swallow my food. "It was the first thing that came to mind when he wouldn't back away from you. Sorry about that." I'm not sure if she's pissed at me for putting it out there.

She reaches across the table, places her hand on top of mine, and squeezes it. I peer up into her eyes. "Thanks for your help. It seems you're always stepping in to help me."

I brush off her comment with a shrug of my shoulder. We both take another bite of our subs. "How long has Jake been hassling you?"

She seems uncomfortable, looking everywhere but at me. "The reunion was the first time I'd seen Jake since Poppy was two. Then he was at the pub that night, and he's come into the shop three times now. It's almost like he forgot I existed until he saw me at the reunion."

"Does he always put his hands on you?" My pulse picks up speed in anticipation of an answer I'm not gonna like. Her eyes dart away from me, then back again as she chews on her bottom lip, tempting me to do the same. Dropping her eyes to the table, she nods imperceptibly. If I wasn't watching closely, I might have missed it, but I was watching her like a hawk. I have to draw on every ounce of my self-control to stay seated and not get up to punch the shit out of something. He's always been a fucking asshole, but to put his goddamn hands where they're not wanted ... that's something completely different. "I don't want his filthy fucking hands on you ever again."

Our eyes lock across the table, stormy gray to blue, as I do my best to convey how serious I am about the situation with Jake. She nods slightly, then drops her eyes to the table. Using my fingertips, I gently raise her face to mine. "It's not your fault he's such a dick, Cass."

"I know." She releases a long breath. "I don't understand why he's back in my space being so freaking demanding suddenly. He didn't want Poppy or me before. It's not like anything's changed." She shakes her head.

"Has he said he wants Poppy?"

"No, it's always about me. It's as though he's ignoring the reality of what ended us in the first place—Poppy."

It's not my business, but I have to know. "Would you go back to him if he wanted to be a proper family?"

She looks over my shoulder, at something out the window, then down to her lunch, biting her lip. Shaking her head in the negative, she says, "Nope."

"Are you sure?" It seemed to take her a while to answer my question, as though she weighed up the options.

"Absolutely positive." She folds her arms on top of the table, leaning forward, giving me the perfect glimpse down her T-shirt.

Hey, I'm a guy. If I get the chance to look, I'm gonna look.

"I'll tell you why if you want to know." I'm not gonna say no, so I nod for her to continue. "I don't love him. I have zero respect for him, and I don't even like him. I haven't for a long time, not even when we were together all those years ago."

I wasn't expecting her answer. "So, why did you stay with him? I remember in high school, you were always on and off. Why not just dump him for good?" She looks over my shoulder again before looking back at me. She's finding it hard to meet my eyes. I get the impression she doesn't want to share any more with me. "It's okay if you don't want to talk about it anymore," I say, giving her an out.

She reaches across the table, and I meet her halfway, twining our fingers together. "No, it's okay. I stayed with him because having a boyfriend made me feel special." She looks up at me. "Stupid, hey?"

"Not stupid. It's how you felt."

She shrugs. "Yeah, but it was pretty pathetic to keep going back to him when I didn't even really like him. My, uh … my dad left my mom when he found out she was pregnant with me. Apparently, he never wanted two children."

What the fuck is wrong with the guys in Cass's life?

"The only male in my life was my grampa, and he wasn't one to make a fuss about his grandchildren. I guess, thinking back, I was looking for the love of a man, even if it was all wrong for me. I kept going back because some part of me always felt I was unlovable, and … well, Jake, I guess … showed me some form of love, even if it wasn't all that great." She shrugs her shoulder, letting out a self-deprecating laugh. "It's all I thought I was worth back then. I know better now, though."

I grasp her other hand, entwining our fingers. "It makes sense you were looking for male attention when you had none growing up. Jake was super popular. I can imagine for a girl, his attention would have felt pretty special."

Her shoulders drop as she nods in agreement, as though she's relieved I understand. And I do. I do understand, even though I hate it. I wish things had been different for her, but they weren't. She was doing the best thing for herself. It's all well and good to look back in hindsight and think about what you could have done differently, but it's unrealistic to judge your choices back then with the knowledge you have now. All it does is create a sense of failure, which doesn't help anyone.

We both eat a few more bites of our subs, enjoying our lunch when Cass surprises me. "So, are we together now?"

I study her closely, not sure where she's going with her question. I feel I need to weigh my answer carefully. I chew my food slowly, using it as my excuse to calibrate my thoughts into a sentence that won't scare her off. "I would like us to be, but I know you have concerns. I'm pretty sure I know what they are, but maybe you could lay it all out for me so we can talk about them. Clear the air, so to speak."

She nods thoughtfully. "Okay. First, I want to say that I *do* really like you, Toby. A lot." Well, that's a fantastic start. "I *know* my view of men is tainted by my experiences, and I apologize because I put you in the same category as the others. Which was wrong of me to do."

I nod, smiling. "Thank you for recognizing I'm not like the other men in your life. I've had a fantastic role model of what a husband and father should be. I know I won't be perfect, that I'll make mistakes, but I want to be in a relationship with you and with Poppy for as long as things work for everybody." Her posture changes. I can almost see her walls being constructed back into place—I've said something wrong. I run the last sentences back but can't work out my mistake. "Talk to me, Cass. I said something wrong, but I'm not sure what."

She shakes her head again, looking everywhere but at me. Her voice is low, almost a whisper, when she asks, "Does that mean, when things get a little rough or difficult, you'll leave?"

It's like I've been physically slapped, as my head snaps back in response. "No. I didn't mean that. I *know* relationships aren't all smooth sailing, that we have to be prepared to put in the work. Great relationships don't just happen. Both parties have to commit to it and work hard to make it a success. I *know* there will be not-so-fun times as well as great times, but I'm more than happy to be there for *all* of it. I meant that if we find we're not compatible, or you decide you don't want to be with me anymore."

"I'm sor—" I cut her off.

"Please don't keep apologizing. I get it. I do. You've only had guys who flake out on you when things aren't going the way they want. It was a fair question, but that's the last time you put me in the same box as them. I'm not them. I refuse to keep being punished for their mistakes. Okay?"

"Okay. I'm sor—" I shake my head with a smile, cutting off her apology.

"Now, tell me some of your other worries where we're concerned."

"Okay, so don't laugh at this, okay?" I nod. "Promise?" I signal, crossing my heart. She draws a deep breath, then, looking over my shoulder, she starts. "A while ago, Poppy asked me if she could ask you to be her daddy." My surprise must be written all over my face because she rushes on. "Of course, I told her she couldn't go around asking anyone to be her daddy. Plus, it was before I knew you were her guitar teacher. Although Mom said once I met you, I might want you to be Poppy's daddy, too." She's rambling now, which is fucking amusing as hell. "Anyway, I'm telling you this because I'm worried if we date, Poppy will get her hopes up, and if, for one reason or another, this doesn't work out, she'll be heartbroken. I also don't want her to lose having you in her life. She's grown to love you so much."

I reach across the table, grasping Cass's hand I squeeze it tight before entwining our fingers together again. "That won't happen, Cass. No matter what happens between us, I'll continue to teach Poppy guitar until she doesn't need me anymore. Okay?" She nods. "What if we dated for a while without telling her? Test the waters; see how we think things will go for us."

Her lips spread wide, filling my soul. "That sounds perfect. Only if it's okay with you?"

"I don't want to be your dirty secret, though, so keeping it on the down-low for Poppy's sake won't be long term ."

She nods in agreement. "I wouldn't want to keep it a secret for long. Just until we're sure."

"Okay. Anything else?" It surely can't be that easy.

She bites her bottom lip. "I *am* concerned about your career—the travel, the fans, touring, your celebrity lifestyle. I'm not sure where we can fit in with all of that. It makes me nervous, to be honest."

A valid concern.

"First, I keep mostly to myself when I'm home. I don't live a rock 'n' roll lifestyle—I'm pretty dull. I spend every Sunday afternoon and evening with my family at my parents' home, while my Friday afternoons are taken with a certain someone's guitar lesson. Other than that, I'm a homebody. It's too much hassle going out in public if I don't need to. Occasionally, I have to do publicity stuff, but that's always pre-planned. When I'm on tour, I'm there to work. It's my job as well as who I am as a person, which is my brand. I'm not prepared to damage either of those things by behaving in a less than appropriate way. I'm not sure what you think happens, but it's not a non-stop party. I don't hook up, get drunk, or do drugs." I brush my hand through my hair. "I hope that puts your mind at ease somewhat. I guess you'll have to trust me and see for yourself." I *have* been thinking about a future as a family man. I know things will have to change, but I don't want to go in too hard and fast with Cass today. I think I've been clear about who I am as a person.

"I actually do believe you."

"Good, now come here." I pull her forward by her hand so I can take the kiss I've been dying for. Licking my tongue across her lips, she opens willingly, inviting me into her mouth. Our tongues slide and tangle, reacquainting with each other.

Even though we were over before we started, I missed her taste, her touch, her scent … I missed … *her*.

We pull away from each other slowly, as if it's the most painful thing to do, then both of us break out in matching grins. I lean forward, stealing another chaste kiss. "Come on. You need to get back to work."

We walk out of the diner hand in hand, and I'm feeling on top of the world. Shane follows close behind. I know he'll give me shit about this later, but at the moment, I don't care. Once we arrive at her shop, I open the door for her to walk inside, knowing I have the goofiest smile on my face because she's agreed to be my girl.

Using my hold on her hand, I pull her back around to face me so I can give her a proper goodbye. With her hand still in mine, I wrap my arms around her, then lean down to take her lips until we're interrupted by someone clearing their throat. Pulling back, I press my forehead to hers as we share a smile. Moving to the side, we make room to allow the customer to enter the store. Cass breaks away, going into florist mode, so I watch her in her element until she's finished and the customer leaves.

"Are you gonna watch me like a creeper all day?" She laughs lightly.

"Maybe. I have nothing else to do." I smirk. "Seriously though, when can I see you again?"

THIRTY-THREE

-cassia-

I CAN'T BELIEVE WE'RE GOING TO SEE WHERE THIS THING between us can go. When I woke up this morning, never in my wildest dreams did I think my day would turn out like this.

"Uh, let me check my bookings." I gesture for him to follow me into the office with a tilt of my head. "Hi, Sam, you can go to lunch now if you like. I have this covered."

"Thanks, Cass. I'm starving. It seems I'm always hungry, even though I snack in between meals." Sam laughs as she stands up, noticing Toby behind me. "Hey, Toby." She turns back to me and winks. I'm sure she'll ask for the lowdown later.

Looking at my calendar, I remember I only have one event this weekend, on Sunday. "Okay, I have a sixtieth birthday on Sunday, which leaves my Friday night free," I say with a hopeful lilt to my voice. "I'll have to check with Mom if she can look after Poppy for me, though. I'm sure it won't be a problem."

He jams his hands in the front pockets of his jeans, which hug his thighs like it's their job. "You wanna go out or come to my place?"

My preference will always be his place. I don't want to

share him with anybody else. "Your place?" It comes out more like a question than an answer.

"Perfect. I'll cook dinner for us. Bring your suit; we can enjoy the hot tub after dinner." Toby pulls me in close to his body, nuzzling the side of my neck before whispering, "Or don't." He nips my earlobe, then pulls back with a cheeky grin on his gorgeous face. He kisses my lips briefly before pulling away and smacking my behind on his way out of the office. Winking over his shoulder, he asks, "Seven, okay?"

"Seven's great. See you then, handsome." He stops at that, turning to face me.

"You think I'm handsome?" Duh, every red-blooded woman in America thinks he's handsome.

"Of course I do. Along with every other woman on the planet." I roll my eyes.

"I don't care about every other woman, only you. Your opinion is the only one that counts." He turns, waving over his shoulder. I hear the door open and close. He's gone. I stand stunned for a moment, then a smile breaks over my face. I jump up and down on the spot like a child, squealing in delight. I'm so freaking happy. I'd better check with Mom that she can babysit Poppy for me before I get too excited.

ME

Hey, are you free Friday night?

I wait for her response with bated breath.

MOM

Hey Love, I don't have any plans. Why?

ME

I have a date

I'm squealing internally as I type. The decision was to keep it a secret from Poppy for now, but I figure it's okay to tell Mom.

MOM

May I ask who with?

ME

You may

MOM

Well ....

ME

Toby

MOM

Oh, I'm so happy you gave that boy a chance. He's such a sweetheart

ME

I know

But don't tell Poppy. We're gonna see how it goes for a while first

I don't want to get her hopes up

Okay?

MOM

Absolutely. I think that's a wise decision

Oh, I'm so excited for you

ME

Thanks Mom

Me too

I message Toby to let him know that Friday night is sorted from my end. I don't even try to play it cool in my texts, making sure he knows that I'm really looking forward to our date.

Friday can't come soon enough in my book.

THIRTY-FOUR

-cassia-

STANDING ON TOBY'S DOORSTEP, I'M EQUAL PARTS NERVOUS and excited. I think the butterflies in my stomach have multiplied on the way over. As I raise my hand to knock on his door, I notice it shaking in anticipation of seeing him again. The door swings open before my knuckles make contact with the surface, revealing a relaxed-looking Toby wearing ripped jeans with a basic long-sleeve T-shirt with a heartbeat line running across his chest; part of the heartbeat makes a guitar. It's very fitting for him; even in high school, he was always caught up in his guitar or notebook during breaks. He has nothing on his feet and his hair's loose around his chiseled face, complete with a trimmed beard. I like this look on him—really like it. *A lot!*

A smile breaks out as he assesses me. I'm wearing something similar to him except I have a watercolor poppy on my T-shirt. I tug my tote higher on my shoulder. "Hey."

He turns to the side, gesturing for me to come in, stopping me as I step in line with him. "Hey." He nuzzles his nose into my neck before placing a gentle kiss there. "You always smell so damn delicious."

I giggle in response as his beard tickles me as much as his

words do. Closing the door, he slides my tote off my arm, placing it on the sideboard in the living room, where we pretty much mauled each other the night of the reunion. I flush with the memory of being pressed up against the window.

"I'm trying to be a gentleman and not maul you the instant you step inside my home, but you make it—" He looks down at his crotch, then back up to me. "—fucking hard." God, his words don't help to cool my overheated body.

The guy's incredibly sexy without any effort.

He smirks at me before taking my bottom lip between his teeth, nipping it gently before soothing it with his tongue. I open with a sigh, inviting his tongue inside as Toby cups my head with both hands, guiding my head where he wants it, deepening the kiss. He steals all the breath from my lungs, leaving me limp, relying on his strength to keep me upright.

"We should definitely stop before I get carried away."

My whole body pouts in disappointment as he pulls away from me.

I'm not ready to stop kissing him, so I grasp onto his T-shirt to pull him back into me to continue the kiss. He guides me until my back is against the window I was just reminiscing about, the coolness of the glass seeping through my clothes to my heated skin. I slip my hands underneath his T-shirt until I feel his warm, smooth skin beneath my touch. His muscles shift and tense beneath my hands as I glide them up to pull him tighter against me. It doesn't seem to matter how close our bodies are—it's still not close enough for me.

He pulls away, leaving us both panting hard, working to catch our breath. Toby rests his forehead against mine as a slow smile spreads across his chiseled face, producing one of my own. "I made dinner—"

"Will it keep for a while? I don't think I can wait any longer to have you inside me." I plead. Remembering the last time—the way he made me wait when I got carried away—I bite my bottom lip to shut myself up. He likes to be in charge of the sexy times, which means I need to be patient, trusting he'll look after me; but it's hard to hold back with him.

He must read the desperation in my eyes because he steps away. "Take off your jeans and panties." He points to the couch. "Bend over the couch. Wait for me. I'll be with you in a minute." His tone is sure, demanding—it says, 'do as I say'.

Why would I argue anyway?

I'm about to get exactly what I want. I do as I'm told and wait, feeling as awkward as hell. My ass is bigger than the average girl's , making me self-conscious about it. I use longer shirts to cover as much as possible. I'm caught up in my head, worrying about the size of my behind so I startle when Toby glides his hand up from the inside of my ankle toward where I want him most. Without missing a beat, his tongue follows the pathway, stopping at the top of my inner thigh, where I hear him take in a deep breath.

"You smell delicious, as usual. I can't wait until I finally get a taste." He reaches for my other ankle, and he repeats the process, following with his tongue. Goosebumps break out in his wake.

He spreads my legs further apart, wedging himself into position. It's then I feel the first swipe of his tongue. It's enough to have me tensing my thigh muscles in anticipation of the pleasure about to be bestowed on me. I know from experience Toby can make my body sing. His tongue swipes through my lips, lapping up the moisture I'm producing to prepare for his onslaught.

My body's on fire as he licks, nips, and plays me like he does the strings on his guitar. It doesn't take all that long, and I'm almost flying over the edge toward my first orgasm. He replaces his tongue with his fingers, causing me to lose all sense of cohesive thought. His fingers are then replaced with his dick as he impales me in one clean thrust. Pushing me down further into the cushions with one hand, he tightens his other on my hip and slams into me repeatedly.

"You're dripping all over my cock. I think you like it a little rough," he grunts between thrusts.

I nod my head, barely able to release the moan from inside me as he slams hard and fast into me over and over again. My hip bones repeatedly connect on the timber frame of his couch as he pushes me down as far as possible. I'm almost upside down, but I'm not about to complain when it feels so amazing.

"You make me lose fucking control. I just wanna keep slamming my cock into your body all night." My walls spasm around his shaft. I'm close to losing control. "Yeah, you like my dirty mouth *and* my hard cock."

"Mmmmmm—"

He wraps one hand around the front of my throat, tilting my head back and to the side. He slams his mouth onto mine as he continues to thrust in and out of me at a steady pace, keeping my orgasm balanced on the brink. I pull away from his mouth slightly so I can see him. The blackness of his pupils almost completely swallows the gorgeous cobalt color of his irises. He looks like a wild man, barely holding onto his humanity.

"Please, Toby." My whispered plea is enough to push him into action. He drags my T-shirt off me then scoops my breasts out of their fabric cage, pinching each nipple, causing me to cry out.

"I'll get you there in good time, Cass. Trust me." He bites my neck before soothing the tender skin with his tongue. He uses one hand on my boob to hold me in place as his other hand finds my clit, pinching it hard before rubbing it in smooth, firm circles. That's enough to send me flying over the edge into oblivion. My vision blurs around the edges, and I'm thankful for the couch holding me up at this point because I've lost all ability to hold myself. His thrusts continue through my orgasm, and it feels like my internal walls are never gonna stop spasming. My legs shake as Toby still thrusts in and out of my pussy. Both of his hands come up to play with my swollen, achy breasts. "Let's get another one. You ready, Gorgeous?"

"I ... I'm not sure I—"

He cuts me off. "Yes, you can. Hold on."

I thought he was pounding into me before, but he really lets loose now, skin slapping against skin, his balls slapping against the inside of my thighs, his fingers tight around my nipples ... and I'm falling again.

Into oblivion.

My body convulses from the tip of my head to the tips of my toes and everywhere in between. It's never been like this before for me, and I'm overwhelmed by how big my emotions are.

It's scary.

Toby follows me over the edge into oblivion, pushing his dick as deep as possible before pausing, his dick pulsing as he fills the condom. His hands smooth up and down my spine, followed by delicate kisses spanning from one shoulder to the other. I love the sensation of his raspy beard trailing over my skin, followed by the silkiness of his hair.

"Fuck, that was fantastic. I'm sorry. I don't seem to be able to control myself with you. I meant to at least feed you dinner first. I was gonna try to be a gentleman." He sounds annoyed with himself. I can't help but giggle at the hopelessness in his voice. "Stop fucking laughing. You're not helping my dick to calm down." He finishes with a groan, sliding slowly in and out of me. I can't believe he's still semi-hard after what we just did. As he slides in and out of my pussy, I can feel him getting harder with each stroke.

Twisting around so I can see him. "You can't be serious."

He leverages himself back up to a standing position, grasping my hips.

"Deadly."

Thrust.

"This is what you do to me."

Thrust.

"Every time you're near me."

Thrust.

"Ever since I was sixteen."

Thrust.

"Why do you think I always had to make a quick getaway?" He smirks, thrusting again, eliciting a moan from me. I'm going to be sore if we go again, but I don't have it in me to stop him. I want this; I want him again.

What the hell is wrong with me?

His hips are slower, more methodical this time around—almost leisurely. He slides almost all the way out before sliding back in slowly, playing my clit with his masterful fingers. He's not in a hurry and I'm enjoying the slow slide of his cock in and out of my pussy, relishing in the sensation of this slow build.

"Oh, yeah, fuck. Tighten those pussy walls around my cock." God, his words undo me, then I break. This time's different—slower, more languid as he breaks along with me—both of us falling over into the abyss together.

We stay connected, Toby lying over my back as I'm still draped over the couch. Sweating, heaving bodies feeling satiated from multiple orgasms within minutes of one another. I close my eyes, allowing myself this moment to just *feel*.

I come back to reality when Toby presses gentle kisses to the side of my neck before peeling himself from me and slowly, carefully sliding his softening dick out of me. We both moan at the feeling of disconnection from the other. I'm worried I won't be able to stand. My legs turned to jelly.

Toby carefully removes my bra before he turns me over to lift me bridal style, carrying me through his home. He disposes of the condom and then steps down into his hot tub. The warm water is heavenly against my jelly muscles and my well-used vagina. I sigh in delight at being wrapped in Toby's arms in the warm water as he places delicate kisses over my face—my heart pounding in happiness.

We sit, wrapped in each other's arms for silent minutes, enjoying the intimate connection. Toby breaks the silence first. "Cass?"

"Mmmm?" I don't want to break the spell surrounding us as the warm air collides with cool, forming a blanket of mist, blocking out the real world.

"I really want this to work between us." The vulnerability in his voice swiftly drags me out of my stupor, so I lean back to study his face. He reminds me of the boy from high school.

Where did my confident lover go?

Looking into his eyes, I need to put his mind at ease. "You remember what I told you at the reunion?" He looks puzzled. I can tell he's working through our many conversations from that night. "I told you I had a crush on you, too. It wasn't all one-sided then, and it's not all one-sided now. I really want this to work, too."

He leans forward swiftly, slamming his lips against mine, but as soon as they make contact, he gentles himself. His lips pressing against mine, exploring softly—quite the contrast to how he just took me bent over his couch. This man is a dichotomy of different facets, and I'm looking forward to learning about each and every part of him.

The kiss slowly deepens. It's a languid meeting of lips, tongues, teeth. He's kissing me as though he's learning every part of my mouth. I adjust myself so I'm straddling his legs, my most private place cradling his hard shaft. His hands cup my ass to slide me back and forth, ensuring he rubs my clit on the way forward.

Pulling away from my mouth, he grunts, "I love your ass. It's like a juicy peach I just wanna bite."

His words are enough to have my pussy convulsing and me coming on a loud, wanton moan. I've never been as vocal during sex—Toby brings out a different side to me, one I like. It turns me on that he loves my ass so much because I've always been self-conscious about it. I think it's out of proportion with the rest of my body. Jake added to my self-consciousness about it when he would often comment about its size and how much it would jiggle whenever I walked or ran.

"I love watching my dick disappear into your pussy between your delicious cheeks. So fucking hot, Cass. Everything about you is so fucking hot—you always make me so fucking hard."

I lean in, quickly pressing my lips to his in appreciation for his words. He makes me feel beautiful exactly as I am; no need to be fancy or try to be something I'm not. I want to show him how much I love his words, so I move off his lap. "Can you sit up on the side of the tub?" He looks confused. "Please."

That seems to do the trick, and he hoists himself up the side of the tub. His nipples peak instantly from the cold air, and I'm second-guessing whether this is such a good idea. It's a little chilly out of the water, but I go ahead. I swim forward, pressing myself between his thighs, using one hand to massage his balls, which have contracted up tight against his body to stay warm. I lean closer, licking his gorgeous shaft from the base to the tip, followed by a squeeze of my hand at the base.

Toby lets out a low groan, then focuses his cobalt stare on me. I make sure to maintain direct, solid eye contact with him as I take his dick to the back of my throat. My gag reflex kicks in for a moment, so I pull back slightly, but I make up for it with an intense suction action as I moan around him. He's no longer a passive participant as he grabs hold of my hair, dragging my mouth up and down his shaft. Even though he's taken over, he's careful with me, not pushing too much, just enough to make me even more desperate to feel his cock inside my mouth. He thrusts forward, so I moan as I swallow deeply around him.

"Fuck, Cass. Your mouth feels so fucking good. Swallow again."

I do as he demands, and he grants me another long groan as he attempts to pull my head away. I try to shake my head to maintain my position, showing I want to take him all the way. His jaw tenses as his brows furrow in intense concentration. I moan around his shaft again and swallow hard. I feel the pulsing of his cock, followed by warm ribbons of cum shooting down my throat. I can't keep up with swallowing it all down. I'm certain I must be a mess, with excess cum and saliva dripping down from my mouth.

He looks down at me with a crooked smile on his handsome face. The glazed look in his eyes almost undoes me. He's looking at me with immense gratitude, as well as care and affection, as he slides back into the tub, pulling me in for an open-mouthed kiss. It's so sexy that he can taste his cum on my tongue. He's kissing me right down to my soul, and I never want him to stop.

Pulling back slightly from each other, we rest our foreheads together as we share a secret smile. Unfortunately, my emotions are getting the better of me. I'm beginning to confuse the intense feelings of lust I have for Toby with love.

It can't possibly be love this early on.

Closing my eyes, I work to center myself by blocking out his potent stare. When I open them again, I'm calmer inside; more in control of my emotions. I remind myself it's all the hormones released by awesome sex, running rampant, which have me feeling so discombobulated.

THIRTY-FIVE

-cassia-

"C'MON. LET'S GET DRY. I NEED TO FEED YOU." TOBY HELPS ME
out of the tub. Together, we race inside, leaving puddles of
water all over his hardwood floors as we make our way upstairs
to his bathroom. Goosebumps cover my skin and his as we
make a run for it. I never got to appreciate his bathroom the
last time I was here. I stop dead in my tracks in the doorway
when I get a look inside. It reminds me of a fancy day spa with
a giant shower head over the open shower area, but it's not the
only shower head. There are ... hang on, let me count. Six. Six
shower heads are coming out of the walls surrounding the
space. It's going to feel amazing.

Toby steps in, turning on the faucet to get the water up to
temperature, before inviting me to join him. Steam fills the
area as I step into the decadent space. I close my eyes, raising
my face to the water surrounding me, soaking up the luxury
when Toby's slippery hands glide up my sides, from my hips up
to cup my breasts. He's soaped up, ready to clean the hot tub
chemicals from us.

Silently, reverently, he washes every single inch of my body,
paying special attention to his favorite part—my ass. I return

the favor, ensuring his gorgeous cock gets extra special attention. As we're drying off, I remember all of my clothes are
downstairs and prepare to head down to grab them when Toby
comes up behind me, slipping one of his sweaters over me. The
arms are way too long while the body comes to mid-thigh, but
it's cozy and warm. An additional bonus is the fabric smells just
like him, which I inhale like a druggy trying to get my next fix.
He passes me a pair of his woolen socks, and I put them on
before we both head downstairs together, holding hands.

He sits me on the kitchen counter, exactly where I sat when
he carefully removed the adhesive residue from my bra. I slide
my fingers across the smooth surface with a smile as I
remember that night as Toby finalizes our dinner. "Can I help
with anything?"

He turns around, smiling. "Nope. You sit and keep looking
gorgeous in my clothes."

It's rare I get spoiled like this, so I happily oblige. "Okay.
Let me know if you change your mind. I'm happy to help."

He presses a kiss to my forehead, then keeps going about
his business. "Whatever you've made for dinner smells amazing. I can't wait to taste it." My stomach grumbles—loudly.
Toby laughs, and I love the deep, rich sound of it; the crinkles
around his eyes, the lightness on his face.

The table's already set, and he places two bowls filled with
the most delicious-smelling dish. I begin to wiggle my way off
the counter when he comes over to carry me across to the
table, sitting me in the chair. "I can walk, you know." I laugh.

"I know. But I want to spoil you. I want to ruin you for any
other man. That way, you won't want to leave me." He's saying
the words as a joke, but I sense it's a sensitive topic for him.

"Trust me, I love having you spoil me, and I'm not thinking
of any other men while I'm here with you." I lean forward to
kiss him gently on the lips. I take the first bite of my creamy
pasta with shrimp, sighing in appreciation of the delicious

flavors. "Oh my god, this is freaking delicious. Did you make this from scratch?"

"Yeah, I like to cook when I have the chance. Of course, I don't bother when it's only me, but this is one of my favorites."

"The avocado's so creamy ... and with the shrimp and feta —it's superb. Thank you so much."

"You're welcome." He smiles at me, and we eat in silence for a few moments, enjoying the delicious meal.

"Where's Poppy tonight?"

I swallow the food in my mouth. "Mom and Violet are treating Poppy and Jasmine to a fairytale princess movie night. A movie marathon at home with all the trimmings. The girls were incredibly excited."

Toby smiles, showing his affection for my daughter. "I'll bet they are." He takes another bite of food, chewing thoughtfully. "What was she like as a baby?"

Now, this is a topic I could talk about all night. "She was such a beautiful baby." He nods. "So happy and easy. She slept right through the night from about six weeks, which was wonderful for me once I got past my anxiousness that she was okay." He takes another bite of food, chewing and swallowing, as I do. "All of her milestones were met at all the right times, and she loved trying new foods as she grew. Her baby years were such a great time. I learned a lot about myself in those early years, too."

"Yeah, like what?"

"I thought I loved my mom, but my love for Poppy surpassed that by miles. I had no idea I could love another person as much as I love her. I learned I'm pretty resilient when I get shocking news. First, when I found out I was pregnant with Poppy. Then learning I would have to raise her on my own. And finally, when I learned my baby was deaf." I suck in a breath. The memory of that event seared into my very soul.

"When did you learn Poppy was deaf?"

"She was born profoundly deaf." Toby reaches across the table, taking my hand in his, giving it a gentle squeeze in silent support. "All babies are given a variety of tests when they're born. To test hearing, they use a probe in the outer ear to send a signal, then wait for an echo to bounce back."

"I never knew that."

I nod. "Yeah. When they tested Poppy, there was no echo. I noticed she didn't seem to respond to noises, loud or soft, at home, so I already suspected that her hearing wasn't the same as mine. When she was three months old, I took her in for more tests, which identified that she was profoundly deaf. She was born with no hearing nerves, so she's never heard a single sound." I take a fortifying breath. "I was hoping, you know—" Toby nods, showing his understanding. "I was hoping the first test was a mistake, but that second test left no doubt. She *was* born deaf."

"It must have been a tough time."

I nod, thinking back to that time, running through the emotions I felt. "It was the toughest. I drove home, handed Poppy to Mom, then went upstairs to my room and sobbed. I cried for her and I cried for me. I didn't want her to have to face the difficulties I imagined she would face throughout her life." Toby reaches across, using his thumb to catch a tear that's escaped. "That night, I watched my baby sleep, and I grieved for everything she would never experience. She would never hear my voice; hear me say the words 'I love you.' Hear the rain falling on the roof, laughter, music."

"I can't imagine being in your shoes, Cassia. You realize, though, you've done an amazing job with her. I don't get the impression she feels she's disadvantaged in any way."

"No. Once I got over my pity party because that's exactly what it was, I put on my mom hat and followed up with the various organizations that work with people like us. I didn't know that ninety percent of Deaf and Hard of Hearing babies are born to hearing parents. I ignorantly thought deaf babies were born to deaf parents. I'd never had anything to do with a Deaf or Hard of Hearing person. I decided I had to learn her world since she couldn't learn mine. I started learning to sign immediately, then began teaching Poppy along the way. She signed her first word when she was only nine months old." A smile spreads across my face. "I was so freaking proud of her. I was running around the house like a complete idiot. I was thrilled because it was the first time I really felt like we could do this. That we could communicate."

"I would've loved to have seen that. It would have been such an amazing feeling after the worry you must have had for her."

"It was such a relief. She blossomed from that point—nothing held her back. I engaged a tutor to come to our home to teach the three of us how to sign. I'm so proud every single day I get to call myself her mom. She's the greatest joy in my life."

"She's an amazing kid. You have every right to feel as proud as you do." He looks away from me, then back again. "She's incredibly easy to fall in love with, Cass."

I can only nod in agreement because Poppy brings out the best in the people around her.

"How about you? How did you learn how to sign?"

"Ah, well. I met Xanthe." He tells me how they met and the friendship that grew between them. "I decided I wanted to learn how to sign somewhat proficiently with my new friends. I also engaged a tutor to teach me. I'm still learning. Sometimes I mess up, but I love it."

It's almost like Toby was preparing himself to become part of our lives. It's mind-boggling.

THIRTY-SIX

-toby-

My admiration for Cass skyrocketed the night she opened up over dinner at my place. It must be difficult for a parent to learn that your child isn't like you. To pick yourself up and work through what needs to be done, putting your child's needs and happiness first is admirable. She says that's the job of a parent, but not all parents put their kids first. Since being friends with Xanthe, I've witnessed firsthand how some parents won't accept their child communicates differently. They insist their child learns to speak and read lips, denying them the opportunity to learn sign language. It's heartbreaking for the child involved.

This last month, sneaking around with Cass any chance we can get has been amazing, but I'm tired of keeping it a secret. It's Cassia's birthday in two days, and I want to celebrate with her and her family. But I can't do that if Poppy doesn't know we're together. I'm not sure what's keeping Cass from telling her we're together because, in my opinion, we're perfect. I want a future with Cass and Poppy. When it's only the two of us, I feel like we're on the same page, but then she keeps putting off telling her daughter and I'm left wondering if I'm in this on my own.

I need to talk to someone who isn't Cass. Pulling out my phone, I press my sister's contact. She answers on the third ring.

"Hey, brother. How are things?"

"Hey, Squirt." I love teasing her about her size.

"Stop it! I owe you a pinch to the side for that." She's laughing, so I know she's not pissed at me.

"You got a minute to talk?"

She senses the seriousness in my tone, responding in kind. "Sure, Tobes. What's up?"

I tell her all about seeing Cass at the reunion and that we spent some time together that night—I don't tell her we hooked up. That part's too personal to share.

"Oooooo, I knew something was going on between you two after the concert. There was this hot, heavy vibe going on between the two of you."

"Uh, you're not listening, Sis. We weren't together then. I had no idea Poppy was her daughter. She didn't know I was Poppy's guitar teacher."

"Awwww, that's such a great story. It's like the universe was pushing you together."

Huh, I never thought about it like that. Maybe ...

"Anyway, I finally convinced her to give us a chance. She agreed on the proviso that we keep it a secret from Poppy until we're more certain about our relationship."

Kate whispers, "I think I know where this is going."

"Yeah, well, I have no doubts, Sis. We haven't said those three words yet, because I don't want to scare her off, but I can't imagine my future without her in it."

"Oh, Toby. That's incredibly sweet. I'm so happy for you."

I pace, the agitation in my body forcing me to move. "Yeah, well, she keeps putting off telling Poppy. It's Cass's birthday on

Friday, so I want to be there to celebrate with her family, but I can't if Poppy doesn't know about us."

"I see."

"I don't know what to do, Kate. I'm tired of seeing her in secret. I would like to do some stuff together as a family, you know. Plus, it's getting harder to keep it under wraps when I see Poppy every week for her lesson."

"Have you talked to Cassia about how you're feeling? What you want? How you see your future together?"

"That's the thing. She's had such shitty luck with the men in her life. She's scared I'm going to be the same."

Kate huffs out a breath. "You remember the trouble I gave Oliver?"

"Yeah. How could I forget? You made him work incredibly hard to be in your life. He has the patience of a saint." I chuckle darkly.

"You, my brother, are going to need to have the patience of a saint. You need to earn her trust. A month isn't all that long in the scheme of things."

"But I want to be part of her birthday celebrations with her family." Again, I can hear myself pouting.

"What's missing out on this birthday, if it means having the rest of her birthday celebrations? Think of the big picture. You need to give her time, Toby. It sounds like she doesn't trust easily—it's something you're going to have to earn. It may take a long time."

She's not telling me what I want to hear, which is frustrating as hell. *Time.* It feels like my enemy at the moment, but I guess I don't have a choice.

"Thanks, Squirt." The misery in my voice is heavy.

"I'm sorry. It probably wasn't what you wanted to hear."

"Nah, that's okay. It's why I called you. I knew you'd give it to me straight."

"If she's anything like me, she's fighting hard against her

demons to let you inside. But she won't be able to stop herself from falling in love with you, because you're the best person I know."

"Thanks, Kate. Love you."

"Love you, too, Toby." She pauses. "Talk later?"

"Of course. Say hi to Oliver for me. Later, Squirt." I quickly end the call, laughing to myself, so she can't retaliate. I'm a shit of a brother sometimes.

I guess she's right. Cass needs time; she needs to see I'm hanging around. She still doesn't trust me one hundred percent. I know this because even though she's on birth control, she won't let me stop using condoms. I almost forgot once, and she went ballistic.

I'M WOKEN BY POPPY JUMPING ON ME WITH THE BIGGEST GRIN. She's already dressed for school, so she must have woken up really early, which is unusual for her. She usually tries to get up as late as she possibly can on a school day. My baby's not a morning person at all. Once my eyes are open, she signs the happy birthday song for me. She's done this since she first learned how to sign the song. I love waking up on my birthday to her wishing me happy birthday this way. We giggle as I pull her in close for a special snuggle, inhaling her strawberry scent.

After snuggles, I dress for work, then Poppy and I make our way downstairs, where I'm greeted with waffles for breakfast—my favorite. Mom makes the best waffles: crunchy on the outside, light and fluffy on the inside. She's been making it for my birthday ever since I was a little girl.

"Awww, thanks, Mom. I'm so lucky to be still getting my favorite breakfast for my birthday."

Mom turns around to face me. Stepping close, she places her hand gently on my cheek. "Happy birthday, Baby Girl."

"Thanks, Mom. You know this day is as much about you as it is about me."

"Oh, don't be silly. I just happened to be there." We both laugh because that's her usual response. Like she was visiting the hospital that day and found me in the parking lot or something.

Violet's busy getting all the toppings organized while Jasmine places the silverware on the table. They both grab me on either side, making a sandwich out of me, and wishing me a happy birthday. It's such a great start to the day, but it would have been nice to wake up in Toby's arms.

I know he's getting antsy with me, wanting me to tell Poppy we're together. I'm unsure what's holding me back. I know he's perfect for me and he adores Poppy so much. He still has Shane driving her everywhere she needs to go to keep her safe. I'm scared he's too good to be true; that as soon as things get a little tough, he'll pack up and leave me. It's what I've seen happen throughout my life. It's difficult to change such deeply ingrained beliefs overnight.

We all sit down to enjoy our special breakfast, which is very decadent for a weekday morning. As we're busy eating the delicious waffles, Mom looks at me knowingly over Poppy's head as she asks, "Will you be seeing Toby today?"

I shake my head in the negative. He wanted to take me to dinner, but I had to turn him down because I always spend it with my family. I couldn't invite him along because, well ... how do I explain his presence to my daughter? It makes no sense for him to attend my birthday dinner. If I were brave enough to take the chance to be open about our relationship, she would know all about him, and I could spend my birthday with the man I've fallen in love with.

If only I were brave.

"Good morning, *Blooms and Balloons*. This is Cassia. How can I help you?" I answer the phone professionally.

"Hey, Cassia. It's me, Kate."

"Oh, hi, Kate. How are you?" I wonder if she's calling about Toby?

"I'm great, thanks. Happy birthday."

"Thank you." I guess Toby must have mentioned my birthday to her.

"Look, I know it's really short notice, but a friend of mine is getting married next weekend, and I was wondering if you could do some flowers for the wedding?" She sounds panicked.

"Sure. What did they have in mind?" I grab my notebook and pencil to record the information.

"Roman and Alice want something simple. What would you suggest?"

I offer her my thoughts, and she chooses blush pink and cream roses. A classic choice for a wedding, and the blooms will be easy to source at short notice.

"Sorry, I can't stop to chat. I'm on a break. The bell's about to ring."

"No problem. I'll chat with you later about the details."

"Thanks for all your help, Cass. I appreciate it at such short notice." Her relief is clear to hear, making me smile. That's what I'm here for. I love to make the planning of an event easier for the organizer.

"You're welcome. Have a great day. Bye." I jot down the notes, then add the additional blooms to my order.

I busy myself putting together an order for a baby shower tomorrow afternoon, a mix of flowers and balloons. It's a lot of fun. The customer has asked me to put blue powder inside the balloons as a surprise for her guests. She plans to reveal the sex of her baby, which I guess is a boy. Sam's taking a long lunch break because she has an appointment with her obstetrician today and Sally's unwell, so I'm here on my own.

The bell over the door tinkles as I'm putting the finishing touches on the order.

I jump in fright.

I find I'm jumpy every time the bell over the door sounds, ever since Jake started showing up at random times, thinking he can put his hands on me. I don't feel safe in my own damn shop, and it pisses me off. As I look up to greet the customer, I automatically grab my secateurs. Doing my best to keep my fear hidden, I welcome whoever it is with a smile. When I see who it is, my shoulders relax, my guard drops, and I put the secateurs down. My smile becomes genuine and my heart rate picks up for a completely different reason. Rushing around my bench to get to him, I leap into his arms before he's ready, almost knocking him on his fine ass.

"Toby! I'm so happy to see you." My day's perfect now. He's the one person I wanted to see but thought I wouldn't.

He laughs. "Woah, Gorgeous. That's some greeting." He's holding me the best he can, my feet dangling off the ground. Finally, I lean in to press my lips against his, claiming the kiss I want for my birthday. When I pull back to look at him, his eyes are sparkling with laughter.

His face is perfect when he smiles ...

Even when he doesn't smile.

He's just ... *sigh*.

"Happy birthday, Cassia," he whispers, leaning forward, taking my lips with his. This kiss is so much more than the kiss I took. He seems to reach down to my soul, owning every single piece of me on the way.

He pulls back way too soon for my liking, sliding me down his body so I can feel every inch—and I mean *every* inch—of him until my feet touch the floor. He doesn't let go until he's sure I'm steady. As I step back, I notice he's holding a gift in his hand. This explains why he couldn't hold me properly. He awkwardly thrusts it toward me.

"Uh, I bought you something for your birthday. I figured I couldn't get you flowers, since ..." He gestures around my shop. "I hope you like it."

To say I'm surprised he got me anything for my birthday is an understatement. The last time we spoke, he seemed pissed at me. I wasn't ready to tell Poppy about us, leaving him out of any birthday celebrations.

"Thank you so much. You didn't need to get me anything —" He steps forward to take the gift away from me with a smirk, but I tuck it in close to my body, protecting it from him. "But I'm glad you did. I love getting presents." I mean, what girl doesn't love to get presents on her birthday? Right?

He gestures with his chin. "Go on then. Open it."

I quickly place it on the bench, opening the card first. It has two mushrooms on the front with the words; *I have so mushroom in my heart for you.* I burst into laughter. I glance up to thank him, finding him standing with his hands in the pockets of his jeans, a gorgeous grin on his face. "It was too funny to pass up. I had to get it for you for your birthday."

"I love it. It's so damn cute." I prop it up on my bench and drag the gift closer. Carefully, I pull at the tape to open the paper so I can see what's inside. When I pull the paper away completely, I'm pretty sure my jaw drops to the ground. I glance up at Toby, then back at the box, then back to Toby again. "Oh, gosh, Toby. You shouldn't have. I can't accept such an expensive gift."

He steps around, lifting my chin with his fingers so I have to look at him. "You can and you will accept it. I wanted you to have it. You said yours was close to dying."

"Well, yeah, but I would have replaced it with a basic model, not a freaking *Kindle Oasis*." Then I realize how rude I've been. "Thank you so much. This ... it's gorgeous. Totally over the top ... but the best present I could have ever asked for."

"You're welcome, Gorgeous. There's a waterproof cover in there, too. I also opened an account for you, so you can buy any books you like. On me."

"Oh, my gosh. Are you serious?" He nods in confirmation. "Thank you so much." He catches me under my ass as I leap into his arms, covering his face in kisses. Shane pops his head through the door, wishing me a happy birthday through his laughter at my juvenile display.

"Can I take you out to lunch for your birthday?"

I pull back, the disappointment in having to turn him down strong. "I can't today. I'm here on my own at the moment. Sam's at her obstetrician appointment, so she won't be back until nearly three. And Sally called in sick this morning." Watching disappointment coat Toby's face has me almost inviting him to join me for my family's birthday dinner tonight. Maybe I should bite the bullet and do it. My gut tells me he's not like every other man I know. He's loyal and committed. He'll always choose to be there for Poppy and for me, no matter what.

He covers his disappointment quickly with a smile. "That's okay. Have you eaten lunch yet?"

"No, I've been too busy. I'll grab something light later."

He nods thoughtfully, his brows drawn down low over his sapphire eyes. The bell over the door sounds, breaking our private moment. "I'd better let you get back to work then." He steps away from me. "Enjoy the rest of your day with your family. Bye."

Stunned at how quickly the mood between us changed, I only have time to wave goodbye before he's gone.

Turning my attention to my customer, I smile. "I'll only be a moment."

I quickly collect everything to carry into my office, buying myself some time to gather my thoughts. Stepping back into the front of my shop, I feel in a more professional headspace and deal quickly with my new customer, creating a unique arrangement for his mother-in-law's birthday. He wants it to be unique because she suddenly lost her husband two weeks ago. Apparently, his father-in-law always gave his wife flowers for her birthday. He didn't want her to miss out this year.

While working on the arrangement and listening to my customer's story, I realize time isn't always on our side. It's the final push I need to invite Toby to dinner tonight, so I text Mom to add two more people to our booking.

MOM

You're sure?

ME

Not really, but when will be the right time?

MOM

I think you're doing the right thing

You can't keep him at arm's length forever

ME

I know

MOM

I'll change the booking

ME

Thanks Mom x

MOM

I'm proud of you for taking a big step forward

I know how hard it is for you to do

The bell over the door tinkles again. Looking up from my phone, I nearly drop it in surprise. Toby's back, and he's carrying a takeout paper bag that smells like lemongrass and coconut. He smiles at me. "Since you couldn't come out to lunch, I thought I'd bring lunch to you."

My cheeks rise to match his and my heart grows exponentially. I'm now one hundred percent certain I've made the right choice to include him in my family dinner tonight.

I step from behind the counter to pull him in for a tight hug, whispering in his ear, "I love you." It sort of slipped out, but I don't want to take it back. His head snaps back, eyes wide in surprise, but I know he's happy I said those three words.

"You love me? It's not even *my* birthday." I nod as my lips spread.

It's true; I love him. It feels so freaking good to say it out loud. I've been feeling it for a while and I've had to work hard to keep it from slipping out over the last couple of weeks. I don't know how to explain how his body language changes; he almost melts in front of my eyes.

"Say it again."

"I love you, Toby Summer."

He pulls me back into his body, whispering in my ear, "I love you so much, Cass." He laughs. "It feels so fucking good to say those words out loud."

He spins me around in the air before planting a rough kiss on me, deleting all humor and raising the heat level to extreme in a matter of seconds. This is a kiss to seal those magic words, reinforcing their importance to each of us. Unfortunately, he pulls back from me sooner than I would like, making my whole body pout in disappointment.

"C'mon, eat while you have a chance." He drags me into my office, then proceeds to lay out a plethora of dishes on the office desk as I clear the paperwork Sam has sprawled all over the surface. He hands me the Pad Thai noodles, giving me the first taste. The flavors burst inside my mouth, eliciting an appreciative moan. Toby pauses eating his crispy chicken, eyes snapping up to mine. He quickly leans forward to steal a kiss, then goes back to eating his chicken as though nothing happened.

"This is delicious. Thank you for spoiling me with lunch on my birthday."

"You're more than welcome, Bun. Where are you going for dinner with your family tonight?"

Here's my chance to invite him along. "We're going to our favorite pizza place. It's the traditional meal for our birthdays." I swallow nervously. "Um, would you like to come along?"

His body stiffens as his knuckles blanch around his fork. I don't think he was expecting an invitation tonight. I mean, I wasn't expecting to invite him along until a little over an hour ago.

"Are you sure?"

"Positively certain. Never felt more sure about anything before. It's time to let Poppy know we're together." I feel almost giddy for tonight, especially at what this means for our relationship. I'm tired of sneaking around, keeping something significant from the most important person in my life. "Poppy will be overjoyed." I observe his face for what I'm about to tell him again. "After all, she asked if you could be her daddy."

Toby's cheeks lift immediately, as his whole face lights up in delight. "You know I would be honored to be Poppy's daddy." He reaches up, cupping the back of my head to pull me forward before capturing my mouth with his. I open immediately, letting him in. God, what I wouldn't give to be somewhere else, so I could have this man inside me. The food is forgotten as we become lost in each other. It's always like this between us. A small spark leads to an inferno in an instant.

"So, is that a yes to dinner tonight?" I whisper against his lips.

"Absolutely, it's a yes. Only because I love pizza." He laughs as he dashes out of the path of my hand, swiping at him in fun.

"Good. I had Mom add two more people to our booking. I

figured Shane would also need to join us since we're out in public."

"Does that mean you're already taking me for granted? Assuming I'm available to have dinner with you on a whim?" He smirks at me.

"You don't have to come if you have plans." I sass back.

"Oh, don't worry, I'll be there for sure. Even if I had plans, I would cancel them in a heartbeat to spend your birthday with you." I think my heart just melted into a puddle; he always says exactly the right thing.

We continue eating our lunch, which surprisingly doesn't get interrupted by a customer. Once we're finished, Toby cleans up the mess, then kisses me goodbye with the promise to see me at dinner after his lesson with Poppy. He promised not to say anything to Poppy, preferring to tell her together at the restaurant tonight.

-toby-
_____

"WE'RE GOING TO DINNER TONIGHT AT *OVER THE TOPPINGS Pizzeria* for Cass's birthday. Can you check it out for us? See if it's not too late to book the place out?"

"Sure, I'll get onto it straight away." He pulls out his phone, searching for the number.

"Thanks, bro."

I feel like I've won another Grammy—actually, it feels better. Cass is showing me a level of trust she hasn't thus far. Introducing our relationship to Poppy is a big deal. One I won't take for granted. Even though Cass hasn't had any positive male role models in her life, I have. Dad was the best man, always patient and supportive. Firm but fair. He was always a solid, steady figure in my life. If I can be half the father he's been to me, I think I'll be doing okay.

A shriek breaks my musing, and Shane steps closer to me.

"Oh my god! It's Toby Summer. It's Toby Summer. I can't believe it. Oh, my god!"

Everyone who happened to be walking down the street, minding their own business, stops to see what the fuss is all about. This is how it starts. One person spots me, then suddenly, I'm surrounded by a mob—usually made up mostly of young women.

"Can you sign my shirt? Oh my god! Nobody's gonna believe me."

"Sure. Do you have a pen?" I often find it best to sign everything thrown my way. That way, I can go on with my day. If I resist, they generally keep following me around until I relent. But I have things to do, so it's best to agree to her request.

"Oh my god! You're gonna sign my shirt!" She turns around to the crowd forming. "Toby Summer's gonna sign my shirt!"

She digs through her purse, pulling out a Sharpie. Man, who happens to have a Sharpie on hand? Shane does, precisely for this purpose, but I usually ask the women if they have one on hand. That way, if they don't and I'm not in the mood, it's a good excuse to get out of the situation. Particularly when someone's as rude as this woman has been. She hands it to me, and I gesture for her to turn around to sign her back.

"No way. I want you to sign it right here." She points to her chest. Damn it. I hate signing women's breasts. I'm not sure what they think is gonna happen if I write across their boobs. Do they think I'll take one look at their rack and fall hopelessly in love?

"Okay, if you're sure." She nods vigorously, reminding me of a bobble doll. "Who shall I make it out to?"

"Deanna. My name's Deanna. D-E-A-N-N-A."

"Sure. Thanks, Deanna. It's always great to meet a genuine fan." As much as I don't enjoy being in the spotlight or having to deal with fans, I'd be a nobody if it weren't for them. I sign as carefully as I can, high up on her shirt, making minimal contact with her breast area. "There ya go. Have a great day."

"Can I have a selfie, too?" Some manners would be appreciated, but people often forget them in these situations.

"Sure." I step next to her, trying not to actually touch her, which is blown out of the water when she wraps her arms around me, squeezing me like a boa constrictor. Shane takes the obligatory photo and then hands the phone back to Deanna, signaling her to move along.

Shane and I spend the next forty minutes signing anything handed to me and taking selfies with strangers who feel they know me like an old friend. In between, he booked out the rest of the restaurant for the evening. The restaurant already had two other bookings besides Cass's, which we couldn't interfere with, but there won't be any others. I'm always aware of the lost revenue, so I pay for the privilege of booking out a restaurant.

To make up for lost time, we head over to Poppy's school together to pick her up for her guitar lesson. I'm not registered to pick her up from school, so Shane heads in to collect her while I wait in the car. I watch her holding Shane's hand, swinging it back and forth between them, as she skips while he walks toward the car. When she spots me sitting in the passenger seat, her whole body lights up with happiness. I step out to greet her properly, barely getting to my feet before she throws herself at me in her usual Poppy style.

Once I set her back on her feet, she signs, "Toby!"

"Hey, Poppy. How was your day?"

"It was the best. It's Mom's birthday today, so we had waffles for breakfast. I love waffles. Then, after my lesson, we're going to have pizza for dinner. You wanna come?" She looks between Shane and me hopefully.

Shit, I'm not sure if I'm allowed to tell her I'm coming to dinner tonight. I catch Shane's eye over the top of the car, indicating for him to situate Poppy in her booster seat. He comes around, guiding her into her seat, ensuring she's safely secured, and allowing me the opportunity to text Cass.

ME

Poppy just invited Shane and me to dinner tonight

What do you want me to say?

It takes less than a minute for the three dots to bounce.

BUN

You can tell her I already invited you guys

ME

Are you sure?

BUN

Yep

See you tonight lover boy

ME

Hey, I'm all man, or do I need to remind you?

BUN

Oh, I remember, but a refresher wouldn't go astray 😊

ME

It would be my pleasure

See you tonight

I wait for a reply which doesn't come. A customer probably came in that she has to deal with. We drive across to *Music for my Heart*. Once we're all out of the car and ready to head inside, I tell Poppy that Shane and I will be joining her and her family for dinner tonight. She jumps up and down with the joy of a child who's been told she's going to Disneyland, not adding two adult males to the dinner reservation. But that's Poppy to her very core.

We spend the one-hour lesson playing the three songs she's mastered, then choose a new song for her to learn. We select a reggae number by Bob Marley, *Three Little Birds*. It's a great song, using three chords, reminding us not to worry about a thing. Poppy loved the video I showed her on YouTube. She eagerly decided it would be her next song and favorite. I sit behind her, demonstrating how to play, with my hand guiding hers, while she watches the colorful display on my laptop monitor. The lesson flies by and before we know it, we're heading back to the car to drop Poppy home.

Once it's only Shane and me in the car, Shane asks, "Do you think I still need to be watching over Poppy? It's been a couple of months since your concert duet went viral."

I think about it for a moment. "I know it's been a while, but what if someone's been waiting for the right time? I would never forgive myself if something happened to her because of me."

Shane nods thoughtfully. "I see where you're coming from, but remember, you have a press tour coming up after Thanksgiving. So who's gonna watch her then?"

I look out of the window, tension building across my shoulders at the thought of being away from Cass and Poppy for any length of time—even though it's only two weeks. "Let me think about it. Okay?"

"Sure. I'll do whatever you want. But I don't want to leave you unprotected while you're away. It leaves you vulnerable to crazies." He looks at me meaningfully. As if I could ever forget what happened a couple of years ago.

-toby-

ARRIVING AT *OVER THE TOPPINGS PIZZERIA*, CASS AND HER family are already inside. I spend a moment observing them interact through the glass window like a creeper, unable to stop the warmth building inside me.

I'm about to walk inside and join them.

Finally, our sneaking around is over. We can be together openly.

There are two other tables, one with an older couple sharing a pizza while looking lovingly into each other's eyes. The other table is a group of young women. They could be a problem, but I'm hoping not. Shane and I don't need to speak to know what the other's thinking about a table of four women drinking wine while laughing over pizza.

I'm not about to stay out here checking out the woman I love from afar when I have the opportunity to join her for her birthday, so I open the door to step inside with Shane close behind. Poppy's facing the door, which means she's the first to catch our arrival, and bolts straight for us, hugging my waist before giving Shane the same attention.

I know he's become quite fond of her over the weeks he's

spent ensuring her safety. She takes each of our hands, pulling us toward the table. Cass offers a secret smile, and I wink back. This, here with Cass and Poppy and their family … is where I want to be—*always*.

Rose steps in to greet me first. "I'm thrilled you could make it on such short notice." She pulls me in, embracing me as she whispers, "I'm pleased my daughter finally came to her senses."

I bow my head, closing my eyes—a shaky laugh bursts out of me. I didn't realize how nervous I was about having Cass's mom's approval. It's always nerve-racking meeting the parents of the girl you're dating, and it's no less daunting doing it as an adult.

"Me too, Mrs. Phillips, me too."

"Rose. Remember?" She chastises me with her eyes.

Cassia steps closer, waiting to welcome me. I want so much to pull her into my arms and greet her the way I need to, but I want to be respectful of Poppy—who doesn't know we're together yet. I grin at her. "Hey, Cass. Happy birthday."

She blows all of my good intentions out of the water when she plants a kiss directly on my lips in front of everyone. I hear a series of gasps from the table of women. Cass flicks her tongue across the seam of my lips and I press in closer to hide my rising cock from the little girls who are standing too close for comfort. However, my hand has a mind of its own, holding the back of her head in place, stopping her from pulling away until I'm ready.

Poppy wraps her arms around both of us, squeezing our bodies together. It's then I remember where I am and the company I'm in. Reluctantly, I pull my lips away, touching my forehead to the woman who holds my heart—sharing a secret grin. Then, out of the corner of my eye, I catch a flash of a camera. Turning in their direction, Shane heads to the table of women. He normally offers them a portion of my time for my privacy in situations such as these. I trust him to do his job, so I bend down to pick up Poppy.

Poppy signs to me. "Mommy told me you're her boyfriend now." I look at Cass because I thought she was going to wait to tell Poppy until we were together.

"I couldn't hold it in any longer. I'm sorry I didn't wait for you." Cass signs to me as she speaks. I can't describe how happy it makes me that Cass was too excited about us to wait. I pull her into me with my free arm, kissing her temple. "I hope you don't mind."

It feels amazing to have both Poppy and Cassia—*my girls*— in my arms. "I don't mind at all, Bun."

We separate, and Violet says, "Hello," warily as we all take our seats around the table. Cass introduces me to her gramma Iris. I feel like I know her already after everything Cass has told me about her. She has a lot of respect for her gramma and they share a strong bond through their mutual love of floral design.

"Gramma, this is Toby. Toby, this is Gramma Iris," she signs as she speaks.

"Well, hello, handsome. It's nice to meet you finally." I go straight in for a hug with my free arm. I come from a family of huggers, so it's natural for me to greet Cass's family in this way.

"Nice to meet you, too." Shane and I pull out chairs at the table.

The red-checked tablecloths add to the traditional feel of the place as two guys work the large pizza oven in full view of the dining area. We chat around the table, comparing our favorite toppings and pretending to be grossed out by Poppy's preference for pineapple on her pizza. The point of difference between this pizzeria and others is that you build your own pizza. There are no boards on display for you to choose from a range of pre-designed pizzas. Instead, customers are encouraged to create their own one-of-a-kind taste sensation. The topping choices are extensive and include your regular options to create a savory pizza as well as sweet options to create a dessert pizza.

We each place our order with the waiter, a teenage boy with a wiry build, curly blond hair, and the unmistakable beginning of a fine mustache. His voice cracks as he introduces himself, preparing to take our orders on his tablet. We order wine for the adults and juice for the girls, which is brought out quickly along with a range of different warm breads. Poppy was quick to nab a seat between Cass and me, allowing me to rest my arm on the back of her chair, allowing me to play with her mom's silky hair.

Shane's sitting next to Violet, and they seem to be getting along. He's smiling freely while answering Jasmine's million and one questions. It's a change to see him relaxing and joining in rather than staying on the outer edges. Even when he spends time with my family, he's always slightly removed from the rest of us. Before joining the military, he was more relaxed around people, but he's different now—more withdrawn, quieter, slower to laugh and join in the conversation.

Pizzas of all varieties are brought out to the table, causing the conversation to die down momentarily as we all get stuck into our creations. Afterward, we all enjoy the birthday cake Rose organized for Cass. A red velvet creation with cream cheese filling and icing to match. Poppy and Jasmine end up with cream cheese all over their sweet little faces, giggling in delight at the reactions of the adults around the table. High on sugar, I pity Cass and Violet when it's time to get them to bed tonight.

As I regard everyone around the table, the night drawing to a close, I wonder what my chances are of getting Cass to come back to my place. I want to wish her a happy birthday properly. Leaning over Poppy, I tuck a lock of Cass's hair behind her ear, then lean closer to whisper, "What are my chances of wishing you happy birthday privately later?"

Her head turns quickly, our eyes connecting. The molten heat staring back at me makes my pulse race, directing the blood in my body toward my cock. *Fuck!* This is not the time nor the place to get a hard-on. "Let me get Poppy home to bed, then I'll come over. Okay?"

"Perfect." I lean in, pressing a gentle kiss to her lips. The same lips I used to dream of kissing in music class. I have to be the luckiest man alive. Our moment's broken by a throat clearing behind us, and I know it's time to pay up in exchange for being left alone during our meal. I excuse myself from the table as Shane does the same. We put some space between our group and the fans who've been reasonably patient this evening.

"Hello, ladies. Thanks for your patience and for being kind enough to wait until we'd finished our meal this evening."

My appreciation is met with various giggles, hair flips, hands pressed to breasts, as well as 'I'm sure you'll make it worth our while' responses.

Shane steps in. "If you would like to give me your phones, I'm happy to take a photo of each of you with Mr. Summer."

The ladies waste no time digging out their phones and opening the camera app before passing them over to Shane. Each one takes their turn, pressing their body as close as humanly possible to mine while posing for the photo. It astounds me to this day that people have no qualms about putting their hands and bodies all over a complete stranger. It's making me more uncomfortable than usual because I know my girls are mere yards away, witnessing these women fawn all over me. I hate it on a normal day, but tonight I feel downright dirty.

Attempting to extricate myself from their clutches, I work to put some space between myself and them, but it's an almost impossible task. They have me sign a menu, personalizing each one. I have to work hard to keep my smile in place as well as my friendly, professional manner intact, as they take every opportunity to put their hands on me. Shane picks up on my discomfort, informing the ladies it's time to move along.

Moving toward our table, I watch for any signs of annoyance from Cass, but I find none. Instead, Rose and Violet are scrutinizing me as I sit down.

"I'm sorry about the interruption to our evening. Unfortunately, stuff like that happens when I'm in public. I've found it best to spend time with my fans rather than ignoring them."

They nod in understanding while Cass turns to me.

"When it's only us, I always forget how famous you are. I think it's great you don't ignore your fans." I sigh in relief at her acceptance of this facet of my life. "But if I see another woman rub her breasts against you or put her hands on you as though she owns you, I'm not gonna be held responsible for my actions." She finishes her statement with a sweet smile, contradicting the tone of her words. Rose and Violet snicker as Shane's lips twitch, suggesting he's holding back his laughter. I notice she didn't sign any of that for Poppy's benefit.

"Are we all ready to head home?" I check with everyone.

A round of yeses sound out, and we all stand, gathering our things to leave the restaurant. Shane's already picked up the tab on my behalf, so I guide the ladies out the door quickly, hoping they're too preoccupied with putting on their coats to notice.

Rose stops near the cashier. "I have to pay for our meal. You all go ahead." She shoos the girls away, but I linger, letting her know the meal has already been covered.

She's not happy with me, making it known that as her guest, it was very rude of me to step in to pay for *her* daughter's birthday dinner. I apologize profusely as we make our way outside to join the others. The girls all pile into one car, Cass lingering beside the driver's door. I say my goodbyes to the girls and Violet in the back seat before stepping into Cass's body and pulling her tight against me.

"Will I see you tonight?" I'm unsure if she still wants to come over after witnessing the women from the other table fawning all over me.

Bringing her smooth hand up, she cups the side of my face. I automatically press further into her palm before grasping and kissing it. "As soon as I can get Poppy to bed, I'll head over. I'm not sure how long that'll take, though. Is that okay?"

"Of course. Don't rush. I'd wait all night for you, Cass." I kiss her palm again, then press my lips to her forehead. "Drive safely." I kiss her lips chastely before nudging her into the car to fasten her seatbelt.

FORTY

-toby-

I FEEL LIKE I'M GONNA COME OUT OF MY SKIN AS I WAIT FOR Cass to show. It's only been an hour since we parted ways at the restaurant, but it feels like so much more time has passed. Then, finally, headlights shine through my front windows, letting me know she's here. I head out to meet her at her car, opening her door before she's aware that I'm there, causing her to almost hit her head on the roof.

Holding her hand to her chest, she chastises me. "Shit, Toby. You scared the crap outta me."

I pull her out of the car and press her up against the rear door. "I'm sorry. I couldn't wait the extra time it'd take you to come to me." Moving forward, stopping her words, I press my lips to hers in a desperate kiss. I'm hungry for her. I can't even wait until I get her inside. It's only when a car full of teenagers careens past, yelling profanities, that I remember where we are. Dragging my mouth from hers is a mammoth task. Breathing heavily, I press my forehead to hers. "Sorry. Couldn't help myself, as usual."

Her giggles lighten the mood. "I love how much you want me. You won't ever hear me complaining about your lack of control." She kisses me chastely. "Now, help me carry my overnight bag upstairs."

"Does that … does that mean you're … are you staying the night?" I finally get the words out past my surprise.

"Yep. Mom insisted I deserved a night away. She promised to take care of Poppy tomorrow. Gramma Iris will deliver and set up the flowers and balloons for the baby shower for me. So you have me all night as well as most of tomorrow."

"This is the best gift, and it's not even *my* birthday."

I can't contain my excitement at having her in my bed all night. To wake up wrapped around her in the morning for the first time. To not have her leave my bed in the middle of the night like a teenager sneaking around after curfew. She removes her car keys, then closes her door while I grab her bag. Locking her car, I guide her up the few steps into my home with my hand nestled into the small of her back. She stops dead in her tracks, sucking in a breath at what greets her.

"Is this all for me?" She glances at me over her shoulder, steely eyes wide. I nod, then press a gentle kiss to the side of her neck, below her ear.

"All for you, Gorgeous."

"It's beautiful." She turns to me, her eyes glittering with the reflection of the candlelight. Pressing upward, she captures my mouth with hers. I drop her overnight bag to the floor and cup her face in my hands, deepening the kiss. As is typical for us, an inferno builds quickly, and I have her pressed against the entry wall without realization. Lifting her underneath her ass, I encourage her to wrap her legs around me, allowing me the pleasure of grinding my rock-hard cock against her soft pussy.

Kissing her roughly, our breaths heavy and uneven, our tongues dueling, tasting, twisting, licking—I *know* I could kiss her for days and be a fortunate man. After a few moments, drawing on every single reserve of strength I have, I pull away, carefully sliding Cassia down my body until her feet make contact with the floor. Ensuring she's steady, I grasp her warm hand in mine and lead her toward the couch, where the wine is resting on the table, along with half a dozen candles. I have more spread throughout the space, giving a romantic glow to the room.

The lights of the bridge in the distance can be seen through the window, and I don't think I've ever felt this content in my private space. The only thing that could make this better would be having Poppy asleep upstairs and Cass's clothes in my closet.

We get comfortable. I pass a glass of wine to Cass, then collect my own. Carefully tapping my glass against hers, I make a toast. "Happy birthday, Bun. Here's to sharing the rest of our birthdays together."

We both sip the sweet wine and Cass leans in to snuggle my neck as she whispers, "Every." Kiss. "Single." Kiss. "One." Kiss. "Until my dying day." It's exactly what I want to hear from her. She pulls back. "Thank you for all this." She gestures around the room at the candles. "You didn't need to go to this much trouble for me."

"You deserve to be treated like a princess. This was no trouble at all." I grasp the back of her head, pulling her lips to mine. Kissing her roughly, tasting the wine, feeling her breath.

Slowly pulling apart, I can see something's bothering her. "What's up?" I whisper, my forehead pressed against hers.

She bites her bottom lip, her eyes skating around the room before settling back on me. "Does it happen often?" My eyebrows pull down, trying to work out what she's talking about. "You know. The fans." Oh, right, *that*.

"It usually depends." How do I explain this without making my life sound unappealing to her? "I don't go out much. Whenever possible, Shane works to ensure I have minimal contact with the public. We didn't have time to plan for tonight, which means we didn't have our usual level of control.

Today was unusual. I was stopped by fans twice. Once, after leaving you this afternoon, then tonight at dinner." I sip my wine as Cass does the same. "When I prepare for my tour, I'm out and about more, which means dealing with fans more often. Then, while I'm on tour, it can get pretty crazy. Otherwise, I work to keep myself as low-key as possible."

Cass nods thoughtfully. "It's to be expected, I guess." She pauses. "It's the first time I've witnessed it up close like that. Those women had seen you with me, yet they had no problem fawning all over you, touching you." She stands, stepping over to the windows, her back to me. "It was difficult to be a bystander. To watch them touch what I think of as mine." And isn't that music to my ears.

I stand quickly, pressing my body close to hers, touching her at every available point. I nuzzle my nose down into her neck, kissing her below her ear. "You're the only woman I *want* touching me, Cass. Remember that." I place several more kisses as she kindly tilts her head, allowing me access. Then, turning her around and pressing her up against the cold glass, I lock eyes with her—stormy gray to calm blue. "I have a two-week press tour after Thanksgiving." She tries to look down between us, but I tilt her chin so I don't lose her eyes. "I plan on telling the world I'm a taken man, Bun. It'll be crystal fucking clear to all women to keep their hands to themselves. I promise." She smiles then, her shoulders relaxing. I'd give anything to be the one to make her smile each and every day. "I can't wait to tell the world you're all mine." I swoop forward, sealing my words with a deep kiss that leaves no room for questions or doubts. "C'mon. I need to take you to bed."

Holding her hand in mine, we lock the front door before extinguishing all the candles. Carrying her overnight bag in my free hand, I guide her upstairs, mentally planning what I'm going to do to her first. Dropping her bag on the chair near the window, I draw Cass into me and wrap my arms around her, erasing any space between us. Her heart beats double time, mirroring my own—it seems we're both worked up. Her hands slide up my back, grasping onto my shoulders as her tits press against my chest. Having her in my arms like this is a dream come true for me; one I never want to wake up from. Tilting my head down, I press kisses to her forehead, and as she closes her eyes; I kiss each lid gently, reverently. I want to worship this woman until there's no doubt in her mind that she's the only one for me.

Stepping back slightly, I remove her clothing piece by piece, revealing her gorgeous body to me inch by glorious inch. Lovingly, I caress my hand from her hip to the indent of her waist, then up further to cup one teardrop-shaped breast. I brush my thumb over her nipple until it's pebbled to my liking; a perfect morsel for my teeth to nip and bite, my tongue to lick and taste, my mouth to swallow and devour.

Goosebumps break out across her body; her shallow breaths come faster. The pulse point at the base of her neck flutters a fast tattoo. My other hand follows the same path up the other side of her body, while I lean down to nip her perfectly pebbled peak, then soothe it with my tongue. I take as much of her breast as possible into my mouth, drawing on the globe with a deep suck. Releasing it from my mouth, I give her other breast the same treatment. It's surreal to touch her in such an intimate way.

Her hands slide up into my hair, releasing the tie holding it back. Tangling her fingers in the strands, she holds me tighter, moaning softly. "I love what you do to me with your mouth. Please, never stop."

I pull away, remaining in position, glancing at her face. "Never, Gorgeous. I plan to have my mouth on you as often as possible for the rest of my days." Crouching forward slightly, I lift her under her ass and as she wraps her legs around my waist, I carry her to my bed, settling her gently on the edge.

Pushing her back, I kneel, spreading her legs wide with my shoulders. She gets the hint, placing her feet on the edge of the bed, dropping her knees, and opening herself up to me exactly the way I like. Resting back on my haunches, I use my fingers to slide open her pussy lips from the bottom up, pinching her clit as I reach the top before sliding back down to begin the process again.

I rub my trimmed beard along the inside of her thighs, making them shake as my fingers continue to caress her pussy. The essence coats my fingers, which I rub along her thigh, then follow close behind to taste with my tongue.

"You taste so fucking good. I want your cream all over my beard, so I can smell you every time I inhale." Finally, I can't hold back any longer. Diving in, I swipe my tongue from the base to the top, feeling her pussy throb as her moisture coats my tongue, covering my beard.

Cass releases a long moan. "Make me come. Please, Toby. Make me come." She whispers over and over, her hips moving to create the friction she needs to fall over the edge. I help her along, thrusting first one, then two fingers into her tight hole. The wet warmth has my dick trying to push its way out of my jeans to get to her. Sliding my fingers purposefully in and out of her body while I suck her clit into my mouth has the desired effect. Cass's hips shoot upward as she spasms around my fingers, spilling her delicious juices all over my face. Her breaths are harsh, her tits rising and falling in rapid succession. It's incredible that I'm the man who gets the privilege of sending her flying into oblivion.

She lays sprawled on her back, her lips widening sleepily across her beautiful face. She looks stunning in this moment, flushed from her orgasm, spread open, ready for me. I slowly crawl up her body, smoothing my hands worshipfully along her tanned skin, leaving goosebumps in my wake, kissing and licking until I reach her mouth. Meeting her lips with a smile of my own, our kiss is slow, languid—quite the opposite of the blood rushing through my body. Her hands reach up to pull me down onto her, pressing her heated body further into the mattress.

As if only just realizing I'm still fully clothed, she pushes at my shoulders. "You need to get naked. Now, Toby."

Her slim fingers tug and pull at my sweater in haste to remove it as if it offends her in some way. Pushing up from the bed, I grab the back of the collar to pull the offending sweater over my head before haphazardly throwing it to the floor. As I free my belt, button, and zipper, allowing me to slide my jeans and boxer briefs to the floor in one swift motion, Cass scoots up the bed, resting her head on the soft pillow. Dark, hooded eyes study me closely, her hands gliding slowly over her silky skin as I climb back on top of her.

My dick bobs forward, trying to get to her, but he'll have to wait a little longer as I reach across to the top drawer to retrieve a condom. Cass reaches out, stopping my hand as my fingers connect with the cool, wooden surface. Then, switching my focus from the drawer to Cass, she shakes her head in the negative. "We don't need it. I trust you, Toby."

My body sags at the level of trust she's chosen to give me tonight. I swallow hard, my dick seeking her entrance. "Are you one hundred percent certain?" I study her face closely for any sign she's unsure or second-guessing herself. "Because once I've been inside you bare, I'm not going back to using condoms ever again." She nods in affirmation. "I need your words, Gorgeous."

She swallows, maintaining eye contact as her response comes out sure and steady. "I'm certain, Toby. I promise. I don't want to use condoms with you anymore. I don't need the physical or emotional barrier."

I don't need any further assurances from her. I quickly get into position, sliding my fingers through her pussy to check she's still wet and ready for me, groaning when my fingers are met with her slickness. Prodding the eager tip of my cock at her entrance, I push her thighs open wider and drive my hard cock to the hilt, my balls nestled against her ass. Rising on my elbows, I kiss her slowly, passionately, tangling my tongue with hers, swallowing her sighs and her moans. Lost in the kiss, our connection, I move—the slow glide out followed by a slow glide in, ensuring I rub her g-spot and clit on the way. Cass's legs wrap around my lower back, moving her hips in time with mine as we make love.

We take our time, kissing, grinding, building toward euphoria.

I'm in no hurry knowing I have her for the entire night and into tomorrow. "I'll happily spend the entire night stroking my cock in and out of your tight pussy, Gorgeous." Her pussy tightens around my shaft at my words—we both groan.

Sweat coats our skin, our hearts speeding up with the exertion, as I lose myself in my woman's stormy eyes, her plush mouth, and her stunning body. This woman stole my heart when I was sixteen years old, and as we've grown closer over these past weeks, I've decided she can hold on to it, keep it, and never give it back.

Our momentum gradually increases, skin slapping against skin. Cass's hands feel sensational, grasping onto my back, digging her fingernails into my flesh. Holding her eyes, I increase my speed and power, building our orgasms toward their mutual peak. Cass's walls squeeze my dick in rhythmic flutters as I grit my teeth to hold on to my own. I want to get her there so I can build her straight into another one.

As she comes down, I gingerly slide out of her and roll to my back, pulling her on top of me where I want her, then slide back into heaven. We lay like that, connected in the most primitive way until Cass is ready for more.

"Mmmm. That was so good."

I pull her head down to me, eye to eye, licking at her lips until she opens for me. Mouths open to the other, sharing breaths as we slide our tongues together. Grabbing her peach of an ass in one hand, I guide her hips back and forth to meet my thrusts. I can't go as slowly this time; the need to release is overtaking rational thought. Increasing my thrusts, I power up into Cass's tight hole as she pushes down, meeting me thrust for thrust. Her silky walls tighten, making my shaft pulse. My balls tighten up, ready to shoot my cum into her.

"Get there, Cass. I can't hold on any longer."

"I'm almost there. Just need—" I circle her clit with my fingers, hoping to push her over the edge, and as I do, she erupts, permitting me to let go. I groan out as my cum fills her pussy. The satisfaction I feel at knowing that she trusts me enough to allow it fills my soul. She flops forward, her head resting in the crook of my neck. Wrapping my arm around her, I use my free hand to stroke her tangled hair away from her face so I can kiss her forehead. With a serene smile on her face, she mumbles, "Love you, Toby."

Placing another kiss on her forehead, I return her words, "Love you, Bun."

-cassia-

T OBY WAS INSATIABLE LAST NIGHT, WAKING ME REGULARLY WITH his mouth on my pussy the first time and his fingers inside me the second. I was thankful I didn't wake up to his dick inside me because I'm not sure I could've handled it without having a flashback to the time Jake came home drunk, thinking it was his right to have unprotected sex with me while I slept.

At one point last night, I pushed Toby away before I realized who I was with. I'll have to explain why at some point—I don't want him to think I was reacting to him because I wasn't. But I'm unsure how to broach the subject with him in the light of day. I know he already dislikes Jake a lot; I don't think it would take much to tip the scales toward hate.

As I roll over, I realize the bed's empty. I'm bereft at the loss of a morning snuggle with my boyfriend.

Boyfriend!

It's rare I get to lie in bed in the morning. Usually, I have to get up straight away to get moving for the day, but having the day off from all responsibilities is affording me a unique opportunity to relax. Snuggling down into the blankets with a smile, I think over last night and the last few weeks.

I've never met a guy more solid than Toby.

Even when he was pissed at me for not telling him about Poppy and breaking things off, he still maintained his connection with my daughter without missing a beat. Because of that, I feel more confident than ever in my decision to open my heart to him fully. To let him into my life and Poppy's life, too.

"You're finally awake, sleepyhead." Toby breezes into the room, looking as happy as I feel, carrying two cups that smell a lot like coffee.

Scrambling to sit up, I hold out grabby hands. "Gimme, gimme, gimme."

Toby chuckles. "I guess you want one of these—" He gestures to the cups in his hands. "And not me." He playfully pouts, looking freaking adorable. Then, handing over a cup of coffee made just the way I like, he leans down, kissing my forehead. I melt into a puddle every time he places a kiss there; it's such a beautiful show of affection and care.

"Well, I want you, too. It's just coffee ..." I leave my statement hanging as Toby slides back into bed, carefully situating me exactly where he wants me without spilling a single drop of caffeinated goodness—quite a skill.

"How'd you sleep?"

Surely he's joking. It's not like we got a lot of sleep last night. "The sleep I *did* manage to get was great. It just wasn't a significant amount because my *boyfriend* kept waking me up," I huff out with a giggle. I give him wide eyes as though I'm annoyed, but I'm really not because those wake-up calls were something else.

Now I'm all hot and bothered again.

I'm not sure my hoo-ha could take him this morning after the night we shared. He wraps his arm around my shoulder, pulling me in tight before kissing the top of my—what I'm assuming—is a rat's nest of hair.

"I'm not gonna apologize for taking advantage of having

my girlfriend in my bed all night. In fact, it would make me happy if that's where she slept every night." He throws it out casually, as though what he said isn't a big deal. I laugh in response because I'm not sure I have the words to respond. We both sip our coffee, enjoying a few silent moments. I guess now would be a good time to apologize for last night.

I look up at him. "Uh, I owe you an apology."

He looks down at me, eyebrows drawn low over his cobalt irises.

"For when I pushed you away. It wasn't anything you did. It just took me a minute to remember who I was with. I, uh … had a terrible experience once, which led to all sorts of major life changes for me." I swallow hard, glancing away. I'm not sure I can tell him anything more; does he even want to know?

He squeezes me, regaining my attention. "You wanna talk about it?"

"You've gotta promise you won't get mad."

His body tenses against mine. I can sense him preparing for what I'm about to share. Finally, he nods in agreement, jaw tight, mouth tight.

"When I was dating Jake, I always insisted on using condoms. You remember how on and off we were? He would always sleep around when we were off. I couldn't trust him to keep me safe, so I kept myself safe." His jaw twitches, but he tilts his head for me to continue. "One night, he came home drunk. I was already in bed and asleep. I woke up to him having sex with me. When I realized what was happening, I tried to push him off me, but he's so much bigger and stronger than me. I couldn't get him to stop. Finally, he came inside me, which I'd never allowed throughout our entire relationship. I was so angry at him that I had to have an STD check because of his selfish ass. That's when I found out I was pregnant— which was a surprise since I was also on the pill. While I would never not want to have Poppy in my life, he took my choice away from me that night." The anger radiating off Toby's body is lethal, and his silence is unnerving. "Say something," I whisper. I desperately need to know he doesn't think any less of me. I know none of what happened was my fault, but other people can be judgmental.

"He fucking raped you is what he did. Not only did he take your choice away from you, he fucking raped you." He goes deathly still, and I'm worried about what he's about to say next as he pulls away from me, ensuring he's not touching me in any way.

Does he think I'm too damaged to touch now?

Am I about to be told to get out of his bed, out of his life?

"I hope you know I would never, *never* do anything like that to you. I will never have sex with you against your will." He swallows, taking his gaze away from me before we lock eyes again. "I'm sorry, Cass, so sorry, if anything I did last night made you feel unsafe or made you feel I was like that fucking asshole." He brushes his hand through his hair in despair as he whispers, "Please tell me you know I would never do that to you." He looks up at me, devastation in his eyes.

I place my coffee on the side table and raise myself to my knees, cupping his face in my hands, his beard tickling my palms. Ensuring I have my eyes locked on his before I begin. "You are nothing at all like him. Not in any way, shape, or form. Don't ever, *ever* think I put you in the same category because I don't." I lean forward, pressing a gentle kiss to his forehead, before pulling back again. "I trust you with the most precious part of my life, my daughter. Toby, I trust you with my heart and my body." His body almost deflates, and I'm unsure if he would still be sitting upright if I weren't cupping his face in my hands. "I know you would never take anything from me against my will. I also know you would never put your hands on me for any other reason than to show me love. I promise."

He leans forward swiftly. I don't have time to brace myself, as his hands cup my face and he takes my mouth in a gentle kiss. He pulls back, each of us holding the other, eye to eye. "I would rather break my own heart before I would break yours. Smash it to pieces all over the floor at your feet as a sacrifice to keep yours intact, Cassia. I love you and Poppy so much."

He leans forward, pressing his mouth to mine; I open willingly, welcoming him inside. Rising, I straddle his lap, feeling his hardness against my feminine folds. Wrapping his arms around me, he presses up, finding my entrance before sliding inside. Sharing breaths, eye to eye, we make love, wrapped in each other, sealing our bond.

"C'mon. I need to feed you. Then I wanna pick up Poppy so I can spend the day with both of my girls." *Could this guy be any more perfect?*

I laugh as he slaps my ass playfully. "Okay, okay. I'm getting up. Not sure my legs are gonna work, so you might have to help me out."

Bending forward, he picks me up as though I weigh next to nothing and carries me into his decadent shower. Washing me from head to toe; he keeps it chaste because I'm a little tender. We dry off and dress quickly, making our way downstairs for breakfast. Toby whips us up some scrambled eggs with toast along with another cup of steaming coffee. Then we're on our way to pick up my girl for a day of fun—just like a regular family.

-cassia-

I FEEL SO FREAKING SICK. I CAN BARELY LIFT MY HEAD FROM MY pillow, but I need to go to work. Making my way downstairs, I find Mom and Violet look to be feeling the same as me.

"Morning," I mutter, only to be greeted by their murmured greetings, which is very unlike our regular mornings in this household. Then it hits: that spasming in my stomach—the need to hold on to its contents before they come exploding out of places they're really not meant to. I make a run for the downstairs bathroom and drop to my knees over the toilet. My misery seems to go on forever. Just when I think I'm done, more seems to come out of nowhere. *Ugh!*

I manage to pull myself up from the floor, flushing away the evidence of my misery until I catch my reflection in the mirror. Bloodshot eyes, clammy, pale skin, and vomit in my hair greet me—gross. I set about slowly cleaning myself up as best I can before heading back to the kitchen.

"I think I have the stomach flu." I manage to say before Mom rushes past me, straight for the room I've just vacated.

"I think we all have it. I need to go upstairs to check on Jasmine. She was burning up through the night." Violet gingerly steps out of the kitchen to check on her daughter, so I do the same. Slowly, following her upstairs, focusing on putting one foot in front of the other, we make it to the top of the stairs before Violet covers her mouth in fear, dashing for the bathroom. I can't believe we all have the same bug at the same time.

I open Poppy's door to find her still sleeping, which isn't unusual for her. I usually have to wake her on a school day. What *is* unusual—she's thrown all the covers off the bed and is lying exposed to the chill in her room. Stepping over to her, I gently place my hand against her forehead, which is burning to the touch. She's clammy and very pale.

That's five for five with the stomach flu on this lovely Friday morning. I wet a cloth, then place it gently over Poppy's forehead, trying not to disturb her too much. The best thing she can do is sleep. I get a bucket to place next to her bed, call Sam to let her know I won't be in today, then call Gramma to ask if she could work with Sally the whole day. Once everything's sorted, I make myself as comfortable as possible, complete with a sick bucket and blanket, on the chair in the corner of Poppy's room, so I can monitor my girl.

I'm unsure how much time's passed when the doorbell rings, causing the lights throughout the house to flash. I wait to see if anyone else will answer it, but it seems I'm out of luck as it rings again. I can't hear anyone making their way toward it. Barely dragging my ass up, I slowly make my way back downstairs to answer the front door. It takes a concerted effort, and by the time I get there, I'm covered in sweat as though I've run around the block a time or two. Looking through the stained-glass inlay of the front door, I see Shane. Shit! I completely forgot he comes through to pick up Poppy for school. I don't want him to get sick; I think it's best to communicate through the door.

"Uh, hi, Shane. I'm sorry. I forgot to call you this morning."

I hear a muffled, "Is everything okay?"

"Uh, no. We all have the stomach flu—all five of us. We won't be leaving the house anytime soon. I'm sorry you came all the way here for nothing."

"That's okay. I don't mind. Can I get you ladies anything to help?"

"No, I don't think so. Thanks anyway."

"Okay then. Bye. I guess I'll see you guys whenever you need me over the Thanksgiving break?"

"Thanks for everything. We'll be in touch. Bye, Shane." I'm about to step away from the door when I remember Poppy has her guitar lesson with Toby this afternoon. "Shane," I call out as loud as I can.

"Yeah?"

"Can you please let Toby know we're all sick and Poppy won't be at her lesson today?"

"Sure, Cass. Take care. Bye."

"Bye, Shane. Thanks."

I sag against the front door as though I've completed a mammoth task. I sigh to myself as I turn, looking at the stairs I have to climb. Then, just as I'm about to head for the kitchen to see what we have in the way of crackers, another wave hits me. I make a mad dash to the bathroom. I get myself cleaned up again, grab what I need from the kitchen, check in on Mom (who's doing about the same as me), then head back to Poppy's room in time to catch her as she sits up, covering her mouth, tears in her eyes. Leaning her over the side of her bed, I grab the bucket for her, holding her hair back so she can expel the contents of her stomach. Her whole body retches. It's painful to feel my baby girl in such a state.

Once she's finished, I slowly lead her to the bathroom, where I deal with the bucket and clean both of us up in the shower. Finally, we both climb into my bed. I replace the sick bucket on Poppy's side just in case. I so badly want to close my eyes to sleep, but I need to make sure Poppy's okay.

I'm not sure if I fell asleep, but my eyes slowly open to the god-awful sound of the doorbell again. *What now?* I lay still, hoping someone else will deal with whoever's there. I can hear muffled voices, so I'm assuming I can relax again, but my stomach's not having it. For the third time this morning, I jump up and dive for the bathroom. At this point, I have nothing left to expel, but that doesn't stop my stomach from trying.

I'm too exhausted to move, so I decide it's a good idea to rest my head on the lip of the bowl for a moment.

-toby-

WHEN SHANE ARRIVED ON MY DOORSTEP WITH THE NEWS THAT Cassia's entire family had the stomach flu, meaning Poppy wouldn't be at our lesson today, I quickly pulled myself together. First, I made a trip to the convenience store and the pharmacy. Stocking up on ginger ale, lemonade, crackers, Imodium, and Ibuprofen. I also bought fruit juice, peppermint and chamomile tea, as well as ingredients to make a chicken broth for them all. Then there was the matter of being granted entry into the house. Rose wasn't happy to see me on her doorstep, and it took quite a bit of convincing on my part to get her to open the front door to let me in. I think I only won the argument because I still had stamina while she's exhausted from the virus.

Now, standing in the bathroom's doorway, looking at my poor love wrapped around the porcelain bowl, I'm relieved I came. I stroke her hair away from her pale, clammy face then carefully pick her up to carry her to her bedroom, where Poppy's already asleep on one side of the bed. She's incredibly weak and out of it; I don't think she's even registered she's been moved. I head back to the bathroom to wet a couple of small towels to care for Poppy and Cass. Meticulously, I wipe each of their faces down with the cool cloth, then rest them on their foreheads. Leaving the room, I check on Violet, who's curled around Jasmine. They're both burning up, too, so I repeat the process with them. Rose is downstairs, asleep on the couch with the TV on low. She doesn't seem to be doing as badly as the others, but she's still mighty unwell. I set a ginger ale beside her with a couple of crackers, then head to the kitchen to make the chicken broth.

Mom used to always make this for Kate and me when we were sick. I swear it has some sort of magic in it because I always felt much better after slowly slurping down a bowl. While it's simmering on the stove, I do the rounds again. Everyone's still asleep. Thankfully, there has been no vomiting since I arrived, but I take the time to rinse each cloth, wipe their faces, and replace the cool fabric on each of their foreheads. As I'm tending to Poppy, her eyes open sleepily, presenting a dull, lifeless gray instead of the cool silver I'm used to seeing from her. She sits up suddenly, eyes wide, gesturing that she's going to be sick. I lean her over the sick bucket next to the bed as I hold her hair out of the way for her. Her little body retching with spasms is like a punch to my gut. Once she's finished, I carry her to the bathroom to clean her up as best I can, then sit her up in bed. Once she's situated, I run downstairs to get her some lemonade I've left sitting out. She sips it slowly before giving me a weak smile and laying back down, falling asleep instantly. Cass must be completely out of it because she hasn't moved a muscle the entire time.

I spend my day going from room to room, ensuring everyone's as comfortable as possible. I have to change Jas because she was sick in her sleep. Messing herself, her pajamas, and the bedding. I felt awful waking Violet to change the sheets. I worked as quickly as possible, then threw everything into the wash.

I'm shattered, and it's only been one day. These viruses can last for longer than a week. I may need to call in reinforcements if the girls keep being sick at the rate they are. During the brief bouts of incoherent wakeful moments, I manage to get a little of the broth into everyone, along with crackers and ginger ale for the ladies; flat lemonade for the girls.

Everyone seems pretty settled at this point, so I think I'll call it a night. I prop myself up in the chair in the corner of Cass's bedroom. This is my first opportunity to check out her space because I've been solely focused on looking after everyone. It's simple, not overcrowded with crap and, interestingly, not a floral pattern in sight.

Sitting quietly, observing my girls, I think about the future with them. Having them move in with me, living with me, spending every available moment together as a family. Planning vacations, as well as holidays together, has me thinking about Thanksgiving coming up in less than a week. I wonder if they'll be well enough to celebrate.

ME

Hey Mom

Would we have space to add six more people to our Thanksgiving?

I don't have to wait too long for her reply.

MOM

Hi Love

Oh, I forgot to tell you, we're having it at Kate and Oliver's this year. She wanted to have all the kids over and they have more room

Who did you want to invite?

ME

I wanted to invite Cass, Poppy, and the rest of
the Phillips family

MOM

Oh, I'm so happy for you Toby. Poppy's just
delightful and her Mom's so pretty

I don't think it'll be a problem, maybe check
with Kate

ME

Okay, thanks Mom

See you soon

MOM

Love you x

ME

Love you too x

I knew she'd be happy to have Poppy around. She's practically been counting down the years until Kate or I made her a grandma.

ME

I heard you guys are hosting Thanksgiving
this year

It takes a few minutes for her to reply. I almost jump out of my chair when my phone eventually vibrates.

SQUIRT

Yeah, is that okay?

ME

Of course. I was wondering if it would be okay
to invite Cass, Poppy, and the rest of their
family? Six people in total

SQUIRT

Of course. The more the merrier

ME

They're all sick with the stomach flu at the moment

SQUIRT

Oh no!

ME

I'm not sure if they'll be up for the holiday, but I figured it wouldn't hurt to check in first

SQUIRT

Oh, absolutely. They're always welcome. Any time

ME

Thanks Sis

Talk soon

SQUIRT

Okay. Love you brother x

ME

Love you too x

Tucking my phone away, satisfied with my organizational skills, I do one last check on the women, then settle down in my chair for the night to sleep.

Coming into awareness slowly, I sense eyes on me. Pretending I'm still asleep, I feel little fingers poke at my beard, followed by little girl giggles. I can't keep my lips from widening as I slowly open one eye, followed by the other. I'm greeted by two little

girls who look remarkably well, considering how sick they were yesterday. I've heard when kids get sick, they go down hard and fast, but they recover equally fast. I never gave it much thought, but looking at the two little sweethearts in front of me, I'm thankful for how fast the girls have bounced back. Their color still isn't what it should be, but they're definitely well on their way to a full recovery.

I sign as I ask. "How are you girls feeling today?"

Jasmine and Poppy both reply eagerly with goofy smiles. Placing their right hand, flat palm, against their lips, then moving it forward to rest it in their left hand. Letting me know they feel 'good'.

I rise from the chair, stretching out the kinks in my neck and back. "Okay, let's get you girls some breakfast." I pick up Jasmine while I hold Poppy's hand as we tiptoe from Cass's bedroom.

I need to keep their food simple today, so I make them some plain toast and give them half a cup of juice each. They happily sit at the table, swinging their little legs back and forth, smiling the whole time. It's great to see them somewhat back to normal.

"How come you were seeping on the chair?" Jas asks me. Oh, no, once this kid starts with the questions, she doesn't know how to stop.

I sign for Poppy as I speak. "I wanted to make sure everyone was okay last night, and well, there wasn't another bed for me. So I slept in the chair."

The girls nod thoughtfully, and I'm hoping that's the end of question time. "But Poppy wasn't in her bed, and I wasn't in mine. You could haf sept there."

Smart kid. Violet's going to have her hands full with this one. "I didn't want to be too far from Poppy and your aunt."

"Do you love them?"

"Yes, I do."

"Are you gonna be Poppy's daddy now?"

"I would like to be."

"My daddy doesn't want me anymore." Her bottom lip quivers as her eyes get that sad look that little kids sometimes have when they're about to cry.

Oh, shit! What do I say to that?

"I'm sure that's not true. I bet your daddy loves you and wants you very much." I look around for something to distract the girls. "How about after we eat breakfast, you guys can have a bath, then we can watch a princess movie?"

"Otay," Jas responds with a serious expression that suggests she means business to get on with the job at hand so she can get to the fun stuff.

Poppy's lips are spread wide as she asks, "You want to be my daddy?"

"Yeah, Poppy, I do. One day."

She throws her arms around my neck, squeezing tightly. Her little heart beats strong and sure against mine.

The girls finish their breakfast. Then, I give them a quick shower because I'm not sure I have the skill set to bathe them. Once they're dressed for the day, I set them up in front of the TV with the movie of their choice, surrounded by their favorite cuddly toys. Watching the first few minutes to make sure the girls settle in, the wild red hair of the princess on the TV reminds me of my sister's.

I leave the girls downstairs to watch their movie and I make my rounds, checking on the adults. They're still pretty out of it, not fully aware of what's going on around them. I wipe the exposed skin of their faces and arms with a cool cloth and replace the drinks on their bedside tables. At least nobody's thrown up today. That's gotta be a good sign.

I think we're up to our third movie of the day. In between,

Poppy and I have done some guitar practice, entertaining Jasmine with our tunes. The girls have managed to glitter-bomb my beard, and I think I've done a pretty good job of keeping everyone fed and hydrated. The final credits are rolling, and I'm about to make a fresh batch of broth for everyone when I spy Cass carefully making her way downstairs. I quickly clear the few steps between us to help her the rest of the way down.

"What are you doing up and about? I'll bring you whatever you need."

She looks wrecked, but still so fucking beautiful. She tries to smile, which looks like it took a lot of effort. "I wanted to check on Poppy. I feel terrible. I've been so out of it that I've totally lost track of time. I haven't looked after my baby girl." Her eyes glisten, filling up to the point a tear escapes down her still-clammy cheek.

"She's good. I promise. The girls have been watching princess movies. They also decorated my beard." I wave my hand around my face to draw her attention to it.

She looks up at said beard, and her eyes widen. She reaches up, pinching it between her fingers. "Is that ... glitter?"

"Yep! I've also kept them fed and hydrated. I even showered them this morning. They're all good. Seriously, go back to bed, Cass. I have everything covered."

"But I'm her mom. I *should* be the one looking after her."

"You don't have to do everything now. I'm here." She sags into me, as though the weight of everything she's had to deal with on her own since she got pregnant has finally been lifted from her shoulders. Wrapping my arm around her shoulder, I guide her the rest of the way to the living room. "You can say hello to the girls; check for yourself they're okay. Then back to bed. Okay?"

"Okay," she sighs.

Stepping into the living room, the girls spot Cass straight

away and head toward her. They can see she's still unwell, so they treat her gently with careful hugs around her legs and waist.

"How are you girls doing?"

"We're good. Toby's been watching movies and playing with us. He's funny, Mommy." Cass's relief is plain to see. She needs to get used to the idea that we're a team now. When one's down, the other picks up the slack. She doesn't have to do it all on her own anymore. I know she's had the support and help of Rose, but it's not the same as having it from a partner.

"That's great. Be good for Toby, okay?" The girls nod vigorously. "I'm going back to bed." She hugs Poppy close, then signs to her, "I love you more than all the stars in the sky and grains of sand on the earth."

I help her back upstairs. "Do you want to have a shower so you can put on some fresh pajamas?"

"I'd love that, but I feel pretty weak. I don't want to fall over in the shower."

"Okay. Give me a sec. I'll make sure everything's okay downstairs, then I'll be back."

I head downstairs to give the girls a snack, turn off the stove, and make sure everything in the kitchen is safe for the girls. I set them up with some coloring in, explaining that I'm helping Cass in the shower. They agree to stay put, so I head back upstairs.

I guide Cass into the bathroom, then turn on the faucets, getting the water up to temperature. I strip off, then remove all of Cass's clothes and help her step into the shower. I wash her body. Even though she's terribly sick, my cock hasn't got the memo. I can't help the erection coming to life as I wash my girl. She barely has the energy to stand, and my dick thinks it's time to come out to play. *Stupid fucker!*

Rinsing us both down, we step out carefully to dry off. I find a clean set of pajamas for Cass, then sit her in the chair while I change her sheets. Once she's settled in bed, I get dressed in the same clothes I was wearing before because I didn't think to bring anything else with me—my sole focus was on getting here as fast as I could yesterday. I dish up some of the broth I've made and carry it with some crackers back up to Cass after checking on the girls.

I do the rounds again, ensuring Violet and Rose are okay, giving them some of the broth, crackers, and ginger ale, too.

"Why are you helping us?" Violet studies me with suspicion.

"Anyone would help you guys out if they could."

"Nope. My husband never once looked after me or Jas when we were sick."

"Well, I don't know him, but I grew up in a house where my parents worked as a team. If one was down, the other stepped up. Simple."

"Sounds like a fairytale."

"It was my reality growing up. I don't know any other way to be."

"I guess you're serious about my sister, then."

"Like a heart attack. Her *and* Poppy."

She nods. "Good." She chews thoughtfully on a cracker, then adds, "Do you love them both?"

"With everything I am, Violet. I want to be the one to take care of both of them. I want to call them mine. Both of them. Not one more than the other."

She nods, giving me a timid smile. "They deserve that."

"Yes, they do. So do you. Don't settle for anything less." She nods. "I helped Cass have a shower before. I'm not comfortable offering you the same service, but I can sit at the door while you shower to make sure you're okay if you feel up to it."

She thinks about it. "Thanks for the offer, but maybe a little later. If that's okay?"

"Sure. I'll check in on you in a while to see if you're up to it then."

"Thanks."

I leave her to it and make my way downstairs to spend time with my girls.

-cassia-

I CAN'T BELIEVE TOBY HAS SPENT THE LAST THREE DAYS looking after all of us. Seeing me at my absolute worst and caring for two young girls while Mom, Vi, and I were pretty much out of it. He's surely going to be rethinking his stance on wanting to be· with me now. No young, attractive, single guy wants to sign up for that.

"Toby's pretty great," Vi blurts out of nowhere as we're all sitting around the kitchen table nursing our tender stomachs with dry toast and ginger ale.

"He certainly is. Did you see the note he left on the kitchen counter about Thanksgiving?" Mom nods toward the sticky note I noticed earlier but haven't yet read.

"No. What about Thanksgiving?"

"We're all invited, Gramma too, to his sister's house for Thanksgiving dinner with his family. So sweet of him to think of us. I've been too sick to do any preparation for the holiday. His invitation is a blessing."

"Do you think Shane'll be there?" Vi asks, and I raise my eyebrows toward her in question. "He, um, he seems really nice. Jas likes him. A lot."

"I'm not sure. This is the first I've heard about Thanksgiving. Don't you think it's too soon to be sharing combined family holidays?" He may have changed his mind since he wrote the note. I don't want to get my hopes up. "His sister's married to Oliver Stone, the billionaire. Remember? I'm not sure they'll want all of us intruding on their holiday."

Vi's eyes widen. "That's right. That man is sex on a stick. So freaking hot. I couldn't keep my eyes off him after the concert when we went for ice cream."

"Violet!" Mom admonishes.

"What? He is. You've seen him!"

"You don't need to talk about him like he's a piece of meat. I brought you girls up better than that." Vi makes a show of rolling her eyes at me.

"Well, I'm sure he's a great guy, but I can only base my judgment on what I know, and since I only know what he looks like …" She shrugs, leaving her statement hanging.

I agree with her. He is hot, but not as hot as Toby. Toby has a raw sex appeal you can't ignore.

"I've actually been to their house. Well, *not exactly* inside their house, but outside. I did the flowers for their wedding." I sigh. "It was such a gorgeous location and even though they could have had anything they wanted for the wedding, it was kept small and simple." I grab my phone. "I'm just gonna check if the invitation is still valid."

"Why wouldn't it be?" Mom's puzzled face is almost comical.

"He might have changed his mind after having to deal with all of us." I glance away. "He saw me at my absolute worst. He probably never wants to have anything to do with me now."

"Rubbish, Cassia. That boy is in it for the long haul. Mark my words."

> ME
>
> Thank you again for looking after us

He answers immediately, as though he was sitting on his phone, waiting for my message.

> TOBY
>
> You're more than welcome, Bun

> ME
>
> I really appreciated it
>
> Sorry you had to see me like that

> TOBY
>
> Like what? Sick? Everyone gets sick

> ME
>
> Yeah, but I was a mess

> TOBY
>
> No one looks great when they're sick
>
> Even though you were sick, my cock still got hard in the shower

Oh, my gawd! Even though I'm not fully recovered, my body heats at his words.

> TOBY
>
> You're always gorgeous to me, Cass

> ME
>
> Thank you
>
> I wanted to check about Thanksgiving

> TOBY
>
> Yeah, what about it?

ME

Are you sure Kate and Oliver want all of us over for Thanksgiving?

It seems like a lot

My phone rings. "Hey."

"Hey, Bun. How are you feeling today?"

"So much better. Still not one hundred percent, but better than I was. Thank you for looking after us."

"You're more than welcome. But you can stop thanking me. You've thanked me enough." He sighs.

"Okay. I wanted you to know how much I appreciated it."

"I know you did. It was my privilege to care for you when you needed it." He pauses. "I already checked with Kate the first night I came over. I want to spend all of my holidays with you and Poppy. If it means dragging your whole family with you to have that, then so be it."

I grow warm all over with his words. He doesn't mess around or play games. He knows what he wants, and then he works toward getting it. For some reason, he wants Poppy and me in his life. I'm incredibly blessed to have him in ours.

"Okay. Only if you're sure."

"We're sure. Kate's inviting the kids from the shelter where she volunteers, so it's gonna be fun. It should be a great day."

"I know Mom was thankful for the invitation. She feels underprepared for the holiday. Poppy'll love to see Kate again. She loved meeting your sister and thinks it's amazing that you're twins. That you were in your mom's stomach at the same time." I laugh lightly. Toby laughs, too.

"Do you need me to pick you guys up, or can you get there on your own? I know my preference would be to collect you and Poppy."

That's his gentle way of telling me what's going to happen,

so I go along with it. I would prefer to go with him rather than show up. "Would you mind picking us up?"

"Of course not, Bun. I'll see you then unless you need anything."

"I think we're all good here. We're taking things slow and recovering. See you on Thursday."

"See you Thursday, Bun. Love you."

"Love you, Toby … and thanks again."

We disconnect the call, and I let Mom and Violet know Thanksgiving is a go.

I'm so freaking nervous. This is only the second time I've met Toby's parents, and I want to make a good impression. The first time was … awkward, to say the least. Toby was shocked to find out I was Poppy's mom, while I was stunned that he was Poppy's guitar teacher. I'm racing around my bedroom, trying to work out what to wear when Violet comes strolling in.

"What's up, Sis? You're all over the place." She plops down on my bed, looking around at the pile of discarded clothes.

Throwing my hands up in the air, I huff. "I dunno what to wear. I want to make a good impression. Plus, I want to erase the last images Toby has of me. I wanna look good, but I can't work out what to wear."

She stands and studies the clothes on the bed as well as the ones still in my closet. "What about these black, skinny jeans with this red sweater? You can wear your knee-high boots. They always look amazing on you."

"You think that'll be okay to wear to Thanksgiving with his whole family?"

"Of course. Why not?"

"I wanna look classy."

"You'll look classy and casual. Sexy even. C'mon, you're running out of time."

"Thanks, Vi. I'll be down in a minute."

She blows me a kiss as she leaves my room. The butterflies in my stomach are going crazy as I get dressed, finish off my hair, and apply a little more gloss to my lips. As I step into the kitchen, Mom's putting the finishing touches to one of the two casseroles she made as our contribution to dinner. Finally, Poppy and Jasmine are ready to go, looking as cute as anything dressed in matching outfits.

The doorbell rings—*he's here!*

I draw a deep breath, releasing it slowly, trying to calm myself as I walk as calmly as possible toward the front door.

Opening it, Toby's waiting on the porch, looking edible in worn jeans with a black sweater that hugs his torso. "Hey." He smiles, sapphire eyes twinkling at me.

"Hey." I step into him, wrapping my arms around his torso and kissing his lips softly. "How are you feeling? You didn't get the stomach flu?"

"I'm great. No sign of sickness. Are you guys ready to go?"

"Yeah, come in. I'll get our coats." He steps inside, closing the door before turning to face the room in time to catch Poppy as she throws herself at him. Gramma Iris steps out of the kitchen, laughing at Poppy's antics.

Toby's holding Poppy on his hip, her arms wrapped around his neck. "Thank you for looking after all my girls for me last week."

"No problem. I was happy to do it." He looks at Poppy, jiggling her on his hip, causing her to giggle.

We gather everything we need and step out the front door. Mom stops dead in her tracks, causing us to walk right into her, almost knocking the casserole out of her hands. I glance up to see what the issue is, noticing a stretched limo parked in front of our house. What the …?

Toby notices us all gawking at the car. "I figured everyone would fit in this. Hope you don't mind."

Mom's the first to respond. "Not at all. I was surprised, that's all. It's very thoughtful of you to organize a ride. I figured we'd be following behind you and Cass."

"This makes it easier. C'mon, let's go." He's nonchalant about organizing such a lavish ride.

We all walk forward to pile into the fancy car. I've never been in a limo before. It feels somewhat over-the-top to turn up to Thanksgiving dinner in one, but I guess it was a fair solution. As we get closer to Kate and Oliver's home, my butterflies become out of control.

I needn't have worried, though, because as we pull up, Toby's entire family steps out to greet us like we're old friends. His mom and dad warmly welcome my mom, while his nan and another elderly woman fuss over my gramma. It's like our families have always known each other—that's how comfortable it all feels. I watch Toby hug his dad in greeting and their easy interaction. I can see the bond they share; the love between them is obvious.

As we're about to step inside, a minibus arrives. Half a dozen kids pile out with a large man and a petite woman hot on their heels. His hair's a mess, as though he's been almost pulling it out. She looks put together with a wide, friendly smile. Kate runs forward, arms open wide, as Oliver follows behind, hands in pockets and a smile on his face. His adoration for his wife is blatantly obvious for everyone to see.

Once all the introductions are made and everyone's inside and settled, Kate and Oliver explain it's a buffet-style dinner today. A long buffet is already set up, waiting for the hot food, a non-alcoholic punch for the kids as well as a 'special' one for the grown-ups. *Lucky us!*

The Stone house is stunning. I remember admiring the home's exterior, but the outside doesn't hold a candle to how warm and inviting the inside is. For such a large house, it feels cozy and welcoming. In addition, Kate's gone all out with holiday decorations, adding to the atmosphere.

Toby hasn't left my side, always finding ways to be touching me, little touches here and there, ensuring we're always connected. It's definitely louder than I'm used to with so many people gathered together to celebrate the holiday. It makes me even more grateful for my family; that it's growing larger by joining Toby and his family.

Poppy's even made new friends, dragging Jas along for the ride. It hasn't taken long for the kids to work out a way to communicate; it always amazes me how kids seem to easily work their way around obstacles. Kate and Oliver hand out a journal to each of the kids they spend time with at the shelter.

"I love the tradition of giving the kids a journal each Thanksgiving. The first year, it surprised me they had anything at all to be thankful for, but they did. So we're keeping it going."

She hands Poppy a journal, too. In purple. "Here, Poppy. I heard purple was your favorite color." I translate for Poppy. Her delight at being included is clear as she quickly gives her thanks, then immediately takes it to Toby to show him her gift.

"Thank you for including Poppy in your journal giving. It was a sweet gesture." I nod toward my little girl and Toby. "She obviously loves it."

"No problem. Once I knew you guys were coming today, I *had* to include her. Unfortunately, Jas is a little young, so I didn't get her a journal. I bought her a coloring book instead." Kate's incredibly sweet, readily including the girls in her gift-giving tradition.

Mom is helping Toby's mom, Emily, in the kitchen along with Roman and Alice, who I learned only married recently. They were the friends in need of wedding flowers at short notice. Roman and Alice are the kids' caretakers at the shared home where they all live. James and David—Oliver and Toby and Kate's dads—are preparing the salad. I assume they were given the simple task, as they're possibly not competent in the kitchen. They all laugh at something Roman said. Mom looks comfortable. It's as though she's known them for years. She has a few friends she spends time with occasionally, but it would be great if she made friends with Toby's parents because I have a feeling he's gonna stick.

Poppy comes running over to me, waving her journal. "Look what I got, Mommy."

"I saw. You know what it's for, right?"

"Yeah. I have to write the things I'm grateful for."

"Exactly."

"It's gonna be a lot of things. I'm grateful for heaps of stuff." I laugh because that's typical Poppy. She finds only things to be happy about. She's rarely sad or down in the dumps. "Hey, did you know one of the other girls is called Ivy? That's another plant name. Just like us."

"Yeah, I heard that. She must be super cool, hey?"

"Super cool."

She runs off back to her new friends after ensuring I'll keep her journal safe. Gramma Iris steps back inside with Toby's nan, Kate, and their friend, Margie. They're all cackling at something and I feel the three of them together will be trouble.

-toby-

IT FEELS RIGHT TO HAVE CASS AND POPPY HERE WITH MY family. They all meld together seamlessly, not that I thought they wouldn't. *Who wouldn't love Cass and Poppy?* The rest of Cass's family is just as cool and easygoing. Cass looks sexy as hell, making it murder to keep my touches chaste in front of everyone. It's been too long since I've had her. Which reminds me, I haven't told her how gorgeous she looks today.

Roman cuts through the noise with a loud whistle.

"Dinner's ready on the buffet, everyone. We'll serve the kids first. Then the adults can get their own."

Cass moves toward Poppy to dish up, but I stop her. "Can I do it?"

Her eyes widen at my question. "Sure. If you want to."

"I want to. Is that okay?" She smiles brightly, which reaches her eyes, giving me an emotional high. Who needs drugs when I have my girls?

"Definitely."

I collect Poppy as well as a plate, and we make our way along the buffet; her pointing out what she would like to eat. I note Shane's doing the same for Jasmine while Violet and

Cassia refresh their drinks with the 'special' punch. Of course, Margie, Iris, and Nan have already had more than their fair share of that punch; Margie and Nan are already wild enough together, they don't need the help.

The kids are all settled at a smaller table with their food, and I collect Cass so we can make our way over to the buffet to fill our plates.

"I can't believe how much food there is. I should have worn my stretchy pants." She laughs.

I snuggle into Cass's neck to whisper, "I love you in these sexy jeans. I'm sorry I forgot to tell you how gorgeous you look today." I kiss her neck, right below her ear. "I'll be happy to help get you out of them later." Pulling away, I wink before moving further along the buffet to get some turkey. We settle in at the table, Cass sitting next to her sister, and me next to mine. Taking turns around the table, everyone shares something that they're grateful for.

Kate nudges me with her elbow. "I guess your patience paid off, Brother?"

"Yeah." I can't stop the goofy smile which fills my face. "You were right. In the end, I didn't need to push. She let me in all on her own."

"I'm so happy for you. She's a great lady and I adore Poppy." She takes a bite of her dinner, chewing thoughtfully, then swallowing. "I can't believe you're pretty much a daddy." Her eyes, which match my own, are looking suspiciously glassy. "You're gonna be such a great daddy, Toby. The best thing about this is I'm now an aunt and I've finally got a sister. Yay!"

"Thanks, Squirt." She shoves her pointy elbow into my side. "Oooomph. Geez, your elbows are deadly weapons." I rub my side in an exaggerated show, making her laugh.

The conversation is loud and is regularly broken up with boisterous laughter. Everyone's having a great time, enjoying fantastic food, surrounded by family and good friends. My heart feels full watching all the people I care about most in the world together in this one space, sharing a meal and enjoying the holiday together. I only hope I get the chance to show Cass exactly how grateful I am for her later on. I have a special surprise up my sleeve that I set up with Rose yesterday for later.

With stomachs full to bursting, we all load ourselves back into the limo, heading back to the girls' home. Hopefully, Rose has already packed an overnight bag for Cass and Poppy so we can head straight to my place.

We arrive at the Phillips' home and pile out of the car, carrying containers of leftovers, which will possibly feed everyone for the next couple of days. Kate always over-caters when she has an event. As we get inside out of the cool air, Rose rushes further inside their home and returns with a duffel, passing it to me. Cass looks between her mom and me quizzically. "What's going on?"

"You and Poppy are having a sleepover at Toby's house." She signs as she speaks. While Cass is shocked at the turn of events, Poppy excitedly jumps up and down in celebration.

Cass is shaking her head, eyes wide. "We can't sleep over at your place." She's making some weird gesture with her face like I should know better than to have a sleepover in front of her daughter. Cass doesn't know Poppy asked me when she could come for a sleepover. It happened at our lesson after Cass's birthday, when she spent the night. I set up a bedroom for her and I can't wait for her to see it. "I don't think that would be a good idea." She's glancing between her mom and me.

"Why wouldn't it be a good idea? Poppy's super excited about it," Rose answers.

"Yeah, but ..." She stops signing. "Do you think that sets a good example for Poppy to see her mom sleeping in a man's bed when we haven't been together all that long? I mean, we've been together for a little while, but Poppy thinks we only got together on my birthday. I don't want to be a poor role model for her."

Poppy stomps her foot. "You stopped signing for me."

I sign, "This is adult conversation."

She crosses her arms with a pout—she doesn't like to be left out of the conversation.

Rose wraps Cass in her arms, beating me to it. "And don't you think it's good for Poppy to see you happy with a man who cares for you both so much? A man who puts you *and* your daughter first?"

I don't want to push her into anything she's not ready for; as disappointed as I'll be if they don't come, I have to let her make the choice. "It's okay if you're not ready, Bun. I understand what you're saying. I don't want you to do anything you're not comfortable with."

She bites her bottom lip, and I want to take over and bite it myself. It's been hell all afternoon, not being able to touch her in the way I really want to. Finally, she looks at Poppy's excited face and signs, "Do you want to have a sleepover at Toby's house?"

Poppy nods like a bobble doll, holding her hands in the begging position under her chin. I watch Cass carefully, observing the moment she gives in. "Okay then. Let's go have a sleepover." Poppy hugs her mom tightly around the waist while I release the breath I was holding, hoping to get the answer I wanted. We all say goodbye and I walk my future family to the waiting limo to take them *home*, which I desperately want to make into a family home with them.

The limo drops us off at my place, and once we're securely inside, Shane heads off, leaving me alone with my girls. The first night I brought Cass here, I never would have imagined I'd have her back in my space with a daughter in tow after the reunion. A daughter I'll proudly call my own one day.

"C'mon, I want to show you your bedroom." Cass sucks in a breath, graphite eyes wide. I take the duffel in one hand and Poppy's hand in the other, then climb the stairs. I show Poppy where her bathroom is on the way. I stocked it with the same strawberry bubble bath, soap, shampoo, and conditioner she uses at her house.

"Oh, Toby. You've gone to so much trouble for her," Cass whispers, her fingers held up to her mouth. "You didn't need to do all this." Wait until she sees Poppy's room.

"It was nothing, Bun. I want her to be comfortable here. I'm hoping you guys will stay over regularly." Maybe I'm pushing her too fast, but I can't help myself. She smiles at me, giving me a simple nod, her eyes suspiciously glassy.

We walk down the hallway. As we get closer to Poppy's bedroom, my stomach rolls in nervousness. I really hope I've done the right thing and they both love it. I suck in a deep breath, readying myself for the reveal to go either way as I open the door. Looking at both of the girl's faces the moment they see the room for the first time, I think I got it right if their smiles are any sign. Poppy doesn't hesitate, moving into the room. Spinning around to look at everything. I even bought her a new guitar and a laptop. That way she can practice while she's here.

"Oh my god, Toby. This is incredible." Cass glances at me before joining Poppy on her exploration. Then, as Poppy investigates everything more closely, Cass steps into me, wrapping me in her embrace. She presses a chaste kiss to my lips. "I don't know what to say. This room is everything Poppy loves. You're incredibly sweet to do this for her."

I wrap my arms around her, locking us together. "I want her to be happy here. I want to make this our home, Cass. I hope you know that." I finish with a kiss on her forehead as she melts into me.

"I never thought Poppy and I would have this." She looks up at me, stormy eyes glassy. "Thank you doesn't seem enough."

"You guys being here is all the thanks I need, Bun."

"I love you so much. I'm gonna show you exactly how much once she's in bed."

"I love you, too. Both of you." I press a kiss to her lips, grinding my hips into her stomach. "I can't wait until later."

Poppy wraps her little arms around both of us, pulling us as tight as she can with the cutest grin on her face. Then, she pulls back to sign, "Thank you, Toby. Thank you. Thank you. Thank you. I love it. I love everything. It's beautiful."

"You're most welcome, young lady." Then, laughing, I bend down to pick her up to include her in a family hug.

Perfect.

My life is perfect!

Cass changes Poppy into her pajamas in case she falls asleep during the movie, then we show her where we'll be sleeping in case she wakes during the night. I had nightlights installed down the passage to help her find her way easily if she wakes in the night and forgets where she is. We head downstairs, where I show Cass the switch I had installed to flash all the lights in the house for Poppy. That way, we can get her attention wherever she is. Cass's eyes look misty again—storm clouds brewing with rain—as she steps in to press a kiss against my lips.

"You are getting so lucky tonight, Mister," she whispers against my ear with a smile, waking up my dick. He's going to have to wait because I promised Poppy a movie tonight and I always keep my promises.

"I'm gonna hold you to that, Bun." I kiss her hard, then

step away, making sure I don't get carried away. We head into the living room, where we load up the Disney Channel.

Did I ever think I'd be subscribing to the Disney Channel at this point in my life? *No.*

Am I happy that I am? *Hell yeah!*

I make popcorn before we settle in for a movie. Poppy takes up her usual position between her mom and me. I stretch my arm along the back of the couch to play with Cass's silky hair and I take a moment to admire my girls.

My house finally feels like a home.

About an hour into the movie, Poppy lays down with her head in my lap and her legs across her mother's. The trust she affords me whenever she does this fills me with gratitude and a sense of purpose I've not felt before. This little girl relies on the adults in her life to keep her safe, to love her unconditionally, and to allow her to be the person she's meant to be. That I'm now part of her circle fills me with a sense of pride that's unparalleled in my life. Even more so than the Grammy's I've been awarded and the albums I've released; or the success I've experienced in my career so far. This right here … *this* is my purpose.

Cass switches off the TV and lights as the credits roll, checking that the front door is locked. I carry Poppy upstairs to her new bedroom as Cass follows behind. As soon as Poppy's tucked in for the night, gentle kisses pressed against her forehead and cheek, I eagerly lead Cass into my bedroom. Or should I call it *our* bedroom?

FORTY-SIX

-toby-

As soon as the door to our bedroom closes, my Bun has me pressed up against it, her lips smashed against mine, hands loosening my hair out of its elastic. I catch up quickly, my tongue swiping against her lips, demanding entry. We get lost in a kiss that's so fucking sexy. My cock's going to have zipper indentations on it at the rate it's expanding and trying to escape my jeans. I switch places, pressing Cass against the door, grinding my cock against her, eliciting a sexy moan which vibrates against my mouth. This woman turns me on like no other, lighting a fire inside me that can only be extinguished by her.

Kissing my way down her neck, I pull at her sweater. She gets the hint, lifting her arms so I can remove the offending item. Her tits greet me, cupped in black lace, presented to me like the gift they are. I'm thankful the lamp's on, so I can appreciate the gorgeous sight of Cass's body. Nuzzling them, licking the nipples through the fabric, I finish with a bite before releasing the front clasp. Kudos to whoever invented the front bra clasp, making life easier for men all around the world. Catching the gorgeous globes in my waiting hands, I knead them carefully, pressing them together and nuzzling them, just the way I dreamed of doing in my teenage bed. The reality of Cass, of being with her, far surpasses any teenage fantasy I could have ever dreamed up.

Cass tugs on my hair until I'm looking up at her; dark eyes, full of lust, look back at me. "I really need you inside me. It's been too long."

"In good time, Gorgeous." I slide down her body, releasing the button and zipper on her jeans. The boots make it difficult to peel the skin-tight denim away from her body, but I'm a man on a mission—nothing's gonna stop me from having my way with her. Matching black lace panties greets me and I take a moment to admire them up close as I inhale her arousal. It's like a fucking aphrodisiac, not that I need any help to get hard when I'm in her vicinity.

Sliding her underwear down her legs, I lift one shapely leg, balancing it over my shoulder, and take my first swipe of her pussy. I moan at her cinnamon taste. I don't know how she does it, but she always has that sweet, woody taste and scent that drives me wild. I get down to business, licking, stroking, nipping her lips, using my fingers to tease her clit.

Three knocks sound on the other side of the door, and I freeze, looking up at Cass. We both know we can't ignore Poppy. She's in a strange house and a strange bed for the very first time. I stand up, giving Cass my sweater to put on, covering her nakedness, and then open the door. Poppy's rubbing the sleep from her eyes as I bend down to pick her up.

Looking at Cass, she signs. "Mommy, I'm scared."

"Baby. You don't need to be scared. C'mon, let's go have a cuddle in your new bed." Cass looks apologetically at me as she reaches for her daughter. I give her a look I hope telegraphs it's okay and tell her I'll be waiting. I think it's best if they have some quiet time together in Poppy's new space to help her acclimate. Thinking I'm no longer needed, I step out of the way so the girls can get past, but Poppy reaches out to grab my hand, pulling me along with them. I guess she wants both of us.

All three of us lay in Poppy's bed, Cass and me on either side, sandwiching her in the middle. Poppy snuggles down under the covers. Feeling safe, she closes her eyes. We watch her as she falls asleep until I decide watching Cass watch her daughter is sexy as fuck. A ghost of a smile crosses her lips as she looks up at me.

"What are you doing, perv?"

"Watching my girlfriend love on her daughter. Did you know it's sexy as fuck watching you as a mom?"

Her eyes drop to Poppy again as her smile drops for a moment. "You have no idea how much of a turn-on it is that you love my daughter as much as you do."

We lay in quiet bliss, watching each other, watching Poppy, enjoying the moment together. Once Cass is certain Poppy's well and truly asleep, she gestures for us to leave the room. Once in our bedroom, I waste no time in picking up Cass to throw her onto the bed, so I can pick up where I left off.

"Get that sweater off. Show me your pussy."

I step back to remove my jeans. She wastes no time. Removing my sweater swiftly and opening her legs wide, she uses her fingers to caress her delicate pink folds for my benefit —eyes hooded and biting her bottom lip. She's a wet dream. I dive down, taking a swipe of her lips, licking her fingers as I do.

"Play with your tits. I've got this."

Her fingers quickly move out of my way, and I watch her glide them up her body until they reach their target. She presses them together, then teases her nipples. Once I'm satisfied she's on task, I leave her to it and focus on my own. Her warm channel greets my fingers with a tight squeeze as I pump them in and out with purpose. Seeking the swollen area that's not as smooth as the rest of her walls, I know I found the spot

I'm looking for. Massaging the area in time with my tongue on her clit, her legs tense around my head as her silky pussy walls tighten around my fingers as she breaks apart beneath my mouth. Her moans and sighs make my dick harder than granite, if that's even possible.

"That's it, Gorgeous. You're a fucking sight to behold when you fall apart." My chest expands with pride that I'm the one to bring her pleasure. I'm the man who will give her the pleasure she deserves for the remainder of my days.

Removing my fingers gently as she finishes, I climb up her body, paying close attention to her breasts with my mouth as my cock seeks her entrance. She's so fucking wet from her orgasm. I have no problem sliding home. Braced above her, our eyes lock, and I pause. Taking a moment to study her face, I absorb her love for me.

"I love you, Bun," I whisper, my lips touching hers, my eyes locked on hers, my breaths exchanging with hers. I don't give her a chance to respond; I press forward to deliver a kiss that expresses the intensity of my emotions.

Joined, not moving, just kissing.

My hair curtaining us from the world.

Her warmth surrounding my cock.

Her breath filling my lungs.

Her love filling my soul.

Moving my cock incrementally in and out of her body, we build a rhythm. Our bodies move together as if we've done this a million times when, in reality, we've only been together like this on a few occasions. If she were living here, we could do this every single day. Slowly, steadily, we build and fall over the edge in mutual satisfaction, sighing and moaning against each other as we continue to kiss.

Cass peers up at me with a lazy smile touching her lips, her eyes serene. "I love you so much." She presses up off the bed to seal her words with a kiss.

Keeping our bodies intimately joined, I roll us to the side so I don't squash her with my weight. Then, using one hand, I brush her hair away from her face, laying a tender kiss on her forehead. "I want you to think about you and Poppy moving in here with me when I get back from my press tour."

Her eyes widen as her lips part, but I stay her words with my finger pressed against her lips. "Just think about it. It's a few weeks away yet. Okay?"

She nods. "Okay. I'll think about it."

We fall asleep, my dick still inside my gorgeous girlfriend.

FORTY-SEVEN

-toby-

I STEP INTO MY BEDROOM AFTER MY MORNING SWIM AND I immediately know something's wrong. I can detect the distinct sweet floral scent of a perfume that I hoped I would never smell again. Feminine underwear lies on my bed like an invitation, one I never want to receive again. Memories flood, knocking me on my ass as my breath leaves my lungs. This can't happen again. I refuse to let her rule my life a second time. My home is meant to be my sanctuary. It needs to be a safe place for Poppy, for Cass, and for me. If this psycho's back and thinks she can mess with my life, she has another thing coming.

I message Shane.

ME

Can you come up to my bedroom to look at something?

Within moments, I hear his heavy footsteps running up the stairs. I haven't taken my eyes off the garments on my bed as he comes up beside me. Looking at him, I see the instant he smells the perfume, and recognition sets in.

I tilt my head toward the bed and he follows, eyes widening as he spots what I found. "Fuck."

"Yeah, fuck."

"I'll call the psych ward to check she's still there."

"You do that, but I don't think she is."

I step out of my bedroom, slamming the door closed in frustration. I need to block it all out. Pretend it's not happening again. Stepping into my studio, I plan to lose myself in my music for a few hours while I wait for Cass to come over.

Making my way out of my studio, Shane catches me in the hallway.

His eyebrows are drawn down, his jaw's tight. "She's still in the facility."

I shake my head. "Are you sure?" *What in the hell is going on?*

Walking back to my bedroom, I open the door to check that what I saw this morning is still there. That it wasn't my imagination playing tricks on me. I wouldn't be surprised since I'm stressed about flying out—leaving Cass and Poppy behind. But then Shane saw it, too. So it can't be my mind playing tricks on me.

We both glance at the bed. The lingerie is still there with that awful odor still in the air, milder now, but still there. I'm fucking confused.

"Does this mean I have a copycat stalker?"

Shane shrugs. "I dunno, man. But she's still under psychiatric care. I made them check her room."

I stand, rubbing the back of my neck, trying to make sense of the situation. Shane's equally confused.

Light footsteps sound on the stairs, and we both step out of the room to see chestnut hair appear, followed by steel-colored eyes together with a smile I want to see every day. Cass comes straight to me, wrapping her arms around my waist. She smells different. I push her away.

"What's wrong?" She studies my face. "You look pale. Are you getting sick?" She holds the back of her hand to my forehead, checking my temperature.

I glance between Cass and Shane. "You smell different. What perfume is that?" Shane catches on, leaning forward, sniffing my girlfriend. I give him a warning look, so he backs away with a smirk on his face.

"You like it? I thought I'd try a new one. It's called Miss Dior."

"No, I don't fucking like it. I like the way you usually smell." Shane's eyes widen comically, and I realize how I spoke to the woman I love.

"No need to be so damn rude. What the hell is wrong with you?" she snaps.

We're both already on edge because I fly out tomorrow for my press tour and we're dreading the time apart. Add to that, finding my room smelling like a past nightmare means I need to temper myself. Shane looks as though he wants to step in to defend me, but I stop him with a shake of my head. Smart man that Shane is, he steps away from us. Leaving me to face the wrath of a pissed-off Cass.

Carefully placing my hands on Cass's shoulders, as though she's a grenade that may explode if mishandled, I pull her into me, snuggling her face into the crook of my neck. Kissing the top of her head. "I'm sorry. I shouldn't have spoken to you like that. Please forgive me." I kiss her again. "I don't want to fight when I won't see you for two whole fucking weeks."

She sags against me. "It's okay … just … don't do it again. Okay?"

"I promise, Bun."

I pull away, pointing over my shoulder. "Do those belong to you?" As her expression changes from forgiving to pissed again,

I realize how my question sounded. I'm not doing very well this afternoon.

"Who the hell else is gonna be leaving lingerie on your bed?" She stomps over to the bed, snatching them up, waving them in my face. "I was planning to give you a sexy treat tonight before you have to leave tomorrow, but maybe I won't."

"Awww, don't be like that." I follow her, tugging her back into me. "Let me explain. Please?"

I sit on my bed, situating Cass on my lap.

-cassia-

HE'S ACTING VERY UN-TOBY-LIKE. I'M NOT SURE WHAT TO make of him. The way he shoved me away from him when I hugged him, it … well, it hurt. He's never spoken to me or treated me like that before—it was a shock. I know he's as anxious as I am about our impending separation, but he didn't need to take it out on me. Now, sitting on his lap, he's scanning the room, looking everywhere but at me. The tenseness in his jaw as well as the frown lines across his brows have me worried.

Finally, he looks at me. "A couple of years ago, I had a stalker." Shane mentioned something about that. "She, uh, she used to come in here and leave her …" He rubs the back of his neck, tensing his jaw. "Her, uh … dirty underwear under my pillow. Her perfume …" He gestures toward me with his head. "Would be all over my bedding, as though she rubbed her body all over my sheets." I can't hold in the gasp as I glance at his bed. "It started with her sending me personal messages on Facebook and Insta. Several times a day, she'd let me know what she was up to, how much she loved me, and send me photos of her boobs and vagina. Never her face." He brushes his hair behind his ear. "Then she started sending me love letters and small gifts. It was constant. Every day, something else would turn up here at the house."

I open my mouth to speak, but I don't know what to say to him. I can tell he's caught up in the memories by the cloudiness in his normally bright blue eyes. I place my hands on his chest because I have to touch him. His heart's beating incredibly fast; I'm worried it's going to beat right out of his chest. "She made a photo album. Like a regular family photo album of us together in different places, with kids, me coaching little league. It was fucking weird. The photos never showed her face and mine was always photoshopped onto different men." I suck in a breath because that's unbelievably twisted—what a sick thing to do. "I would sometimes come home to find my favorite meal set out on the dining table, with the table set for two, candles, the works. Then it escalated to the underwear and messing around in my bed." He releases a heavy sigh, so I wrap my arms around his shoulders to offer him support. "It took months to work out who it was and to actually catch her. The woman was very unwell. She ended up in the psych ward. She put me through hell, Cass ... and ... when I walked in here, smelled the perfume and saw the lingerie, it took me back there." He locks eyes with me. "I'm sorry I reacted the way I did."

I cup his face in my hands, pulling his face forward to place a gentle kiss against his smooth lips surrounded by soft bristles. "Thank you for sharing with me. I completely understand your reaction. It must have been an awful experience for you. I'm sorry I brought back those memories. I thought sneaking in to leave my lingerie displayed on your bed would be a sexy tease." I kiss him again. "I assume that's why you employed Shane."

He nods. "It definitely gave me the excuse I needed, but it's also why I've been protective of Poppy. People go to extreme lengths sometimes, and I didn't want her caught in the crossfire."

"I get it now. I do. But I also think it's time to call Shane off her watch. You need him while you're away. We'll keep Poppy close. I promise she'll be safe."

He shakes his head, his jaw tensing. "You don't understand how creepy these people are, Cass. They wait for any opportunity. That woman stalked me for months. The stuff she did ..." He glances away again before looking back at me.

I can see his fear and concern for Poppy, but I don't think she'll garner the same attention as Toby did with his stalker. "How about you take Shane with you?" He's already shaking his head. "Listen, please. I'll sleep better at night knowing you have him with you. If it makes you feel better, we'll keep your guy, Len." I only hope he sees reason. I soften him up some more, grinding down on his dick as I kiss him (maybe soften him up was the wrong phrase because he's as hard as a rock).

He kisses me back, grasping the back of my head to take control, pressing his dick harder into the softest part of me. Pulling away, pressing my forehead to his, I implore, "Please. For me?"

He huffs out a breath. "Okay. But I want you to know I'm not happy about the swap. Shane's been giving me a hard time about it, too. He thinks the risk to me is higher than to Poppy at this point."

I agree with Shane. "I think he's right." Toby nods lightly.

"Uh, do you mind if we have a shower?" he asks sheepishly. "I really need to get that smell off you."

I wriggle off Toby's lap, pulling him up with me to head to the shower. "Sure thing. I'll give this perfume away. You'll never smell it on me again."

He kisses my shoulder. "Thanks, Bun."

Toby treats me to some extra attentive loving in the shower, and even though it wasn't what I had planned for our last night together for a while, I'm certainly not complaining. What that man can do with his nimble fingers is nothing short of astounding. He certainly keeps my lady bits happy.

But more than that, he keeps *me* happy. I've never felt so safe, so cherished, so loved before. I know he would do anything in the world for Poppy and for me.

FORTY-NINE

-cassia-

WE STAND ON TOBY'S FRONT STEPS IN THE EARLY MORNING. The chill surrounds us as we say our final goodbyes. "Why can't I come to the airport? Sam and Sally can hold the shop for a little while."

"I would love for you to come to the airport. Hell, I'd love it if you'd grab Poppy and jump on the plane with me, but there'll be too many people. I don't want to draw more attention to the fact that you guys are going to be here unprotected. Our photos are already all over social media. I'm terrified someone's gonna come after you guys. Humor me, please. Stay as close to Len as you can. Try not to go out more than necessary. I know I'm asking a lot, but it would make me feel better."

The tension radiating off his body is intense. I can feel it transferring across to me; making me feel unnecessarily worried. I push it down—I don't want him to sense that I'm worried. We don't need both of us getting worked up. "I can do that for you. Just work, school, and home for us for the next two weeks. But only because I love you." I agree with a smirk, punctuating it with a cheeky peck on his lips.

His body sags as he releases a long breath, kissing me on

the nose. "Thanks, Bun. I appreciate it. And I only worry because I love you guys. You and Poppy are too important to me to put at risk."

I think the events of yesterday are still raw for him, making him more anxious than necessary. "I know. We'll be careful, I promise."

We share one more intense kiss, then I drag myself away from him to head to work for the day as he heads to the airport to begin his press tour. This time it's only two weeks.

How will I feel when he's away for months at a time for his actual tour?

Work is terrible. This place is usually my sanctuary, but today it's not offering the peace I typically feel when I'm here. Looking up into the corners of my little shop, I sigh at the sight of the hidden cameras Toby insisted on installing. I can't believe how quickly they worked to get them in. He said it would make him feel better to have the cameras recording inside since I didn't have Shane standing outside. He doesn't have as much faith in Len as he does in his best friend, so he wanted additional measures for my safety and Poppy's. I reluctantly agreed to give him peace of mind.

I can't concentrate no matter how hard I try. My mind is constantly wandering to Toby—wondering what he's doing, where he's at, who he's with. Not that I don't trust him. I do—one hundred percent. I just miss him and it hasn't even been a full day.

Toby and I have been messaging regularly back and forth for the last three days, but it's not enough. I miss him so much. I miss his smell, his touch, the rasp of his beard against my skin, the warmth of his body. He told me to be secure in my room, on my own, ready for his text tonight. So here I am. Poppy's in bed, and I'm in my warm fleece pajamas, reading the latest Bratva romance by Bree Porter on my Kindle. My phone vibrates with an incoming message.

TOBY

I miss your sexy ass

ME

I miss you too lover

TOBY

I want you in my bed

ME

I miss your bed so much

TOBY

I'm gonna fuck you for a whole day and night when I get home

ME

Promises, promises 😏 😉

TOBY

I always keep my promises

The things I'm gonna do to you

ME

What sorts of things?

TOBY

You're gonna sit on my face so I can eat your pussy for starters

I can't believe I'm sexting my boyfriend. I'm squealing inside like a teenager receiving her first love note.

ME

Yeah? That sounds so good

TOBY

Yeah, you're gonna cover my face and beard with your juices, so I can taste and smell you for hours

My dick will be so hard from licking your pussy

Then I'm gonna fill your pussy with my fingers, while you fuck my face

ME

Can I suck on your cock while you're eating my pussy?

TOBY

Fuck yeah

I'm so fucking hard for you

ME

I'm so wet, god I miss you

As I'm about to slide my hand into my pajama bottoms, my phone rings, scaring the shit out of me. I press to accept his call, holding the phone up to my ear.

"Is your door closed?" His voice is gritty—god, he's sexy. He's as turned on as I am.

"Yeah," I whisper.

"Good. Take your pajamas off." He's not messing around.

I put the phone on my nightstand, quickly stripping down until I'm completely bare. "I'm naked." I didn't realize how breathy my voice was until I heard him groan on his end of the phone.

"Good girl, now tell me … how wet are you?"

I dip my fingers down to my pussy. "I'm so wet, Toby. I wish you were here to lick up all of my cream."

"Slide your fingers down to your beautiful pussy and let me listen to them slide in and out of your tight hole."

Oh, god. His words.

I move the phone down to my pussy, then do as he told me. The noises I'm making are obscene.

I put the phone back up to my ear. "Did you hear how wet I am for you? Are you hard?"

"I'm so fucking hard for you. I'm stroking my cock so hard right now, imagining your tight pussy strangling it." His heavy breaths fill my ear.

"Mmmmmm. My fingers don't match up to your dick, but your words, they get me so hot."

"Rub your clit, Gorgeous. Just the way I would, small circles."

"Oh, god, Toby. It feels so good. I'm getting close. Are you close?"

"Yeah, Gorgeous, I'm close. Rub harder, then slide two fingers inside you. Imagine it's my fingers fucking you."

"Oh, oh, oh …" My pussy spasms around my fingers as my legs shake. I've never had an orgasm like this before while talking to my boyfriend over the phone.

"Yeah, fuck, I can feel your pussy squeezing my cock so hard. Mmmmhm." He grunts as he comes undone. "Fuck, that's messy," he huffs out as he laughs mildly.

His statement's so unexpected that I laugh, too. "Oh, Toby. I miss you so much and I'm not talking about your dick. Though I miss that, too." I chuckle.

"I miss you too, Bun. I'm counting down the days."

"Me too. I saw you on The Tonight Show. Jimmy's such a funny guy." Watching Toby on television was surreal. I used to follow his career intermittently once he got big via social media and interviews on TV, but it's somehow different now I've spent time with him on a personal level.

"Yeah, he is. Not just in front of the camera, either. He had me in stitches beforehand, too."

I lower my voice. "I love how you're letting everyone know you're off the market. Thank you." I don't think he truly realizes how much it means to me that he's sharing his personal life with the world, so women back off.

"I needed to make it clear that my woman doesn't like sharing. Just as I don't like to share either." His voice is deeper, raspier as he tells me he doesn't like to share.

"You sounded so good last night." His voice is incredibly rich and warm. "I loved the new song. Is it going on the album?"

"Yeah, I wrote that one when you weren't giving me the time of day." He chuckles, but it's forced.

"I'm sorry about that. I was trying to protect myself when I really didn't need to." My stomach turns as I remember how I ended things abruptly with him. I'm thankful he didn't give up on me.

"No problem, Bun. It all worked out how it was supposed to."

I wake with a start, my phone stuck to my face. I must've fallen asleep while we were talking. I'm still naked as the day I was born from our sexting session. My body warms as I remember our text messages and conversation last night.

FIFTY

-toby-

I HATE BEING AWAY FROM HER. FROM BOTH OF THEM.

I've decided I'm definitely not doing my normal tour when the album releases. It's too hard being away from her and Poppy for any length of time. I know for a fact I won't make it if I'm away from them for six months touring the country. I *don't want* to make it without my girls for that long.

They're my priority now. The music's great and all, but they're my future, my world.

I answer the door to my suite, finding Peta standing with three cups of coffee. I take them from her so she can step inside. She's a petite firecracker who always has my best interest at heart, but I don't think she's going to like what I'm about to tell her this morning. "Morning, Peta."

"Morning." She breezes past me, making herself comfortable at the small dining setting where Shane's already set up. "Morning, Shane." I follow behind, placing the correct coffee in front of each person as Shane grunts his response. He barely tolerates Peta on a good day, and he's in a crap mood today for some reason. "Now, what was so important that you needed to see me desperately this morning?"

I don't quite know how to break it to her, so I think I'll just rip the band-aid off. "It's about the tour for this album."

"Yeah, I'm still finalizing the dates and venues. Then I'll work on seeking suitable support talent in each location. You wanna go with local talent, right?"

"Yeah, about that. I don't want to do an extensive tour this time."

Her eyes narrow as her back straightens; she looks like an angry pixie. "What the fuck, Toby? I've already invested months of time and effort into planning the damn thing. You can't just up and decide on a whim you're not doing your normal extensive tour." She's almost yelling at me as she finishes. I almost feel the need to protect myself against a physical attack.

"I have different priorities now."

"Oh, do tell. What are your priorities now?" she snarks at me.

"Cassia and Poppy. I don't want to be away from them for too long."

"You've been, what, fucking this chick for a month, maybe two at the most, and now you're going to throw everything away we've worked for? Are you for real?" She practically snarls.

"Watch your fucking mouth, Peta. I won't have you speaking about Cassia like that. She's the real deal for me and I have Poppy to think about, too. It's not only about me anymore." I stand abruptly, tipping my chair over in the process. "You fucking work for me. Remember that. Make it work."

"I know I work for you, asshole. You can't throw something like this at me, expecting me to be all, 'okay, Toby, sure thing, Toby.' We're talking about your career, *which*, until a few months ago, *was* your priority. So forgive me for not responding in the way you expected," she snarks at me, rolling her eyes.

She looks across at Shane, who always keeps out of these conversations. "Did you know about this?"

He shakes his head in the negative. "Nope. And as far as I can tell, he's the boss, which means he gets to decide what he wants to do with his career. How he wants it to progress." I'm surprised he spoke up on my behalf, and I think Peta is too, because she slams her mouth shut, sagging back into her chair.

Shaking her head, she seems resigned. "Shit. Okay. What do you want to do then?"

"Well, I was thinking four cities, two nights in each. Allow three days in between for setup, pack down, and travel. We would need the largest capacity stadium in each city to make it work." She's nodding as she types like crazy to get everything down. At least she seems somewhat on board with my new plan. "If we make the final concerts at home, that makes the whole time away less than three weeks in total." Which makes it more tolerable.

"I think it's workable. Limiting your appearances makes you more appealing, anyway. The whole playing hard to get thing could definitely work in our favor." There she goes, putting on her marketing hat. "Okay, let me work with that. Are you still looking at early June?"

"Yeah, that still works." I can hopefully convince Cass to come along and bring Poppy, too. It wouldn't be too long for her to be away from her shop. Sally's reasonably competent, and I think she's looking for someone else to help.

"Okay, I'll get onto it and let you know. Luckily, we haven't set dates or have tickets on sale yet." She looks pointedly at me as she stands from the table, taking her now cold coffee with her as she hurries to the door. "You owe me big time for messing me around." She slams the door behind her, and Shane breaks out into laughter.

"She's an angry pixie today."

I nod. "That she is, but I *did* throw her a curveball. So it's understandable." I shrug, taking a drink of cold coffee.

I've been doing interviews all over the place for the last ten days. I've just about had enough. Can't these guys come up with some original questions? I've been answering the same questions repeatedly; I could almost answer them while I'm asleep.

The thing that pisses me off the most is when they play the video of Poppy and me at her debut performance. I get she has star appeal, but I refuse to use our performance together to further my career. Peta always thinks it's great when they pull the footage out, but I shut that shit down real quick. Social media's been blowing up about my overprotectiveness of the girls in my life—opinions are divided about whether I'm too controlling and protective while others think I'm 'so sweet'.

I don't care what anyone thinks. They're my girls, and I don't want anyone messing with them.

-cassia-

WORKING OUT BACK IN MY WORKSHOP, I'M COUNTING DOWN the days until Toby comes home. We've messaged, talked, and sexted every single day—but I miss him so much. I don't think it registered how much I've grown used to seeing him at some point every single day. If I'm not spending time at his place, he's visiting me at the shop or at home. Every single female in my family adores him, too.

"I'm going to lunch now. See you in half an hour."

"No problem, Sally. Can you pick me up a salad, and I'll pay you back?"

"Sure." She heads out to lunch. She's a great kid. I'm beyond thankful to have her here helping me in between her classes.

I have a huge wedding this weekend, so I'm putting together all the greenery today for the table arrangements. That way, I only have to add in the fresh flowers tomorrow. I hear the bell over the door tinkle, and I step out with a professional smile, ready to …

I freeze in my tracks when I see who it is.

"Wh— What are you doing here?" My heart beats a million miles a minute as I tremble.

"Can't I come to say 'hi' now? You think you're too fucking good for me now that you're fucking a star? He's telling everyone in America that he's fucking you and in love with *my* fucking daughter," he practically spits at me as he shouts. "You're my fucking family. Not his!"

Shit! I never considered how Toby's interviews would negatively impact us. He was worried it would bring out the crazies for him, jealous girls who feel he belongs to them, but neither of us banked on Jake. "It's not like that, and you know it. You have no reason to be stopping by. We have nothing to talk about." My voice comes out steady, concealing my panic.

He moves lightning-fast around the counter to stand toe to toe with me. I tilt my head back to peer up at him. The veins in his neck and forehead are bulging, and self-preservation kicks in—the urge to step away from him is overpowering. As I make the first move to do so, he grabs my wrist.

"Ow, let go, Jake."

Out of my periphery, I see Sam step out of the office. "Leave her alone, or I'll call the police." Her voice is shaky, and she looks scared out of her mind as she holds her hand protectively over her protruding belly.

He snarls at her, releasing my wrist to step toward her. With only eight weeks to go, Sam's bump is significantly larger.

Jake gets right into her space, pushing at her shoulder. "Call the fucking cops," he snarls like an animal. "I ain't doin' nothin' wrong."

"You're intimidating us. That would be enough."

She steps back to head into the office, and his whole body seems to grow—the space he's taking up is overwhelming; his anger is like a living organism. Grabbing Sam by her forearm, he flings her full force across the small space. It's like the whole thing happens in slow motion as I let out a panicked scream. I can see what's going to happen, but I can't do a damn thing to stop it. She sickeningly smashes against the counter, baby first, then crumples to the floor, cradling her belly, sobbing. Jake bends down with his arm raised back, ready to inflict a blow. I quickly scramble onto his back, pulling on his arm with everything I have in me, screaming bloody murder.

He stands, attempting to dislodge me, but I hold on for dear life, scratching at his face like a madwoman. I sense we're moving, but I'm not wholly aware of it in my crazy attempt to get him away from Sam. Agony explodes down my back as he slams me into the solid wall—my head flies back, connecting with the brickwork. My vision goes blurry around the edges and it's tough to hang on, but I would rather take the brunt of his anger than he do any more damage to Sam and her baby.

"That's your baby in there, you fucking motherfucker!" I scream at him, trying to get my finger into his eye socket. I need to get him away from her.

Where the hell's Len?

I try to glance out the windows to see what's going on, but my vision's still fuzzy, and too much is happening at once.

"Stop fucking scratching me, you bitch!" He grabs my left forearm, twisting and pulling hard. Agony in my shoulder overwhelms me, forcing out a blood-curdling scream. I release him, having no other option as intense pain rushes through my system, almost causing me to black out—but I can't.

I have to fight.

He'll go after Sam. He never wanted the baby, and this is his chance to get rid of it. He's like a raging bull—his face red, saliva coating his mouth.

He slams me into the wall again. Without any purchase, I slide down it to the floor in a puddle of useless arms and legs. He takes the opportunity to kick my ribs, smashing them and forcing the air out of my lungs. Gasping frantically, I struggle to get any air and panic, which won't help me in trying to catch my breath.

I can't die.

I have Poppy to look after.

He can't do this to me, to Sam, to Poppy, to Toby, to my family.

Who in the hell does he think he is?

Does he think he can come into *my* shop and attack Sam and me?

My inner thoughts give me the strength to get up so I can keep fighting. I'm not going to let him do this to us.

He must've thought I was down for the count because he turned his back on me, moving his attention back to Sam. "I never wanted this fucking kid." He lands the punch to her stomach that I tried my best to prevent. We both scream at the same time.

He must spot my movement as I fight hard to sit up, working myself into a standing position to protect Sam, because he stomps over to me and, lifting his foot, he slams it down on the lower half of my right leg.

More excruciating pain floods me as I feel the snap of bones.

Falling to the ground, blackness fills my vision as I fall into oblivion …

… *feeling like a failure.*

FIFTY-TWO

-toby-

Out of the corner of my eye, I see Shane standing out of camera shot, reading something on his phone—his face is like thunder. I can almost feel his anger radiating off him from here. He looks up at me, gesturing that he's stepping out. It's not like I can acknowledge him while I'm in the middle of my interview.

Once I'm done, the host thanks me for my time and I step away from the cameras and crew. Peta's standing to the side, eyes red and puffy, her bottom lip trembling with Shane beside her, looking as though he wants to kill someone. They glance at each other, then back to me. Dread settles in my belly, my gut telling me something's terribly wrong.

Looking between the two, I swallow the feeling of dread. "What's going on?"

Shane takes hold of my arm, guiding me away from the few people around us into a private alcove. He glances down at his feet, and when he looks back up at me, his eyes are glassy. "What the fuck's going on? Tell me."

"Uh, I don't know how to tell you this."

Peta starts crying. I'm assuming it's not the first time by her puffy red eyes.

My hands fist on my hips as adrenaline begins coursing through me to prepare for whatever they're about to tell me. "Just fucking tell me. What's wrong?" Their behavior shows only one thing—shoring up my feet, I brace for bad news.

"Cassia and Sam were attacked in the shop around lunchtime today."

"What!" I yell as I start moving. I need to get to Cass. "Where are they? Are they okay? What happened? Who the fuck attacked them?" Even as I ask, my gut tells me I already know who it was. I'll kill the motherfucker myself.

Shane and Peta fall into step with me. Peta's almost running to keep up. "They're in *Mercy Vale*. Sam's being prepped to deliver her baby via c-section, and Cass ... Cass is still unconscious."

I break into a run. "Get me on a plane, now!"

"You're already booked. A car's out back to take you guys to the airport. I'll sort everything out here, then I'll fly home. You guys can go. I'll find my way back to the hotel," she rushes out between sobs.

We get to the car in record time, thanks to the adrenaline powering me. Peta tries to hug me, but I'm in too much of a rush. It's going to take fucking hours to get to my girl.

"Toby. I'm so sorry this happened. I hope they're gonna be okay." I don't even acknowledge her in my rush—the anxiety of getting to my girl overwhelming all my senses. My heart is shattering beneath my ribs and will only be whole again if Cass is okay.

Sitting in the car on the way to the airport, I can't stop my leg from shaking or my foot from tapping impatiently on the floor of the car.

"What the fuck happened?" More importantly. "How did it

happen? Where the fuck was Len?" He's next on my list of motherfuckers I need to kill.

Shane takes a deep breath. "Apparently, Len was at lunch when the attacker came into the shop. When he came back, Cass was unconscious, and the guy had just kicked Sam in the stomach." *Fuck!* "He fought with the attacker, but he got away. He contacted local law enforcement. They're going to study the footage from the cameras inside the shop." He turns away, swallowing hard. "I'm sorry, Toby. I should have listened to you and stayed behind with the girls." Thank god we installed those cameras.

As furious as I am about what's happened, I can't let Shane carry that guilt. "You didn't know something like this would happen. None of us did. Don't go down that path, man." I grip his shoulder and squeeze, punctuating my point. "Can you tell me anything else? Do we know who did this to the girls?" My gut tells me I already know, but I need it to be said. I need to hear that motherfucker's name.

"Len thinks it may have been Jake. He's not sure. He didn't get a good look at the guy in the chaos before he escaped. Len says the guy was like a raging bull." Shane shares a look, suggesting he also thinks it was Jake. He hadn't been around for a while, but before that, he *was* getting handsy with Cass. Something's obviously tipped him over the edge, and he's snapped.

"What about Poppy? Is she okay? Is she safe?" I don't think I could handle having both Cass and Poppy victims of Jake's brutality.

"Fuck, I'll check in with the school. Give me a minute."

It's two-thirty in the afternoon. She *should* still be in school. Watching Shane's face carefully as he talks with the school officer, his face blanches and his jaw tightens. "Call the cops. Call them now and get them down to the school. He's already landed her mom in the hospital." He hangs up, immediately making another call.

"What the hell's happening? Is he at school? Is Poppy safe?" *Fuck!* I squeeze my knees tight to the point of pain in an attempt to keep myself still, but it's getting harder by the second.

Shane covers the mouthpiece. "He's causing all sorts of trouble in the office, yelling and cursing, throwing chairs around the room. But they won't release Poppy because he's not on the approved list." He holds his finger up, indicating he'll be a minute. While he's talking to the police, I stare out of the window, unable to contain my thoughts. My body thrumming with adrenaline.

When we arrive at the airport, I don't wait for Shane to jump out of the car. I know he'll follow. Instead, I sprint to the check-in desk to tell the woman who I am. Peta's worked her magic because Shane and I are immediately taken through the back passages to the correct gate and onto the plane without delay. As the plane fills, it's taking everything inside me to sit still. I need to get to my girls. I need to lay my eyes on them. The suffocating feeling is overwhelming and all-encompassing. The sheer terror Cass and Sam must have felt during the attack. Anger pulses through me at the weak excuse for a man who thinks it's okay to beat on women.

I'm going to go after him with everything I have. He's going to be sorry he was born. I'm not some weak sixteen-year-old kid he can bully around anymore. I'm going to make that son of a bitch pay for what he's done.

Shane gets off the phone after several calls. "Cass's family knows what's happened. They're on their way to the hospital. Do you wanna contact your family, or would you rather I do it?"

I shake my head in the negative. "I'll do it."

"Do it now, before we start moving, and you have to turn your phone off."

I nod.

With shaky hands, I pull up my contact list, pressing Dad's number. He answers on the fourth ring. "Hey, Son. How are all the interviews going? Your mom and I have watched every single one."

As soon as I hear his voice, I break down. I unashamedly let the tears stream down my face. Shakily, I whisper, "Dad."

His tone changes. He's immediately on alert. "What's wrong? What happened? Are you okay?"

I shake as my tears turn to sobs, and I struggle to take in a full breath. I feel more than see Shane slide my phone out of my hand. I drop my head into my hands, allowing the feelings of hopelessness and anguish to break free, barely aware that Shane's relaying the terrible events of today to my father. He disconnects the call and wraps an arm around my shoulders, letting me have my breakdown.

"Let it out, Toby. Once we're home, Cass is gonna need you to be strong. Let it out now." As the plane prepares for takeoff, I sit, sobbing in my best friend's embrace.

FIFTY-THREE

-toby-

WE BARGE THROUGH THE HOSPITAL EMERGENCY DOORS TO FIND my whole family and Sally in the waiting room. Kate immediately engulfs me in one of her hugs, which I desperately needed.

"I'm so sorry this happened to Cassia. It's awful," she mumbles against my chest. When she looks up at me, blue eyes exactly like mine rimmed in red greet me; her nose red and her cheeks blotchy. We're particularly close, which means she'll be experiencing my pain as though it's her own, just as I did when she hit a rough patch with Oliver. I'm not sure if all siblings are as close as we are or if we're close because we're twins. I smooth my hand down her hair and raise my eyes above her head, making eye contact with Dad. He's scrutinizing my face carefully for signs of distress. I think I got all of my tears out on the plane. I tip my head to let him know I have myself together, and he returns the gesture.

Mom's holding onto Nan as they walk forward together. Oliver steps in to peel Kate away from me, giving me a very serious tilt of his head. His whole body's drawn tight. I can feel his anger over the attack from here. Mom and Nan step into me, giving me their love and support in the only way they know how—hugs and fussing.

"This is awful. Who would do such a terrible thing to such a lovely woman?" Mom's completely bewildered.

We've never had anything like this happen to anyone we've known. It's so far out of the realm of our experiences to date that it's difficult to understand why someone would do something so heinous. However, Shane and I know exactly who's responsible for this horrendous crime against two women who did absolutely nothing to deserve his hate and anger.

"I have a pretty decent PI I use if you need him." Oliver offers.

"Thanks, but the guy's already been arrested. The police caught up with him at Poppy's school. He was trying to get to her and went berserk when they wouldn't let him have her." Thank god the school only allows the kids to leave the grounds with a registered person.

Mom gasps. "It wasn't random?"

I shake my head. "No. It was Cassia's ex, Poppy's father." Mom covers her mouth with a shaky hand, tears rolling down her cheeks. "But why?"

I shrug. I have no words for what he's done. I don't want to think about what his plans were for Poppy. But I'm beyond grateful he couldn't get his hands on her.

Shane messaged Rose to let her know what we found out and that we were on our way to the hospital. Cass's entire family is in shock, which is entirely understandable.

Dad wraps his arm around my shoulder, squeezing me close to his body. He heard my sobs over the phone, and I know he's worried about me. After all, he is a psychologist.

"You want me to stay with you or head back to the shop to get the footage for the police?" Shane asks.

"Go get the footage and take it to the police. That's the

priority. We need all the evidence we have to make sure he gets put away."

Shane nods, looking uncomfortable. "Uh … did you want to … uh, watch the footage?"

"Why on earth would you want to watch what happened?" Mom butts in, her normally steady voice high-pitched.

Dad steps across to her, wrapping his arm around her. "It has to be his choice, Em."

She looks up at him. "I know. But it'll be horrible to see exactly what happened." Dad squeezes her shoulder, and she acquiesces.

"Yeah, I do. Make a copy to keep. I'll watch it when I'm ready." My gut's rolling. I don't know if I'll ever be able to watch the attack, but I want to have the option. Shane nods, saying his goodbyes to everyone else before pulling me aside.

"Give Cassia my love. Okay?" I nod and Shane turns around, walking purposefully out of the hospital to make sure Cassia's attacker gets the fullest punishment possible.

Rose walks toward us down the corridor, her face pale and blotchy, her eyes red and swollen. I meet her partway, not thinking twice about comforting her. Her body sags into mine as her hands clutch the sides of my shirt.

"Oh, Toby," she sobs into my chest.

Rubbing my hand up and down her back to soothe her, I whisper, "She's gonna be alright. She's gotta be."

"I don't understand for the life of me why Jake would do this to her."

"Did you know he's been hassling her since the reunion? He wants her back." I suck in a breath. I feel that all my talk about Cass and Poppy in my interviews may have been the catalyst that pushed him over the edge. "How is she? Can I see her?"

"Well, that's certainly no way to treat a woman you want to have in your life." She huffs, stepping away from me and acknowledging my family. "Thank you all so much for coming."

"We can't express how sorry we are this happened to your daughter. How is she?" Mom steps in to embrace Rose.

"Thank you. It's certainly been an afternoon." Her voice is shaky as her gaze skates around all of us. With a sad smile, she takes my hand in her own. "She's awake." She nods as if confirming to herself Cass is okay, swallowing harshly as though to gather her emotions. "She has a concussion, broken ribs, and a bruised spine. The lower half of one leg is broken, and they've put it in a cast. She also had a dislocated shoulder, which has been corrected, as well as bruising on her arm."

My stomach rolls and I'm worried I'm going to be sick. Hearing the results of the attack reignites my fury. "Can I see her, please?"

"Of course. Come on. I'll take you to her room."

I turn to my family. "Thanks for coming, but you may as well go home. I'll let you know how she's doing. Maybe you can come back to visit tomorrow." I don't want to share Cass with any more people than her mom and gramma at this point. "I'll tell her you all came and that you give her your love."

They all nod, hugging me as they leave. Rose and I make our way down the corridor toward my love. "I have to warn you. She's pretty bruised and sore."

Words escape me, so I only nod, swallowing down my bile. I'm doing my best to keep myself together because Cass doesn't need to see me broken; she needs my strength and my love more than anything.

Arriving at Cass's door, we both pause. Rose checking with me if I'm okay, and me taking a deep breath in preparation. Finally, she opens the door, and the world falls out from beneath my feet as I lay eyes on the woman I love.

Anger rises, but I push it down with equal force.

I don't know how anyone who calls himself a man can put his hands on a woman in anger and cause so much destruction.

I take four strides to reach Cass's bedside, and as soon as she sees me, tears immediately run down the side of her beautiful face, and her bottom lip quivers.

I want to take her in my arms, but she's so fucking broken.

Leaning down, I gently wipe her tears with my thumbs, laying a gentle kiss on her forehead, which appears to be free of bruising. Then, gently pressing my forehead to hers, I lock eyes with my love.

"I love you so fucking much. I'm so fucking sorry, Cass," I whisper against her lips.

She lets out a sob, and I softly cup her head, breathing in her pain. "You're safe now. He's been caught and they'll have to lock him up." I feel her nod gently, and I still her head. "Don't move, Bun. I don't want you in any more pain than you already are."

We stay like that, with me bent over her bed, dull gray eyes to blazing blue, sharing breaths until her eyes close and she dozes. When I look up, Rose and Iris are watching us closely.

"Would you mind staying with Cass?" She looks back at her mom. "We feel terrible, but we need to get home to check Poppy's really okay." Rose is worrying the end of her shirt with shaky fingers. "Mom also promised Cass she'd work with Sally to get everything ready for the wedding this weekend. We know she's in good hands with you."

"Of course. I'll be staying with her until she's discharged. Then I'll be taking care of her."

Rose nods as though she already assumed that's what I'd do. "Violet's home looking after Poppy and Jasmine. She'll probably want to come to see her sister's okay for herself."

"Sure. That's understandable. My family is worried about Cass, and they barely know her. I can't imagine what it's like for you guys." I swallow hard, dropping my eyes back to Cass. "If it were Kate, I'd want to be where she was."

"Thanks, Toby."

"Uh, hug Poppy from me, please. I felt homicidal at the thought of Jake getting to her and what he planned to do."

With glassy eyes, they nod, kiss Cass gently goodbye, then come around to me. Rose places both of her warm hands on my cheeks, peering up at me.

"She's incredibly lucky to have you. They both are." She pulls my head down to kiss my forehead, the same way my mom does. Iris hugs me, kissing my cheek. Then they both head out of the room with one last look at their daughter and granddaughter.

Alone with my girl, I pull up a chair. While holding her free hand, I study her. The bruising on her face and forearm. The tangles in her hair and dried tears on her face. Down her body to the cumbersome cast on her leg. I can't see her torso, but I imagine it's pretty bruised, considering she has bruising down her spine as well as broken ribs. My jaw tenses, and I know it's going to be that way for a while yet to come. My phone buzzes.

SHANE

I watched the footage of the attack

You should be fucking proud of your girl. She fought him like a champion to protect her friend

I look back at Cass, sleeping soundly. Tears track down my face as pride fills me for the strong woman she is.

ME

Thanks bro

SHANE

I've taken it to the police and filled in the necessary paperwork

ME

I appreciate it, thanks

SHANE

No problem. Let me know if you need anything

ME

Will do

I sit watching my girl. Unsure of how much time has passed. A doctor walks in as Cass begins to wake, her eyelids slowly lifting, revealing her graphite gaze, locking me in place.

"Good evening, Cassia. How are you feeling?"

"She's been asleep—" I glance at my phone. "For about an hour. She's just waking up."

"Good, she needs to rest, but we don't want her sleeping too long with that concussion."

Trying to lift her head, Cassia whispers 'hello' to the doctor.

"Stop moving, Bun." Her eyes snap to mine, blinking back tears.

The doctor steps closer to Cassia. "Where are you feeling the most pain, Cassia?"

"Everywhere hurts," she whispers with a shudder.

"Okay, we'll get some pain medicine for you in a moment." The doctor flashes a light in Cass's eyes, records something on her tablet, then looks back up. "I need to talk with you about the results of our tests." Then she looks at me. "Would you mind stepping out of the room, please?"

The hackles on the back of my neck stand on end.

I'm not leaving her.

Now or ever.

Cass places her hand on my arm, squeezing it. "Toby's my boyfriend. I'm okay with him staying, Doctor."

She nods. "Okay." Dropping her eyes back to her tablet, she runs through Cass's injuries and what treatment they've done so far. "I also wanted to let you know the baby's fine. It's early enough that the injuries you sustained in the attack didn't impact the embryo." She smiles as though she's delivered news we were waiting to hear—I'm confused as fuck.

Why is she calling Sam's baby an embryo?

Cass looks relieved. "Thank you, Doctor. I'm so glad Sam's baby is going to be okay. I was so scared that ... that he ... he ... what he did ..." A loud sob escapes, preventing her from finishing. I brush her tangled hair away from her face, trying to calm her. The violent sobs can't be good for her broken ribs.

-toby-

THE DOCTOR LOOKS CONFUSED. "WHO'S SAM? I WAS TALKING about you." Her eyes widen. "You didn't know you were pregnant?"

My eyes snap to the doctor as Cass blurts, "What?"

"I'm sorry, I thought … I assumed you knew. Our tests show you're roughly six weeks pregnant." She looks at both of us with an expectant smile. When we don't respond in kind, her face drops. "Uh, I'll go sort out some pain medication for you and leave you two to talk."

Cass's brows wrinkle as she bites her lip. Her focus has turned inward, and I sense she's thinking about the news the doctor just delivered. I'm fucking ecstatic that we made a baby, but the longer she's turned inward, I worry she's not feeling the same. I squeeze her hand to draw her attention to me. She looks everywhere but at me, her eyes flitting around the room, trying to find somewhere to settle. She attempts to pull her hand away from mine, but I cover it with my free one to keep her in place. Finally, she looks at me, a steady stream of tears tracking down her bruised cheeks.

She doesn't want this.

She doesn't want a baby with me.

My heart cracks with the pain of knowing she doesn't want to have a baby with me.

"I ... I'm so sorry, Toby."

"Shhh, shhh. It's okay." No matter what she wants to do, I'll support her. It's what you do when you love someone unconditionally, even if they don't love you the same way.

"I religiously take my pill every day," she sobs. "I don't understand what happened. Oh, god! I should have insisted you keep using condoms." She looks devastated, and I feel gutted that I'm the cause. "I'm sor-ry, Toby. I didn't mean for this to happen."

I stroke her hair gently, calmly. "Shhh, shhh. It's okay. It's not your fault. It's mine. This isn't only on you. I was there as well, remember?" I smile sadly because my heart is breaking. "Neither of us meant for this to happen, but I can't say I'm unhappy about it."

She sucks in a sharp breath, then cries out in pain.

"Calm down. You can't afford to get yourself worked up. We'll work it out. Whatever you wanna do, Cass. I'm here, standing with you, supporting you. I promise."

More tears track down her face, and I fear I've said the wrong thing. "You mean, you're ... you're not upset? You're not angry with me?"

"Hell no. I'm fucking ecstatic that I knocked you up." My chest puffs up with pride.

She blinks rapidly. "Wha ... What did you say?"

I stand up, cupping her face carefully in my hands, locking my eyes on hers to make sure she hears me correctly this time. "Cass. I'm so blessed to have you and Poppy in my life, but this ... you being pregnant with my baby ... it's everything to me. *You're* everything to me. You *and* Poppy, this baby ... I couldn't be happier. You hear what I'm saying, Bun?"

She nods the best she can with me cupping her face. I lean down, pressing my lips gently against hers. A breath gushes out of Cass as she whispers against my mouth, "I thought you'd be mad."

"Never, Bun. Never."

Cass shakes her head, closing her eyes. "I was scared I was gonna lose you," she whispers on a shaky breath.

"I love you so much, Bun. I'm not going anywhere. We're doing this together. You're not alone this time." She opens her eyes, locking them onto me, and I smile, trying to reassure her.

A nurse enters the room, breaking our moment. "Sorry to interrupt, but I'm here to give you some pain relief."

Cass and I share a look. I know we're both thinking the same thing. I don't want her in pain, but is it safe for the baby?

"Will it be safe for our baby if I take that medicine?"

"Yes, it's totally fine at this stage of your pregnancy. Your baby is well and truly protected and safe."

Cass tries to adjust her position, sucking in a sharp breath and scrunching up her face. "Take the pain relief, Bun. You need it to heal properly."

She studies my face closely for long moments before turning toward the nurse. "Okay. I'll take it."

"Good choice. We don't want you in distress. It's better for you and the baby." The nurse goes about her business. She's an older woman who seems to be all about efficiency. Her movements are swift and precise before she leaves us alone again.

I haven't left Cass's side since I arrived last night. There's a sharp knock on the door, followed by two police officers stepping into Cass's room.

"Ms. Phillips, we would like to have a word if you're up to it."

"Surely, this can wait a few days. You have the footage from the shop. Isn't that enough?"

"I'm sorry, Sir, but we need to follow up with everyone involved." They turn back at Cassia, who nods.

"Can you remember what happened?" asks the second officer.

"Most of it, I think."

"Would you mind running through it for us?"

She nods again, glancing at me, then back to the officers. Slowly but surely, she walks us through the attack yesterday afternoon. My blood boils with violence for that cocksucker. I wanna get my hands on him and break his fucking neck. Vivid images play out in my mind of what I want to do with him.

Through tears, shaky breaths, and plenty of stops and starts, Cass shares the events of her attack. All the while, I hold her hand in support. Hearing her describe her attack in graphic detail, blow by blow, makes me feel so goddamn proud of her. The way she tried to protect Sam. Which reminds me, we need to find out if Sam and her baby are okay.

"Thank you, Ms. Phillips. We'll be in touch."

I want to hold my girl after listening to her recount the events of yesterday. I have no fucking words to express how brave I think she is. But I'm scared I'll hurt her if I hold her the way I want to.

Cass looks at me. "Would you mind doing me a favor?"

"Anything, Bun. What do you need?"

"I need to know how Sam and her baby are. Can you please try to find out?"

I gently squeeze her hand. "Of course. I'll find out for you. First, though, I need to tell you something." I brush her hair, which is still tangled from her ordeal, away from her face. "I am so fucking proud of you, Cassia. What you did yesterday … you were so goddamn brave. I don't know too many people who would have stayed and fought rather than run to save themselves." I lean forward, kissing her lips, as more tears track down her face. "I love you so much, Bun. So much," I whisper.

"Thank you," she whispers back, her lips touching mine. "It was probably stupid, really. I'm a mom. I could have ended up much worse than this." She indicates down her body. "How would that have helped Poppy?" More tears track down her cheeks.

"Don't think about it now. You're okay. I'm sure Sam and her baby are okay. Jake's been locked away. He won't be able to hurt you again." I kiss her again. "I'll see what I can find out about Sam." I don't want to leave her alone, but I know she's worried about her friend and I don't want her to get upset. "Be back in a minute."

I step out of the room to find Shane and Violet standing outside the door. "Hey." I lean in to hug Violet. "I was about to see if I can find any information about Sam and her baby. You mind sitting with Cassia?" Violet looks as though she's been crying nonstop since she found out about the attack.

"Hey." Shane pats me on the back. "Sam's up in maternity. She had the baby last night."

"Oh, okay. Maybe I don't need to leave Cass to find out. Come in to say hello." We step back inside the room.

Cass's eyes widen as her lips spread in happiness at seeing Shane and her sister. He steps toward her, kissing her forehead. "Hey, Cass. How are you feeling?"

"A bit sore and sorry for myself, to be honest," she responds with a sad smile. "But thankful it's not worse than what it is."

"I watched the footage from the shop. You're a badass. I'm honored to call you my friend. What you did for Sam. The way you fought with everything you had. You were ... are amazing. Don't forget that."

Cass's eyes are glossy as she blinks rapidly at Shane's praise. It means a lot coming from someone like him. He steps back, allowing Violet to step forward. She's frozen on the spot, her eyes tracking all over her sister's face and body.

Cass holds out her good hand to her sister, which seems to wake her up. She rushes forward, gently grasping her sister's hand as a loud sob breaks free and the girls cry together. We step back to give the sisters their privacy.

-cassia-

MY WHOLE BODY ACHES AND THROBS. MY MIND'S SPINNING. I've been attacked, hospitalized, and found out I'm six weeks pregnant. Sam had her baby boy, and I'm being discharged today.

It's been a lot.

Toby hasn't left my side. I'm missing my Poppy desperately, but I didn't want her to see me lying helpless in the hospital. I've decided, though, I'm not leaving here until I visit Sam. Toby rolls me toward my friend, and as Sam comes into view, tears fill my eyes.

She's okay.

Shane told me she was okay and the nurses also told me, but until this moment, until I saw her with my own eyes, I didn't fully believe them. The relief that fills me is overwhelming, and I'm grateful I'm sitting down, or else my legs may have let me down. Sam takes one look at me, covers her mouth, and begins to cry. Big, fat tears roll down her face. Toby rolls me forward quickly.

"Don't cry, Sam. We're okay. You're okay. Your baby's okay.

I'm okay." I reach forward with my good arm to brush her hair away from her face, and she settles a little at my touch.

Toby quietly steps out of the room, giving us time together. I know it was difficult for him to do because he hasn't left my side since he arrived at the hospital.

"Thank you for everything you did, Cass. I … I don't know what would have happened if you hadn't been there. My baby —" She breaks into a loud sob, unable to finish the sentence.

"Shhhh. Shhhh. Everything worked out okay. We're all safe now. He can't hurt any of us anymore." Sam nods slowly. "Now, where's your beautiful baby boy?"

A smile forms as she sniffs and wipes away her tears. "He's in the NICU. I just came back from seeing him. He's so small, so helpless."

"You know he's in the best possible place. They'll care for him and give him everything he needs."

She nods. "His skin's so soft." She smiles, almost to herself. "His feet are tiny." She shows me with her thumb and forefinger. I remember when Poppy was that small. I lay my good hand on my stomach, thinking about the time I'll get to meet this little one.

"I can't wait to meet him. What's his name?"

She locks eyes with me. "Phillip." My eyes widen in surprise. Surely she didn't … "I named him after you because you saved his life."

More tears trickle down my face as pride fills me down to my soul. "I'm honored, Sam, but I didn't do anything anyone else wouldn't have done."

"I don't care. If you hadn't been there to distract Jake, I don't know what he would have done." The thing is, I feel it's my fault to begin with. If Jake hadn't come after me, he wouldn't have hurt Sam. I feel the heavy burden of guilt for bringing that asshole to her doorstep.

We catch up for a while before Toby steps back into the

room, suggesting we head home. We say our goodbyes, and Toby rolls me out of the hospital. Lifting my face to the sunshine, I soak in its warmth while I carefully suck in a lungful of fresh air. I have to be in a wheelchair for a few weeks until my shoulder's healed because I can't manage crutches at this point. Communicating with Poppy is going to be a little slow for a while, too. I'm going to need to manage signing with one hand, something I haven't done a lot.

As we're driving home, Toby announces, "Once you're able, you and Poppy are moving into my place." I look across at him, eyebrows raised. "I'm not having you away from me any more than absolutely necessary."

"You don't think it's too soon to live together?" I sass at him. Secretly, I love that he wants us in his space as much as he does.

"Nope," he snaps out, sharp as a whip. "I've wanted you since I was sixteen. I've already waited too long."

I laugh at his grumpiness about the topic and point to my leg. "I won't be able to manage three flights of stairs in your house for a while."

"No problem. I've set us up in the guest room on the first floor. I figured we'd stay with your mom until you're out of the wheelchair and she feels happy enough to let you go." His tone is all business and I don't have any inclination to argue with him at this point. I *want* to be with him as much as he wants to be with me.

We pull into the driveway. My heart soars, finding Poppy standing on the front step waiting for us, with Mom, Violet, and Jasmine behind her. I want to jump out of the car and run to my little girl. Give her all the love I haven't been able to give her since Friday morning.

Toby quickly jumps out of the car, coming around to my side with the wheelchair as Poppy runs down the few steps to the grass, bringing her closer to me. Toby opens my door, and

Poppy stops cold when she sees the sling holding my arm in place, the bruising on my face, and finally the cast on my leg. Mom prepared her; told her that someone had hurt me, but I think hearing about it and seeing it are two very different things for a seven-year-old. Her bottom lip trembles as her eyes fill with tears. I want to wrap her up and pull her in tight, which is impossible at the moment. Every time I move or forget about my ribs and breathe a little deeper, they send agonizing pain shooting through my body.

"Mommy. Are you okay?" I can only nod in answer.

Toby quickly helps me out of the car, and it takes me a moment to recover from the burst of pain caused by the movement. Then, we all head inside slowly and carefully, Toby carrying me up the steps before situating me on the couch.

Carefully Poppy—more carefully than I've ever seen her be —sits beside me on my right. Wrapping my arm around her carefully, I pull her in close, kissing the top of her head. We sit side-by-side for long minutes as Toby brings in my wheelchair while Mom makes us all a coffee.

Violet smiles at me. "It's good to have you home, Sis." She teases out the bottom of her hair with her fingers. A tell that she's bothered about something.

"It's good to be home. I missed you all so much." I sign one-handed.

"Aunt Cass. I missed you." Jas comes barreling toward me with the speed of a toddler, but her mom's quicker, scooping her up to hold her next to my face so I can kiss her chubby cheek. She giggles as I tickle her with my good hand.

"Come on, girls, I'll put a movie on and we can all chill out together," Vi signs as she speaks, pulling up the movie channel so the girls can choose an old favorite. And that's how we spend our afternoon, with me dozing while the girls giggle at the antics of the characters on the screen.

-cassia-

I'M FEELING ESPECIALLY GRATEFUL THIS CHRISTMAS. I HAVE Toby in my life, a baby on the way, and in a few weeks, we'll be living together like a proper family. It's something I've always dreamed of but figured would never happen.

Not for me, anyway.

But here I am, living the dream.

Toby's been living in a house full of women since I came home from the hospital. I have to admire his patience with the girls. He spends hours sitting and playing with them.

We plan to tell my family about our surprise baby this morning as part of their Christmas gift. I can't wait to see their faces. I'm so freaking excited. This time is completely different from the last time I got pregnant. I *know* he wants this baby as much as I do.

Before we tell the rest of my family, we want to share the news with Poppy first, just the three of us. Sitting on my bed, Poppy's almost bouncing out of her skin, waiting to find out the special present I told her she would get first thing this morning.

"Merry Christmas, Mommy!" She leans forward, gently pressing her body against mine. She learned very quickly that she had to be super gentle with me. "Merry Christmas, Toby!" She throws her body at him—gone is the gentle little girl. He kisses her forehead with a smile and a laugh.

"Merry Christmas, Baby Girl!"

"Can I have my special Christmas surprise now?" She's practically vibrating with excitement as she signs.

Toby and I look at each other. He tilts his head, letting me take the lead. "Well, we were wondering how you'd feel about being a big sister?"

"I would love that so much. When can I be a big sister?"

I look at Toby, and we share a proud smile. "How about in August? I already have your baby brother or sister growing in my stomach."

She looks between the two of us before jumping off the bed and running around the room like a headless chicken. I'm relieved she's happy about it. I was worried she'd be upset because she's been an only child for such a long time.

She stops dead in her tracks. "Really?" She looks at us expectantly, as though we're playing a prank on her. Toby and I both nod with wide smiles as she throws her little fists up in the air, jumping on the spot. "Can I see the baby?"

"Not yet, Baby Girl. Soon, though. We'll go to a special doctor where they'll take a photo of what's inside my stomach."

"Okay. But you're gonna have to stop calling me Baby Girl because I won't be the baby anymore." She doesn't seem sad about losing that title, which is a huge relief. "Can I tell Gramma?"

Toby nods, letting me know he's okay with her sharing our news. "Okay. But you have to wait until after all the other presents are opened first. Okay?"

She nods. "Okay."

"Alright, let's get ready for opening presents. Did Santa come last night?"

"He sure did. You should see all the presents. There's so many." Her eyes are wide as she runs from the room.

Toby helps me into my wheelchair, and we follow behind. Mom, Violet, and Jasmine are already in the living room waiting for us.

"Merry Christmas!" Mom calls out as she makes room for me next to the tree, bending forward to hug me.

"Mewwy Chwistmas, Aunt Cass." Jas sings out to us from her spot almost tucked underneath the tree. She can't possibly get any closer to the presents if she tried.

I giggle, then suck in a sharp breath, and then wince at the pain caused by the breath I just sucked in. My ribs still hurt if I forget and carry on as though they're not broken.

"Merry Christmas, guys," Vi calls out from the kitchen.

"Merry Christmas, everyone. Thanks for waiting for us. Is everyone ready to open some presents?" I sign as I speak.

Shouts of yeses fill the room along with arms raised high in celebration, and we get down to the important business of opening gifts.

An hour later, Poppy and Toby are making music videos on the creator cam he bought for her, complete with a green screen. Mom and Vi are picking up all the wrapping paper. Jas is playing with her new dollhouse, courtesy of Shane and Toby, while I sip on a decaffeinated latte made for me in my brand-new coffee machine, courtesy of my very generous boyfriend. Once I'm recovered, he's gonna get very lucky.

He loved the personalized wooden guitar picks Poppy and I

had made for him with various phrases, like 'You're my guitar hero' and 'You're my pick' engraved on them. I also got him a hemp bracelet to match the leather bands he likes to wear. This one has an outline of a guitar made from stainless steel as a feature to join the two ends. He put it on straight away. I keep catching him rubbing his thumb along the band.

Once everyone's back in the living room, I let Poppy know she can share our news. She makes sure everyone's sitting quietly, and she has their undivided attention. Then she signs, "I'm going to be a big sister!"

The silence seems to last forever; Mom and Violet look between Toby and me. Mom pointedly looks down at my stomach, then back up to my face, eyebrows raised in question. I nod like a bobble doll, tears filling my eyes. She jumps up, picking Poppy up off the floor, giving her the biggest snuggle, before sitting her on her hip and dancing around the room.

Violet steps over and cups my cheeks, looking into my eyes. "I'm so freaking happy for you." She looks across at Toby. "For both of you. This is such amazing news." She picks up Jas in happiness. "You're gonna have another cousin. Aunt Cass has a baby in her tummy."

Jas looks down at my stomach, as if she can see the baby, and then wiggles free of her mom's arms. Coming right up to me, she places her hands carefully on my stomach. She leans forward, speaking softly, "Hello, baby." My heart melts at Jasmine's cuteness.

Mom wraps her arms around Toby, holding him tight. "Thank you for making me a gramma again. This is the best news we've had in a while. Oh my gosh, Mom's gonna be so excited to be a great-gramma again. I can't wait until she gets here so we can tell her." She leans in, cupping my face, much like my sister did. "Thank you, Cassia. You two are going to make a great team." She kisses my cheeks and then steps away, looking as proud as can be, her eyes glassy, her smile wide.

We gather everything we need to take with us and pile into our cars to make our way to Kate and Oliver's home. Once again, they generously invited my entire family along for the fun. The afternoon is spent eating too much and opening more presents. I don't think I've ever experienced a Christmas quite like this before. We normally only have our little family together for the day, meaning it's pretty quiet. As I absorb the love, happiness, and friendships around the room, my smile grows as warmth fills my entire body. This is going to be my future. Holidays spent with family and friends—it's amazing to know there are so many more people to love Poppy.

Toby sits next to me. "Are you ready to tell everyone our news?" His sparkling eyes give away his excitement at sharing this news with his family.

"Yep. Go get Poppy, so we're all together. Then you can tell them." He kisses my lips too briefly for my liking and heads off to find our girl. It was easy to think of Poppy as *our* daughter. He loves her as much as I do. Poppy and I are his top priorities all day, every single day.

He brings Poppy in close to me before gaining everyone's attention. Everyone's watching him expectantly, eyes wide, waiting. I can't imagine what they think the news will be. My family all have knowing smirks on their faces, while Poppy's almost coming out of her skin with excitement.

He clears his throat and looks down at me with a wink, then back to his family and their friends. "Cass, Poppy, and I are expanding our family. Poppy's going to be a big sister!" he signs as he speaks.

At first, everyone's silent again. Then it's as though they all absorb the meaning of Toby's announcement at the same time as they all cheer, moving forward en masse toward us, engulfing us in warm hugs and loud congratulations. Even though they already treat Poppy, and Jasmine for that matter, as their grandchildren and nieces, I *know* this will be even more special because this baby will be part of Toby.

FIFTY-SEVEN

-toby-

I FEEL STUPIDLY NERVOUS AND OUT OF MY ELEMENT AS CASS, Poppy, and I wait in the obstetrician's waiting room. Women in various stages of pregnancy are seated around the room. Some on their own, some with small children, some with their partner. We thought Poppy should be here to see her brother or sister for the first time. She's practically bouncing in her seat with excitement.

A nurse steps into the room. "Ms. Phillips."

I can't wait to change her surname to Summer. Poppy's, too.

I indicate to Poppy that it's our turn. Standing, I push Cassia forward; with her arm still in a sling and her leg in a cast, it's been a necessary requirement. Cass is sick of it, and it's been hell watching her in pain, watching her frustration grow over the things she struggles to do at the moment.

Her gramma had to go back to working full time, pulling in a friend to help her and Sally out while Cass and Sam are out of action. It's been tough on Cass to let things go. She attempts to do as much of the paperwork for the shop as she can from home, but it's not enough for her.

The nightmares are the worst. More often than not, I'm woken up by her thrashing around in bed, crying out in pain because she's moved more than she should, fighting Jake in her sleep. I feel helpless as she lies sobbing, half in a dream, half awake. She's been casually talking with Dad about everything that had happened that day as well as the stuff that had happened years ago. He won't tell me anything they talk about and Cass just says she's 'getting there'.

"Hi, I'm Kelly. If you could, please follow me. I'll get you set up and ready for Dr. Hart." We step into a clinical room, which could do with being a little warmer. "I'll just check your weight and blood pressure. Are you able to stand on the scales?"

"Sure. But won't the cast on my leg make my weight incorrect?"

"That's okay. The doctor will consider all of that."

I help Cass onto the scales and the nurse records the measurement on her tablet. "Do you mind helping Ms. Phillips onto the table?"

"No problem." I pick Cass up to carry her over to the table, eliciting a giggle from her.

"I'm pretty sure she didn't mean you had to carry me here."

I kiss the tip of her nose. "I'd carry you everywhere if you'd let me."

Moving the wheelchair out of the way, I sit down next to the bed and situate Poppy on my lap, ensuring she has the perfect view of everything that's going on. First, the nurse takes Cass's blood pressure, recording the numbers on her tablet, and then takes Poppy's for fun.

"Okay, that's all for me. Dr. Hart will be in shortly."

"Thank you, Kelly." She smiles as she leaves us in the room alone.

We play eye spy with Poppy to keep her entertained until

the doctor walks in a few minutes later. He's young and good-looking, and I'm not too fond of the idea that he'll have his hands on my girlfriend.

"Good afternoon, Ms. Phillips. Mr. Summer." A hint of recognition fills his eyes, but he remains professional. "And who is this young lady?"

Cass signs one-handed as she speaks, introducing Poppy to the doctor. He makes a big fuss of shaking her hand and congratulating Poppy on becoming a big sister. His award-winning smile stretches right across his face as he makes sure Poppy's included.

Maybe he's not so bad after all.

He washes his hands in the sink, then sits on the other side of Cass, pulling on a pair of gloves. "So, you think you're around ten weeks pregnant? Is that right?" Cass uses her free hand to translate for Poppy, as she normally does in public situations.

Cass nods. "It was picked up in a test when I was in the hospital for these." She gestures to her shoulder and leg. "They said the hCG levels suggested I was around six weeks pregnant. That was four weeks ago now."

He nods. "Well, let's take a look to see if they were right. First, please lift your shirt and lower your pants to your bikini line. Did you have a big drink of water before your appointment today?"

"Yes, I did. I have to warn you. I'm getting pretty close to needing to go to the bathroom."

"Excellent, we should be able to get a good, clear picture of the baby." He holds up a tube. "This may be a little cold, but we need to use it to help with the equipment."

Cass nods. "I remember from when I was pregnant with Poppy." Poppy's eyes are glued to her mom's stomach and everything the doctor's doing.

He squirts the gel on her stomach, then uses a flat probe to spread it out, pressing down firmly on Cass's midsection. He fiddles around with some buttons on his computer, and the screen comes to life. Poppy's eyes snap to the screen while I watch my girl's face light up at the sight of our baby in her belly. Finally, I look at the screen, and my breath catches at what I see.

Our baby.

The one Cass and I made together.

Seeing the little body complete with little stumps for arms and legs and a huge head on the screen makes it real. I mean, I knew it was real, but it was an abstract type of real. Now it's really real. It's fucking amazing to see the life we created in a grainy black-and-white image on the screen. The doctor freezes the image and uses the mouse to draw some lines.

"I'm taking some measurements to get an idea of your due date."

"Is everything looking okay, Dr. Hart?"

He looks at me. "Everything's looking perfect, Mr. Summer."

"Okay, judging by my measurements, your baby is about 3.3 cm from crown to rump." He inputs the figures, then looks at us. "I'd say you'll be due around August thirteenth."

We had done some calculations ourselves and had come to the same conclusion if the blood test had been accurate. Cass'll still be able to travel with me for my tour. She resisted at first, using the shop as her excuse, but her gramma said she didn't mind stepping in again to help, which took that excuse out of the equation. Every excuse she came up with, I found a solution.

"Are you ready to hear your baby's heartbeat?" He fiddles with something on the computer, and a rhythmic whooshing sound fills the room as the heartbeat line shows along the bottom of the monitor.

My own heartbeat ceases for a moment, then restarts as I

listen to the fast beats of our baby's heart. I grasp Cassia's hand and soak in the moment, appreciating the wonder on her face as tears slowly escape, tracking down her cheeks. Poppy's mesmerized by the moving image, steeling her eyes away from the screen to look at Cass's stomach in awe.

Dr. Hart points to the screen. "Can you see the little flutter right there?" I release Cass's hand so she can translate. We both peer more closely at the monitor, then nod. "That's your baby's heart. The flutter you see are the chambers working to pump the blood around your baby's body."

"That's amazing." I'm in awe of the technology. I'm in awe of Cass. That she's able to grow a human inside her body. Her stomach's only got a slight bump at this stage, barely noticeable. It's hard to believe that what I see on the screen is inside her body.

Cass squeezes my hand as she whispers, "You know, Poppy will never *hear* her baby's heartbeat like this." More tears stream down her cheeks, and she releases my hand to wipe them away.

"She may not *hear* it the way we do, but she'll see it, and she'll be so in tune with everything, she'll probably *feel* it." I lean forward to kiss the back of her hand.

"Now, let me move around a bit here and we'll take some photos for you to take home for your album. We'll also send them to your phone if you like. Be sure to check we have your correct numbers."

He takes photos and prints them out, handing them straight to Poppy. "Here you go. Your little brother or sister," Cass signs for her.

Her little face lights up as she looks down at the images. She places them carefully on the bed to sign, "I'm gonna make a special photo frame when I get home." She holds the images up for us, then presses them against her little chest close to her heart. She's going to be a great big sister.

-cassia-

MOVING INTO TOBY'S HOME FEELS SURREAL. I'M WORRIED I'M going to wake up and it's all going to be a dream. Poppy was so freaking excited. She made sure to pack every single toy she had; she didn't want to leave anything behind—even though I told her she'd still have sleepovers with Gramma, Aunt Violet, and Jasmine. She's currently upstairs, situating all of her favorite things in their new homes while Toby and I share a glass of wine on the couch. Well, he has wine; I have sparkling water.

Thank goodness I no longer need the wheelchair as of yesterday, and I can use crutches now that my ribs and dislocated shoulder have healed. It makes it so much freaking easier to get around and communicate with my daughter. Toby wasted no time. He made it clear. As soon as the wheelchair was gone, Poppy and I were moving in with him—and here we are. I was given the okay to use crutches yesterday, and we moved in today.

"She's so excited to be living here. It's all she's talked about since I told her we were going to be living with you." I sip my water.

"I doubt she's even half as excited as I am seeing both of you here in our space."

He's had no trouble talking about his home as our home. He's made numerous adjustments to his home and life for Poppy and me. The flashing lights attached to the doorbell and the switches on each floor to flash the lights throughout the house to get Poppy's attention wherever she is. Her beautiful little girl's bedroom. All of our favorite bathroom products are in the bathrooms, and our favorite foods are in the cupboards. He's even made space for Poppy in his studio. He makes me feel like we're the most important people in his world.

He leans forward, kissing me until I'm dizzy—lucky for me, I'm sitting down and can enjoy it without losing my balance. He makes my body heat in anticipation for later, when Poppy's in bed and it's only the two of us. Pulling back, he's toying with the ends of my hair, eyes focused on the strands as he whispers, "How are *you* feeling about moving in?"

"Do you want my honest answer?" He nods slowly, swallowing hard. "I'm honestly happy to take this step with you, even though I'm a little scared. This is a big step for Poppy and me. I genuinely want this to work out more than anything." I kiss his lips gently then whisper against them, sapphire eyes to charcoal, "I feel deep down in my heart … this is where we're meant to be, here with you. Making a family. Together for always." I blink quickly, working to keep my tears at bay. The lump in my throat makes it hard to get the words out. "A *real* family full of love."

"That's exactly what we are, Bun. A *real* family." His mouth comes down onto mine and I open eagerly to greet his tongue. Grasping the back of my head, he directs the kiss, deepening it until we're sharing each other's breaths. He pulls away before I'm ready, our foreheads pressed together as we each catch our breath. "I'm gonna marry you, Cassia Phillips, and adopt Poppy as soon as I can."

Pulling back to see his face more clearly, I open and close my mouth several times before anything comes out. "What?"

"You heard me, Bun."

"Are you asking me or telling me?" I'm trying my best to be sassy; however, I'm not sure I'm pulling it off. I'd say yes right now to this man. I don't need a romantic, down-on-one-knee proposal from him.

"I'm warning you, so you can be prepared for when I ask you properly." He smirks and winks at me. "Now, where's my other girl? It's time for lunch."

Holy cow! This man's so sexy. I can't wait until tonight.

FIFTY-NINE

-cassia-

"I'M SO NERVOUS." I'M HAVING TROUBLE DOING UP THE buttons on my blouse because my hands are so freaking shaky and I'm certain I'm going to throw up any minute.

"You have nothing to be nervous about. I'm not gonna leave your side." Toby takes over, doing up my buttons. "I much prefer undoing these, by the way." He winks as he secures each button in its corresponding hole, bringing a smile to my face and distracting me from my thoughts.

Once I'm dressed, I head out to the kitchen to grab a glass of water. Toby smacks my ass, almost causing me to spill it on the blouse he just secured for me. His hands shoot out to prevent it from falling, and we both laugh. I certainly don't have time to change. My nerves already have us running late.

On the way to the courthouse, I fidget with the fabric of my pants, picking at imaginary lint. Toby reaches his hand across to stop my fidgeting, glancing at me before returning his eyes to the road. "It's going to be okay. He can't hurt you anymore."

I swallow down my nervousness. "I know. It's just ... I never thought I'd be in this situation."

"I know. Nobody should have to go through this, Bun." I love it when he uses my nickname. "You know you weren't the only one. He's dangerous, Cass. The sooner he's put away, the better for everyone."

I nod. "I know." And I do. I'm not nervous about sending him behind bars. I'm worried they won't.

"You've told your story. Everyone else shared theirs. There'll be no reason for the jury to set him free."

I nod. "Thanks for the pep talk. I needed it."

"Any time, Bun."

Toby parks the car and then helps me out. Shane and Len arrive at the same time we do, and we all walk into the courthouse together. Sam's standing off to the side with an older woman who looks like an older version of her. We head in her direction.

"Hey, Sam." We hug in greeting. "How are you doing? How's Phillip?"

Her face lights up at the mention of her gorgeous little boy. "He's doing great. I love being able to snuggle him without all the wires. It's so exciting, but I'm also a little scared. I don't want to mess up being a mom."

"You won't mess it up, Sam. You'll be a great mom." I glance at her mom. "Plus, you have your mom to help you. My mom was invaluable to me when Poppy was a baby."

Toby notices the time and ushers us inside, ready for the final proceedings. Things happened incredibly fast after the attack. I'm not sure why, but I think our case has been pushed through quicker than what would usually happen. It may have had something to do with new policies being pushed through regarding domestic violence. I think the Governor wants to make a big show that he supports victims of domestic violence and he won't tolerate it in our State.

We sit together with Becky, the woman Jake beat up five months ago. When I met with the district attorney to give her my statement, she told me Jake was already considering a plea deal for an attack in which he killed an unborn baby. Apparently, he didn't want that baby either, so he beat Becky, kicking and punching her stomach repeatedly. She was taken to hospital and tragically lost her baby at twelve weeks. I share a deep connection with her; she's been through so much at the hands of Jake. It seems he started to become violent and unpredictable after our reunion.

On the other side, Jake sits with his attorney. Laying eyes on him turns my stomach, and I suck in breaths to keep from expelling the small amount of breakfast Toby insisted I eat. I fold my hands together tightly in my lap, attempting to steady the shakiness, but the one thing I can't stop is the way my heart beats. It feels like it's going to pound right out of my chest, and as I swallow down each breath; I feel like I'm struggling for air. Sensing my discomfort, Toby places his hand on my thigh. His touch and genuine concern help to settle me. I'm able to slow my breathing to get myself under control.

Jake's mom sits in the seat behind her son, fidgeting with her necklace, looking everywhere but at us—Jake's victims. My heart breaks for the kind woman I remember—her son has put her in a terrible position. She doesn't deserve what she must have been through since everything he's done came to light. But it goes to show the good person she is, that she's here to support her son even though he doesn't deserve it.

The bailiff breaks into my thoughts, calling the court to order. "All rise for Judge Albercombe." We all stand and the proceedings get underway.

I get distracted in my thoughts, remembering the days spent in this courtroom listening to Becky and Sam recount their stories. Becky's story was very much like mine.

She was woken in the middle of the night by a drunken Jake having sex with her. When she tried to get him to stop, he kept

*going. Then he wanted her to abort the baby when she told him
she was pregnant as a result of the rape. The one thing I can say
about Jake is that he's consistent—a consistent asshole of the
highest order. I'm sure it makes me a terrible person, but I'm
grateful Jake didn't do to me what he did to Becky and Sam. He
never actually tried to kill my baby.*

*The days after the attack were horrendous for all of us. I
remember the remorse written all over Len's face about stepping
away to grab some lunch, leaving us exposed. Of course, he
wasn't to know what was about to happen—the man's entitled to
a break.*

*Sam was worried she would be judged because she got pregnant on
purpose. Love can cause you to make questionable choices sometimes. It took a lot of support and encouragement on my part to
get her to be completely honest on the stand about her pregnancy.
She didn't want him to be seen as a victim. She didn't want the
jury to sympathize with him and let him off the hook. I understood where she was coming from, but he nearly killed their baby
that day. I got the distinct impression during the attack that it was
one of his goals. He wanted that baby gone from this world, and
it was only the quick actions of the paramedics and doctors which
ensured Phillip came into the world as safely as he did.*

I glance at Jake's mom. She looks pale as she closes her
eyes, sucking in a breath. This must be incredibly difficult for
her to hear. She has grandchildren I'm now certain she never
knew existed.

*I remember when it was my turn. As I made my way to the stand
on my crutches, I made eye contact with the jurors, hoping they'd
listen to everything Jake had done and bring down a conviction
against him that will put him behind bars. Finally, I was sworn
in, and my mouth went dry, my hands shook, and my vision went
fuzzy around the edges.*

I found my talisman and locked eyes with him, stormy gray to calm blue. I managed to take deep breaths as I started at the beginning of our story, all the way back to high school. As I walked the jury through all of my experiences with Jake, I felt the knots loosen, and it became easier to speak my truth.

Recounting the night Poppy was conceived was tough. In my mind, I was taken back to that place and time—my shakes intensified, and I had to grip my hands together to steady myself. I sought Toby again, and he centered me with his unwavering support from across the room. I was grateful I'd already shared my story with him; that he wasn't hearing it for the first time. I don't think I could have made eye contact with him if he was hearing it for the first time, along with the jurors and judge.

Moving forward in time, I recounted what happened when Poppy was two. I remember the audible gasp Jake's mom let out at her son's violence against me, as I protected Poppy against his fist. The fact he thought he could correct her hearing with a fist to the head showed how unstable he is. The only thought that kept me moving forward with my story was the hope we'd all be safer if he was locked away. I remember pushing through my discomfort to share the last few months.

The prosecutor warned Sam and me that he wanted to show the footage of our attack to the jury. We agreed with him, but when it came time for it to be shown, I wasn't certain I could watch it. Toby wrapped his arm around my shoulder, tugging me into his body as the footage began to play. The images were so clear. The sounds of violence and hate couldn't be ignored. I felt like I was living through it all over again: every punch, kick, and stomp. I remember the way the jurors responded to Jake punching Sam's pregnant belly. They didn't bother disguising their disgust and horror at the events they witnessed. It was difficult to watch myself lying unconscious on the floor as he kicked her belly right before Len entered the picture, pulling Jake away from us and fighting with him for several minutes before Jake escaped from the shop.

The trial has been a long process. I feel like I've been put through the wringer. I'm exhausted, mentally, emotionally, and physically wrung out. There's been so many horrible details shared and it's been a lot to absorb.

I don't know whether to feel better or worse that I wasn't the only woman he was mistreating and assaulting. Maybe if I'd said something to the police sooner, none of this would have happened. The shame and guilt I feel surrounding my younger self's choices are overwhelming, and it's difficult to reconcile that girl with the woman I am today. There's no way I would tolerate anything like that ever again. I only wish I'd come to this point sooner. Looking around at the other women sitting nearby, they both appear to feel the same way I do.

I'm so caught up in my head that I almost miss the judge's ruling.

"On one count of manslaughter in the first degree. Guilty. On one count of attempted murder. Guilty. On four counts of assault with intent to cause harm. Guilty. On one count of destruction of property. Guilty." He looks around the court-room. "Jake Robert Simmons, you have a track record of abuse and violence against women, which this court will not tolerate. I hereby sentence you to serve twelve years in the state penitentiary with a minimum sentence of five years before consideration for parole." He bangs his gavel. "Court dismissed."

He stands to leave. Everyone seated on our side of the court seems to release a collective breath. My body sags into Toby's as the guards lead Jake away, but not before he says something to his mom, which has her shaking her head as tears trail down her cheeks.

Stepping out of the courthouse, the gray skies greet us,

threatening rain—the weather matching our mood. This event has fundamentally changed me. The nightmares. My persistent wariness of being alone in my shop, which was once my sanctuary. The constant tangled thoughts over past actions and what I should have done differently.

I want to go back to a simpler time when monsters didn't attack women or murder unborn babies.

"Cassia. Cassia." A woman calls out as Toby and I carefully make our way down the courthouse steps. I know exactly who it is. I carefully turn around on the step, keeping myself as steady as possible on jelly legs. She takes a couple more steps down, coming closer to me. "Cassia," she whispers, her bottom lip trembling.

"Mrs. Simmons." Tears flood down her cheeks at her name on my lips. As much as I think her son is an appalling excuse for a human being, I don't feel any of that for her. She was always kind, warm, and welcoming to me. "Please don't cry." I want to reach out to her, but I'm unsure if my comfort would be welcomed.

"I ... I'm so, so sor— ... sorry. I h— ... had no idea ... about any of it." She blinks quickly, fiddling with her necklace. She takes a few moments to compose herself. "I feel as though I didn't know my son. I mean, I knew he had a temper, ... but ... this. I had no idea. I can't believe I have grandchildren that I never knew about. Never met." Searching her bag for something, she pulls out a handful of tissues. "I feel so ... responsible for everything that's happened." She sobs into the tissues, her whole body shaking. I look at Toby, silently asking him if I should comfort her. He gives a single nod, so I lean closer, placing my arm around her shoulders, rubbing my hand up and down her arm, attempting to calm her.

"Mrs. Simmons. Please don't take the blame for Jake's behavior. It's all on him." I try to keep my voice soft, soothing.

She nods, but I see the doubt in her eyes. "But *I'm* his mother. I *should* have known."

"How could you have? He was very good at showing people what he wanted them to see." I had no idea his temper could get this bad, and I dated him on and off for years.

"Thank you, Cassia. You're too kind. But this guilt … it's something I'll carry with me until my dying day." She pulls away from me, having gathered her composure somewhat. "Please take care of yourself and your daughter." Her hand snakes up to her necklace again as more tears escape her eyes. She's genuinely upset at the thought of having grandchildren she didn't know about.

As she goes to step around me, down the steps with her head down low, I call out to her, "Would you like to meet your granddaughter?" I'm not sure what possessed me to invite her into our lives, but none of this is her fault. When I was younger, I remember feeling hurt she hadn't made an effort to meet Poppy or support me, but now I know she had no idea about any of it. I don't want to punish her for her son's behavior. Her steps come to a stop, and she turns to face me, an incredulous expression.

"Really? You would let me meet my granddaughter?" she almost whispers, her chin trembling.

I nod. "Yeah, I would. Poppy's amazing. You shouldn't miss out on getting to know her." The more I think about it, the more comfortable I feel with the idea. I know Jake's mom is a kind and loving person. I know she'll love Poppy with all of her heart, and why wouldn't I want to give that to my daughter? "Do you still live in the same house?"

"Yes, I do. But … are you sure?" Her eyes are open wide, shining bright with hope.

"Yep. How about we let the dust settle a little? Then I'll organize a time with you to bring Poppy over for a visit?"

She steps into me, embracing me tightly. "That would be

wonderful, Cassia. I'll look forward to it." As she steps away, she looks a little taller; a little happier. After what she's been through recently with Jake, I'm glad I could give her something to look forward to.

After watching her walk away, Toby pulls me to his side. "You're such a good person, Cassia. I don't think too many women would do what you just did."

Pressing my head against his shoulder, I sigh. "It's not her fault Jake's such a monster. She shouldn't be punished for her son."

He nods, kissing the top of my head, making me feel cherished. "C'mon. Let's go home."

SIXTY

-cassia-

STEPPING THROUGH THE DOOR OF *OUR* HOME TOGETHER—IT still feels surreal to be living here with Toby—he slips my coat off my shoulders and down my arms, hanging it in the coat closet. He's always doting on Poppy and me, making every single day special. Today, after everything at the courthouse, I know, I *just* know, he's going to take good care of me. Poppy's staying over at Mom's tonight because I wasn't sure how I would feel after the judge delivered his verdict.

He steps into me from behind, wrapping his arm around me beneath my breasts. A sigh escapes me at the feel of his hard body pressed against mine. He uses his other hand to smooth my hair away, giving him clear access to my neck.

Nuzzling down into the space between my shoulder and neck, he whispers, "I plan to make long, slow, sweet love to you, Gorgeous. Starting now." He presses a gentle kiss with a glide of his lips across my heated skin.

This man turns me on just by being in the room. When he actually touches me, I have no hope of resisting him and why would I? Turning me around, he presses me up against the foyer wall, reminding me of the first night we reunited, when I did the very same thing to him. He swoops down, licking across the seam of my lips, and I open with a sigh as I sag against the wall. He wastes no time connecting our mouths completely. As Toby kisses me, I wrap my arms around his head, removing the elastic holding his hair so I can run my fingers through the silky strands.

I love his hair—the softness of it.

I love it when his weight's on top of me as his hair creates a private curtain around us, shielding us from the outside world.

Our tongues slide and taste each other, exchanging breaths, sighs, and moans. He presses his hard dick against me and my hips automatically seek the friction only he can give me.

I've learned to relax. To let Toby lead during our sexy times. He's always diligent in doling out my pleasure before his own; I don't need to worry. I *know* he'll get me where I need to go, which is so damn hot!

Pulling away, we both catch our breaths as our foreheads kiss. "I'm gonna need a bed for this. I wanna take my time." He bends forward, picking me up bridal-style, carrying me up three flights of stairs as though I weigh next to nothing. He stops next to our king-size bed, sliding me down his body slowly, my bump sliding against his taut stomach until he's sure my feet are firmly on the ground.

His hands instantly snap up to the fasteners of my blouse. "I've been dying to undo these little silver buttons since I did them up for you this morning."

The tension I was carrying in my shoulders begins to slip away as my body prepares to be taken care of in the best possible way. As each inch of skin is exposed, Toby leans forward, kissing down the front of my body. I sigh at the gentle press of his warm lips against my flesh, pausing on my bump and leaving a trail of goosebumps as his soft beard tickles me.

"I love how soft your skin is. I always want to have my hands, or better yet, my mouth, on you."

"I love having your hands and mouth on me. You always make me feel so good."

I jump slightly as he nips at my belly button before releasing the button and zipper on my pants. I won't be able to wear these pants much longer. He slips his hand inside my underwear, stroking my pussy lips, and my belly quivers.

"You're already so fucking wet and I've barely touched you," he whispers, as his fingers slip through my folds easily.

"I just have to look at you and I'm wet. My body knows what you can give me and instantly prepares for your touch," I whisper, as my hands reach forward to stroke the hard outline of his cock through his trousers. "Mmmmm." I look down at his crotch. "Can I have a taste?"

"Not yet. I need to take care of my pussy first." He grunts as I squeeze his shaft.

He pushes my pants and underwear down my legs, then takes my hand to help me step from the discarded items before helping me to remove my ankle boots. He flicks open the front clasp of my bra and slides his calloused fingers underneath the straps, sliding it and my blouse off to join the rest of my clothes on the floor.

Goosebumps erupt all over my body and my tender nipples do their best to gain Toby's attention. Leaning forward, he takes a bite of one, then soothes the sting with his tongue. I shudder as his mouth closes over the nipple and sucks—hard. Massaging the other breast with his hand, he pulls back. "I can't wait to watch you nourish our child with these pretty tits."

His mouth. How he uses it. The words he says. It's such a turn-on. Moisture slicks my pussy lips and I clench my thighs together in a lame attempt to lessen my reaction to him. *It doesn't work.*

He picks me up underneath my ass, laying me out on our bed like an offering. His fingers smooth down to caress my body, followed closely by his talented mouth, pausing over the bump of my stomach. If you didn't know me, you wouldn't know I was pregnant when I'm fully dressed. Naked, though, the curve is visible. Toby takes every opportunity to caress and kiss it. Each night, he talks and sings to our baby while he lovingly rubs body butter over my torso, making me fall more in love with him; if that's even possible. His kisses reach my pubic bone and, after giving me a sexy smirk, he literally dives in.

Tasting.

Licking.

Biting.

Sucking.

Fingering me until I'm a writhing mess of need, on the verge of exploding. Then, pushing my legs further apart with his shoulders, he sucks hard on my clit as his two fingers press up against the front wall of my pussy. Violent spasms erupt out of nowhere, and I fall into bliss—a trembling, quivering mess of liquid bones and muscle. I flop my hand up to my forehead as my lips spread wide. A sigh escapes as I lie in post-orgasmic bliss.

Toby climbs up my body like a panther, all slick and sure, pressing a gentle kiss to my lips. I can smell my arousal on him as I run my tongue along his lips, tasting myself as he groans.

"You know how fucking sexy it is when you want to taste your cum on my lips?"

"Mmmmm." I run my fingers through his hair. "Can I taste you now? You taste so much better than I do." His cock jolts between us, tapping my stomach. "I think your cock wants me to." I smirk sassily.

He sits up. Then he helps me upright as he gets into position at the edge of the bed. After tossing a cushion to the floor between his feet, he directs me exactly how he wants me— kneeling between his legs on the floor. Taking one of my hands, he wraps it around his cock, then grips the back of my neck, guiding my mouth toward his magnificent cock. As far as dicks go, I've only seen two in real life, so I'm no expert, but to me, his dick is perfect.

"Lick the tip, then suck it into your gorgeous mouth. I wanna see my cock resting on that delicious bottom lip of yours." He uses his hand at the back of my neck to gently guide me forward. "In high school, I used to imagine your plump lips surrounding my dick. It never took me long to come with that vision in my mind."

I groan. Knowing he masturbated to thoughts of me in high school should be creepy, but it's not. Instead, knowing he's wanted me for so long boosts my desire to please him. I take his cock in my mouth, pressing my tongue along the underside of his dick, as I moan long and low from my throat. His hand tightens on the back of my neck as he pushes me closer to his body, sending his cock further into my mouth to the back of my throat. Taking a deep breath through my nose, I manage to contain my gag reflex, swallowing around his shaft. He groans, thrusting his hips toward my face.

"Your mouth feels so fucking good, Gorgeous."

His praise turns me on, urging me forward. Increasing my strokes and sucks up and down his shaft, sliding it out of my mouth and back in with a suck. I cup his balls gently and use my finger to massage his taint. Even though I've just had an orgasm, doing this to him has me heating, preparing for another one. His grip tightens on my hair, and as he pulls on the strands, his hips thrust in time with my ministrations.

I moan, and he groans.

Before I can stop him, he has his dick out of my mouth, me on his lap, and his cock in my pussy in one swift action.

Straddling his thighs, we remain still, joined in the most intimate of ways. The connection we share reaches right down to my very soul. I thank the heavens above that Toby came back into my life. Then, with our eyes locked, we begin to move, slowly, surely, with purpose and promise. With one hand resting on his broad shoulder, I tangle my other hand in his hair, drawing him forward to my mouth. Lips open, our tongues caress each other as we build toward our peak.

My pussy walls flutter and begin tightening around his dick. In response, his dick jolts and grows impossibly thicker, putting more pressure against my g-spot. Finally, his hand snakes down, and his fingers press against my clit, sending me flying into the stratosphere. My whole body shudders as my pussy walls tighten around his shaft, gripping it with force.

"Fuck, yeah. I want your pussy strangling my cock every single day of my life. It feels like heaven." He slams his mouth over mine and thrusts deep, holding himself inside me as his pulsing dick releases his cum. I wrap my arms around his shoulders, pulling him in tight to me, every inch of my skin touching every inch of his.

Sweaty, slick skin against sweaty, slick skin.

Hearts pounding a matching rhythm.

Panting breaths gush in and out as we attempt to fill our lungs.

He brushes my sweaty hair out of my face and presses a delicate kiss to my forehead, the tip of my nose, then my lips. My sighs are met with a gorgeous smile.

"You're so fucking beautiful, Cass." He kisses me again. "When you come." He bites his bottom lip. "I'm the luckiest bastard in the world." He kisses me again. "Thank you."

His genuine gratitude for what some men take for granted increases my love for him and the man he is. I return his kiss, deepening the connection until I don't know where he begins and I end.

"I love you, Toby Summer." I kiss him again, stealing his breath in the same way he steals mine. "Thank you for being the man who showed me it's okay to open my heart." I press my forehead to his. "Thank you for loving my daughter and me as deeply as you do."

We stay locked together. Slick bodies pressed tightly, his dick nestled inside me for long moments. Connected physically, mentally, emotionally, and spiritually. This man is the one and only for me, just as I am the one and only for him.

After snuggling for a while, both of our tummies let out a hungry grumble, sending us into fits of laughter. I didn't eat much before court. It's now mid-afternoon after an intensive round of lovemaking, so I'm not surprised I'm starving. Finally, Toby rises out of bed, pulling me up with him.

"C'mon, Bun. Let's feed you and the bump." He steps over to the drawers and throws a T-shirt at me. "I got you a little something."

Aww, he's so sweet. He watches me closely as I smooth the T-shirt out on the bed, immediately bursting into laughter at the text on the front.

'Guitarists Finger Faster'

Toby smirks, then pretends to be offended that I'm laughing at the gift. He runs his hand through his messy hair to push it out of his face, contracting his bicep, drawing my eyes there. He notices, tensing the muscle even more.

I roll my eyes; he's such a guy.

"I thought it was appropriate." He smirks and shrugs as he pulls on a pair of jeans, doing up the zipper but leaving the button undone.

I put the soft T-shirt on, then step over to my boyfriend. Wrapping my arms around his naked torso, I peer up at his face. "I love it. Thank you."

He tilts his face forward, kissing the tip of my nose. "I love you, Cassia." His voice sounds raspy, and as I study his face closely, his eyes show me how deeply he means those words.

Pressing up on my toes, I press a tender kiss to his soft lips. "That works out perfectly because I love you, Toby Summer. I love you as my partner, my lover, my friend, and the father of both of my children."

epilogue

SIXTY-ONE

-toby-

I STEP INSIDE *CRISTO'S TAVERNA* AND GIVE MY EYES A MOMENT to adjust to the dimness. Shane's close behind as usual; he knows why I'm meeting Rose for lunch. I'm sure Rose has her suspicions, but I didn't elaborate on why I wanted to meet here today. The host greets me by name, possibly because there's no mistaking who I am since I'm a regular here and I booked out most of the restaurant to ensure my privacy. I did a similar thing when I met Cass for lunch, back when I was trying to convince her to give us a shot. It's the only way to ensure a modicum of privacy.

Rose is already seated at the back table I prefer, perusing the menu. She glances up as I approach, giving me a smile that reminds me of her daughter. She stands, embracing me tightly. "My, aren't I lucky to be invited out on a weekday to share lunch with my favorite guy?"

"Hey, Rose. Thanks for agreeing to have lunch with me today." We both sit. "You're gonna love the food here. I brought Cass here a while ago. She enjoyed the authentic Greek cuisine."

"Anything I don't have to cook tastes pretty good to me." She laughs.

The waiter brings a bottle of water to the table, filling our glasses. "Would you like to share a bottle of wine today, Sir?"

I look to Rose for her input. "Sure. That'd be lovely."

"What do you like to drink?"

"Sweet white, if that's okay with you?"

"Definitely. That's Cassia's preference, too." I let the waiter know, and he steps away to get our drinks.

I gulp my water to soothe my dry throat. My hands are shaking so badly that Rose notices. Peering at me with a raised eyebrow and a small smile, she sits forward in her chair, resting her chin on her hand.

"It's lovely of you to invite me out to lunch, but I assume you have an ulterior motive for sharing a meal with an old lady."

"Wow, Rose. I'm hurt you think my intentions aren't what they seem." I hold my hand over my heart, giving her my best 'hurt feelings' face. "I was at least going to ply you with excellent wine and food before getting down to business." I smile at her and she laughs.

The waiter returns with our wine, pouring each of us a glass. "Are you ready to order?"

I look at Rose. I know she already perused the menu, and I know what I like here. "Do you know what you'd like?"

"Yes, I do. I'll have the kokinisto me manestra thank you."

"A great choice, Ma'am. And for you, Sir?"

"I'll have my usual, thank you."

"Certainly." He heads back into the kitchen with our order.

"And what is your 'usual'?" She takes a sip of her wine.

"I always enjoy the moussaka whenever I eat here. It's always a tasty choice, not that you can go wrong with anything on the menu." I rearrange my cutlery, centralize my glass, and unfold my napkin before folding it up again.

Rose places her hand over mine. "What is it, Toby?"

Tucking a lock of hair that's escaped my hair tie behind my ear, I sip my wine, hoping for liquid courage. "Uh, well, I have something I wanted to talk with you about."

She pulls her hand away to fiddle with her necklace, her eyes wide, as her shoulders rise around her ears. "Are Cassia and Poppy okay?"

"Oh, yeah, yeah. There's nothing wrong." I glance away, then back at Rose as her shoulders drop and she takes another sip of her wine. "I, uh, well … I … I wanted to … uh—"

Her eyes are twinkling as she fights a smile. "What are you trying to say?"

"I'm gonna ask Cass to marry me and ask Poppy if I can adopt her," I blurt out. "Geez, I had this entire speech worked out, and that was not how I was going to start the discussion." I huff out a breath. I'm so goddamn disappointed in myself.

"Oh, Toby. That's wonderful news. I'm beyond happy for the three of you." She stands, stepping around to me with her arms open wide, and I get up to meet her. She wraps her thin arms around me tightly, whispering, "I couldn't have asked for a better man for my girls."

My entire body, from the top of my head to the tip of my toes, relaxes. I knew I was tense because of my nervousness, but I didn't realize *how* tense I was. "Thanks, Rose. I appreciate you saying that." I squeeze her back, then we release our embrace.

Sitting back in our respective chairs, Rose is beaming, and I feel like I can breathe again. I don't think I've ever felt this nervous in my life, even when performing in front of thousands of people or sending a new song out into the world. The waiter brings our food, and we both dig in. It's probably good I got the difficult part out of the way because I can actually enjoy my meal.

Rose looks at me with excitement. "I hope you're going to do it soon. I'm not sure I'll be able to contain myself for long."

"I was planning on doing it this weekend." I tell Rose about my plan as we enjoy our delicious meal. She nods along excitedly, giving me praise for my choice of location as well as my craftiness.

We finish our meal, talking some more about Poppy and Cassia before Rose needs to leave for an appointment with a new client. Shane and I walk her out of the restaurant, parting ways with a tight squeeze and a kiss on the cheek. I feel lighter than I did when I walked into the restaurant.

I turn to Shane. "Did you enjoy your lunch?"

"Yeah, the food here is always great. I assume you got the all-clear from Rose for the weekend?" He smirks at me.

"Yep." I pop the 'p' like an adolescent. "She said, and I quote, 'she couldn't have asked for a better man for her girls'." I blow on my fingernails, pretending I'm buffing them on my shirt as my face cracks into a broad smile. I'm on top of the world. "Now I've just gotta put my plan into place."

"Well, I can't see a 'no' anywhere in your near future if that helps." He slaps me on the back. "Where to next?"

"I need to get to the jeweler to pick up Cass's ring. Then we can pick up Poppy from school and take her for ice cream. I have something I need to ask her."

Poppy orders her regular peanut butter crunch, while I order the macadamia crunch, and Shane has a raspberry swirl. The three of us find one of the back booths to enjoy our frozen treats in relative peace. Poppy's working like crazy to lick up the ice cream as quickly as possible. Cass and I always make sure there's ice cream in the house because it's one of the few things we can use to bribe her to do her chores. Shane sits on the same side of the booth as me, blocking me from public view, so we're left alone.

Once I finish my ice cream and my hands are free, I rub them down my jeans to wipe the nervous sweat away. I ask Poppy about her day, checking in with how her friends are going. I know I'm delaying what I really want to talk about. I can't believe how nervous I am to ask a seven-year-old if she thinks what I want to do is okay. Once I've calmed myself down and I'm satisfied Poppy's in a good place, I bring up the purpose of our outing.

"Hey, Poppy. You know how much I love you and your mommy, right?"

She nods and passes her ice cream to Shane. "I love you, too. And I know Mommy loves you lots. She's always kissing you." She screws up her cute little nose.

Good, I'm glad she thinks it's gross to kiss a boy. I hope she feels that way until she's at least thirty.

I ask her to come and sit next to me. Shane stands, allowing Poppy to sit in the booth while he blocks us from the rest of the customers with his body. Wrapping my arm around her shoulder, I kiss the top of her head and breathe in her little girl's strawberry scent. Pulling away, I put some space between us so we can talk.

"There's something I want to ask you, and I hope you think it's okay."

She nods, indicating I should get on with it.

I swallow down the buildup of saliva, taking a deep breath. "Do you think it would be okay if I asked your mommy to marry me?"

Instantly, her face lights up brighter than I've ever seen, and her hands move fast. "Will that mean you'll be my daddy?"

I smile. "Yeah. We'd be a family. The three of us, and when the baby comes, we'll be a family with the four of us."

"Yes! Yes! Yes! Please marry Mommy. I want us to be a family. I want you to be my daddy." She throws her little arms around my torso, squeezing me as tight as she can. I suck in a gulping breath and Shane gives me an 'I told you so' look.

I explain some aspects of my plan to Poppy, and she offers her input as well as a couple of suggestions for tweaks that could work in my favor. Gotta love a smart kid.

At six months pregnant, my Bun looks spectacular. She has that pregnancy glow about her, making her even more gorgeous than she usually is. The last three months, having Poppy and Cass living with me, have been more than I could ever have asked for. They've made my house feel like a home, full of the love and warmth I'm used to having. The three of us have started creating our own special traditions, like breakfast for dinner on Sunday nights after we've spent the afternoon with my family.

I can't wait for the weekend when I can put my plan into place to make them both mine permanently.

As Cass comes down the stairs after putting Poppy to bed, I carry hot cocoa for each of us over to the couch. She sits down with a heavy sigh. "Today was nuts. I'm not sure what's going on, but we were busier than usual. Sam was only in for a couple of hours, then she had to head home to feed Phillip. I'm exhausted."

"I know Sally's a big help, but have you given any thought to hiring another floral designer to help you out? What are you planning to do when the baby's born?" I lift her feet and she swivels her body so they're resting on my lap. I begin massaging them for her as she drinks her cocoa.

"Yeah, I definitely have. I have my eye on a new, upcoming floral designer. She's won a couple of local awards, so I've been putting together a proposal to woo her to my shop." She moans as my thumbs dig into the arch of her foot, waking up my dick. Settle down, buddy. I'm looking after our girl in a different way for now. I shift my legs, making room for the expansion.

"Oh, yeah? How are you gonna woo her?" I swap to her other foot.

"Well, I was hoping a couple of tickets to your final concert might do the trick. She's in your core demographic. Maybe even some backstage passes?" She looks at me with hopeful eyes. As if I'd ever deny her anything.

"It's all yours, Bun. Anything you need to get her on board and into your store." She leans forward, offering me her luscious lips for a kiss, which I happily accept. Pressing my lips against hers, I cup the side of her head, directing and deepening the kiss the way I want it. Her breath mingles with mine. Our tongues tangle together. She tastes like cocoa and my Bun —my favorite flavor. "I actually, uh … have something I wanted to talk to you about."

She pulls back, studying my face carefully. "What's wrong?"

"Nothing's wrong, I just … uh … wanted to ask you something really important to do with Poppy." I struggle to get the words out. Reaching forward, I drink my cocoa to coat my dry throat, noticing my hand shaking as I grip the cup.

It's certainly been a day full of anxiety for me.

"Well, it's something. You seem a little … out of sorts." She nudges me with her toe, connecting with my dick. She looks up at me questioningly. "Are you excited to see me, or is that a banana in your pocket?" She giggles, breaking the tension I brought between us.

"I'll show you exactly how happy I am to see you later." I wink, twisting around to face her more directly. "You know how much I love you and Poppy?"

"Yeah, we both know how much you love us. We love you,

too." She leans forward, kissing me again, settling my nerves slightly.

"Well ... uh ... I was wondering how you'd feel about me adopting Poppy. I want both of our kids to have my last name. It's important to me that our kids have the same surname." Cass's face goes soft as she offers me that ghost of a smile that she often does. "I mean, I know Poppy's not mine biologically speaking, but I think of her as mine. I love her as though she's my own and I would do anything, *anything* at all to keep her safe and happy—" Cass cuts me off with a press of her smiling lips against mine. I pull back slightly, whispering, "Is that a yes? Would you be okay if I asked her?"

She presses another light kiss against my lips. "Yes." *Kiss*. "Absolutely." *Kiss*. "One hundred percent." *Kiss*. "Yes." *Kiss*. She pulls back further, putting more space between us. "You're gonna make her so happy. I can't wait to see her little face when you ask her."

"You're sure?"

"Never been more certain about anything in my life. I know how much you love her, and I know how much she loves you. I love how you think of her as your own. How you support and care for her. She's one lucky little girl to have you *choose* to be her father."

"I would consider it an honor to be Poppy's daddy." I lean forward, kissing my girlfriend, hopefully soon-to-be fiancée. I spend the next few minutes running through my plan for the weekend with her. Only sharing the parts I need her to know. We clean up our dishes, lock the house, then head upstairs to bed, where I take my time to defile the woman I hope to make my wife.

SIXTY-TWO

-toby-

I'M AS NERVOUS AS ALL GET OUT THIS MORNING. THE BEAUTY of my plan is that Cass thinks I'm nervous about asking Poppy if I can adopt her, and Poppy thinks I'm nervous because I'm going to ask her mom to marry me. I barely tasted the chocolate chip pancakes I ordered for breakfast. Cass kept smirking at me over her decaffeinated coffee, while Poppy kept nudging me with her elbow when her mom wasn't looking.

Shane has the goods in his pocket, and he's set to take photos on his phone for me at the important moments.

"Are you girls ready to head out for my surprise?" I wink at Cass while I nudge Poppy.

Poppy's practically vibrating with excitement, as she pretty much climbs over me to get out of the booth we're sitting in. Cass and I laugh at her energy. Once I'm up, I help Cass slide out of her seat. She's finding moving around a little awkward. She says it gets even more difficult closer to the end. Watching her grow round with our baby has opened up a whole new level of overprotectiveness I have for her. She says I'm hovering and fussing too much, but I want to help her out as much as possible. I want to make her life as easy as possible while her body's working hard to create another human being. She needs to get used to it because I can't see myself stopping anytime soon.

We all climb into the car to make our way to the Japanese gardens. I came by earlier in the week to check it out, making sure the cherry blossoms were in bloom and to work out exactly where I want to propose to my girls. Large wooden doors greet us at the main entrance, and as we pass through, the tranquility of the gardens can be felt instantly. The weather is absolutely glorious for my plan.

Poppy stops inside the entrance for a moment to take in her surroundings with Cass in tow. A pond full of koi greets us, along with superb large pines towering over the pathway, creating a shady canopy for the lush greenery surrounding us. We wander over a low wooden bridge, past the open tea house on the right—we'll stop in there before we leave today.

The large Buddha statue greets patrons, and I snap a couple of photographs of my girls with him. I remember seeing a photo of *The Doors* posing with this very statue. We stroll further into the gardens on this perfect spring day, walking along the pathways which meander through carefully manicured plants and miniature trees. We're getting closer to the spot I've chosen. I asked Poppy to distract her mom when we reached the stone steppers.

Poppy looks at me and I give her the signal we agreed on over ice cream. She grips her mom's hand, pulling her to a stop between a pond full of koi fish on the left and a two-tier water-fall on the right. A realistic statue of a couple of herons rises out of the pond on the far side—it's the perfect location. Shane stayed back to take photographs. As Poppy signs to Cass about the fish in the pond, I get down on one knee, the ring safe in my pocket. With the sun at my back, I draw in a deep breath, waiting for Cass and Poppy to turn around.

She turns around, and it takes her a moment to register

that I'm down on one knee in front of her—with my heart in my throat and hope in my eyes. Her eyes widen as she looks between Poppy and me. She was expecting me to ask Poppy about the adoption, and I will, but I wanted to have Cass as my fiancée first.

I make sure to sign as I speak, even though I'm shaking like a leaf, to make sure Poppy doesn't miss out. "Cassia." I half-smile. It's all I can manage while I'm this nervous. "I've had the biggest crush on you since I was sixteen. Never in my wildest dreams did I think I would actually be lucky enough to call you my girlfriend. But today, I'm a man kneeling in front of the woman I've fallen deeply in love with—the woman I want to share my life with, through good times and bad. When I think about the future, you're all I see. All I want." I smile up at her. "I promise to love you and our children with every beat of my heart. Will you do me the honor of marrying me? Becoming my wife?"

Now that I have all of that out, I look at Poppy and Cass properly. Poppy's holding her hands in the begging position, a cute smile on her face, wide-open eyes peering up at her mom. Cass's hands are clutched up against her chest, eyes glassy, a ghost of a smile on her lips as her chin trembles. She glances between Poppy and me, taking what seems like a hundred minutes to respond. I'm not sure she's going to respond, but she seems to become aware that I asked a question that requires an answer.

At first, she begins nodding slowly, teasing me. Then a smile slowly spreads across her gorgeous face. "Yes. Yes! *Yes!* I want to marry you and spend our days and nights together. Yes! I want to build a family with you. You're all I want, all I see."

I quickly get to my feet, scooping her body into mine for a luxurious kiss to seal our promise to one another, to our family, our future. Then, keeping in mind that we have young, impressionable eyes on us, I reluctantly pull away.

"We'll finish this kiss later, when we don't have little eyes on us," I whisper against her lips, forehead pressed to forehead. Cass nods in agreement. Both our faces split wide in a grin.

Poppy nudges me, pointing to my pocket, reminding me about the ring. *Shit!* I forgot to give Cass her ring. I pull it out of my pocket, and, holding her left hand steady, I slowly slide the platinum hand-engraved band on her slender finger. The three-carat solitaire diamond sits proudly on her finger, held in place with platinum petals, making it appear almost like a flower. I already have the matching platinum hand-engraved wedding band in the safe at home.

Cass studies the ring closely for several moments before looking up at me.

"It's gorgeous, Toby. So simple and pretty. I love it so much. Thank you." She leans forward, laying a hard kiss on my lips as Poppy wraps her arms around both of us. I hope Shane's getting all of this on his phone. Bending down, I lift Poppy up to join us. We stand, the three of us in a tight embrace for several moments. Soaking in the feel of my two girls in my arms, I absorb their goodness—the perfection of my family.

We wander deeper into the garden until we come across the Peace Lantern. This is where I want to ask Poppy an important question. I already asked Cass to distract Poppy at this point, allowing me the time to get down on one knee for her. When the girls turn around, I'm in position and the confused expression on Poppy's face is almost comical. She looks up at her mom before looking back at me. Cass nudges her slightly closer, and I suck in a deep breath to prepare for this next part.

"Poppy." I sign shakily. "I love you so much, even before I knew who you were. From the first moment I laid eyes on you, I knew you were going to become an important person in my life." She smiles shakily. "I was wondering if you would do me the honor of becoming my daughter? I would really like to adopt you so that you'll legally be mine."

She pounces on me, tears trickling down her cheeks, her little girl face split in a wide grin. She kisses my cheek and snuggles her face into the crook of my neck. I hold her close, rubbing my hand up and down her back. Cass squats down, pulling the three of us in tight, much the same way Poppy did a few minutes ago.

Poppy pulls her head away, putting some space between us. I look at her with hope and butterflies in my stomach. She brings her hands in front of my face and then, with a broad grin, she shows me two thumbs up. She jigs them up and down to make her point. I pull her forehead to my lips, pressing a relieved kiss there before tucking her in tight. After several moments, I let her down to stand on her own feet and dig into my pocket for the Return to Tiffany red double heart tag pendant. I got the one with the red heart because poppies are red. I thought it was fitting. I show her the necklace, then put it on her.

When I glance up at Cass, her face is glowing and her gray eyes are like storm clouds holding back the rain. Poppy shows Cass her necklace as she signs to Poppy how lucky she is to have me for her daddy. Poppy reminds Cass that they're both lucky. I have to interrupt them at that point because *I'm* the luckiest one of all.

I have one more surprise for my girls. I want to give it to them on the bridge that's shaped like half a drum, with the reflection in the water completing the other half. Together, with Poppy skipping between us, we head toward the bridge. Shane passes me the item I need for this part and then moves into position to capture the memories for me. Climbing the steep wooden structure, using the crossbeams for support, we

440 • DEBRA ST JAMES

reach the top, which matches exactly how I'm feeling—like I'm on top of the world.

"I have something I want to share with both of you." They both watch me in anticipation. I pull the CD out of my hiding spot. "I finished recording my latest album, as you both know. It's been mastered and pressed. I have the finished product here." I hold it up for them to see.

"The artwork's gorgeous, Toby. This looks amazing."

"Turn it over and look at the back." Cass turns it over, and I watch her studying it closely. I know immediately when she sees what it is I wanted to show them. With wide eyes, she looks up at me. I tip my chin, indicating she should let Poppy see. She passes it to Poppy so she can see. Her eyes snap up to mine as confusion fills her face.

"I hope you don't mind, but I put our song from the concert on my album. In addition, I've listed you as co-arranger, which means you'll earn royalties." I raise my eyebrows, waiting for her to notice what I've done.

Her face falls as tears fill her eyes so quickly they can't be contained, running down her precious cheeks. I look up at Cass in question, and her face mirrors her daughter's. My heart sinks to the bottom of my feet, through the bridge, and into the water below with a hefty splash.

"I'm sorry. I thought you'd like it." I shove my hand through my hair in exasperation. I can't believe I fucked up so epically. "I'll redo the CD and take it off. No problem. I'm sorry." My hands can't keep up with my verbal apology and I'm certain I've messed up some of my words. I drop to my knees in front of Poppy, raising her chin with my fingers as I wipe her tears away with my fingers. "I'm sorry, Poppy."

She shakes her head in the negative, then slowly signs, fingerspelling her new name. "You made my name Poppy Summer."

"Yeah. I'm sorry, I shouldn't have done that."

Her lips spread in a shaky smile, and she looks up at her mom as her smile grows wider. "He wrote my name, Poppy Summer."

Cass nods. "Yeah. I saw that." She has a watery smile as she looks down lovingly at her little girl, tucking a lock of hair behind Poppy's ear.

Poppy looks back at me. "You really *do* want me to be your daughter."

"Yeah, I do. You're the best daughter a man could ever wish to have. I love you, Poppy." She throws her body into mine, and with our arms wrapped tightly around each other. I stand on top of the bridge, on top of the world, with one of my girls in each of my arms.

Over Poppy's shoulder, I ask Cass. "Did I do the wrong thing? Was it too much?"

Cass shakes her head. "It was perfect, Toby." She comes in, closing her arms around us. "Thank you for loving us the way you do."

Would you like to attend Toby's final concert and bear witness to the birth of their child?
Sign up for my newsletter to get your ticket for the bonus epilogue here:
https://tinyurl.com/secondchancesummer-bonus

Toby's twin sister, Kate, finds her HEA in
Loving Summer.
A grumpy/sunshine billionaire romance
A steamy, low-angst, stand-alone contemporary romance about a grumpy, determined hidden billionaire and a penny-pinching, tenderhearted teacher doing her best to protect her heart.
https://books2read.com/dsj-lovingsummer

Shane's journey is an emotional one as he works to overcome his past. Read his healing story as he finds his HEA in
Everlasting Love.
A scarred cinnamon roll Hero/single mom romance
An emotional, steam-filled contemporary romance about a damaged cinnamon roll veteran who believes he's undeserving of the sexy single mom with a sweet daughter even though they may be exactly what he needs.
https://books2read.com/dsj-everlastinglove

pinterest

I put together a Pinterest board for Toby and Cassia's story. If you're interested, you can check it out here:
https://tinyurl.com/secondchancesummer-pinterest

debra's books

The Summer Twins
Loving Summer | *Kate Summer & Oliver Stone*
Second Chance Summer | *Toby Summer & Cassia Phillips*
The Summer Twins | Complete Series
Spin-off Novella
Loving Roman | *Roman Armstrong & Alice Reed*

Kisses
Stolen Kisses | *Emma Miller & Theo Drivas*
Moonlit Kisses | *Max Stanfield & Molly Lewis*
Unexpected Kisses | *Sarah Stanfield & AJ*
Kisses | Complete Series

Monday Knights | *novellas*
Enemy Kisses | *Finn Brady & Harriet Dubois*
Wicked Kisses | *Lincoln Kingsley & Sophie Chalmers*

Everlasting
Everlasting Love | *Shane Sutton & Violet Jamison*
Everlasting Promises | *Hope Sullivan & Benjamin Taylor*
Everlasting Vows | *Nixon Steele & Abigail Steele*

Debra has a list of her books available on her website.

You can find them here:
https://debrastjamesbooks.com

connect with debra

stalk me

You can stalk me pretty much everywhere!
https://debrastjamesbooks.com/connect/

How about joining my Facebook group?
https://www.facebook.com/groups/DebsBibliomaniacs

newsletter

Join Debra's newsletter to receive important updates before anyone else. Newsletters will be sent once a month unless something exciting is happening.
https://debrastjamesbooks.com/newsletter/

thank you

Thank you for taking the time to read my second novel. I hope you've enjoyed spending time with Toby, Cassia, and Poppy as they found their happily ever after. Writing a book is a funny thing, it's as much a journey for the author as it is for the reader and I've loved every minute of writing these stories.

Thank you for taking a chance on me; for reading my book. I truly do appreciate your time. If you've enjoyed reading about Toby, Cassia, and Poppy, I'd love to hear from you.

I would like to thank Mr. St James and our two sons for their support and patience with me when dinner was late, or I didn't listen as attentively as I should have, or I didn't want to leave my cave because I was working on this baby.

I would also like to thank my beta readers, Stacy, Wendy, and Kelly (who stepped in at short notice). Your feedback and support meant the world to me. The fact that you were prepared to give up your valuable time to help me polish my story helped me immensely.

about the author

Debra St James is an author of spicy, slow-burn contemporary romance that features cinnamon roll heroes who listen to their women's hearts and their words. She takes her time to weave a detailed tapestry of genuine characters, real-life struggles, love, and romance to create engaging stories that will have you so immersed in the story that you'll never want to leave. Her stories are always guaranteed to take you on an emotional journey that ultimately ends with a HEA!

Debra loves to read romance. Her family often finds her with her nose stuck in her iPad, swooning over her latest book boyfriend. She writes part-time from her Perth home, which she shares with Mr St James and their two sons, whose antics often make her roll her eyes and laugh in equal measure.

Writing a novel had never been on her radar. One morning, she was enjoying a coffee by the river and a story sprouted, seemingly from nowhere. At 51, she pulled up the Pages app on her phone and began to type, giving life to her debut, *Loving Summer*.

The rest, as they say, is history!

Debra xo

- amazon.com/author/debrastjames
- facebook.com/debra.stjames.books
- instagram.com/debrastjames_books
- bookbub.com/authors/debra-st-james
- goodreads.com/debrastjames
- pinterest.com/debrastjamesbooks

www.ingramcontent.com/pod-product-compliance
Lightning Source LLC
Chambersburg PA
CBHW060813120726
47909CB00006B/1904